MAGGIE SHAYNE

KILLING ME SOFTLY

MIRA®

Recycling programs
for this product may
not exist in your area.

ISBN-13: 978-0-7783-2793-6

KILLING ME SOFTLY

Copyright © 2010 by Margaret Benson.

For questions and comments about the quality of this book please contact us
at Customer_eCare@Harlequin.ca.

www.MIRABooks.com

Printed in U.S.A.

To my critique group, the Packeteers:
Cactus Chris Wenger,
Micki Malone aka Michele Masarech,
Gayle Callen aka Julia Latham,
Laurie Lance "Bugs" Bishop, Theresa Kovian and
Ginny Aubertine. I couldn't have written these
books without your brilliance and brainstorming.
More importantly, no writer could dream up friends
as beautiful and as true as all of you.
You are loved, and deeply, deeply appreciated.

Prologue

It had been sixteen years since I'd killed anyone. But I was going to kill someone tonight.

It had also been sixteen years since I'd taken the Thunderbird out of the garage, where I kept it under lock and key. Garage, hell, it was more like a crypt. I'd thought the killer inside me would die, given time. So I'd buried him in my subconscious, and I'd buried his car in my garage, even covered it up with a death-shroud tarp. I'd covered up the trophy wall, too. I'd told myself never to set foot inside that garage again.

But I had.

Every now and then, *his* voice would get to me, and I'd go in, start the T-Bird up, let it run, listen to it purr and feel that old thrill I used to get when we had been on our way to take another victim. Sometimes I would even slide the phony pegboard wall aside, to look at the cinder-block it covered. To look at all their faces. So pretty. Always smiling. Always young.

I'd taken the T-Bird out tonight. And the kit. I'd brought the kit along, as well, though I had no intention of using it. I nearly always had the kit at hand. It was a way of testing myself, I think. A way of making sure I was the one in charge, the one in control. That I could resist the urges of the beast within.

I was going to kill the rookie cop, yeah. But it would be a simple kill, just a bullet to the back of the head and a scene made to look like a home invasion gone bad. It wasn't the nemesis within me committing this crime. It was me, all me, this time. And I had no choice.

But my alter ego was with me, coming along for the ride, getting a hell of a thrill out of the whole thing. He loved killing. He loved it way more than I did. And that was saying something, because I'd come to relish it myself. There was no other rush quite as potent.

Still, this wasn't going to be like the others. This wasn't about the rush; this was about necessity.

Getting inside the house was easy. It would've been easy even for a virgin without any kills under his belt. For me, it was child's play. The small brick house's door wasn't locked. There was no security system. Every light in the place was turned off. A cop oughtta know better. Even a rookie like him.

There had been a party earlier in the evening, but the guests had cleared out. The doorknob turned easily in my hand, and I stepped inside, into inky darkness. I paused there, just inside the door, giving my eyes time to adjust. It was darker inside than out. A different kind of darkness. Heavier. Denser.

Still, I managed to see a little. And I could tell what I would have been seeing, had there been any light, just by the smells permeating the place and assaulting my sensitive olfactory receptors. Overflowing ashtrays. Half-filled beer bottles, some of which had been used as ashtrays, so the scents of sour beer and wet tobacco mingled in the air, nearly making me gag on them. Stale potato chips and spoiling dip melted together in plastic recyclable bowls, adding to the pungence.

My senses were always heightened when I was getting ready to kill. They were heightened to hell and gone tonight, maybe because it had been so long. I was shivering with it, feeling everything. Even the rub of my black clothing against my skin was arousing to me.

I moved carefully, slowly, taking my time and knowing I had plenty. All I wanted. The rookie wasn't going to wake up. So I took my time, enjoying every second of it. Walking soundlessly through his darkened home I felt, I thought, like a hunter must feel when stalking prey through a dense jungle. But not just *any* prey. I'm talking an elephant or a lion. Something that could kill you just as easily as you could kill it. Something dangerous.

Though you might disagree with me, given the nature of my victims, I've never believed there is any animal more dangerous than a human being. I never will. It's the intelligence. It's the mind that makes it so. Be it a young, beautiful woman, or tonight's prey—a young man in his prime. A cop.

I made my way to the bedroom, measuring every step I took. It didn't feel as if it had been as many years as it had—sixteen since my first time. Her name was Sara,

that first one. I remembered every detail of her face—
and of her death. I was as sharp and as tight tonight as
if I'd killed only last week. Or last night. Maybe the
years had mellowed my nerves and honed my skills.
I wasn't even shaking or sweating the way I usually
did when I got into the same room with the evening's
chosen one.

Silencing my thoughts, I listened, and heard slow,
steady breathing from beneath a mound of blankets on
the bed. My heart pumped a little faster. The compul-
sion came to life within me, like a fire in my blood. I
felt that dark, hungry twin, alive inside me. I'd kept
him silent for a long while, trapped in some kind of
induced coma—until now. Now he was wide-awake.
I closed my eyes and reminded myself—and *him*—
that this was going to be different. We were not going
to start up again. Not like before. It would be just this
once. It was necessary.

We had no choice, really. He knew, you see. Or, at
least, he suspected.

Gently, we pulled the covers back.

And the dark twin within my soul roared in delight,
even while I shook my head in denial. For the person
in the bed was not the man I had come here to kill.

A young woman was lying there instead. She was
sound asleep and reeking of beer, but still, beautiful. In
the darkness, her skin appeared pale and flawless. Her
hair was long, straight and sleek. Just the way I liked
it. It looked to be light brown.

It had to be, my newly awakened twin whispered to

me. *That's your favorite shade, isn't it? She's here for us. I knew she would be. So did you. Come on, don't deny it. You knew.*

What I *knew*, I reminded myself, was that the voice, the twin, was not real. It was nothing more than a part of my mind, a twisted part, the part I'd managed to ignore all this time. Though I'd never silenced him entirely. Even while he'd slept, I heard him in my dreams. Maybe he only slept while I was awake, and vice versa. I wished he would shut up now, though, because this was not what I wanted. Not now.

You knew she would be here, he pressed. *Sooner or later, she had to be. That's why you used the T-Bird tonight. It's why you brought the kit in with you.*

But he was wrong. I carried the kit as reminder— a testament to the power of my will and my ability to control the impulse. To control *him*.

Bullshit. You brought it for this. You brought it in hopes of finding this very moment—this moment we both knew would come. It's a gift! You've been waiting sixteen years for this! Take it out. Come on, take it out. You know you want to.

No.

Yes. And you know you will. We will. *Why fight what we are?*

My hands trembling, I slid the backpack off my shoulders and, reaching inside, pulled out the leather bag. The one that hadn't seen use in the sixteen years since I'd taken my final victim and framed another man for the crime. It was about the size of a shaving kit, with a zipper on three sides. I felt alive again as I slowly unzipped it, careful not to make too much noise and yet exhilarated at the risk that I would be heard. I leaned over her. I felt passion I hadn't felt in a decade and a half. My heartbeat pounded in my ears, as my skin heated and my hands tingled. It seemed as if my other half melded with me as I crept to the head of the bed and stood between her and the wall behind me. So I could get her from behind and watch her face in the mirror that topped the dresser on the opposite side of the room.

I took the black silk stocking from the kit and slid it carefully beneath her neck, all without disturbing her drunken sleep. Her skin was warm against my gloved fingertips. I heard the twin inside me groan in delicious anticipation as we pulled the stocking into position. As we began to pull it tight. And then tighter. And tighter still.

She came awake fast. Her eyes flew wide, and her hands rose to clutch at her throat. I pulled the stocking even tighter, lifting her upper body off the bed as I did, so that she, too, could see the entire game play out in the mirror.

As I'd hoped, the sight enhanced her terror. Seeing me there, behind her, all in black, big and powerful, steadily choking the life out of her. She knew there was no hope. She thrashed in the bed, mouth opening wide, face turning red. A rush, not unlike the one produced by a hit of Ecstasy, only much, *much* better, washed through my body like a warm, vibrant, all-encompassing wave as we slowly, steadily, squeezed the life out of her. She wasn't so pretty anymore, with her tongue swollen and filling the space between her parted lips.

When her eyes rolled back in her head, I let go of the stocking and turned to the case again. I took out the two custom-made shot glasses, with the artwork on them that so seemed to reflect the predator inside me. The crimes we committed together. I took out the copper flask, as well, and I poured both shot glasses full of whiskey.

After a moment, she started to rouse. Her eyelids trembled rapidly, before they fully opened, then widened as she realized I was still there. She opened her mouth to speak, and I gripped her chin with one hand, forcing her teeth open. I poured her shot of whiskey into her throat. She couldn't swallow; she began to choke. Without letting a second tick past, I dropped the glass and grabbed the black stocking again, and this time I pulled it tighter, jerking it harder, twisting it with all my might and easily crushing her throat with that soft bit of black silk.

I heard the gurgling as she drowned in the whiskey. I saw the foamy spit running over her lower lip and her chin. Her eyes bulged as if they would pop, tears running from the outer corners. Her entire body jerked and spasmed. A single purple vein in her forehead expanded and pulsed beneath her blue-tinted skin.

And then it stopped pulsing.

There was a palpable change when they died. I always

knew the very moment when it happened. There was no more awareness on their part, no more struggle or shock or fear. There was just a sudden absence of...of *everything,* really. And, with it, came a rush of release within me that made an ordinary orgasm pale in comparison. There was nothing like this feeling. *Nothing.*

As life fled the girl's body, as I *felt* it flee, the sensation continued trembling through me. It lit me up. I felt it in every nerve ending, in every deliciously sensitized inch of my skin, in the quivering of my stomach and the aftershocks convulsing my muscles. I eased the pressure on the silk stocking, my head tipping back, my eyes falling closed as I sighed and shuddered in delectable bliss.

Then slowly, cell by cell, my brain came back online, like a computer being rebooted. The lights came on in order. The hard drive began to whir. The pleasure ebbed into a warm glow that filled my body and would last, I knew, for days. But the delight receded enough to allow rationality and practical considerations renewed access to the forefront of my mind.

I hadn't accomplished what I had set out to do tonight. Not precisely. But I could still achieve the end I'd intended. I'd just need to take a slightly different, and perhaps more torturous, path to get to the same destination. I could still do it. I knew how.

And besides, this way was so much better.

You're right, I told my twin, alive and wide-awake inside me now. It was. God, it was. It's been so long.

Sixteen years too long.

I nodded. Then quickly stopped myself. It won't happen again, though. As good as it was, I can't let it happen again. I won't.

Oh, who the hell are you kidding? You're back, my friend. You're back, and you're glad of it. You've missed this. You know you have.

Ignoring the one who, in that moment, felt like my oldest and dearest friend—and the only one who ever had or ever would understand me—I released the stocking that had seen so many throats before, slid it from around her neck and returned it to the case. I had other work to do this night, to make this go the way I needed it to. But first, there was one more thing.

I picked up the second shot glass, from where I'd set it on the nightstand, put it to my lips and tipped it up, swallowing my celebratory drink.

My *nightcap.*

It was tradition, after all.

1

Bryan Kendall awoke with a crushing headache that turned into blinding dizziness when he rolled over. It was only then, as his hand swung out and hit something cold and hard, that he realized he wasn't in his bed.

He was on the bathroom floor.

"Hell," he muttered. "Must've been some party."

He tried to think back but remembered nothing, and really didn't care all that much at the moment. He had a case of cottonmouth that made anything short of the house being on fire uninteresting in comparison. He needed liquid. Any liquid. Now.

He opened his eyes, then squeezed them shut against the morning light slanting in through the bathroom windowpane. The sun seemed unreasonably *bright* this morning. Gripping the sink with one hand, he pulled himself up onto his feet, then leaned over it and cranked on the taps. He bent closer, cupped his hands and drank. The lukewarm water wet his mouth but was nowhere near enough to quench his thirst. His head was spinning and pounding, his stomach churning, and it occurred to him that this didn't feel like an ordinary hangover.

He'd never been drunk enough to pass out on his own bathroom floor.

Lifting his throbbing head, he peered into the mirror and then closed his eyes again. This was too much effort. He needed to drink a vat of water, take a handful of aspirin, crawl into bed and sleep for another eight hours or so. Then he could try again.

He turned in the direction of the door and shuffled through it, feet dragging, because the percussion of actual steps was too painful. It was only a few feet to the bedroom and a few more to the bed, and then he was sinking gratefully onto the queen-size pillow-top mattress, pulling the covers over himself as he rolled onto his side. His arm hit Bette before he remembered she was there.

"Sorry, babe," he muttered, closing his eyes and letting his head sink into the pillow.

She didn't answer. Good. He hadn't woken her. Feeling cold, he tightened his arm around her waist and snuggled up a little closer. But she didn't move. Didn't roll up onto her side and press her back to him the way she normally would. Didn't stroke his forearm where it draped over her.

And she felt cool.

Colder than he did.

Frowning, he lifted his head and looked at her in the early-morning sunlight that was just beginning to stream in through the tiny gap where the curtains didn't quite meet. She was lying on her back, staring at the ceiling, eyes open wide. Something hit him as he stared at her, and it felt as if he'd stuck his finger into a live socket. It slammed into the middle of his chest, just like a shock, and woke him entirely. Bryan blinked to clear the haze from his vision and sat up straighter. A chill ran up his spine, as if some part of him knew what he was seeing before his mind caught up.

"Bette?" He reached out to touch her cheek and found it unnaturally cold. Not cold as if she'd been outside in a snowstorm, but cold like raw meat. There was a huge difference. And that was when his brain caught up to what his instincts had already known.

Bettina Wright was dead.

Dead!

Bryan scrambled backward out of the bed, suddenly more wide-awake than he'd ever been in his life. He stood there for a moment, staring at her, gasping for breath. "Bette?" he said. "What the hell? What the *hell?*" Finally the cop in him kicked in. He ran around the foot of the bed, to her side and bent to feel for a pulse, but stopped himself when, again, he felt how cold she was. His brain was ten steps ahead of him now, thinking, telling him to drag her off the bed, onto the floor, start CPR, call the EMTs. But he didn't do any of those things, because reality had outshouted training. She must have been dead for several hours. There was nothing he, or anyone else, could do for her now. She'd been lying here, getting stiff and cold, while he'd been passed out in the bathroom. Useless.

He struggled to remember anything that might have happened last night that would have given him a clue something like this could happen. He didn't think she'd seemed sick or particularly tired. She hadn't complained about anything. He knew she didn't do drugs, nor would he have had any at the party. Hell, most of the guests had been cops.

Had her heart given out without any warning at all? Had this been some kind of allergic reaction or alcohol poisoning or—

"Oh, no." He spoke aloud, as his gaze settled on her neck. On the ligature marks there. They were obvious, even in this feeble light. "No no no…" Backing up two steps, he jerked the curtain wider and let the sun pour in on her body. The angry, bruised ring around her neck was unmistakable, as were the still-protruding tongue and dried spittle on her chin. Bettina Wright had been strangled to death in his bed while he slept, drunk, in next room. She'd been murdered while he'd been ten feet away, too plastered to help her.

He was a cop, for God's sake, and he'd—

Hell. Oh, hell.

He looked around the room again, spotted his cell phone and picked it up, then he walked back through the house without touching anything. He was wearing jeans, and nothing else, and he didn't grab anything on the way. His home was a crime scene now. Jesus, he couldn't believe it. Bette. Dead.

He opened the front door, using a sock he found on the floor and only two fingers to turn the knob, trying

not to smear any prints. Then he left the door open
and sat on the front steps, where he flipped open the
phone. There were two men who were more important
to Bryan than anyone else in his life: his father and his
mentor, retired cop Nick Di Marco, and he wanted to
phone them both at the same time, but since he had to
make a choice... Of the two, Di Marco was physically
closer and could get to him faster. Decision made.

He called Nick, then held his head in his free hand
while waiting for him to pick up.

"Di Marco, and this better be good, being 6:00 a.m.
on a Saturday, pal."

"Nick?"

"Kendall? You sound like hell." The older man
paused. "Are you okay?"

"No. I... It's Bette—"

"Who?"

"The girl I'm...sort of seeing. She's...she's dead,
Nick. She's fuckin' dead." Bryan's voice broke, but he
kept forcing out words. "Strangled, I think. In my bed.
Damn, Nick, she's—"

"Whoa, hold up, hold up. Where are you right
now?"

"Sitting on the front step. She's inside. She's dead.
How could I not have *heard* something? How could
I—"

"You sure? You do CPR? You check for a pulse?"

"She's cold, Nick. She's ice fucking cold."

Nick swore under his breath. Then, "Have you called
anyone else?"

"No. I—"

"Okay, okay, we do this by the book. It's the only way to go here. You're a cop—you do this right. You gotta be beyond suspicion, you got that?"

"Sus-suspicion? Shit, Nick, why would I—"

"You're there, aren't you? You woke up with her. You're the last one to see her alive, the one to find the body. You know how this works, kid. You're a cop."

Everything in Bryan tightened until he thought he was going to break. "Yeah. I mean…yeah."

"Hang up and call your father. I'm gonna call the chief, and I'll get there by the time he does. You just wait for us. Don't call anyone else—don't, for the love of God, call her family. Just your dad. Tell him to get here *A-SAP*. I'm on my way. Don't go back inside. Don't touch anything. Don't take a shower or change clothes. Just sit there, you understand?"

"Yeah. Yeah. I just—"

"I know, kid. You hang in. I'm on this. I'm gonna be there in a matter of minutes, okay?"

"Okay."

"Just breathe. It's gonna be all right."

"Okay."

"Where's your sidearm, Kendall?"

Bryan blinked as he thought for a second and remembered where he'd put the gun the last time he'd had it out. It had been a while. He'd been on paid leave since a recent hostage standoff, waiting for the department shrink to give him the all clear. "In the lockbox, hall closet."

"You sure no one else is in the house?"

Bryan's head came up slowly, and he looked behind him through the still-open door. "I didn't really check."

"Don't. Get yourself a little distance away, but maintain line of sight, just in case."

"Okay."

"Be careful, kid. I'll see you soon."

Bryan closed his eyes, disconnected and felt as if his world had turned upside down. He got to his feet and looked back inside the house, feeling a little more certain there was no one lurking inside. Then again, a few minutes ago, if asked, he would have been fairly certain he wasn't going to find a dead woman in his bed.

So he walked several steps down the driveway, but only got as far as his brand-new, candy-apple-red Mustang Shelby GT, before he had to stop and throw up. And he didn't think it had anything to do with the alcohol he'd imbibed the night before. Dammit, how could Bette be dead? Much less strangled? Maybe he was wrong. Maybe he'd imagined the marks on her throat. Maybe the chief had been right to put him on leave, and he did have some kind of PTSD or something going on, and he'd just imagined all of this. Maybe if he walked back into the house right now, he would find Bette sitting up in bed and griping about being late for whatever early-morning class she had.

He could almost believe it. He nearly turned and walked back inside. But something stopped him. The weight of the phone on his hand, he guessed. He needed to call his dad.

He wanted to call Dawn instead.

He wanted to hear her voice right now even more than he wanted to quell the waves of nausea battering his stomach. But that wasn't going to happen. He and Dawn hadn't spoken in five years. There was too much space between them now. Too much hurt. Too little effort to remedy or even address it. He couldn't call Dawn, even though hearing her voice on the phone would make things better in a way nothing else could.

No. Not even Dawn could fix this.

He opened the car door, sat down inside and stared for a long moment at the dark, hulking shape in the distance, where the waterfall that gave this town its name shot off the end of a rocky ledge and tumbled down. The craggy flat-topped beast of a cliff was positioned in such a way that the waterfall itself was nearly always in shadow, making it dark and ominous looking, rather than cheerful or sparkly, the way most waterfalls seemed. Shadow Falls, the landmark, was not beautiful. It was downright spooky. But Shadow Falls, the town, had been the place with an opening on the police force after he'd finished college. And it was only an hour from what he considered home. And so it was perfect.

Or he'd thought it was.

But the town seemed far from perfect right now. Because it concealed something in its shadowy depths.

Something evil. A cold-blooded killer was lurking here. And he'd never even known.

Sighing, Bryan called his father, fifty miles away in his hometown of Blackberry, Vermont.

2

Nick Di Marco was a big man. And it wasn't entirely a physical thing. He was tall enough at five foot eleven, and his shoulders were wide and solid, even though he was lugging around some extra belly fat these days. His once raven-black hair was streaked with silver, his intense brown eyes lined with crow's-feet that made his smiles more infectious, and his frowns downright scary. Beneath all of that, he was the best cop Bryan had ever had the honor to know. Retired or not.

And he wasn't the only one who felt that way. Di Marco was a hero cop, and everyone in Shadow Falls knew it.

So Bryan felt a little lighter when he saw Nick get out of his black, big-as-a-boat, old Crown Victoria and come striding toward him. Bryan got out of his own car, whose payments were as much as his rent, and tried to hide the fact that his knees were shaking. It was warm outside, the summer sun already beating down on them.

Nick threw his arms around Bryan, and it was no pat-on-the-back "guy" hug; this was a full-blown, real thing that squeezed the air right out of his lungs. "You okay, kid? You okay?"

"I don't know."

"You're okay. You're gonna be okay." Nick clapped a big palm to the back of Bryan's head and crushed it to his shoulder for a second, then released him and backed off enough to search his face. "You call your dad?"

"Yeah. He's on his way."

"Good. That's real good, Kendall." Nick turned his head as another vehicle came skidding to a halt along the roadside. Chief MacNamara had driven the Bronco with the Shadow Falls Police Department logo—a black waterfall inside a circle made up of the words themselves—on the front doors, and the bubblegum lights on the roof. At least those lights weren't flashing.

Chief Mac got out, thick shocks of unruly white hair sticking up all over. His face showed all the ruddy puffiness of a lifelong drinker, and his belly backed up the story. He was fat enough that he sort of swayed heavily from side to side when he tried to walk fast, which was what he was doing now.

"Somebody want to tell me just what the *hell* is going on here?" he demanded a little breathlessly.

Nick nodded. "Tell him, Kendall. Tell us both."

Bryan took a deep breath and nodded once. "I had a party last night. To celebrate getting the okay to go back on the job Monday." He nodded at Nick. "You were there—you can vouch for that part."

Nick nodded and glanced at the chief. "It was no big deal. A few twelve-packs and some chips. Mostly cops, a few faces I didn't know. A dozen, maybe eighteen, people at most."

"You left early," Bryan said, eyes lowered, gaze turned inward. "A few more people showed up later on. I think I remember most of them—I don't know. I must have drunk way more than I thought. I woke up on the bathroom floor. Everyone had gone. I headed to the bedroom, wanted to get a few more hours of sleep—and Bette was there. And…" He lifted his head, looking the men in the eyes, first Nick and then Chief Mac. "She was dead," Bryan said. He had to force out that final word, and his voice broke when he said it. "She was already cold. And there are ligature marks around her neck."

The chief gaped, his jaw dropping as if its spring had broken. He took a step back, turned to stare at the house and pushed a hand through his crazy white hair. Then, swearing a blue streak, he started forward, hurrying toward the house with that swinging gait of his.

Nick clapped Bryan on the shoulder to get him moving, and in spite of his resistance to the notion, Bryan fell into step, the two of them following close behind the chief.

"You didn't hear anything?" Chief Mac asked without looking back.

"No."

"Careful, don't touch a damn thing," the chief went on as he stomped through the house and into the bedroom. Just inside the bedroom door he stopped, and his voice, when he spoke again, was lowered. Maybe out of respect for the dead. "In fact," he added, "stay out of this room, Kendall. Di Marco, get in here. But be careful."

Nick went into the bedroom with the chief, while Bryan stood in the doorway, his eyes riveted to the blue-tinted skin of Bette's face, those sightless red eyes, the grotesquely twisted mouth.

The chief looked closely, not touching anything. "Strangled. Sure as shit. And she— Holy fuck."

"What?" Bryan asked from the doorway, even while the chief gripped Nick Di Marco's wrist and nodded at the nightstand.

Bryan followed their gazes and saw what was sitting there. A shot glass with a black scythe painted on it, a red rosebud above, severed from its stem by the blade and trailing tiny red droplets.

It was a design the three men had seen before.

"That can't be," Di Marco whispered. "There's no way." And despite the whisper, his voice trembled. "Sniff the glass, Chief. Check—"

"Whiskey," the chief said after leaning over and inhaling. He turned to Nick. "Check her mouth."

Nick nodded and leaned close to the dead woman, his face so near hers it might have seemed to an outsider that he was about to kiss her. Without touching the body at all, Nick sniffed, and then he jerked upright again. "Whiskey," he said. "God, this can't be happening."

"What?" Bryan asked. "What...what the hell is going on, Nick?" But he had a sinking feeling that he knew.

"Is that your shot glass, Bryan?" Nick asked.

"No."

"It's a trademark, Kendall," the chief said. He came out of the room, flipping open his phone as he did and hitting buttons. "Calling card of the Nightcap Strangler."

Bryan blinked in shock, processing that, along with all that he knew about the old case—which was probably a lot more than either of these two men realized, considering that all the files and all the evidence was currently taking up space in a storage bin in his garage. The three of them walked out of the house and stood in the driveway again, and the chief ordered up a crime-scene investigation unit and an ambulance.

When he hung up, Bryan faced him. "Chief, how can this be? The Nightcap Strangler was caught, what? Sixteen years ago? Nick, you caught him. You put him away. You solved it. It was the biggest case of your entire career. He's in prison."

"Not anymore, kid," Nick said softly.

Bryan blinked, puzzled for one terrifying moment before he remembered that the convicted serial killer had died in prison three weeks ago.

"He bought it in a fight," the chief said. "Didn't you see it in the papers? So there's no way this was him. Unless..." He looked at Nick, not finishing the thought.

"No way did I bust the wrong guy, Chief. No way in hell."

"You're confident about that?"

Nick was offended by the question. He looked mad enough to punch something, Bryan thought. "He was guilty as hell. And you know that, Mac. You know it as well as I do!"

The chief nodded, keeping his trademark calm. "I also know that we never released certain details to the public. No one knew what the design on the glasses was, Di Marco. Or the specifics about the kind of whiskey he used. No one but you and me. Unless you told your protégé here," he added with a look at Bryan.

"I never discussed the details of the Nightcap case with the rookie, Chief."

"Right. You're his mentor, and you never talked to him about the case that made your career? He never asked? You wrote a book, Di Marco. They made a freaking movie. You telling me you never talked about it with Kendall here?"

"That's what I'm telling you." Nick braced himself, getting in the chief's space, his chest thrust out, chin up, challenging. "Now why don't we get to what *you're* telling *me?* Are you saying a rookie cop turned into a copycat killer just 'cause he took a couple of classes from the retired cop who solved the case? 'Cause I think that's a stretch, even for you, Mac."

"He shot a guy last month, Nick."

"In the line of fucking *duty!*" Di Marco shouted.

"He was cleared of any wrongdoing. It was a clean kill. You know that."

"It was a clean kill and it left him a basket case," Chief Mac argued.

"According to *you*." Nick jabbed a finger in the chief's direction, and for a moment Bryan thought he was going to actually poke him in the chest with it. He only barely missed doing so. "The department shrink says he's fine."

"Now," the chief said.

Because he hadn't *seemed* fine right after the shooting, Bryan thought. Then again, who would have?

Bryan had never shot a man before. He'd had no choice, though. The guy had his girlfriend in a headlock, a knife at her throat, and he was getting ready to use it. There had been no question. Hell, she'd been bleeding already when Bryan had taken the shot. He was the only one with a clear line. He'd had no choice. But he damn well didn't like it.

"Yeah, *now,*" Nick repeated. "And *now* is when this killing went down. The kid didn't do it, Chief. Come on. You know the kid didn't do it."

"Quit talking about me like I'm not in the room, you two," Bryan said. He kept his tone level, his voice low. "I'm standing right here. And I didn't do it. I'll tell you both, I didn't fucking do this. I had no reason. I *liked* Bette."

"*Liked* her?" The chief bit back whatever else he'd been about to say, sighed, compressed his lips. "All right, Kendall. You liked her. You were, uh, *seeing* this Bette—"

"Bettina Wright," Bryan filled in.

The chief pulled out a pad and jotted the name down. "You were seeing her pretty regularly?"

"We were friends."

Chief MacNamara looked at Nick. "If he's gonna start lying already, about something so obvious…"

"I'm not lying," Bryan said.

"She was in your bed, son."

Di Marco drew a breath, released it. "Come on, Kendall, be straight with the chief. It's pretty clear there was more between you than just…friendship."

"There really wasn't. We were friends. We got along great, but neither of us wanted anything serious."

The chief blinked, looking blank. Di Marco rolled his eyes. "I think this is some of that shit the kids over at the university call 'friends with benefits,' Mac.

"I'm old, not dead, Di Marco. I've heard the term. I just never thought anyone really lived that way."

Di Marco shrugged and turned his attention back to Bryan. "So you two never fought? Didn't argue? There was no jealousy?"

"I knew from the beginning she was still gun-shy after her ex-boyfriend—and that's where we oughtta start, right there. That bastard *was* jealous. Didn't want her for himself, but it sure as hell drove him crazy to see her with anyone else. Even me, even though we were just—"

"Just friends," the chief muttered.

Bryan nodded, knowing how lame it sounded.

"Okay," the chief said with an exasperated sigh. "Look, we have a lot more to go over, Kendall. We need to take you in, get your statement, get a list of every other person who was at the party, get the name of this ex-boyfriend of hers, and anyone else you can think of who might have had a motive, notify her family—"

"Hell," Nick muttered. "Worst part of this freakin' job."

"What freakin' job?" MacNamara blurted. "You've gotta be real clear about something, Di Marco. You're retired. You teach criminal justice now—you don't practice it."

"I teach criminal profiling," Nick corrected. "And I just decided to *un*retire."

"That's not—"

"Don't say it, Mac. Don't say it's not possible when we both know it is."

"You're the kid's mentor, practically a father figure. You don't call that a conflict of interest?"

"It's my case."

Chief MacNamara met Nick's steady gaze.

"If it's anything to do with the Nightcap Strangler, Chief, even a copycat who somehow had inside information, then it's my case. Always has been. Nobody knows more about it than me. Nobody else is gonna have the foundation of information and knowledge that I have. And if it turns out I fucked up and sent an innocent man—"

"You didn't," MacNamara said.

"If I did, then I'm *damn* well gonna be the one to make it right."

The chief nodded. "I might be able to pull some strings."

"Then pull them. Cut through the red tape. Call me a consultant or some bullshit like that if you have to, but get me in on this—*officially* in on this." Then he turned to Bryan. "You said your dad's on his way?"

"Yeah."

"Call him and tell him to meet us at the station, okay? While you do that, I'll call you a lawyer and your union rep, have them meet us there, as well."

"Come on, Nick. I don't need a lawyer."

Bryan saw the grim look that flew between Nick Di Marco and Chief Mac, and for just a second his heart seemed to freeze in between beats. "Damn, is it really that bad?"

Nick met his gaze, but his wasn't steady, and his smile was clearly forced. "Probably not, kid. But we might as well prepare for the worst, just in case. Don't you think?"

"Nick…" Bryan could hardly ask the question, but he had to know. He had to. "Nick, tell me you don't think I did this."

"No, kid. I don't think you did this."

Bryan looked at the chief, hoping and maybe even half expecting him to say, "Neither do I." But Chief MacNamara only lowered his eyes, shook his head and led the way to his waiting SUV.

Bryan thought he was going to throw up again before he got in.

* * *

Dawn pulled the pillow over her head and hugged it around her ears, but the damned phone kept right on ringing. It was set to go to voice mail after four rings, because four rings was more than she ever wanted to hear. But this caller had just hung up and dialed back when that had happened. And then had done it again.

At ten rings total, Dawn peered out from beneath the pillow. She could see, from the Caller ID feature on her television—which had been left on all night long, just as it was every night—that the call was coming from her mother. Her birth mother, not the one who'd raised her. Blackberry Inn, the screen announced.

She reminded herself that she was lucky to have found her birth mother at all, after fifteen years with each of them believing the other to be dead. She adored Beth, and had been raised beautifully by the woman she considered her mother, Julie Jones. But even though she loved Beth dearly, Dawn wasn't ready for another conversation where every other sentence revolved around the life and times of Bryan Kendall.

Bryan, the son of Beth's husband, Josh, had been Dawn's first love. And she'd broken his heart when she'd left him behind in Vermont five years ago.

Hell. It didn't seem as if Beth was going to give up until she answered, and it would be rude to just yank the line out of the jack.

Sighing, she rolled onto her side, grabbed the phone and brought it to her ear. "Hi, Beth."

"Dawn. God, I thought I'd never get you. Are you all right? You don't sound well."

Dawn rolled her eyes, and reached for the water glass on the nightstand, but it was empty, and the one half full of diet cola was also half full of vodka. And it was too early in the morning for vodka.

She hadn't needed to resort to vodka in quite a long time. But last night she'd had that feeling—that creeping, pins-and-needles-in-her-spine feeling—that told her something was coming. And that her normal bedtime dose of Ativan wasn't going to be enough to keep it at bay this time.

She'd thought, at the time, she'd been sensing that the dead were going to start talking to her again—asking for her help, pestering her, the way they had before she'd run away from her life and her gift and her family. And Bryan, her first love.

Now she thought maybe all she'd been sensing was the approach of this phone call. Which was, after all, likely to be almost as unpleasant as the "gift" she'd turned her back on. "I'm fine," she said. "Why so urgent?"

"You've got to come home, Dawnie. You've got to come home right now."

Dawn blinked and looked at the clock on her cluttered nightstand. It, and the framed photo of her and Bryan, arm in arm, in happy teenage puppy love, were the only two things there that really belonged. Beside those were the empty water glass, the partially ingested vodka diet, a box of tissues, an empty prescription bottle and another one that wasn't empty, the bowl of Chinese noodles she'd had for dinner and an open package of peanut M&M's.

She had to shove some of the junk aside to see what time it was, and as soon as she did, she felt a lot less guilty for her reluctance to answer the phone. "It's first thing on a Saturday. Is someone dead?"

She was kidding, being sarcastic and snotty, and feeling totally justified in both, until Beth said, "Yes. Someone is dead."

Dawn sat up straight and blurted his name as everything inside her turned to ice. "Bryan—"

"Bryan's...he's fine. No. He's *not* fine. His dad is with him, and he's physically fine. At least, I think he is."

"Good God, Beth, will you just tell me who's dead already? I'm having heart failure here!"

"A girl. Her name is Bette—Bettina something or other. She was...she was murdered last night. Apparently in Bryan's house. In his...in his bed."

"What?"

"He had a party last night. Had too much to drink. Woke up this morning to find this girl dead in his bed."

"Drugs? God, that's going to mess up Bryan's career big-time. Or was it...?"

"She was murdered."

Dawn swore in a way she'd never before done in front of either one of her mothers.

"Dawn, they've taken Bryan in for questioning. Josh

just called from the station, and he says it doesn't look good."

"Doesn't look good?" Dawn frowned at the phone as if it were deliberately being vague. "Doesn't *look* good? As in, they actually think he *did* it?"

"I don't know. I guess…I guess so."

"Well, they can't! That just doesn't make any sense," Dawn said. "Bry's a cop, for crying out loud."

"Yes, a cop who's been suspended for the past month."

"What, still? All because he shot that guy?"

"He's been cleared of any wrongdoing, but he was required to meet with the department psychiatrist to be sure he wasn't suffering from post-traumatic stress. She just gave him the all clear, and he was scheduled to return to work on Monday. Hence, the party last night."

"He was celebrating," Dawn said.

"Apparently."

Dawn closed her eyes, shook her head, offering a token argument, because she couldn't seem to stop herself. Force of habit, she presumed. "I don't know what good my coming back would do, Beth."

"Yes, you do," Beth whispered. "You know you do."

"Did he…ask for me?"

"He needs you, Dawn. If they don't arrest him—"

"Arrest him?"

"If they don't arrest him, Josh is going to bring him

home. Dawnie, you know you can help. Even without the...the ability you inherited from your father—"

"There is no ability." She didn't bother reminding Beth that any mention of Dawn's long-dead father was strictly off-limits. The man had been a powerful medium—as well as a murderer. His gift and his mental illness, so twisted up in his mind that he couldn't tell the real voices from the imaginary ones. The ones that told him to kill. With his dying breath, he'd passed his gift on to his teenage daughter, promising to return to her. A promise he'd kept, and one that had sent her running across the continent to escape.

And she *had* escaped.

"The dead don't talk to me anymore, Beth. It's... it's gone." Thanks to AA—Absolut and Ativan in her case.

"I don't believe that," Beth said softly. "I know it drove your father insane—and I know that scares you, Dawn. So I hope, for your sake, it's true. But even without that, Dawn, you can help. You and Bryan were like—you were like Nancy Drew and the Hardy Boys."

"One Hardy Boy."

"The way you figured out what was going on in Blackberry five years ago when your father found me here—when he thought God was telling him to kill me... If it hadn't been for you and Bryan..."

"That was five years ago, Beth. A lot of water has gone under the bridge since then. Bryan's the one who went on to become a cop. I just fix cars—"

"You restore classic cars for collectors. Don't undersell yourself."

"Yeah, well, it's a far cry from crime solving."

"He needs you, Dawn. And *I* need you. I'm scared. Josh sounded awful on the phone. Bryan's his son, and this is going to be hell on him, no matter how it comes out. I need to be there for him, Dawn, but *I'm* scared, too. I need you. The family needs to face this together. Please, baby, please. It's time you came home."

"There are just...so many ghosts."

"Yeah. Well, now there's one more."

"Beth—"

"Dawn," Beth said, and her tone had changed from pleading to the voice of absolute authority. "I didn't raise you—didn't even get to know you until you were practically grown. But I *am* your mother and I'm speaking to you as a mother right now. There's a ticket waiting for you at the airport. Your flight leaves at 1:16 p.m., your time. Get up, pack a bag, call your boss and get your ass home. I'm not asking you. I'm telling you."

Dawn closed her eyes. "I'm a grown-up now, Beth. You can't tell me what to do."

"I just did, kiddo. I've put up with your hiding and your wallowing and your—well, to be blunt, your cowardice, for five long years, but I'm done with it now. You're tougher than this. Stronger. Your family needs you, and I hate to say it, Dawn, but if you let me down again, I'm just not going to forgive you. Not this time."

Dawn blinked and stared at the phone, but Beth was

gone. She'd disconnected. So Dawn replaced the receiver on its cradle and peeled back her covers. Her birth mother had just called her a coward. She had never once even hinted that she felt that way. Dawn had thought Beth understood why she had to run away, had to stay away, from that place where so much had happened. Where her murderous maniac of a father had died at long last after a string of murders and assaults. From that instant when he'd spoken his dying words to her, told her his so-called gift was hers from then on.

Gift. Who the hell called insanity a gift?

Oh, there was more to it than just madness. The dead really did talk to Mordecai. But he couldn't tell the voices of the dead from the voices of his own insanity, and in the end, he'd nearly destroyed everyone he'd ever loved. Even her.

His "gift" was nothing she wanted. Nothing she would *ever* want.

She flung back the covers, shuffled into the bathroom and cranked on the shower taps. Shrugging out of her robe and letting it fall to the floor, Dawn stepped into the spray. Then she stood there with her head hanging down, and Bryan's face front and center in her mind's eye. He must hate her for walking away without a word five years ago. He must hate her for ignoring every effort he'd made to get her to talk to him, to at least tell him why. He must hate her by now. He *ought* to hate her. And she couldn't blame him for it, but God, she didn't want to see that hatred in his eyes. Not face-to-face, up close and personal. She didn't think she could take that. It would hurt too much.

They'd been so in love. It had been new and fresh, and fun. She'd met him when his father had fallen for Beth, and it had felt as if they were meant for each other. So young and inexperienced, that when they finally made love for the first and only time, it had barely lasted five minutes.

She smiled softly when she thought of that completely unsatisfying, awkward night when they'd lost their virginity to each other. It was the sexiest memory of her entire life.

Damn, she didn't want to go home. She really didn't. But there was no point in arguing about it. She was going. Today. And deep down inside, now that she had no choice in the matter, she couldn't wait to see Bryan again.

3

"It wasn't the three hours of questioning that got to me," Bryan said to his father. He had one hand braced on the mantel and was staring into the Blackberry Inn's oversize fireplace as if there were dancing flames to contemplate. Which there were not. It was midsummer and still too warm for a fire, even in Vermont. But staring at the dark, empty hearth kept him from letting his eyes get stuck on one of the countless photos of Dawn, or him and Dawn together, that littered every room of this place.

She was on her way. Right now. Beth was picking her up at the airport in Burlington, an hour away. She would be here soon. Any minute now, and he could barely believe he was going to see her again for the first time in five years. He was going to see her again, now, in the middle of the biggest mess he'd ever landed in. He was going to see her. And it was going to rip his guts out.

"So what did?" Josh asked.

"What did what?" Bryan glanced at his father, sitting

in the big rocker recliner with a cup of coffee and looking less like the relaxed, content innkeeper than he had
since he'd first arrived in this town. Not that he ever
really fit the stereotype, with his athletic build and good
looks. Bryan took after him, and thanked his lucky stars
often for his father's genes.

But Josh had relaxed a lot since retiring from govern-
ment work to run the inn alongside his wife. Tonight,
though, Bryan could see the lines of tension creasing his
brow. He was worried about his only son. This whole
thing had his stoic, easygoing father shaken, and that
scared him.

"You said it wasn't the questioning that got to you,"
Josh said. "So what did?"

"The lawyer." Bryan's glance slid sideways, from his
dad's worried, rugged face to the photo on the end table.
Dawn, leaning on a classic Dodge Charger, wearing
overalls, a wrench in one hand and a smudge of grease
on her cheek. Must have been one she'd sent them from
California. He jerked his attention away from it and
tried to stay focused on the subject at hand. The lawyer
his father and Nick had sent to his rescue.

"I'm a cop. I hate lawyers," he said, elaborating on
his previous statement.

"That's fine—until you need one."

"That's just it, I *don't* need one. Or at least, I
shouldn't. I didn't *do* anything."

"You woke up in bed with a murder victim, son."

Bryan thinned his lips. "The mouthpiece wouldn't let
me say a hell of a lot. Kept interrupting when the chief

was questioning me, telling me not to answer. Hell, he made *me* think I looked guilty."

"It's for the best, Bryan. You have to protect yourself."

"I know that. I just—I know what I think when a suspect lawyers up and won't talk. I hate like hell to have my colleagues thinking that way about me. Especially Chief Mac. I'd prefer to just tell him everything and ask him to help me sort it all out."

"I know."

Headlights slid over the walls as a car pulled into the driveway. Bryan closed his eyes slowly, tried to brace himself for whatever feelings were going to assault him at the sight of Dawn. But he was damned if he knew which ones to expect. It had been so long. Part of him hated her, and part of him ached for her. And all of him resented the fact that she wouldn't be here at all if his life wasn't on the line. He wondered if he was supposed to be grateful she would rush home because he was in crisis. He wasn't. He was angry that it took a crisis to get her here. Hell, he hadn't blamed her for running off without a word after all that had happened. Having the dead just start talking to you had to be bad enough. Having your dead father leading the crowd of ghosts to your door was too much, especially when your dead father had been a homicidal maniac.

So she panicked. She freaked. She ran away. No goodbye, no warning, nothing. She was just gone. And he could have forgiven that, if she had just called after things calmed down. But she didn't call, and she didn't write. She spoke to Beth, her birth mother, and anything Bryan learned about her life came through her. Second-hand news of the woman he loved. It was insulting.

There was no excuse for letting it go on for five long years. None.

Still, he turned toward the front door as footsteps crossed the porch. He strained his eyes when he saw the foggy outline of her beyond the frosted-glass panes. And then the door opened and she walked in, Beth close behind her.

Dawn met his eyes, and he just stood there, mute, staring at her and thinking his heart was going to pound a hole in his chest, and wondering if it would fall onto the floor before or after it stopped beating.

Her hair was still long. Still its natural shade of dark honey and amber gold, perhaps with a few lighter high-lights, no doubt thanks to the California sun. But her face had changed. Grown thinner. Her cheekbones were more prominent than before, which might be partly be-cause she was older now, but he thought it might also be that she'd lost weight. Hell, she was so damn thin. And the tender skin underneath her eyes seemed pink and puffy. As if she'd been crying.

Over him?

Hell, who was he kidding?

He wondered, briefly, what she was seeing as she stared at him. What changes was she noticing? He imagined he'd changed quite a bit, too, in the course of five years.

Finally she said, "Hey, Bryan. How are you holding up?"

Just like that. As if there wasn't a weeklong conversation that should happen before that casual hello. He shrugged. "Damned if I know. I don't think it's all had a chance to sink in yet, to tell you the truth." He moved toward her, but not too close, just enough to reach out and take the suitcase from her hand. "How about you?" he asked. "You look…tired."

"Gee, thanks."

He shrugged, not overly concerned that he'd sort of insulted her just then. Hell, she'd done worse to him, hadn't she?

"It was a long flight," Beth said quickly. "Naturally she's tired."

Bryan could see the worried looks passing between Beth and Josh from the corner of his eye, though he couldn't really take his eyes off Dawn. "You've lost weight," he said.

"That doesn't sound like a compliment, either," she replied.

"It wasn't." He sighed and lowered his head, turning toward the stairs. "You didn't need to come, you know. There's not a damn thing you can do."

"Hey, don't think I didn't try that argument, Bry. Beth didn't buy it, and she wouldn't take no for an answer. So I'm here. Deal with it."

He was halfway up the stairs when he replied, "I've got enough to deal with already, thanks." He finished climbing the stairs, avoiding the muttering going on behind him. The three of them discussing his mental state, no doubt. Then he was out of range, at last. He headed down the hall to the room Beth had chosen for Dawn and set her suitcase just inside the door. Then he kept going, to the next room, his room, and once inside, he closed the door, sat on his bed and lowered his head to his hands. Damn, damn, damn. He hadn't wanted to snap at her. He'd wanted to wrap her up in his arms and hold her, just hold her, for a long, long time. He'd wanted to feel her right there, against him, warm and alive, more than just a memory.

Which made it even more irritating that she, apparently, had no such sentimental notions about him.

"I'm sorry," Dawn said. "I should have—maybe I—"

Beth hushed her. "You two have a lot to talk about, to work through. It's high time, Dawn. It's past time. Adults do not just stop communicating with people they care about. They talk it out."

Dawn pressed her lips together more tightly to avoid saying anything that might sound rude, since several snotty rejoinders were knocking against her teeth in an effort to escape.

Josh closed a hand on her shoulder. "He was glad to see you, hon. I realize it didn't seem that way to you, but I know him better than anyone else in the world. He was glad to see you, and more than that, he needs you. He needs you more than he needs anything or anyone right now. So I'm asking you to swallow your pride and be there for him."

She nodded, not believing a word of it. It would have been nice to believe it, but it just didn't make any sense. Bryan hated her. And she couldn't blame him, because he had every reason to hate her. *That* made sense. But she didn't argue with Josh. She just said, "I'll try my best."

"Good." He smiled. "I think I jumped ahead a little, though." And then he hugged her. "Welcome home, Dawn."

"Thanks, Josh." She relaxed and hugged him back. "Thanks. It's good to be back."

"It is?" he asked.

She smiled at him and shrugged. "Well, it might be too soon to tell. But it feels good at the moment."

Beth said, "It does my heart good to hear that."

Dawn felt bad. Her lack of enthusiasm had probably hurt her mother's feelings, and that wasn't what she'd intended. "I think I'll go on upstairs," she said. "I'd like to take a shower, freshen up before dinner. It was a long flight."

"Food'll be on the table in an hour."

"All right." Dawn hugged her mother. "Thanks for picking me up."

"Thanks for coming. Just take it slow, okay? Just take it nice and slow."

Dawn nodded, unsure what it was her mom wanted her to take so slowly, but not wanting to open the can of worms she thought lay behind that comment. So she headed up the stairs, but slowly. With every step she took, she half expected to see some shady, vaporous apparition, or to hear some disembodied voice. Most of all, she expected to encounter her long-dead father, demanding that she accept her "gift." Her "calling," as he'd referred to it.

She hadn't seen or spoken to a dead person since she'd spent her first night in San Bernadino. Maybe that was due to the Ativan she'd been prescribed by the first doctor she'd trusted with the truth. Or maybe it was something to do with the distance, as little sense as that made. She only knew she didn't want to come back here and face the ghosts again. She didn't want the damn gift that had become so twisted and corrupt it had rotted her father's mind, turning him into a murderer who honestly believed he was doing God's will when he killed.

She didn't want any of it.

She entered her room and stood there, just inside the open door, looking around but seeing nothing. No ghosts. "If I hear even one peep, see even one misty shape in the night, I'm out of here. I hope you're getting that."

"Loud and clear."

She nearly jumped right out of her skin as she spun around to see Bryan leaning against the door frame. One hand on her chest, she closed her eyes slowly and willed her heart to slow down.

"Sorry. I didn't mean to give you a heart attack."

She took a deep breath. "It's okay. Come on in, Bry."

"You sure?"

She nodded and stepped aside to give him room to pass. He walked in, looked around the bedroom. "You, uh, you alone in here?"

She smiled. "Yeah, I'm alone." Bryan had been matter-of-fact about her "abilities" ever since she'd first told him about them. He hadn't doubted her. Hadn't thought she was crazy. Hadn't been all weirded out about it. It had barely fazed him, except that he worried about her. And in return, she'd walked out and left him a note that really didn't say a damn thing.

"So, uh, no ghosts in California, huh?"

"Not for me, at least. I haven't…heard from any of them since I first got there."

"Why do you suppose that is?"

She lowered her head, not meeting his eyes. "I don't know. Distance. Medication. Vodka, when the other two aren't enough."

When she glanced up again, he was frowning, studying her face and probably getting ready to comment on her methods of ghost-dodging. But he seemed to change his mind. "And now that you're back?" he asked.

"Nothing yet. I hope to God there won't be."

He nodded, sighed heavily. "You told Beth it wasn't me you were running away from. That it was them. You said you needed time. But I don't think you were being entirely honest."

"I don't want to talk about that, Bryan. About us.

About what we had. It's history. I know I hurt you, and I'm sorry. But I did what I had to do, and it was five years ago. I'm just not up to rehashing it all. Not now."

His eyes narrowed. She thought she saw a flash of anger, but he banked it fast. "It's not all that important, anyway," he said.

Her brain immediately registered it as a lie.

"Look, Bry, can we just skip all that for the moment? Just focus on what's going on here and now instead? 'Cause this is a big thing, you being implicated in a murder. All this ancient history between us, it can wait. Can't it?"

He met her eyes. "It's waited for five years already," he said. "*I've* waited for five years."

"You weren't exactly *waiting*," she said. "I mean, this poor woman—she died in your bed, after all."

He lifted his brows and took two steps closer to her. "Does that bother you, Dawn?"

"Of course not." But she averted her eyes when she said it, cursing herself afterward for being so obvious.

"Did you think I was going to be celibate for five years? Did you really think one night losing our virginity to each other was going to sustain either of us for the next half decade? 'Cause that's crazier than talking to dead people."

"Let it go, Bry. I'm not up to this, not yet."

He watched her face for a moment, as if waiting for her to give something more away, and when she didn't, he finally nodded. "Fine. It's waited five years—it can wait a little longer."

She lifted her head and, gingerly, put a hand on his forearm, where it hung by his side. His biceps were big and hard. They hadn't been before. His shoulders were broader, and his hair, as brown as milk chocolate, was longer than she'd ever seen it. She liked it long. It would be a shame when he had to cut it again to return to his job as a cop. *If* he was able to return to his job as a cop.

She thought about saying so, then realized she'd been standing there with her hand on his biceps for a good minute and a half, in silence.

"I want to help you get through this," she said. "I want to help however I can."

"There's nothing you can do."

"You know better." She lowered her hand, reluctantly, but her eyes replaced it. Damn, he'd beefed up. "God, don't you remember what a kick-ass pair of amateur detectives we were?" she asked, forcing her eyes to move upward and lock with his.

"I thought we weren't going to talk about the past."

She sighed deeply. "I don't care how difficult you try to make this, Bryan. I'm staying, and I'm going to try to help."

"That's kind of a switch from 'Beth wouldn't take no for an answer,' isn't it?"

"Oh, come on. I would have come whether she asked me to or not, once I knew what was going on with you.

Don't pretend you don't know me well enough to know that."

"I'm not sure I know you at all anymore."

She probed his eyes, looking for the emotion behind the words. Was it just anger, or was there also hurt, frustration, even worry? Or maybe a combination of all of the above? He must be going out of his mind with everything that had happened in the past twenty-four hours. And yet she resented him snapping at the friend who had come all the way across the country to help him. "You going to be an asshole the whole time I'm here, then?"

"Probably."

"Well, just so I know up front. Look, I want to take a shower before dinner, so—"

"Right. Go for it. I'm out of here."

He turned to go, but she went after him, grabbed his shoulder to turn him around, and then jerked her hand away as if the contact burned. Because it had. His shoulder was even more changed than his biceps. Big and hard, and so very different from her memories of him.

"What do you mean, you're out of here? You're staying for dinner, aren't you?"

He met her eyes, and his face, harsh before, softened just a little. She had to wonder if that touch, no matter how brief, had hit him the way it had hit her. Like a fingertip to bathwater that was way too hot, making you pull it back fast and hiss through your teeth. Making your nerves jump from lazy complacence to screaming awareness.

He sighed and said, "Yeah, I'm staying. And I'll try not to be an asshole the *entire* time."

He almost smiled.

She almost returned it.

"That's good," she said. "Because I want to know everything, Bryan. Everything that happened, everything you can remember, including the stuff you haven't told Josh or the police or your best friend." She tightened her lips, thinking that *she* used to be his best friend. Wondering who filled that role today. And why the very thought was like a knife in her chest.

He studied her for a long moment, and slowly something changed in his face. It was as if he were thinking of something troubling, something he hadn't thought of before. He reached out, and to her utter surprise, he ran his fingertips from the crown of her head down over her hair, to where it hit her shoulder. "Dawn, I don't know how safe it is for you to get too close to this. Or to me. Hell, I don't know if it's even safe for you to be here right now."

She frowned. "Why?"

Beth called his name from downstairs, and he hesitated, then nodded as if making a decision. "There's a lot to this you don't know. But I'll fill you in after dinner, okay?"

"Okay." She could have sagged in relief just then. Because for that moment he had seemed like the old Bryan. It had felt as if nothing had changed between them. But only for a moment. As soon as she smiled up at him, she saw the door behind his eyes slam closed. The moment was gone, and he was tense and defensive again.

Beth called again, saying, "Nick's on the phone, Bryan."

"Coming," he called. Then he lifted a hand, a half wave that might have started out as something else—a touch, maybe—before morphing into the kind of half-hearted wave strangers offered one another. "See you at dinner, Dawn."

She nodded and watched him go, then closed her bedroom door, leaned her head briefly against it and wondered why her heart was contracting into a tiny stonelike lump in her chest and her throat had tightened to the point where it was hard even to breathe.

She was feeling too much. *Way* too much. And way too soon. But at least she'd forgotten to worry about the dead.

Odd that they hadn't bothered her yet. She wondered why, then decided it was best to just count her blessings, as she headed for the shower.

Bryan really hadn't intended to be a jerk. But damn, there was something infuriating about being in the same room with Dawn, and he didn't think it was due to stress over being a murder suspect.

Now she sat across the dining room table from him, nibbling halfheartedly on her pot roast. She seemed to be ignoring the mouthwatering scent wafting from her plate to her nose. She barely touched the gravy-soaked vegetables and potatoes. She looked as if her mind were entirely elsewhere.

For the first time Bryan wondered if she was seeing someone back on the West Coast. God, what if she was so touchy simply because she missed her lover?

Suddenly he couldn't stand the smell of the food, much less eat it. He started to push himself away from the table.

"It's just us here now, Bryan," Josh said, finally breaking the tense silence that filled the dining room as surely as the aroma of Beth's continuously simmering potpourri. "You can tell us everything. It's not going any further."

Bryan felt the bottom fall out of his stomach at his father's words. "Tell you everything? What, exactly, is it you think I'm not telling you?"

Josh's eyes widened, and he shook his head hard. "No, no—"

"God, Dad, tell me you don't think—"

"I *don't* think you did it! I know you didn't do it, son. That's not even within the realm of possibility. Come on, Bryan. I *know* you."

Bryan felt the sudden weight leave his shoulders a little as he let himself believe his father's passionate declaration.

"I just meant," Josh went on, "that you can tell us everything that happened. Everything you remember. Things your lawyer wouldn't let you tell your colleagues."

Bryan lifted a brow. "Are you wearing a wire or something?"

Dead silence fell on them like a shroud. Around the table, every eye was glued to Bryan, every expression mortified, especially Dawn's. Then Bryan shook his head, sighed and said, "I was kidding, Dad."

"Damn, Bry, this is no time for humor." But Josh sighed his relief all the same.

"Guess not. But you're all so damn glum." Bryan looked around the table, including Dawn in the observation. "Look, I haven't been convicted yet. Hell, I haven't even been charged. And I'm not going to be. I have faith in the system."

Josh stabbed a chunk of meat with his fork. "Yeah, well, I've spent most of my life in the system, and I'm not so confident in it that I'm willing to trust my son to it." He set the fork down, meat still attached, and tossed his cloth napkin onto the table in front of him. "Look, Bry, the only way to ensure you don't end up being arrested and charged is for us to find out who did this ourselves. And to do that, we need a place to start. The more you can remember, the better off we'll be."

Bryan nodded slowly. His father knew his shit. He'd spent years as an agent with the DEA. "I know, I know. But that's just it. I don't remember a damn thing. There was the party the night before. Things were getting…a little rowdy, I guess. But everyone seemed to be having a good time. I drank. A lot. More than I normally would have, though I didn't think I was going overboard all that much."

Josh's head came up. "Did they ask you for a blood sample when they questioned you?"

"Yeah. Freaking lawyer didn't want me to agree to it. But I overruled him. Hell, I'd already admitted to being drunk, so it wasn't going to hurt to have them know the blood alcohol level. And as for DNA, it was my house. My DNA's all over it. So I gave it."

"Good," Josh said with a firm nod. "So there was the party. And you were drinking. And…?"

"And that's it. I woke up on the bathroom floor. The house was empty, but I didn't remember when everyone left. I felt like hell, decided to go back to bed to sleep it off, dragged my ass into the bedroom and found Bette lying there, already cold."

"I'm so sorry, Bryan," Dawn whispered.

It wasn't her words that hit home in his brain. It was the way she reached across the table and gripped his forearm. He looked up fast, met her eyes as his skin sizzled beneath her palm.

"I've been so focused on the fact that you're a suspect in this, I haven't told you how sorry I am that you lost someone you cared about."

Her eyes backed up every word. She really meant it. He could only nod and grunt his thanks. She took her hand away, and he wanted it back. Touching her—being touched by her—was something he'd missed more than he'd realized until now.

"I mean it," she said.

"I know you do," he replied.

"Nick tell you what he told me on the phone?" Josh asked.

"There was whiskey in Bette's throat, and in her lungs," Bryan said softly. "Glasgow Gold, he said."

"Yeah. Maybe you don't know what that means, but—"

"I know what it means," Bryan said, and he met his father's eyes.

Josh's face fell.

"What does it mean?" Dawn asked.

"*How* do you know?" Josh whispered, as if she hadn't even spoken.

Bryan knew she was confused, but he had to get this out to his father now. There was no point in doing less than laying his cards on the table where his family was concerned. He didn't want tidbits of information surfacing later on and shaking their belief in him. With a deep sigh, he said, "Two weeks ago, I signed out all the files on the Nightcap Strangler case."

Dawn dropped her fork. "*Nightcap Strangler?* Bryan, that sounds like the name of some kind of…of a serial killer or something."

"It is," he said. "Or was."

She blinked. "What the hell is going on?"

Bryan set down his silverware. "There's a lot you don't know."

"Like that Bette was killed by a serial killer, you mean? And that now they think it might be you? A *serial killer?* God, Bryan!"

"It's even more complicated than that. The Nightcap

Strangler was a man named Johnny Lee Jackson. He was arrested sixteen years ago, and there hasn't been a killing fitting his M.O. since. He died in prison just last month. I think this has to be a copycat crime."

"But why?" Dawn asked. "Why would this…this copycat want to kill *your* girlfriend, in *your* bed, while you were sleeping in the next room?"

"I don't know why."

"Yes, you do," she accused. "Bryan, what were you doing with those files? The timing of this, of you going through those old files, that can't be a coincidence. The police certainly aren't going to see it as one. What aren't you telling me?"

"Nothing."

Dawn noted, though, that Beth and Josh were looking at him with the very same questions in their eyes. Oh, none of them believed Bryan was capable of murder, but there was clearly some kind of link between him and those crimes—or this criminal.

And Dawn had the feeling he knew what it was.

"I think this is all about Nick," he said, confirming her belief.

Josh nodded as if he understood, while Beth kept staring at him, waiting for further clarification.

"Nick?" Dawn asked. "*The* Nick?"

"Nick Di Marco," Bryan said. "He was one of my professors back in college, my mentor. We're tight. Hell, I trust him more than anyone in the world, except maybe my dad. Anyway, he's the cop who solved the Nightcap

Strangler case sixteen years ago, before he retired from the force and took up teaching."

"I know," Dawn said. "I'd forgotten what they called the killer, is all." She'd heard all about Nick the super-cop, and his book and his movie deal, from Beth. If she'd ever actually lived in Blackberry, she would probably have heard about him far sooner. He was the nearby town of Shadow Falls's version of a living legend.

"I think Bette was chosen because of her connection to me and *my* connection to Nick," Bryan said. "Some-one is trying to set me up, but I think they're also trying to get to him, somehow, through me. But whoever it is, it's not the Nightcap Strangler. Probably just some lunatic with an obsession or a bad case of hero worship. A wannabe."

"A wannabe who somehow got information only known by the police?" Josh asked.

"And by Nightcap himself," Bryan said.

"He could have told someone, a friend, a relative—even a cell mate."

"Do you think this copycat will kill again?" Beth asked softly.

"Oh, he'll kill again," said a new voice from just beyond the screen door off the foyer. They all turned, and the man standing there went on. "I just hope Bryan here is safely behind bars or surrounded by cops when he does." He grinned, and every part of his face joined in on the smile. "Can't get a better alibi than that now, can you?"

4

Dawn was startled, probably because of the dark feeling that had crept over her entire soul as the dinner conversation had unfolded. Nightcap Strangler. Serial killer. Copycat crime. A dead girlfriend. And all of it tied up with Bryan. What the *hell?*

"Hey, Nick," Bryan said, his expression lightening. "Dawn, come meet Nick." Bryan got up, and she followed him out of the dining room, across the living room and into the foyer. Beth and Josh remained at the table, and Dawn could hear them speaking softly, probably trying to reassure each other that everything would be all right.

Nick, who looked as if he'd been buff once but now had the proverbial muffin top spilling over his belt, pushed the screen door open and entered, still smiling. He had blue eyes that won you over with a single glance. His hair looked like onyx in a snowstorm. And when his warm smile landed on Dawn, it somehow managed to broaden.

"You've gotta be Beth's little girl, Dawnie. I've been hearing about you for years. It's good to finally meet you. I'm Nick Di Marco, an old friend of Bryan's."

Dawn couldn't help but return the infectious smile. Somehow his demeanor made the tension she'd been feeling a few moments ago fade away.

"Hello, Nick. I've been hearing about *you* for years, too. Bryan tells me you're the man he trusts most in the world, after his dad, and that's saying something." She extended a hand, and Nick took it. His was big and very warm, but she felt the strength beneath the friendliness.

"Sorry we're meeting under such dire circumstances," he said, and then he shifted his gaze to Bryan. "You didn't tell me how closely she fit."

Bryan frowned hard, but nodded at his mentor. "I didn't even think about it myself until she got here."

"She can't set foot in Shadow Falls, Bryan. She might not even be safe here in Blackberry, even though it's almost an hour away. You know that, right?"

"I know," Bryan agreed.

"Whoa, wait a minute." Dawn was shifting her curious blue eyes from one of them to the other. "Fit what?"

"She's got the look," Nick said. But he said it quietly, as if he didn't want Beth and Josh, who were still in the other room, to hear.

Bryan ignored her question and said, "I *know,* Nick," he said. "I was going to get to that."

"Get to what?" Dawn frowned at Bryan, puzzled and irritated at being ignored.

He quickly covered her hand with his and gave it a squeeze that made her heart beat faster, despite the situation.

"Nick, go on in and have something to eat. I'll be back." Then, finally, Bryan met Dawn's probing stare. "Come for a walk with me?"

She looked down at his hand still holding hers and felt such a rush of confused emotions that her eyes started to burn. She blinked against the feeling and nodded once, not quite trusting herself to speak, because her throat was so tight. Bryan was in more trouble than she had begun to imagine, and it seemed she cared a whole lot more than she had allowed herself to acknowledge.

Bryan walked Nick to the dining room and waved him into a seat as Beth invited him to join them for the meal. "Dawn and I are going for a short walk. We'll be back soon," Bryan told them.

"Don't parade her all over the neighborhood, Bryan," Nick said. "The more people who see her, the greater the risk."

Risk? Dawn shot Bryan a "what the hell is he talking about" look as he returned to her. But he just took her hand and gave it another squeeze, then walked with her to the door. The screen door creaked, and as they stepped outside and let it close behind them, she felt the warm kiss of a summer night and heard the crickets chirping in a way she hadn't heard in five long years. God, she'd missed Vermont.

They walked down the porch steps, and Bryan seemed to be avoiding looking at her, even though she was staring at him as she kept in step at his side.

He released her hand as they walked, and hers felt cold without it, despite the warmth of the evening.

"Why am I...at risk, Bryan?" she asked.

He sighed, coming to a stop. They'd followed a walkway that wound through a garden that hadn't been there when she'd left. It took up the entire side lawn, and was dotted with statues and benches. The air was almost thick with perfume, and even though it was already dark, there were still bees bumbling from blossom to fragrant blossom.

Bryan sank onto a bench, and she sat down beside him. "Dawn," he said, "Bette looked...similar to you."

"She did?" She tipped her head to one side, and for some reason her mind went in the opposite direction from murders and death and serial killers. It went straight to him—to *them.* "You were dating someone who looked like me? What's that mean, Bryan? Are you saying you never—"

"It wasn't like that with Bette and me. We were friends."

Dawn lifted her brows. "Some friends."

"I'm not telling you this to make you think I still— Dawn, that's not what this is about. You're blonde, slender, taller than average. You have blue eyes, and you're between nineteen and twenty-five."

"That's an odd way to put it. You know perfectly well I'm twenty-four."

"Bette was twenty-three."

She nodded. "So we were close in age. And we looked kind of alike. But it was just coincidence that you were dating her, right? It had nothing to do with her resemblance to me."

"Right."

"So why bring it up, then?"

"Because...that description—the age range, the body type, the long straight hair, light brown to blond—it also fits all the original victims of the Nightcap Strangler."

An ice-cold finger slid down Dawn's spine, and she sucked in a breath, suddenly very clear as to what he was getting at.

"All of them? And how many would that be, Bryan?"

"Seventeen original victims that we know of. Eighteen, if you add Bette. The thing is, whether this is a copycat or Nick arrested the wrong guy, you won't be safe in Shadow Falls. And Nick's right, you might not even be safe here in Blackberry, Dawn."

She nodded three times, slowly, firmly, while her mind raced. But even before her brain reached a practical conclusion, her lips were moving. Her emotions were doing the talking tonight, it seemed.

"I'm not leaving," she told him.

"Dawn, look, I can't let you risk your life—"

"It sounded like you don't think this guy will kill again."

"Nick thinks he will. And believe me, Dawn, Nick knows this case a whole lot better than I do."

"I can take precautions," she said quickly. "I can color my hair. Slouch when I walk so I look shorter. Get some tinted contacts."

Bryan sighed, shaking his head and, she sensed, constructing logical arguments in his mind. But then she closed her hand around his, and he went very still. She'd been hoping her touch still had the same effect on him as his did on her. And it seemed that maybe it did.

"I'm *not* leaving you, Bryan."

He stared into her eyes for a long moment. She tried not to start arguing with herself as to whether what she was feeling for him now was friendship or something more. It wasn't the same emotion she'd felt for him before. She'd been a girl then. Barely out of school.

What she felt now was different, and it was too soon to know exactly how. Besides, figuring that out wasn't the most important thing right now. What was important now was getting through this. "I mean it," she said, feeling the need to drive the point home. "I won't leave you."

"Sure you will," he said. "It's only a matter of time."

She frowned, because that had sounded bitter, and as if it had nothing to do with the subject at hand. But before she had a chance to defend herself, she heard the distinct sound of carefully placed footsteps on the path behind them. She swung her head around startled.

Bryan surged to his feet and stepped in front of her so fast that it shocked her. She sat there staring up at the back of his T-shirt, noticing how his wide shoulders offset his narrow hips. God, he was built. This was not the lean, lanky nineteen-year-old she'd left behind. His arms were cut, probably all flexed out like that because of the way he was clenching his fists at his sides, as if ready to take on all comers in her defense. It made her belly clench up and her heart beat faster.

"Wow," she whispered.

"Who the hell is there?" Bryan demanded.

"Hey, Kendall, is that you?" The steps came closer.

"Rico?" Bryan's fists unclenched, and she heard his breath flowing out all at once, like a mini-windstorm. Glancing over his shoulder at her, he said, "It's okay. It's my partner, Rico Chavez. We call him Rico Suave—he's pretty smooth with the women."

By the time he finished his explanation, Rico was coming toward them along the garden path. He was a relatively short bronze-skinned hunk with black curly hair cut close to his head, and when he saw Dawn, he hesitated. "Sorry, man. I hope I'm not—"

"It's fine," Bryan said. "Rico, this is Dawn Jones."

"Oh." Rico's thick brows went up as he stared at her a little too intently. And then he asked, "*The* Dawn?" And Bryan groaned and nodded.

Rico came closer, better to check her out. He smiled,

a bright white smile in that copper-skinned face, and offered her a hand, then sent a not-so-subtle nod of approval Bryan's way.

So apparently Bryan had told his partner about her. That warmed her way more than it probably ought to.

"Don't you believe anything they say about my man, here," Rico said. Then he looked at Bryan, and his smile turned serious. "I got your back, Bry. I hope you know it. No question. I don't doubt you."

Bryan nodded. "Thanks, Rico. That means a lot to me."

"I think they're close to, uh…" He shifted his eyes to Dawn and then back to Bryan again.

"Arresting me?"

Dawn felt her blood run cold, not even believing the words had crossed Bryan's lips. "No," she whispered. "No, that can't be."

"Sorry, man," Rico said. "I don't think it'll be tonight. Maybe tomorrow, though. She's got your skin under her nails, your hairs on her pillow—" He bit his lip. "Sorry."

"That's bullshit," Dawn blurted. "He was *sleeping* with her. Naturally his DNA would be all over her."

Then she pressed a hand to her suddenly queasy stomach and turned her back on both of them. She realized she wasn't just sick at the thought of Bryan going to jail, but at the thought of him making love to another woman. God, why would it hit her this powerfully? And why right now? Had she really thought he'd been celibate all this time, just because *she* had?

"There's no sign of anyone else, man. Not in the bed or on the body," Rico explained.

"Why is that so strange?" Dawn demanded. They both looked at her, questioningly, so she went on. "You didn't say anything about the Nightcap Strangler raping his victims."

"You're right," Bryan told her. "He didn't rape any of them."

"So, whether this is him or a copycat, he won't be raping them, either. Right? So why expect to find his—"

Bryan held up a hand to stop her words. But Rico was nodding hard. "Yeah. Yeah, she's right. I said the same thing to the chief not two hours ago, but damn, it's like talking to a brick wall." He sighed, sounding angry. "I figured you'd need time to decide how to make bail. Listen, man, I got a few grand stashed away, if you need it."

"Thanks." Bryan put a hand on his shoulder, lowering his own head. "For the warning *and* the offer. But mostly for believing me. I appreciate it more than you know."

Rico nodded. "*De nada,* partner. Good to finally meet you, Dawn."

"Nice to meet you, too, Rico," she said. And then Rico turned and headed back toward the house.

Dawn turned to blink up into Bryan's eyes. Hers were wet, but she hoped he wouldn't see that in the growing darkness. "They're going to arrest you."

"I'll make bail. And we'll find out who did this and—"

"Maybe...maybe I can help," she told him. "*Really* help, I mean."

Bryan seemed blank only for a moment; then he apparently got what she was saying and shook his head, backing away a step as he did. "You mean...you mean by trying to revive the ability you've spent the past five years trying to get rid of? No. No way, Dawn."

"Just listen. How better to find out who killed Bette than to ask her? And who else are you going to get to do that for you?"

He continued shaking his head. "Do you hear what you're saying?" he demanded. "You've been hiding out from this gift you call a curse for five years. You threw away everything we had because of it. Now you're just going to welcome it back with open arms?"

"To save you from life in prison? Yeah, Bry, with open arms. *Wide* open."

He pushed a hand through his hair and tipped his head up toward the glittering stars above them. "You left home over this," he said. Then he lowered his head and stabbed her eyes with his. "You left *me* over this."

"We're not going to talk about that. We're not going to waste our time and attention on what's gone by, Bryan. There's nothing we can do about it, anyway. It's in the past. We need to focus on finding out who murdered that poor girl."

"It's not in the past. Not for me. You destroyed me, Dawn." He drew a breath, still holding her eyes.

"I'm sorry," she whispered, not liking what she saw in his eyes just then. Anger. Unexpressed until now, so it had festered. She'd really ruined things with him, and done it in spades. She hadn't left any room to fix it now.

So she decided to change the topic, because that one hurt too badly to think about. "You still haven't told me why you were going through all those files on the Nightcap Strangler case. Are you going to?"

"Yeah, but you can't tell Nick."

She nodded, but she thought she already knew. "You were beginning to suspect that he'd arrested the wrong man, weren't you, Bryan? And I'll bet the real killer found out somehow, was afraid you were going to catch him and killed Bette to distract you—or maybe even to frame you. That's it, isn't it?"

He held her eyes a moment longer, then smiled a little, all that pent-up anger seeming to dissipate as his gaze roamed her face. "You're still some kind of aspiring Nancy Drew, aren't you, Dawn?"

"I'm too old to be Nancy Drew." Then she shrugged. "But yeah, I guess I am still into the crime-solving thing. I just didn't realize it until I got here. You have to admit we were good at it. Helped save our friend from a homicidal headcase before we were out of our teens. I'm right, aren't I?"

"No, Nancy. You're dead wrong. It was a great theory, though."

She frowned hard, not sure she'd heard him right.

"The thing is, Nick is getting an award next month—

a Lifetime Achievement Award from the Vermont Association of Law Enforcement. And it's a big deal. They asked me to present it at their annual convention, and part of that involves putting together a speech. You know, the highlights of his career and all that."

She felt her brows push against each other. "*That's* why you were going over the files?"

"It's the case that made him famous. I was going to do this whole multimedia presentation. Big screen behind me, featuring the cover from his book, maybe a clip from the movie they made out of it. De Niro played him, you know."

"*Everyone* knows."

"The thing is, I had to sneak the hard copies of the files out of the department's records room. Some of the boxed evidence, too. I didn't sign them out, the way we're supposed to, because I didn't want anyone to know. And if I'd accessed them electronically, I'd have had to log in, and that would have left a trail for sure."

"You risked your career to present an award?"

"Hell, no," he said. Then he tipped his head back again as if searching the night sky for assistance. The crickets kept chirping, and the stars kept twinkling, but neither of them offered him any help. "It wasn't risking my career. It was a little sneaky, but it's an old closed case, and if I got caught and explained my reasons to the chief, he'd have let it go and played along."

"Then why didn't you just tell him in the first place?"

"Because the committee was adamant that no one can know. That's the way this award is always given out—no one knows who will get it before the big night. It's as closely guarded a secret as the Oscar winners are. I even had to sign a confidentiality agreement."

She nodded. "So then does *anyone* know you took the files?"

"Only you. Beth and Josh will know before the night's out," he said. "I have to tell them."

"Had you returned the files yet, before all this happened?"

"No. The night I took them, I gave Nick a ride home—his car wouldn't start. I didn't even know he was coming in that day. He's retired from the force, but he still pops in. I was still on suspension—had to make up an excuse to go in at all. But that's beside the point. The point is, I wasn't expecting to see him, much less have him in my car. I ended up sticking everything inside a picnic cooler I'd left in the trunk of the Mustang, so he wouldn't see it."

She closed her eyes, thinking he couldn't look more guilty without actually trying. "Where's everything now?"

"Stashed in my garage." He sighed. "The police are still going over the house, but they'll get to the garage soon enough, and when they find those files..." He lowered his head and shook it slowly.

"It's going to look bad," she admitted.

"Yeah." He looked up at her again. "I don't want Nick to know about this award if he doesn't have to,

Dawn. It's supposed to be hush-hush until the night of the ceremony. It's a big deal."

"Yeah, you've made that clear. But so's your life."

"If I have to reveal why I did it to get out of this mess, I will. Believe me. If they find those files in my garage—or if they go looking for them for background information on the current investigation and can't find them—I'll explain myself. But not until and unless I have to. Okay?"

"Okay." She looked into his eyes, felt a little rush of something very familiar, and didn't have the will to censor herself. "We're gonna solve this thing, you know. You and me. Just like old times."

"Maybe not quite like old times," he said softly.

For a second the tension pulled tight between them. And then, to break it, she took his hand and began pulling him along the path behind her, back toward the inn.

"Where are we going?"

"To the inn, to get your car."

"To go where?" he asked.

"To Shadow Falls. You're taking me to your house."

He stopped, using his weight to stay put, despite her tugging. "My house is currently cordoned off with crime-scene tape. And for all we know, there are cops there even as we speak."

"We're going, anyway." She tugged again. "If there are police there, we'll just keep on driving. But if no one's around, we can take the opportunity to get those files out of there."

"No. I can't let you tamper with evidence, Dawn. You'll wind up sharing a cell with me."

She looked up into his face, still gripping his hand. "I can think of worse things." She almost wished she could bite back the words, but instead she averted her eyes, ignored the heat rushing into her face and went on. "Besides, we're not just going for the files. We need to get inside the house. Into the bedroom."

"Why the hell would you want—"

"Because the place where Bette died is probably the best place for me to try to make contact with her."

"I'm not gonna let you do that for me, Beth."

She was encouraged, though, because he stopped holding his ground and instead let her pull him along the path beside her. They crossed the garden and emerged onto the lawn, where the winding footpath continued all the way to the front door. They were nearly to the porch steps when a speeding vehicle came squealing around the curve in the road. Headlights blinded her as she turned in alarm.

Brakes screeched, rubber burning on the pavement, and something flew past, hurled by the driver, smashing right through the Blackberry Inn's living room window.

Bryan swore and raced toward the car, but it was already peeling out, fishtailing twice before the tires gripped the road, and speeding away.

He grabbed her upper arm and ran with her, up the

front porch steps and into the inn. Beth and Josh, Nick and Rico were all standing in the foyer, and Rico's gun was in his hand. Broken shards of glass littered the floor, and in their midst lay a brick with a piece of paper wrapped around it.

"Is everyone all right?" Bryan shouted.

"Yeah," Josh told him. "Everyone's fine."

"You see anything, Bryan?" Nick asked.

"Black, Olds 88. Probably a '93 or '94. Vermont plates, too dirty to make out. Passenger-side taillight was broken."

Dawn blinked at him, completely awestruck.

"Dawn?" Nick said.

She couldn't take her eyes off Bryan. This was a side of him she'd never seen. Damn. He really *was* a cop. She'd known it, but she hadn't *known* it. "What?"

"Did you see anything Bryan didn't?"

"Hell, he lost me at black. And I wouldn't even have been sure about that much."

"Beth, can you get me a zipper bag and some salad tongs, please?" Bryan asked.

Beth rushed away and returned with the requested items. Bryan knelt beside the brick, and used the salad tongs to pull the paper off and unfold it. It wasn't hard to read. Just one word. *Murderer.*

Dawn could see that it hit Bryan as powerfully as if the brick itself had nailed him in the belly. He actually flinched back from it.

Nick knelt beside him, took the tongs from his hands and used them to tuck the note into the plastic bag.

Then he pushed the brick in, as well, lifted up the bag, closed the zip top and handed it to Rico. "You want to take this to the station, or you want me to?"

"I'm headed back there, anyway," Rico said, and he took the bag and sent a sympathetic look at Bryan. "Hang in there, partner. This is just some ignorant jackass who wouldn't know a good cop if one was pulling him out from under a bus. Just hang in."

"I'm trying." Bryan walked away from the others, head down.

Dawn went after him, put her hand on his shoulder. "We'll go do what I said," she told him when they were out of earshot. "It'll help."

Bryan shook his head. "No. Not tonight. It's not safe, Dawn. Besides, it's not legal. I think we should do this by the book. I get caught tampering with evidence, I'll look even more guilty than I already do."

She didn't think it was possible for him to look more guilty than he already did, but she decided not to say so. Instead, she just nodded slowly. "All right, Bryan. If you're sure."

"I am. Besides," he said, "I feel like I ought to call Bette's parents tonight. And that's gonna be—"

"It's going to be hell. Did you ask your lawyer about doing that? 'Cause it sounds to me like something he'd advise against."

"I did, and you're right. He said no way. I'm doing it, anyway."

He turned and walked up the stairs. Dawn watched him go, more determined than ever to help him. But when she looked toward the front door, her mind made up to go to his house alone, she froze as a shiver of fear worked up her spine.

Okay, maybe it would be stupid to go to the scene of a serial killer's latest fun fest, in the dead of night, looking like the victim. Yeah. That was it. It wasn't anything to do with the paralyzing fear of facing a dead girl in the darkness.

She would wait till daylight. That was what she would do.

A hand closed on her shoulder and she turned, knowing it was Nick before she looked at him.

"That brick through the window bullshit shook you up, didn't it, Dawnie? You all right?"

She nodded. "Just tell me Bryan's going to be okay."

"We're gonna make sure of that, little girl. All of us together. He's glad you're here. You know that, right?"

She smiled, liking the man's easy, reassuring way. "I wasn't so sure at first. And then I thought maybe he was, and then I wasn't sure again."

"He is."

"I hope you're right, Nick."

"About him being glad you're here? I *know* I'm right."

"I meant about us making sure he's going to be okay. We have to find out who killed Bettina Wright."

"I hear you," he told her.

"Don't you worry, Dawn," Beth called from the

doorway into the dining room. "Nick is one of the best cops who ever served. The chief has put him back on duty, so he has all the authority he needs to help Bryan. And Josh is no slouch, either," she added with a look behind her at her husband, who was carrying dinner plates into the kitchen. "To say nothing about Rico. And whether you know it yet or not, Bryan's very good at his job, as well. And then there's you and me," Beth went on. "There's no way we won't solve this thing."

Dawn sighed, nodding and wishing she felt as confident as Beth did. "I'm gonna head up to my room," she said. "It was nice meeting you, Nick. Really nice. I'm glad Bryan has you on his side." He smiled warmly at her, and she felt a connection with him. Then she turned to the others. "And that goes for you, too, Rico. Night, Beth, Josh."

"Night, Dawn," Beth called after her as she hurried up the stairs to her room.

Once inside, with the door closed behind her, Dawn closed her eyes, took a breath and nodded firmly, knowing what she had to do. She went to her bag, which she had yet to unpack, and fished out the pills she used to keep the dead at bay. She took out the bottle of vodka she'd thought she might need if the pills weren't enough here, where the ghosts had always been waiting. Then she went into the adjoining bathroom and emptied both of them into the toilet. She didn't want to have them around at all—if the ghosts started showing up again, the temptation to medicate them away might be too great to resist. Best to remove temptation once and for all.

She looked up at the ceiling then. "All right, here's the deal. I'll talk to the dead girl. Bettina Wright. But no one else. Okay?"

She waited, goose bumps rising on her arms, demanding she rub them away. But nothing happened. There were no disembodied voices. No pictures hurling themselves off the walls. No misty figures hovering six inches above the carpet.

"Yeah, well, I probably need to give it some time. The Ativan's probably still in my bloodstream."

That was most likely it. And even more reason to wait until morning to go to Bryan's house—the scene of the crime. Maybe by then she would be able to see Bette.

She sank onto the bed, put her hand over her eyes and couldn't believe she was actually *hoping* to talk to the dead again. Her father had been right, after all. You couldn't run away from this thing. She wondered if he'd ever tried. Maybe that was how he knew.

Damn.

5

"You look like hell, Bryan." Beth met him at the foot of the wide staircase and pressed a hot mug of freshly brewed morning coffee into his hands.

"Thanks." The fragrant steam wafted up to his nostrils, waking up a few more brain cells, he thought, and took a deep sip. Then he took another as he walked with Beth into the kitchen.

"Didn't sleep, did you?"

"Tossed and turned until around five. Then I finally passed out."

"From sheer exhaustion, I'll bet. You think you can eat?"

"He'll force himself," Josh called from the sunny breakfast room off the kitchen.

"He's right, I will," Bryan said. "I need to try to keep myself strong through this. Keep my mind sharp, be quick on my feet. It'd be too easy to stop eating or sleeping at all."

"Go on out with your father, Bry. I'll bring you a plate."

Bryan nodded and sipped more of the coffee as he walked through the kitchen, which smelled of bacon and, God help him, cinnamon rolls. He hoped he didn't look too much like a zombie as he stepped into the sun-drenched breakfast room, which had been added on three years ago. The frame was hardwood, gleaming boards that curved, so that the room looked like the rib cage of a capsized ship. And in between those ribs, nothing but glass.

Josh sat alone at one of the three round tables. Bryan was surprised. Not at the lack of guests—he'd known Beth would cancel any reservations and hustle out the stragglers when all this broke. She would want her full attention on him and his troubles. And on Dawn and her return. But he'd expected to see Dawn there at the breakfast table with his father.

"She's not here," Josh told him before he could ask. "Sit down, relax. She'll be back."

"Where is she?"

"Borrowed the car," Beth said, entering the sunroom with three plates heaping with food, one balanced on her forearm. She put one in front of each of the men, then took her own and sat in the empty seat between them. "She said she wanted to take a drive. Maybe pick up a few things in town."

Bryan lowered his head, and stared at his plate. "And you let her go? Alone?" He lifted his eyes again, spearing his father with his gaze. "Didn't Nick tell you—"

Josh laid his napkin down while Beth paused, her first bite halfway to her mouth. "If there's something you feel I should know about, son, then you need to tell me yourself. What is it?"

Bryan closed his eyes. "Of course Nick didn't tell you—for the same reason I didn't say anything yet. He probably didn't want to scare the hell out of you both. Especially Beth. He's old school about protecting the weaker sex."

"If he thinks Beth and Dawn are the weaker parts of this family, he doesn't know them very well," Josh said, sending Beth a reassuring—and adoring—look.

It didn't seem to soothe her at all. "What does Nick think he's protecting me from, Bryan?" Beth asked.

"From knowing that every one of the victims of the Nightcap Strangler was between five foot six and five foot ten, slender, had long, straight, blond to light brown hair, was in her early to mid-twenties, was—"

"You mean they all looked like Dawn," Beth said, rising from her seat. "But...but you don't believe this *was* Nightcap. You said—you said it was a copycat."

"Either way, she's not safe running around in public by herself," Josh said. He rolled his eyes. "Did she say where she was going?"

"Did she ask directions to my place, by any chance?"

Beth nodded. "She said she wanted to just drive past it, see where you lived, where it all happened. Like it might spur her thoughts or something."

"She's going to do more than drive by," Bryan said.

He pushed back from the table. "I'd better go after her." Getting to his feet, he hesitated, reaching back down to grab the cinnamon roll and the coffee.

"But, Bryan," Beth said. "Couldn't you get into trouble for going there? It's a crime scene, and—"

"I'm not going to tamper with evidence. I just need to go get Dawn." He cupped Beth's head and leaned down to press a kiss to the top of it. She wasn't his mother. His own mom had been killed in an airline crash when he'd still been in his teens. But Beth treated him as if he was her own offspring, and he loved her as much as if it were true. "It'll be okay."

Dawn drove around a bend and had to stop the car. Ahead, in the distance, she saw a tall, flat-topped rock formation with water shooting off the end of it and plunging downward into oblivion. Beside her, a green road sign read Welcome to Shadow Falls.

The waterfall wasn't typical, wasn't what she'd expected—no glittering cascade glinting with the sunlight. The rock was dark, nearly black, and its mass, along with the taller cliffs around it, kept the sun from hitting the falls at all. She supposed at some other time of day they might sparkle and shine. But this early in the morning, the water looked murky and dark.

And she felt an answering murky darkness pooling in the pit of her stomach, but forced herself to put the car into motion again. She didn't drive into the village, but skirted around it, following Beth's directions, and soon she found the side street where Bryan lived. The houses were a good distance apart, each one surrounded by privacy and trees and open space. Eventually she found his house number, pulled into the driveway and sat for a moment in the car, looking around. Ahead of her was the garage. Beside her on the right, all too close beside her, was the house itself, the house where a woman had died.

Bryan's place was a cozy, modest-size ranch-style home near the village itself. It was all made of red bricks. The shutters were black, as was the trim. Must be a guy thing, she thought. There was a small concrete stoop, with three steps and wrought-iron railings. A little black mailbox was attached to one side of the door, beneath an outdoor light without a bulb.

"Honestly, Bry. You're a *cop,* for crying out loud. Where's your outdoor light? And the thorny hedges under all the windows? And the alarm-company-logo lawn sign?"

Of course, he wasn't there to answer, and she was just killing time. She was scared. And she wasn't ashamed to admit it. At least, not to herself.

She had to get those files before the cops did. And that was the least intimidating of the two tasks she'd set for herself when she'd rolled out of bed at five-thirty to shower and get dressed. She'd left the inn by six, all in hopes of getting this job done before Bryan figured out what she was up to and tried to stop her.

She pulled on the rubber gloves she'd stolen from Beth's kitchen drawer, opened her car door and looked around again. It was only seven now, and the traffic along the road was light. On a Sunday morning, it ought to be. Seeing no one, she decided now was the time. And once that decision was made, she knew she had to move fast or risk being caught. Quickly, she trotted around to the side of the garage, tried the door there and found it unlocked. She opened the door, and went inside.

Bryan's garage was as neat as a pin. And the picnic cooler he'd described to her sat in plain sight on a shelf in the back.

She hurried back there, grabbed it and dashed out the door again, pausing in the doorway to look around, before she popped the trunk. She slung the cooler inside and slammed the trunk closed again. Then she turned, looking and listening.

No one. Not a car passing, or a curious neighbor peering anywhere in sight.

Cool. "Mission accomplished," she whispered.

Sliding back behind the wheel, she started the car and backed out of the driveway. Then she drove ahead a block and a half, and parked along the roadside, where the car would be less likely to attract notice.

The first part of her mission was complete, she thought. If she didn't do another thing, at least she'd done that. She'd recovered those incriminating files. Maybe she and Bryan could get them back into the police department records room before anyone realized they were missing, rather than misfiled.

Now, though…now she had to tackle a much more daunting task.

She had to creep inside Bryan's house and hope there was a dead girl in there, waiting to talk to her.

She was tense. That was pretty much to be expected. There were certain physical sensations that always used to hit her when the dead were getting restless and yearning for a visit. She would feel it every time. A little shiver up her spine. Goose bumps on her forearms. The hair on her nape rising with static electricity. A little bit jumpy, a little bit restless. A weight in the center of her belly, like a lead ball in her solar plexus. Shivers. Chills. Hiccups, sometimes.

Right now she felt taut and jumpy. But as she walked down the road, she didn't feel any of those other things that usually signaled a close encounter of the dead kind.

Bryan's driveway was on her left, and she turned to face his house. Yellow tape had been strung up all the way around the place, supported by wooden slats thrust into the ground like miniature fence posts. Stepping over it was easy enough. The tape was only knee-high. It wasn't meant to be a physical barrier but a warning. Notification that if you crossed it, you were breaking the law. No way to plead ignorance, not with neon-yellow tape glaring at you. A few more pieces zigzagged across the doorway. Gloves still on, she tried the knob, but it was locked, so she proceeded to walk around the house, looking for another way in.

A window was open about two inches. She pushed it up farther, and reached inside to push the curtains apart and look around.

There was no one inside, of course. The place was a mess, though. Clearly no one had cleaned up after the party Bryan had mentioned. It was odd to think of a night of celebration and joy morphing into a morning of violence and death.

She swallowed hard, because she could feel the death there. It was heavy in the air, impossible to describe, but vivid all the same.

"I'm coming inside now, Bette. I hope you're going to talk to me."

And then she climbed in through the window, hoping to get this over with before anyone caught her there.

The place reeked of old beer and stale junk food. It was all she could do not to start cleaning up as she moved through the living room, trying to step lightly and not disturb anything. She hated the idea that she might contaminate evidence, but she was fairly certain the forensics team had already gone over the place thoroughly. Hell, there was fingerprint dust everywhere, which made damn little sense to her. There'd been a party. There would be dozens of sets of prints on everything in the place.

Underneath the mess, she thought, Bryan's place was nice. Spartan, but nice. His sofa was deep-brown rich leather, and there was a recliner that matched except for being just a shade lighter. His throw pillows were green, sage like the carpet. She would have added other colors to break it up, but it was all right as it was. For a guy. He had hardwood bookshelves lined with law-enforcement texts and true-crime stories, and memoirs written by, for and about cops.

Hmm.

She moved closer, scanning the shelves but not touching. Yes, there it was. *Nightcap,* by Nick Di Marco. Biting her lip, Dawn pulled out the book, touching nothing else, and tucked it into the back of her jeans. She'd heard enough accolades about Bryan's mentor that she'd fully intended to read his story, or at least see the movie, but hadn't gotten around to it. Having met him, she was even more curious. She liked Nick Di Marco. Besides, if this killer was copying the Nightcap Strangler, she'd better educate herself on the old case as much as possible.

A small smile pulled at her lips, though most of her was feeling pretty dire. Still, she had to admit, it was exciting, playing amateur detective again.

She would have tucked the book into her purse, only she'd left it in the car. And that made her ask herself if she'd remembered to lock it.

Hell, she wasn't sure.

Sighing, she moved through the living room, glimpsing the kitchen off to the right. It was white. Way too white. But she didn't explore it further. Instead, she headed for the hallway to the left, which had to lead to the bedrooms. But she paused at an end table, noticing a framed photo there. A familiar one. It was the same one she kept on her nightstand. A shot of the two of them, her and Bryan, more than five years ago, when they'd been madly in puppy love, arm in arm, smiling into each other's eyes. A candid moment Beth had captured without telling them. She'd sent an eight-by-ten to Dawn six months after she'd left. And apparently she'd given a copy to Bryan, as well. Hell, it was even in the same antique-looking pewter frame.

Sighing, she moved past it, down the hall, but when she stepped into the bedroom doorway, she stopped cold, too terrified to move any farther. The feeling of death was stronger here. It was heavy in the air, and dense and sort of cold, but not in a physical way. She didn't think she could describe that feeling if she had to, but she knew it when she felt it. And she felt it here.

If Death were really a being, the way people imagined he was, then he definitely left an aura behind when he came to call. She wondered briefly if he were more a comforting angel or a frightening reaper. And then she wondered if the whole sense of him was only in her imagination.

Her gaze moved to the stripped bed and froze there, and she felt her breath catch in her throat. She tried to swallow past it, failed and tried again. Sweat trickled between her brows. She *never* sweated. Her hands were trembling, palms damp. And she knew it was fear of what was about to happen. Fear of facing the ghost of a recently murdered woman. Fear that her father would show up alongside the unfortunate Bette, and that once she opened this door, she would never be able to force it closed again.

"Just get it over with, Dawn," she ordered herself in a harsh whisper. And then she lifted her chin and looked around the room. "Bette? Are you here? Talk to me, okay? Tell me who killed you."

She stood there, her knees feeling weak and shaky, her stomach slowly joining in her body's rebellion, waiting for a reply. Dreading it and hoping for it at the same time. In the past, ghosts had appeared to her many times. Sometimes they were so real she'd mistaken them for the living, until some angle or change in the light showed her that they were translucent. She'd had a lot more trouble hearing them than seeing them. So she expected to see Bette and hoped she would be able to hear her, too. But no apparition floated into the room. No reply came. She sat there for a half hour, waiting. But there was nothing. And she could tell by the lack of those telltale physical signs that there wasn't going to be anything.

"This is unreal. This is…this is freaking…" Dawn lowered her head, shook it slowly and took one last look around the bedroom before finally turning and walking out again. She clambered out the same window through which she'd entered, then closed it behind her, leaving a gap she estimated was close to what it had been before. She peeled off the gloves, stuffed them into her jeans pocket, then turned to head down the driveway.

She was halfway to the road, her eyes on her feet, her mind deep in thought, when a man's voice said, "Bette?"

Hell.

She lifted her head fast and met the striking dark eyes of a good-looking guy with a shiny shaved head, muscles bulging under his T-shirt. She didn't know him. But he was not, she determined after only a split second, a ghost.

He looked her up and down with a hostile expression clearly meant to frighten her. "Who the hell are you?" He made it sound like an accusation.

"No one." She kept walking, refusing to let him intimidate her with his size and the tattoos that were like ink sleeves, covering both arms as completely as the black T-shirt covered his torso. Didn't the killer always return to the scene of the crime? Just in case, she yanked her cell phone from her pocket, flipped it open and pressed the nine and then the one. Her thumb hovered over the one as she continued to the sidewalk and turned, putting her back to the stranger as she picked up her pace.

She heard his steps following and figured he wasn't giving up as easily as she'd hoped, and that maybe she ought to at least try to get his name, but first she needed to be sure he wasn't about to kill her.

Predators preyed on the weak. So she had to appear just the opposite, right?

She stopped and swung around, holding up the phone and glaring at him. "Just make me hit this button, pal, and I'll have cops crawling all over you. Who the hell do you think you are, trying to scare a woman you don't even know? Are you the one who murdered that girl? Is that it? You gonna try for me, too, now? Huh?"

His eyes widened as she spoke, and he took a step

back, holding up his hands. "Whoa, whoa! That ain't it at all. You're way off."

"Am I?" She patted herself on the back inwardly for the show of strength and how well it had worked—even while reminding herself not to let her guard down. "Then what the hell are you doing here?" she asked. "That house is a crime scene, you know."

"You...you a cop?" he asked.

She didn't say yes or no, just held the phone up higher, and while she had it up there, she slid her thumb to the camera key and pressed it, taking his picture without him being any the wiser.

Damn, she was good at this, she thought with an inner smile.

"Identify yourself, or I *will* call the cops."

"Jaycam," he said.

She frowned. "What the *hell* is a Jaycam?"

"I am. Bettina, she was my girlfriend. They told me she was..." His eyes shifted, down and to the right. "Murdered. I heard it happened right there, in that house. The rookie cop she'd been banging did it. Bastard should have been in prison already, then my girl would'a been safe."

"Why do you say that?"

"He shot that guy last month."

She nodded slowly. "The way I heard it, he didn't have a choice. It was investigated, he was cleared—"

"Cops take care of their own." He lifted his chin toward the house. "They'll let him get away with *this,* too. Cover it up some way. Pin it on someone else. He'll walk. Shit, he'll be back on the job. While Bette's rotting in the ground. You wait and see."

She almost felt a little sorry for him, the way his voice broke just then. And yet she didn't see a hint of moisture in his dark eyes. Maybe he was faking it. "I'm sorry for your loss," she said. "But just so you know, I had nothing to do with it."

"I didn't say you did. He's gonna pay, though. You mark my words, that bastard is not gonna get away with what he did to Bette."

She swallowed hard, or tried to. Her throat was suddenly very dry. And there was no point in trying to talk him down. He was either grieving and furious, or covering up for the fact that he was the killer. Either way, he was dangerous. "I have to go now," she said. Then, stiffening her spine, she turned her back to him again and hoped he wasn't going to bash her over the head or grab her by the throat.

"You look like her," he said as she walked away. "You'd best stay away from that bastard, or he'll freaking kill you next."

"Thanks for the warning." She still had her phone in one hand, but she patted her jeans pocket in search of her keys with the other, and then realized she'd left them in the car, which meant she hadn't locked it, which meant she would be lucky if it was still there.

But it was. She saw Beth's Audi up ahead, right where she'd left it. If her luck held, her purse would still be inside it. She didn't hear Bette's pissed-off boyfriend following her, and she didn't turn around to see if he was still watching her.

At least not until she saw Bryan's Mustang pull over behind her borrowed vehicle. That made her look back over her shoulder in a hurry.

Jaycam was still back there, watching her, and looking intently now at the Mustang.

Dawn broke into a run, heading right to the driver's door, jumping behind the wheel and starting it up almost in one motion. Then she was peeling away from the curb, knowing full well that Bryan would follow.

She glanced in the rearview mirror and saw him pulling out behind her. Then she looked the other way. The idiot with the ridiculous name was walking toward the street as they flew by, but they were leaving him behind.

She sighed in relief, not seeing a third vehicle parked anywhere nearby. Maybe he'd arrived at Bryan's on foot. Which might mean he lived close by. They would have to find out.

Glancing sideways, almost as an afterthought, she saw her purse lying tipped over on the passenger seat, its contents spilled all around it. She must have pulled away too fast and knocked it over. At least it was still there. She tugged the book from the back of her jeans as she drove and tucked it into the purse, then scooped up the other items one-handed and crammed them in, as well.

She drove until she'd put a couple of miles between herself and the hulking, sulking alleged boyfriend, and then started looking for a place to stop. She was still shaking like a leaf, and she needed a break, wise or not. There was a diner just at the edge of the village she had yet to explore.

She pulled into the parking lot alongside the Cascade Diner, and Bryan pulled into the spot right beside her. Sighing in relief, she laid her head down on the steering wheel and tried to get her still-tensed-up muscles to relax.

And then Bryan was there, opening her door. He laid a hand on the back of her neck. It felt cool on her skin, and she felt the breath sigh from her lungs all at once. One touch from his hand and the tension just rushed out of her. She hadn't expected that.

"What the hell was that all about?" he asked softly.

She drew a fresh breath, lifted her head and regretted it instantly, because his hand fell away. "You said you and Bette were…friends. The sex was casual. You weren't…in love or…?"

"We weren't in love."

She nodded. "Well, she was cheating on you. Or with you. Or something." She watched the frown that bent his brows, and then she pulled out her cell phone, pulled up the photo and turned it to show him. "With this guy. He says his name's Jay something. Jaycam, I think."

Bryan looked at the photo and nodded. "His name's Jeremy Cameron. I suppose he thinks Jaycam sounds tougher. He's a punk. Bette dated him for six months, then ditched him back in March, and he hasn't gotten over it yet."

She blinked slowly and held his gaze. "He have a record?"

Bryan nodded. "Possession, assault and a burglary conviction. He did five years for the burglary."

"What are the details on the assault?" she asked.

Bryan looked impressed by her question. "It wasn't a girlfriend. Wasn't even a woman. It was another tattooed, much-arrested jackass who pissed him off in a bar one night."

She nodded. "Still, he's got a temper and is capable of violence. I think he makes an awfully good suspect in Bette's murder, Bryan. Don't you?"

"He would, if he had enough brains to pull it off. The guy who killed her got in and out of my place without me even knowing it. He killed her without leaving any trace evidence, and he managed to copy a sixteen-years-ago serial killer's M.O. to a T, including details that were never released to the public. Which he must have been pretty damn smart to get hold of. He look that bright to you?"

"People can be smarter than they look. Where does he live, Bryan? Near you?"

"Ten miles from me, at least. Shitty apartment above a bar in a dirt-poor neighborhood."

"I didn't know there were bad neighborhoods in Vermont," she muttered.

He smiled. "Very few."

"And what does he drive?" she asked.

Bryan frowned at her. "You know, I don't know. But I'll find out."

"Ten to one it's a black Olds 88 with a broken taillight."

"I think that's a pretty good bet." He turned and glanced at the diner, then back at her. "You have breakfast?"

"No, I wanted to leave before you got up and stopped me. You?"

"Not really. I was just about to when I found out what you were up to. You wanna get something here?"

She met his eyes, smiled at him and nodded. "Yeah. We can get to work solving this thing."

Bryan rolled his eyes, but she knew he wasn't going to be able to keep turning her down. He reached past her, snatched a baseball cap off the passenger seat and handed it to her. "Tuck your hair up underneath that, put on a pair of sunglasses and stop walking around Shadow Falls wearing a Victim Here sign, would you?"

"If you insist." As she did what he asked, she felt something she hadn't felt in five long years.

She felt taken care of. Watched over.

She'd been taking care of herself for so long, she'd kind of forgotten how nice that sort of thing could be every now and then.

It was early enough that there were a lot of patrons still enjoying their breakfast. Most looked at Bryan as he passed, then looked quickly away, making him feel like a leper.

Only one met his eyes and said, "Mornin', Officer Kendall."

"Mornin', Nate," Bryan replied to the older man. "You enjoying your summer break?"

"I prefer working. Can't wait to open the lodge when the snow flies."

"I'll bet. Hope it's a good winter for you and Sugar Tree."

"You and me both, son. And I hope your…problems… work out the way they ought."

"Thanks." It hurt a little that the confirmed town grouch, Nate Kelly, was the only one to wish him well this morning. But it touched him, too. He and Dawn made their way to a vacant table and sat down.

And then she leaned close to him and whispered, "I got the files from the garage."

It shook him, her leaning close like that. Even with a table between them, it seemed intimate and made him wish it really was. "You shouldn't have done that," he whispered back. "Taken that risk, I mean. I don't want you to end up being charged as an accessory, Dawn."

"That can only happen if you're charged with murder. And you're not going to be."

He lowered his eyes. "I think it's actually pretty close to happening already." When he glanced up at her again, she looked stricken. At least, he thought she did, behind those oversize California sunglasses. Sparkles glittered from the sides of them. *Sparkles,* for crying out loud.

The waitress came and took their orders, filled their

cups—his with coffee, hers with tea—and hurried away again.

"We'll go over those files together. Tonight," Dawn said, when they were alone again. "I say this Jaycam is a great suspect. And there have to be others. Maybe someone with nothing against Bette at all. Maybe their issue is with you."

"I've been thinking about that."

"And?"

He licked his lips, glancing around the diner, narrowing his eyes on one man who'd taken a seat at the counter just after he and Dawn had come in. The guy was hunched over a newspaper that was open to the same page it had been since he first sat down.

"And?" Dawn asked again.

Bryan shifted his attention back to her. "And I haven't been on the job all that long. Most of my work has been pretty mundane. I mean, until that hostage standoff two months ago, I never even had to draw my weapon, much less fire it."

She nodded slowly, took a sip of her tea and then waited silently as the waitress brought their food.

She didn't even look at her omelet, just waited for enough privacy to continue the conversation. "What about that?" she asked.

"Take a bite and I'll tell you."

She stared at him, blinked behind the dark lenses. "Huh?"

"Take a bite of your omelet and I'll tell you." He nodded at the food. "You don't look good—wait, scratch that. You do look good. You *always* look good—you just don't look *well*. As in healthy. So take a bite."

She sighed and picked up her fork, scooped up a big piece of the omelet and popped it into her mouth.

He nodded in approval. "The guy I shot had family. Parents too decrepit to be a threat. Friends who didn't really give a shit if he was alive or not, he was such an asshole to everyone. And one brother. No record, but the guy hates my guts and made it clear he wasn't going to let it go when it hit the press that I'd been cleared of any wrongdoing in his brother's death. I got several threats from him right after—three phone calls, two letters, all documented. They started a watch file on him at the department, even sent a couple of officers by to read him the riot act, tell him he could end up doing time for harassing a police officer if he didn't cease and desist. I haven't heard from him since."

She nodded. "He got a name?"

He pointed at her fork. She took a bite, and he smiled, because of the way she rolled her eyes as she did it. "His name is Everette Stokes. His brother, the one I shot, was Merle."

"Okay, so now we have two suspects. Stokes and Cameron. I'm going to need a notebook."

Bryan held up a hand to stop her and nodded to her left. She stopped speaking and looked up to see what he'd already seen.

The man from the counter. He'd finally got off his stool and headed over to the two of them. Bryan's mind clicked into cop mode instantly. Five-nine, one hundred and eighty-five pounds, stocky and solid, sandy-blond hair cut short and doctored with too much gel so he looked like a hedgehog on top, blue eyes, no scars, one pierced ear. Cheap suit that was trying to look like a nice one. He had good taste but not enough money to go with it. No visible trace of a weapon. All of that in one sweeping glance.

Then the man was speaking to him. "Sorry to interrupt. You're Bryan Kendall, right?"

"Depends on who's asking.

"Doesn't matter, I already know. You're Bryan Kendall. And who are you?" he asked, turning his attention to Dawn.

"I'm—"

"She's none of your business."

"Why are you in disguise, miss?"

Bryan held up a hand toward Dawn. "Don't say anything. He's a reporter."

Then he looked at the guy for confirmation of what he'd guessed.

The guy sighed. "Mitch Brown, *Burlington Gazette*."

"That would explain why I didn't recognize you," Bryan said. "So you came all the way from Burlington? I must be big news."

"The biggest. I already know the murder was a carbon copy of the work of the Nightcap Strangler. A crime spree solved by your friend—some say best friend, some say mentor—Nick Di Marco. I also heard they're going to arrest you for the murder today," he said. "Any truth to that?"

"It's not like they'd give me the heads-up, Mitch."

"And what about you, ma'am? What were you doing out at Officer Kendall's house? It's a crime scene, you know."

Dawn blinked. "What makes you think I was—"

"I saw you walking down his driveway and back to your car. Who was that guy you were talking to?"

She licked her lips, shifting her gaze to Bryan and then back to the reporter. He didn't tell her to be quiet again, partly because he knew she was smart enough not to say too much, and partly because he knew it would piss her off if he acted like he thought otherwise.

She said, "Look, I really have no comment on any of this. But I don't want you thinking I've got anything to hide. So who I am is an old friend of Bryan's. My name is Dawn Jones. I'm from the West Coast, and I drove by his place out of curiosity and nothing more. The guy was a stranger, hitting on me. I shot him down."

"Really? Because, frankly, miss, it looked to me like you were a little bit afraid of him."

She shrugged. "Can't help what it looked like to you, can I? Although now that I think about it, thanks a lot for being chivalrous enough to come to my rescue. Oh, wait, you didn't, did you? You just stood there, watching a lone woman being harassed by a tank of a man, in the very same spot where another woman was murdered only days ago. Sweet of you. Do you think you could leave us alone to enjoy our breakfast now?"

He was rocked by her firm put-down, and it took him a moment to regroup. Bryan admired her even more than he had before and had to fight not to smile at her tactics.

And then the guy cleared his throat and said, "Actually, I'd like to get a statement first. Bryan Kendall, did you kill Bettina Wright?"

"No."

"Do you know who did?"

"Not yet," he said. "And that's all I have to say. So if you don't mind…"

The guy turned back to Dawn again. "Just one more question, and it's a repeat. Why are you in disguise, Ms. Jones?"

"I told you, I'm not." Sighing in frustration, she took off the sunglasses, pulled off the baseball cap and shook her head slightly so her hair fell around her shoulders. "Happy now?" she asked.

"Look, I'm just doing my job here."

"Yeah, well, unless your job includes making sure my omelet gets cold before I can eat it, take a hike, okay?"

He smiled slightly, nodded fast and backed away, his entire demeanor suddenly friendly rather than aggressive. Bryan rolled his eyes, because he knew precisely why that change had occurred. It had taken place the second the man had seen Dawn without the getup.

She was that beautiful. Beautiful enough to stop a man in his tracks and change his entire train of thought.

Damn, he'd missed her.

She refocused on him. "I don't like that guy, Bryan."

"He liked you," he said.

"I don't care. Remember his name, if it's even real. Mitch Brown. It sounds made up to me. We should do a…a background check on him."

"If you finish your omelet, I'll get Rico to do it today."

She smiled and shoveled another huge bite into her mouth, still grinning as she chewed.

He knew why, too. This was feeling more and more like old times, and he was kind of glad it felt as good to her as it did to him. Hell, he knew the past was gone, that they couldn't go back. But this part of it, this team-sleuth thing they had going on, it was as good as it had ever been. Better, maybe. He hadn't wanted to enjoy having her back—but he *was* enjoying it, in spite of himself. And in spite of the fact that his entire life had been turned inside out.

They were still good together. And he was damned glad of that.

And yet, he was worried. "Put that gorgeous hair back into hiding. We need to finish our breakfast and get you out of sight again."

"You think the Nightcap Strangler is staking out diners, looking for me?" she asked.

"I think if you keep catching the attention of every red-blooded male in Shadow Falls you'll find something more interesting to do than help me solve a murder."

She tipped her head to one side and smiled, and he

knew she'd enjoyed the compliment. Damn, he had to be careful here. There was one thing he needed to remember, besides the fact that she was just the kind of woman the Nightcap Strangler, or his number-one fan, went after.

He also had to remember that she was going to leave him again. Either as soon as this was over, or as soon as she started seeing ghosts again. Whichever came first.

6

Seven hours later, Bryan's father dropped a hot-off-the-presses copy of the *Burlington Gazette* on the dining room table just as they were all gearing up for dinner. The first thing that caught his eye was a photo of Dawn—an old one. And it was just underneath a banner headline.

Nightcap Strangler Back from Dead
Have Cops Turned to Psychic in Desperation?

"What the hell?" Bryan said as he read the headline.

"What?" Dawn asked, leaning over his shoulder, looking at the paper. "Oh, no."

Bryan began to read aloud, halfway down the page. "'Dawn Jones was spotted today at the scene of the crime. Five years ago Ms. Jones was instrumental in saving the life of Blackberry, Vermont, chief of police Cassandra Jackson, some say because of her ability to communicate with the dead, a talent her notorious father, the late Mordecai Young, claimed to possess throughout his criminal career.'"

She blinked and lifted her head. "Where did he get that photo of me? It's old, but…"

"Probably found it on the Net somewhere," Josh said.

"So I guess keeping you from being seen is off the table," Bryan muttered. "I don't like this."

"We've really got to look into that reporter now," Dawn said. "How does he know all this stuff about me?"

"I don't know, Dawn." Bryan put his hand over hers where it rested on his shoulder.

"Don't hate him too much," Josh said. "He's listing off suspects like appetizers on a Ruby Tuesday's menu. No names—he probably doesn't want to get sued—but he's punching a lot of holes in the police department's case against you, Bry."

"Really?" Frowning, Bryan looked more closely at the article.

The phone started ringing just then, and Beth went to get it, then held it out. "It's Nick. He said to put him on speaker." She thumbed a button, and said, "Go ahead, Nick."

"You got a reprieve, Kendall," Nick said.

Bryan lifted his head, looking at the phone. "What do you mean?"

"There's a reporter, a Mitch Brown. You see his piece in the Burlington paper?"

"Yeah, I was just starting to read it now."

"Well, he claims there are people who need to be ruled out before anyone makes any arrests. He lists Bettina's ex-lover, the brother of the guy you shot in that standoff and an English lit professor who knew every one of the victims the first time around and, it turns out, knew Bettina, too."

Bryan heard Dawn's sigh of relief, felt her hand tighten on his shoulder. "That's one more suspect than we have on our list," she whispered.

Bryan nodded but tried not to get his hopes up. "I'm far from cleared, though."

"True, pal. But you aren't going to be arrested today. This reporter did you a huge favor. The evidence hasn't changed in the least, and you still look guilty as hell, but the chief doesn't want the press turning on him on this one. So he'll give it another day or two, make sure he's covered his bases, not to mention his ass. Although I'd still like to kick this reporter square in the balls for plastering Dawnie's photo on the front page."

"I really don't think I'm in any danger, Nick," Dawn said.

"Yeah, well, you didn't live in Shadow Falls when the original Nightcap was stalking pretty girls who looked so much like you they could be your sister. Women were living in fear, Dawnie, and I remember it all too well. You be extra careful and stay safe until we get this guy, whoever he is."

She nodded, warming a little at Nick's protective attitude. He was a decent guy. "Thanks, Nick. I will."

Then she frowned, and Bryan could see the wheels turning in her mind. "Nick?"

"Yeah?"

"Who is this college professor Brown mentioned in his article?"

"Dead end. Nice lady, name of Olivia Dupree. I looked at her during the first round of this mess. And it's true enough, every one of the victims knew her. Most of them were students, and she was, too, at the time, so it makes sense they would know her. Bette did, too. But that doesn't mean anything more than that the killer moved in the same circles they did, or was picking his victims from among the student body."

"Oh."

She seemed deep in thought then, so Bryan took over. "Thanks a bunch for calling, Nick."

"I'm glad to have some halfway decent news for a change. Have a good night."

"Will do. Night, pal."

Nick hung up, and Bryan sighed and turned to Josh and Beth. "What do you say we order pizza, rent some movies and try to put all this out of our minds and have a normal evening?"

His dad met his eyes and nodded. And he alone, Bryan thought, understood why he wanted a normal night tonight. It was because he knew this reprieve was only a temporary one. This might be his last normal evening for a long time.

I yanked the newspaper from the seat of the Thunderbird, pulling it toward me and blinking down at it in the glow of the dashboard lights. Mitchell Brown. Bastard. He was getting in my way, and if it continued, he'd be next.

No, he won't. The voice of the murderer inside me disagreed, just as he always did. *It's kind of fun, don't you think? He's throwing suspects out there because it'll sell more papers than a simple open-and-shut case would do. That's all.*

"I'll fuckin' kill him."

You'll fuckin' kill her, my twin said. And as he said it, he shifted my eyes to the front of the newspaper again, where the pretty girl's photograph didn't come close to doing her justice. I'd *seen* her. She was way hotter than the grainy old black-and-white shot.

I swallowed hard and looked away, toward the house I'd been watching.

I told you it wasn't going to be just a one-time deal.

"I don't have a choice," I told him. "The rookie has to go down for this. It's the only way. To make that happen, there has to be one more."

One more? His laughter filled the car, loud enough that I had to cover my ears to try to shut it out, but of course that did no good whatsoever. *One more? Listen to you! There are going to be lots more, my friend.* Lots *more.*

"But not that one," I told him, shifting my eyes to the newspaper again.

"Oh, buddy, you're not getting this, are you? That one is going to be the best one of all. Now get your ass

moving. You know better than to linger too long. Some-one could see the car.

"No one would link it to me, anyway," I said, but I opened the door and got out. The night air was cool on my face. I walked toward the silent darkened house and tugged the ski mask down over my face as I did. My gloves were on already, my kit attached to my belt.

Apparently my twin had decided to shut the hell up. He was still with me, though. I could feel him riding along, aroused as all hell. He was slowly stroking his erection while I did all the work. And how fair was that?

I was erect, too, though doing nothing about it. That would come later, away from here, in private, where no DNA could get left behind. Not here. Not now. No matter how turned on I got.

I found all the windows closed and locked. So were both doors. But that wasn't all that much of a challenge to me. I knelt in the rear of the house and tapped the glass of one of the two casement windows there until I hit it hard enough to shatter it. A few pieces tumbled inward, onto the basement floor, but I was confident she wouldn't hear it two floors above, where she slept. God, I loved houses with basements. The bigger, the better.

I wiggled the rest of the glass loose, piling it on the ground beside the window, until I had a clean open-ing that wasn't going to cut me on the way through. DNA again. You had to be careful with that shit. Then I

squeezed through, feet first, and landed on the basement floor.

Nothing of interest there. A typical musty-smelling
basement with a furnace, and piles of boxes here and
there. I was interested only in finding the stairway up,
and I did so without much trouble at all.

The door at the top wasn't locked. Of course it wasn't.
I was a little amazed at how scared most women were
about their cellars—it was a rare one who'd venture
down to check the breaker box in the dark. And yet none
of them ever put locks on their cellar doors. As if what
they were so afraid of could only wait down there. As
if it would never emerge into the aboveground sections
of the house.

It's emerging now, baby!

"Shut up," I whispered. But I couldn't even pretend
I wasn't feeling the same exhilaration he was. My skin
was tingling, my heart beating faster with every step.
I could already see her delicate hands clawing at my
gloved ones. I could see her body twisting and turning
uselessly as I choked the life out of her. It would be
good. And though I was only doing it because it was
necessary, thanks to that damned reporter, I knew I was
going to enjoy it. Maybe even more than the last one.

But not as much as the next one!

"There won't be a next one. This is unavoidable,
but—"

*There will be. And you already know who. Hell,
you're wishing it was her right now, tonight. Let's pretend, why don't we? Let's pretend this one is her. It'll*

*be easy in the dark. And then we're going to leave what
we brought, just to scare the hell out of her, because
it'll be even better if she knows we're coming for her
next. Her fear...God, we can eat it with a spoon, that
delicious fear, from now until we take her. She is going
to be our masterpiece, my friend. You know she is. The
culmination of our life's work together.*

I caught myself rubbing a hand over my bulging
hard-on, right through the pants I wore. I shivered with
pleasure but stopped myself. And then I walked up the
stairs to the second floor, walked into her bedroom and
stood looking at her as she slept.

I'd been determined to ignore him, my twin, my
alter ego. But as I stared at her, the face I saw was not
hers.

And a few seconds later, when I tightened the black
silk stocking around her throat, it wasn't her I saw come
awake in stark terror, eyes widening, hands clawing at
mine and then at the stocking itself, her body twisting
like a fish on dry land. Dying. It wasn't her I saw dying,
surrendering her life to the power in my two hands.

It wasn't her I saw.

It was the beautiful Dawn Jones.

Dawn was up early, earlier than everyone else in the
house. To be honest, she'd barely slept at all. Last night
had been too...too much like a blast from the past. She
and Bryan had watched a few episodes of *Magnum,
P.I.* on DVD, because the show was a shared favorite,
despite originally airing long before their time. Bryan's

dad had turned him on to it. Then Bryan had turned her on to it, and it had become one of their things.

So they'd watched TV and laughed at the shortness of the shorts on Tom Selleck's long, hairy legs, and praised the cleverness of the voiceover method of narration, and picked apart the flaws in the mysteries being solved. Beth and Josh had turned in early, but she and Bryan had stayed up, made brownies, eaten them topped with vanilla ice cream and talked and talked and talked.

They talked about the Blackberry Inn, and some of the more interesting guests who had come and gone. They talked about some of the hot rods she'd worked on in San Bernadino and their celebrity owners. They talked about baseball and restaurants, holidays and friends in common. They talked about everything except the murders and their relationship. Bryan had ruled those two topics off-limits from the beginning. At first it had driven her crazy—all those files, which they'd moved to the trunk of the Mustang, just waiting to be pored over. She was itching to dig into the case. But she did understand why Bryan needed a night off from all that. And given that Nick felt the reporter had bought Bryan some more time, she didn't mind all that much.

But as the night had worn on, it had begun to feel... intimate between them again, especially near the end, as the credits of the final episode ran. The room got all quiet, and when she looked at Bryan, sitting close beside her—but not touching—on the sofa, he was staring at her with an expression in his eyes that told her very clearly that he was thinking about kissing her. And she knew that if he did, she would take him straight to her bedroom for the rest of the night. And he would regret that.

She almost considered it, anyway. But then she closed her eyes, lowered her head. "I don't know what's going on with me yet, Bry. I really don't."

"What do you mean, you don't know what's going on with you? You've been taking pills, drinking too much and eating too little. You haven't been taking care of yourself at all. But at least the ghosts have left you alone. You came back home to help me get out of this mess I'm in—we both know you wouldn't be here otherwise. And I think we both also know that you'll be heading back into hiding the minute this is over. Right?"

She took a deep, slow breath. "The pills are to keep… keep the ghosts away."

He lifted his brows. "They have *pills* for that now? I don't remember hearing about that in the latest round of FDA approvals."

"The shrink thought I was imagining them, and attributed everything to anxiety and post-traumatic stress over my father's death. But the irony is, it turns out they work as well for real ghosts as imaginary ones."

"And the vodka?"

"I wasn't drinking much. I just thought I might need something extra while I was back here. I really expected them to inundate me."

"Uh-huh."

"The thing is, Bryan, they haven't. I haven't seen a single ghost since I've been back."

"Well, with the pills and the booze..."

"I dumped them. I haven't taken a pill or even a drink since I've been here."

He shrugged. "Then maybe you don't need them anymore."

"But, Bryan, you don't understand. I *wanted* to see one. I wanted to get Bette to tell me who killed her. But...even at your house, even sitting on the bed where she *died,* I didn't—"

"You went *inside?* Dammit, Dawn, I told you not to do that. It's a crime scene."

She rolled her eyes. "You're missing the point. I don't think I...have it anymore. I think I've lost it, Bryan." She got up off the sofa and paced to the TV, bent to take the DVD out and replace it in its case, just for something to do so she didn't have to watch him searching her face for answers she didn't have. "I've spent the past five years hiding from a curse—or a gift—that I didn't think I wanted. Or could even handle. My whole reason for moving so far was to get away from my dead father and his dead pals."

"And now?" Bryan asked. "If you can't talk to dead people anymore, does that mean your reason for living on the West Coast is gone, too?" He came up behind her, closed his hands on her shoulders, turned her to face him. "Are you saying you're thinking you might stay, Dawn?"

She stared up at him and was scared to death by the hint of hope she saw beginning to light up behind his eyes. God, she didn't want to hurt him again. "I don't know. I mean, no, of course I'm not staying here. I've got a good job—"

"You're a genius with classic cars. You could get a good job anywhere."

"It might come back," she whispered. "Even though it's gone now, it might come back."

"It might not."

"But I think I...I *want* it to come back."

Bryan frowned, blinking at her and looking almost as confused as she felt. "But you *hate* it."

"I could help you, Bryan, if only I still had it." She pressed her lips tight, lowered her eyes. "Dammit, I'm sorry. I'm so sorry I turned my back on my gift. My father warned me there would be repercussions, but I just thought it was more rambling from a homicidal lunatic."

"It was."

"But now I don't know. I want it back, Bryan."

He drew a deep breath. "Just for my sake?" he asked softly.

"Honestly? I don't know. I really don't know. Maybe I want it to come back just this once and then vanish forever. I don't know if it's ever coming back or if it's really gone for good, and I don't know if I'm staying here or going back to California. I don't know anything. And that's why I can't...can't...I can't—"

"You can't let things get beautiful between us again."

That was a hell of a way to put it. And yet it *had* been beautiful between them. It had been young and innocent and perfect. And she wanted it to be that way again. "It wouldn't be fair."

"To you? Or to me?"

She licked her lips and lowered her head. "I need some time, Bryan."

"I wish I could tell you to take all the time you want. That I can wait. But, Dawn, you know I might not have time to give you. And I really would like to settle things between us before time runs out. I know I said I didn't want to talk about the past, about us, but—"

"I have to believe we'll have time to work through things, to have that talk. We *will*. I promise."

He looked into her eyes so deeply she felt as if he were touching her soul. "I'm going to hold you to that."

She nodded, reached up to him and brushed his hair away from his forehead. Her fingers trembled against his skin, and her body seemed pulled toward his. More than anything in the world, she wanted to stand on tiptoe, give in to that pull and kiss him.

But it wouldn't be fair to him, or to herself. Her father's gift—the one she'd called a curse—had been the center of her existence for five years. Everything she'd done had been because of it. To think that it was just gone—that it might have been gone for quite some time now, and that everything she'd done had been utterly without reason—shook her to the core of her being. She wasn't even sure who she was without it. Hating it, rejecting it, had been her life up to now.

"Thank you for coming home, Dawn," Bryan said softly. "I'm really glad you're here."

"So am I. Good night, Bryan." And in spite of all her mind's warnings not to, she leaned up and pressed her lips to his. His lips were warm and soft and moist. The kiss was quick. Too quick. Then she turned and hurried up the stairs to her room without once looking back.

And then she hadn't slept.

She made a pot of coffee and took the first steaming cup out onto the front porch. It was 6:30 a.m., and already the sun was pouring down on the green, green hills of Blackberry.

She sat on the porch swing, wrapped snug and warm in one of the thick fluffy Turkish robes her mother offered for sale to customers. It was violet and bore the Blackberry Inn logo on the left breast. She wore matching slippers. Both welcome-home gifts that had been waiting in her room for her.

As she sat there sipping, listening to the chorus of birds singing madly, happy she'd decided to try the vanilla hazelnut creamer, a familiar Crown Victoria pulled into the drive.

She saw Nick Di Marco behind the wheel and waved hello, even as he cut the engine and got out. He smiled, but she knew immediately that something was wrong.

Nick's smiles tended to involve his entire face. This one barely even involved his mouth. Hands thrust into his pockets, he came up the steps, then leaned back against the railing, facing her.

"Hey, Dawnie," he said, and gestured back toward his car. "What do you think you could do with this to make it pop? Anything?"

"Hell, yeah," she said, eyeing the Crown Vic. "I'd start with some bodywork to smooth out the rough spots, then a custom paint job and some tinted glass. Then make it ride low and put in some ground effects. Shoot, Nick, she could be a real collectible, if you wanted." She lifted a brow. "But you're not into that kind of thing, are you?"

"You kidding? I had the hottest car on campus, back in the day." He grinned.

"Really? What kind?"

"You first. What do you drive, back at home?"

"Seventy-four Corvette Stingray. Metalflake red, but a deep red, like wine, you know?"

"Convertible?"

"T-top. Immaculate. Not much to a collector, but I really love my car."

"I'll bet you do." He lowered his head, shook it slowly. "That's such a pretty smile. I feel like a bastard for having to chase it away first thing in the morning. But I got no choice here."

She braced herself for bad news. "I figured. You're here awfully early for a casual visit. And with it being an hour's drive, you must have been up at dawn."

"Never really slept," he said. "Everyone else still asleep?"

"Yeah. Beth's closed the inn to customers until this… well, you know." She held up her mug. "Coffee?"

"No time." He licked his lips.

"Well, why don't you tell me the bad news and get it over with, then? I can pass it along, and that way you can get back to work."

He nodded, not even denying it. "Bryan might take it better coming from you, anyway," he said. "Though I don't really know how anything could make this feel better at all." He drew a breath, then said, "They've found another victim."

She came out of her seat, because of all the theories that had been swirling in her brain as to what his bad news might be, that was not among them.

"Same description, same M.O., right down to the whiskey."

"Oh, my God."

"They're gonna arrest him today, Dawnie. No question in my mind on that. He's still the most likely suspect, and no judge in the world will risk leaving a serial killer running free. No matter what the newspaper says."

"Bryan is no serial killer. You know that as well as I do." She was staring at her slippered feet beneath the robe, but then her head came up fast. "But he was here all night. He was right here with me and Josh and Beth. It's proof that he's innocent."

"Families lie to protect their own," Nick said. "Juries

know that. And it could be said that he had time to slip out sometime during the night. But I suppose it's worth something. And I believe you. I believe in Bryan. That's why I brought these." He pulled a manila envelope from under his jacket. "Crime-scene photos, the initial report, statement from the husband, who came in from working graveyard a little after midnight and found her." She reached for them, but he pulled the envelope back. "I don't want you looking at this stuff, Dawnie. At least, not alone."

She nodded, her expression solemn. "I won't, I promise. Thanks for the warning, Nick."

He clasped her shoulder, his grip solid and warm. "We're going to get him out of this, honey. I promise you that."

"I know we will," she said. Then she nodded at his car. "Go ahead. I'll…I'll break the news to everyone."

"Hang in there, kid," he told her. "I'll be back later on—when they come for him. Moral support and all that."

"Yeah." Tears burned behind her eyes, and her throat was tight. "Thanks. I'll tell him."

Nick turned, jogged down the steps and back to his car. Seconds later, he was driving away.

There was a terrible feeling rising inside her. More than a feeling—a *knowing*. Something terrible would happen if Bryan went to jail. Something irreversible. Dawn waited until he was out of sight, and then she turned and ran into the house, up the stairs, flung Bryan's bedroom door open and lunged into his room. "Bry!"

But he wasn't there.

She stood still for a second, a little breathless, listening, and she heard the shower. "Fine. Great, in fact." Moving to his closet, she opened it, scanned the inside and yanked out a duffel bag. Then she went to the dresser, tugged it open and began pulling clothes out and stuffing them in the bag. A couple of pairs of jeans, some underwear, socks, T-shirts. She went to the closet, grabbed some button-down shirts and a hoodie, and crammed those inside, too.

She was still packing when he came in from the shower, and she felt him go still, staring at her for a long moment while she kept right on doing what she was doing. And then, finally, he spoke.

"Dawn? Hon, what are you doing?"

"Packing."

"Yeah, that's obvious, but—" He moved to her, caught her shoulders in his hands to stop her frantic movements.

She stood staring at him, the duffel in one hand, his running shoes in the other. He had to see the tears in her eyes.

"Dawn, slow down and tell me what's going on, will you?"

She shook her head. "There's no time. We have to get out of here, Bry. We have to go now."

"I'm not going anywhere until you tell me why."

She looked frantically toward the door, as if expecting

the cops to kick it in at any moment. And then back at him. "Another woman was murdered. Nick was just here. He brought the file." She nodded toward the bed where she'd dropped the envelope.

Bryan released her instantly and went to the bed, opening the envelope and pulling out the photos.

"Nick's sure they're going to arrest you today, Bry. We have to run. Something bad's going to happen if you go to jail. I can feel it."

"I thought you'd lost your…gift? Which was talking to the dead, not ESP, as I recall."

"I can't see dead people anymore, that's true, but this feels just as real. I know it in my gut, Bryan. We have to go. We have to hide out and solve this thing. I *feel* it, I'm telling you."

"I'm not running. I'm a cop. If I run I look guilty, Dawn, don't you see that?"

"No."

"We have to do this by the book. If they arrest me, my lawyer will arrange bail and I'll be out the next day—"

"Even if the judge thinks letting you out might cost another woman her life?" she asked. "No, Bryan. We have to go. We have to run." With that she raced into the bathroom and grabbed things almost blindly, shoving them into the bag. His aftershave, his razor, his deodorant and toothbrush.

"I told you, I'm not… Oh, God."

"What?" She lunged back into the bedroom, half expecting to see the police at the doorway. But instead she only saw Bryan, his face as pale as one of the ghosts who used to plague her, his eyes stricken as he stared from the photo in his hand to Dawn, then back again. "What is it, Bryan?"

He opened his mouth, closed it again, licked his lips. "You're right. We need to go. Let's grab your stuff from your room and—"

Moving fast, she snatched the photo from his hand.

The woman in the photo lay naked on a bed, completely uncovered, her eyes wide open, her swollen tongue protruding from her parted lips, bruises on her neck. Beside her, on the nightstand, was a shot glass with a scythe slicing through a rosebud painted on it. She didn't see what could have upset Bryan so much— and then she did.

Lying artfully on the girl's chest was a tiny gold heart-shaped locket. It had a delicate chain, and it was painfully familiar to Dawn.

Frowning, she yanked the other photos from Bryan's hand and flipped through them, ignoring the horror of looking into the face of death, focusing instead on finding a better shot of the locket.

And then she did. A close-up, just the locket and the dead woman's pale skin taking up the entire eight-by-ten glossy.

She swallowed hard, because the initials carved in the locket's face were clear. DJ & BK.

"That's my locket. The one you gave me for my birthday that summer when we first met," she whispered.

He nodded. "I put a lock of my hair inside it."

"It's still there."

"Where was it the last time you saw it, Dawn?"

"I…I don't know. I keep it in a little velvet drawstring pouch in my purse, so that it's always with me wherever I— My purse. My *purse!*" She raced out of the room and down the stairs, snatched her purse from the coat hook just inside the entry door and ran back up the stairs again. She went straight to Bryan's still-unmade bed and dumped her bag's contents on it. "I left my purse in the car when I was at your house, and I forgot to lock the doors. When I got back it was spilled all over the place." As she spoke, she pawed through the contents, pushing aside lip balm, keys, breath mints, receipts, pens, checkbooks and a large wallet. "It's not here." She blinked, lifting her head and meeting Bryan's eyes. "It's not here, Bry. Not even the pouch. Someone took it.… Maybe that Jaycam guy, or that reporter, Mitchell Brown—he was there. Or…or anyone else. God, it could have been *anyone.*"

"It *wasn't* anyone, though. It was a murderer." He moved up beside her and started scooping the items off his bed, shoving them back into her handbag.

It occurred to her then, hit her like a bullet, that she'd been that close to a murderer. A serial killer. Copycat or not, this guy was officially a serial killer now, one whose victims all looked like her. And he'd been close enough to her to lift something from her purse.

"Why didn't he just kill *me?* If he was that close to me, why didn't he just— Bryan?"

Bryan closed the flap on her bag. He slid the long strap onto her shoulder. "What are you…?"

"You were right—we need to get out of here." He picked up the duffel she'd packed for him, zipped it shut and took her hand in his. Dawn grabbed the pile of photos and the manila envelope as he pulled her with him into the hallway. She hurried along in his wake as he headed down the hall to her room and flung open the door. Their roles had reversed completely. It was Bryan now, stalking through the room, snatching up items and cramming them into her suitcase—though most of her things were still packed. She'd been hesitant to unpack, because that would be like admitting she might stay a while, which she'd had no intention of doing, at least at first. She'd been changing her mind, but now she didn't know what to think, much less what to do.

"Get dressed," Bryan said. "Be quick."

She nodded, and snatched up the jeans and T-shirt she'd been wearing the day before, pulling them on with her back to Bryan, then tossing her robe to him and watching as he added it to the stuffed suitcase.

He ignored the empty pill bottle on the nightstand, but within maybe thirty seconds, every other item in the room was stowed. He grabbed her laptop, putting it in last, before closing the suitcase.

And then he had her hand again, tugging her with him into the hall and down the stairs.

"What about Beth and Josh?" she asked. "Shouldn't we wake them, tell them—"

"We'll call them later. Before the police get around

to tapping the phones, I hope." They crossed the foyer and were out the door, down the porch steps and climbing into his Mustang before Dawn could say more.

He slung the bags into the backseat and got behind the wheel. Then he fired up the car and backed out of the driveway, shifted and drove down the road.

"Where are we going?" she asked.

"I don't know, Dawn. All I know is that I'm *not* going to wake up to find your body lying cold beside me. I'll fucking *die* before I'll let that happen."

"And that's what you think it means—my necklace being on her body? That I'm going to be the next one he kills?"

He met her eyes, and his were harder and colder and more intense than she had ever seen them. In that moment, her gentle childhood sweetheart looked downright dangerous.

"Over my dead body," he said. "And let me tell you this, Dawn, if I go down, I'm taking this bastard with me. There's no way I'll let him near you. No fucking way. Not *ever.*"

7

They'd driven for an hour, putting a solid fifty miles between them and Shadow Falls. And they'd passed that entire time with barely a word spoken between them. She knew he was deep in thought, probably working through a lot in his head. So she thought she would just give him the quiet. They were as good together in silence as they'd always been. They'd never needed constant talking to connect.

They'd been blasting the MP3 player the entire time, and many of the older songs took her back in time. The newer ones were recordings she liked, a lot of them songs she had added to her own collection. They still seemed to be on the same wavelength. And then she decided it was time to discuss what they were doing.

"We can't go too much farther, Bry," she told him.

He frowned at her. "Sure we can. The more distance we put between you and the killer, the better."

"We're not going to be able to solve this thing if we go too far away."

He swung his head to look at her, his eyes widening. "*Solve* this thing? You still think I'm going to let you play Nancy Drew with this? Dawn, your *life* is in danger. Haven't you figured that out yet?"

She pursed her lips, trying to figure a way to reason with him and knowing she wasn't going to do it with her brain spinning the way it was. There was too much going on in there: too many choices, too much information, too many questions. She glanced up as if seeking help from beyond and, like a beacon of hope, saw a Dunkin' Donuts sign up ahead.

"Take this exit, will you? I need food, and I need coffee."

"I don't want to stop."

"Stop, or I'll open the door and jump."

He frowned at her. She tried to soften the threat with a wobbly smile. "I'm scared, Bry. For you *and* for me. And I want a freaking cup of coffee, so just don't argue about it, okay?"

The desperation—which was the main emotion she'd seen in him since he'd spotted the locket in the photo—finally faded from his eyes. A softness returned to them. The softness she was used to seeing whenever he looked at her. God, how she'd missed it.

She'd missed it for five years now. Five damn long years. Five years too long.

He flipped on the signal light, and took the exit. Then they followed the signs pointing the way to nirvana, and went to the drive-through window rather than take even the slightest chance of being seen. He ordered two breakfast sandwiches, two large coffees, four bottles of water and a half dozen assorted doughnuts. Then he glanced her way and took in her raised eyebrows.

"Just in case we're on the road a while," he said. "We'll need sustenance."

"Sustenance? We eat all that, we're going to have to stop someplace for bigger jeans."

He laughed, his face relaxing. His dimples flashed and made her go soft inside, and she felt that same old warmth suffuse her. "It's been a while since I've heard you laugh," she said softly. "It's good to hear that sound again."

"I'm sorry if I've been acting like an ass all morning. It shook me, thinking that bastard might come after you next."

"I know. Just like it shook me to think you might be arrested today. Neither of us has really been thinking straight, Bryan. In a way, it kind of says something about us, don't you think? About…you know, how much we still…care about each other."

"Caring was never the problem. Caring too much, maybe." He shrugged, then they fell silent as he accepted two bags from the girl at the drive-through window. He handed them over to Dawn, then drove around the building and out of the parking lot, only to continue down the street until he came to a grocery store with a lot of cars in its parking lot. He pulled into a spot among them and cut the engine.

Dawn had already set the coffee in the cup holders in the console between them. Then she dug out the sandwiches, handing him one and unwrapping her own.

"I don't know what to do," Bryan confessed. "But every instinct I have is telling me to put you on the first possible flight back to California."

She took a bite of her sandwich, chewed it slowly and washed it down with a sip of the still-too-hot-to-enjoy coffee, holding his eyes the entire time. Then she said, "But you know I won't go."

"Dawn..."

"I won't go, Bryan."

"What if he kills you?"

"What's to stop him from following me home and doing it there? Would I really be any safer? He knows who I am. He's been through my purse. He probably has my home address, my social security number and my credit card and bank account numbers. Shit, he could have made impressions of my house and car keys if he wanted to. So why would I be any safer there?"

"He wouldn't follow you."

"You don't know that."

He sighed, shook his head and started eating. She ate a little more, too. Then she said, "On the other hand, what if he tries to come after me while I'm here? What if he tries to kill me but we're ready for him? Expecting it?" She nodded as the idea took root and began to grow. "That's it, I think. We can set a trap for that bastard. That's how we'll catch him and clear your name."

"Yeah, set a trap and take him by surprise. Good plan, except for the part where we use you as bait. Oh, and also, except for the little fact that he *wanted* us to know he'll be coming after you." She frowned, studying his face. He went on. "Think about it. Why else would he plant that locket on the victim?"

"Maybe he just did it to make you look more guilty, Bry. It has your initials on it, after all."

"He could have bought something with my initials. He took this from *you*. He *wanted* us to know you're in his sights. So we can pretty much figure he'll be ready for a trap, as well. That might even be just what he wants us to try."

Dawn mulled that over as she ate her sandwich. "He couldn't have *bought* a lock of your hair, though. Maybe what he wants is for you to send me packing so he can have a clear shot at me." She tipped her head to one side. "Or maybe he just wants to send me running scared, so he can have an easier time framing you for his crimes."

"Right. He's that impressed by your amateur sleuthing skills, as reported thirdhand by a Burlington journalist."

She shot him a pseudo-insulted look. "A journalist who *also* mentioned I was rumored to be in contact with the dead. A murderer might get a little nervous about someone who could talk to his victims. I go home, he might feel a little more at ease. He's just trying to scare me away."

"Even assuming he believes you can talk to ghosts, are you saying a guy who kills women for kicks and then decides one particular woman is a threat to him figures the solution is to scare her into leaving town? Makes *perfect* sense."

"Read my lips, Bryan. I'm. Not. Going. Home."

"Okay, okay, you going home is off the table."

"Thank you."

"So then, what do we do?"

She popped the last bit of her sandwich into her mouth and chewed. "We investigate. We figure out who he is, and we bust him. We can do this, Bryan. But not with you behind bars, and Nick doesn't think you'll be granted bail, since there's been another murder."

"He's probably right."

"So that's the first thing we know for sure. We have to keep you out of jail—"

"And you alive," he put in.

"And me alive. So we stay in hiding while we dig. Are we agreed on that much?"

He nodded. "I think it's our only option. If I'm behind bars, I can't be sure you're safe."

"My hero."

He shot her a mildly offended look, but she smiled away the sting. "Hey, I'm just saying I'm not entirely helpless. Besides, there's your dad and Rico, and Nick, if we need reinforcements."

He nodded. "I know. I know. I just—"

"You'd go nuts worrying if you couldn't watch over me yourself." She lowered her head. "I'm surprised— gratified, too—that you still…you know…give a damn, after what I've put you through."

"I'm not entirely dense, you know. I get that you were

running scared. Hell, if I had ghosts popping out of the woodwork, pestering me day and night, I'd probably want to run and hide, too."

He was trying to ease her mind, probably because she might end up dead if things went badly. But she knew he'd been terribly hurt and angry, and that he wasn't over those feelings. Not by a long shot.

"Looks like I was running for nothing," she said. "They won't talk to me at all now, not even when I ask."

He shrugged. "They're just people. Dead people, but still, people are people. There's only so much rejection people can take before they just stop trying."

She shot him a look, knowing that statement had been personal, and that he meant it. And even though she'd already surmised as much, it hurt a little to hear it.

He fished out a doughnut and began eating it, making it clear he didn't want to continue that leg of the conversation. It almost made her laugh the way he held an open napkin underneath his face as he ate, catching every crumb that fell, to protect his precious Mustang.

Personally, she thought new cars all belonged in junkyards. They had nothing on the classics. "So what did you pay for this thing?" she asked.

"Forty, give or take. A steal for a Shelby."

She snorted through her nose, and when he shot her a look, she shrugged. "I paid five grand for my 'Vette. And now it's showroom-worthy."

He shrugged. "I wouldn't give five cents for a Chevy."

"Yeah, yeah, I know. You always were a Ford guy. But you'll never win that argument with me."

"I have backup now. Nick's in total agreement."

"Oh, well, if Nick is on your side, then I *must* be wrong. Even if I *am* the one in the car biz."

He grinned at her, and she smiled back. The volley was an old familiar one, and it had broken through some of the tension that had been building between them again.

Sighing, she got back to the more immediate considerations. "We need to let your parents know that we're safe, and what we're planning. Otherwise, they'll worry themselves sick."

He nodded. "We should go to the bank and withdraw some cash, then get moving, so we'll be far away once the police start checking my accounts."

He lowered his head. "I hate this."

"I know. So I'll distract you with something you'll probably think is even worse. We need to ditch this car," she said.

Bryan had finished the doughnut, wadded up the napkin and was tucking it into the empty bag that had contained the sandwiches, but he stopped to look across at her, his expression one of horror. *"Ditch?"*

"Figure of speech."

He closed his eyes. "This car is my baby," he said, stroking the dash. "We need to store it somewhere safe."

"Airport garage? They have security cameras."

He shook his head. "That's the first place the police would check. And if they find her, they'll impound her and start tearing her apart, looking for trace evidence. I can't leave her anyplace that obvious."

He looked at Dawn, then sighed. "And don't pretend you don't get that."

"I *totally* get that. She *is* a great car, by the way." She shrugged. "For a new model, I mean."

"Yeah."

"Let me call my boss," she suggested.

Bryan lifted his brows. "What good will that do? He's a continent away. Besides, are you sure you can you trust him?"

"Yes. Not that the police would think to contact him, anyway. He deals with garages all over the country, and he might know one around here where we could stow the car and even get a loaner without too many questions asked."

"That's a really good idea, Dawn." He shook his head. "You're the one who should've been a cop."

"I dislike rules and regulations too much. I'd have been drummed out my first year."

"Beats facing a murder rap your second."

She put a hand on his shoulder, but the heat that moved from his body to hers at that touch made her wonder if it was a good idea. She resisted jerking her hand away too fast, though—that would be obvious—and just left it there, letting that feeling move from his flesh into hers. She could have closed her eyes at how good it felt.

"They'll be all over our cell phone accounts," she said softly when she finally removed her hand, speaking to cover her awareness of the physical pull that still lived between them. "Once they figure out we're both missing. In fact, we can't be sure that hasn't happened yet."

"You're right. Is yours turned off, by the way?"

She nodded.

"Good. So, steps one and two, we find a pay phone and we find a bank. After that, we'll drive back toward Shadow Falls and get a place to hole up, because that's the exact opposite direction they'll assume we were heading."

She lifted one brow. "That's really good."

"Yeah, well, I'm *supposed* to be good at this stuff."

He put the car into gear and pulled back into traffic, this time looking for anyplace that might still have a pay phone. It took some doing to find one. They were going out of favor these days, when everyone had a cell. But eventually they located a gas station with a pay phone outside it.

"Be careful what you say, Bryan." Dawn knew she didn't need to tell him that. But she felt compelled, anyway. "We can't be sure our parents' phones haven't been tapped already."

"Yeah, the minute they figure out we've gone off the grid, they're going to be all over Beth and Josh."

"It's a shame. If we needed help—"

"They'd try, anyway, and they'd end up being charged themselves." He cupped her head with his hand, then ran it downward to the nape of her neck and gave a gentle squeeze. "Just like you're probably going to end up being."

She held his eyes so he could read her expression clearly. "I don't care."

"You should."

"But I don't. So 'should' doesn't matter. Now, let's just call Josh and Beth, so they won't worry. The longer we wait, the more likely the cops will have already been there."

"Okay. And then your boss, about the car. And then we find a bank and take out massive quantities of cash."

"See?" she said, trying to sound cheerful. "I told you we make a great team. Already we have the beginning of a plan."

"Some beginning. No place to stay, and no idea what the hell to do next."

"Oh, don't you worry about *that*," she promised. "I've got all *kinds* of ideas of what we can do next."

He sent her a quick look to show her he was well aware that her words could be read with a sexual slant. She was glad to see he was keeping his sense of humor. Hell, if anything, he seemed more upbeat, more animated, more *there*, than he'd been ever since she got back.

Was it the excitement of being on the run? The fear

of being caught, making him feel more alive? Was it the hunt for a killer?

Or could it be that just being with her was responsible for the change? Because damn, it was having that effect on her, being with him. She felt like a desert experiencing its first rainfall in five years. She felt as if she was coming to life, blooming again. And that frightened her.

Bryan knew something was wrong the minute Beth picked up the phone. Her usual greeting, "Blackberry Inn, may I help you?" sounded stiff and false.

"Beth, it's me. Don't say my name. Just tell me, are the police there?"

"Yes, Melissa, of course I remember you. You're one of our favorite guests. I hope you're calling to tell us when you'll be back."

Bryan heard voices in the background. Someone who sounded like the chief asked, "Who is it?"

"I just wanted to let you know we're okay. Dawn's a target now, so I had to get her out of there."

"Yes, we guessed as much."

"I'll try to get in touch again."

"Probably not the best idea."

He blinked and realized they must already be putting taps on the phones. He'd better hurry.

"We're not going far. Just looking for clues. Don't worry."

"Well, now, *that's* easier said than done. We can't wait to see you again, though."

"Tell Dad I love him."

"Give me that phone!" someone said, and Bryan knew beyond any doubt that it was the chief's gruff voice. Something in Beth's face must have given her away. He heard Chief Mac, shouting, "Is this you, Kendall? If so, you'd best get back here ASAP! Do you have any idea how guilty this makes you look? For the love of—"

Dawn, who could clearly hear the chief's outburst, took the phone from Bryan's frozen grip and placed it on the hook as quietly as possible. "No point listening to him."

"I know." Bryan swallowed hard. "But he's my boss, and it's a hard habit to break, listening, *obeying,* when he gets to yelling like that."

She nodded. "I understand."

"I don't know if you can. I'm one of the good guys, Dawn. But I feel like a criminal here. Running, hiding, using a pay phone… How the hell did I get here? A fugitive, for crying out loud."

"You're an innocent man. And you're doing the best you can. But if you want to go back, now's the time. We can make something up, say we were just out for a joyride with no idea they'd be coming to arrest you today. We can go back without making things any worse—if we do it now."

He met her eyes, only to immediately see Bette's overlaying them in his mind. Lifeless, cold, dead eyes. "No way in hell," he told her. Then he picked the phone back up and handed it to her. "Your turn to talk to *your* boss."

Nodding, she took the phone.

An hour later they were backing Bryan's beloved Mustang into a garage full of cars, most of them looking more than a little battered. Which made sense. It was a body shop. And while they did some restoration work, most people didn't bring cars in unless they'd been banged up. And there were some sad cases there.

Bryan stopped when the guy in the overalls gave the signal, then shut off the engine and sighed, his hands opening and closing on the leather steering-wheel cover.

"If my boss says we can trust this guy, we can," Dawn said. "Stan Murphy is a stand-up guy, Bryan. Your baby will be fine."

He hoped so. He opened his door, turned to face the shop's owner and held out his keys.

"Don't forget to hit the trunk release, Bry," Dawn said.

He pressed a button, and the Mustang's trunk popped open. Then he tossed the keys to the man in the overalls, who stood waiting.

A smile appeared from within a respectable crop of salt-and-pepper whiskers, and a grease-stained palm opened to catch the keys. "Don't look so glum, pal. She'll be as safe as in her mama's arms. Promise." He pocketed the keys and extended his hand again. "Dane Babcock. Good to meet you. Any friend of Stan Murphy's is a friend of mine."

Bryan shook the man's hand, searching his brain for a false name to give.

"Never mind, pal. Stan said no names. But I know who you are. I read the papers." He bobbed his head slightly. "He also said you were good people, you two, that I could trust that, so I do. Hell, Stan got me started in this business. He's sent me more clients than I ever would have found on my own. I owe him. So if there's anything else I can do for you..."

"Thanks," Bryan said. "But this is plenty, really. We'll owe you a big favor and then some. And we can't thank you enough."

"Nah." Dane Babcock turned and crossed the concrete floor, weaving among wrecks waiting to be repaired and other cars already being worked on, partially done, blotched up with primer and body putty. "I'm sorry it's not what you're used to," he said, nodding toward a turquoise-blue 2005 Taurus without a scratch on it.

"Hey, it's just what we need," Bryan said. "Thank you."

"She runs great. Got a tankful of gas, too."

"I'll return it with a tankful, then."

"Keys are inside. I...thought you might be in a hurry."

Dawn smiled at the guy. "Thanks a lot. I'll tell Stan what a great help you were. And we won't forget this. You ever need anything—well, we'll get in touch later when things settle down."

"You do that. You can keep the car as long as you need it. Be safe, okay?"

"Thanks again." Bryan went to the Mustang and took the stuff from the trunk and backseat—including the picnic cooler that still held the old files on the Nightcap Strangler. As he was carrying things from one car to the other, Dawn snagged the keys and opened the Taurus's trunk. He loaded everything in, then got behind the wheel as Dawn got into the passenger side. She looked at him, a sympathetic expression on her face. He shrugged. "Hell, at least it's a Ford."

Babcock opened the overhead garage door and stood to one side as they exited. He waved as they passed, and then they were on the road and driving away.

"Phase one of our plan is complete," Dawn said. "We have a safe, unrecognizable car, a tankful of gas, some cash, and we've let Beth and Josh know we're safe. Now we can move on to phase two—a place to hole up."

Bryan nodded as he drove. "I've been thinking about that. I think we should get the hell out of here, head to the other side of Shadow Falls and find a motel or something."

"Yeah, and we should switch motels *and* towns every day," Dawn put in.

He nodded. "You're getting ahead of me. I'm not planning to be on the run for too many days, you know."

"I'm all for optimism. So we drive, we scout out a place to crash and then…?"

"Spend the afternoon with the files," Bryan said

quickly. "Make a list of suspects that looked good sixteen years ago and take a second look at each of them. Start getting current contact information—"

"I have my laptop in my suitcase," Dawn said. "That'll help."

"Good. Then we talk to them."

"Won't that give us away? Put us at risk of being caught?" Dawn asked.

"Yeah, but if we don't solve this thing, there was no point in running at all. Because sooner or later, they'll catch us."

"The cops—or Nightcap?" she asked.

"Both."

She lowered her head and rubbed her arms, as if his words had evoked a chill. "I'm scared, Bryan."

He reached over, closed his hand around hers. "I know you are. I'm gonna keep you safe. We'll nail this guy. I promise. You believe me?"

"You've never broken a promise to me before. That's kind of been *my* forte. So, yeah. I believe you."

"Good."

"But there's one more really important thing to do first, Bryan. And you can't say no, okay?"

He looked at her. "Okay. What is it?"

"We need to eat." Her very serious expression was replaced by a broad grin. "I'm starved."

He couldn't help but smile back. Leave it to Dawn to find a way to lighten the mood just when he was feeling the weight of the world on his shoulders. "I don't know what the hell I've done without you for the past five years, you know that?"

Her smile wavered a little. "I've…missed you, too, Bry."

There was a tense silence that stretched into more. Finally he broke it. "So let's find a motel we can afford to pay cash for, get a pile of takeout from whatever's close by and then we can feed our faces and work our cases."

"Is that police talk?"

"Nope. I think you said it once, back when we were playing detective in our teens. It stuck with me. Always makes me smile when I remember it. Silly damn thing to say."

"I used to be a silly kid."

"Used to be?" he asked. "You haven't felt silly in a long time, have you, Dawn?"

She frowned hard, considering the question. "Now that you mention it—no, I don't think I have. Not since I left home."

"Seems to be coming back to you," he said. "Along with your appetite."

"I don't think I'm going to feel very silly about much of anything, until we find out who did this and get you in the clear."

"And you out of danger," he said. Then he spotted the on-ramp and they hit the highway once again.

8

"Ten o'clock, Bates Motel, Nowhereville, Vermont," Dawn said into an imaginary microphone. "Pizza and wings having been devoured, and my partner and I have moved on to serious investigative work, using our tried-and-true method known as 'spreading papers through-out the room in hopes something will catch our eye.'"

Bryan lifted his head, met her eyes, tried to smile at her lame attempt at humor. But he looked tired, and he looked worried. His lighter mood from earlier that afternoon had been beaten down by the daunting task of trying to solve a crime without the resources he was used to.

Nearly every piece of evidence that proved interesting had him reaching for his cell phone, wanting to call someone in authority to double-check on something, only to realize he couldn't. He was completely on his own in this. Well, except for her.

His eyes were puffy, with half-moon shadows, and he needed a shave.

And while the way he looked elicited her worry and her sympathy, it also turned her on to no end. That un-shaven scruffy look was—well, it was one she'd never seen on Bryan before. And it was sexy as hell.

He set aside the stack of papers he'd been reading. He was sitting on the motel room floor amid papers, photos, cardboard boxes, file folders and a stack of motel-issue notepads they'd swiped from an unattended housekeep-ing cart.

Dawn let her eyes roam his face for another second, then said, "It's after ten, and you look wiped out. Why don't we call it a night and try to get some sleep?"

"Not yet. Not until we've made a game plan for tomorrow."

"Okay, well, I think we've pretty much agreed that we need to start talking to the people of interest on our persons-of-interest list, right?"

"Right."

"Okay, so we've got Bette's ex-boyfriend, Jeremy Cameron, aka Jaycam, the tattooed hulk who couldn't take no for an answer and returned to the scene of the crime."

He nodded. "And we've got Everette Stokes, the brother of Merle, the gun-wielding wife beater I shot in that hostage standoff last month. He threatened me repeatedly."

"And we've got Professor Olivia Dupree, over at Vermont State, who knew all the victims sixteen years ago, as well as now. Including the unfortunate Nadine Burmeister, who was found this morning."

"Did we establish that?" Bryan asked.

"The reporter did, but check the info Nick gave me this morning." Dawn dug back through the piles, found the photos of the most recent victim and tried not to see the woman's dead face as she flipped each one, looking for what she wanted. "There," she said, turning the photo toward him. "There, on the bookshelf just to the right of the bed. Check out the titles on some of the spines."

He frowned, picked up the photo and leaned closer. "Those are textbooks."

"Yeah, English lit textbooks. Isn't that what our professor teaches over at VSU?"

"Yeah, it is." Bryan tapped the photo against his palm repeatedly, almost as if he were trying to shake something loose from it.

"Hell of a coincidence, isn't it?" she asked.

Bryan nodded slowly, still staring at the photo. "We have to figure out if any of them could have known about the art on the shot glasses—enough to copy it, even. Not to mention the brand of whiskey."

"Wouldn't be the first time someone hacked into the system. And anyone with a record could have gotten the info from Nightcap himself." She shrugged. "Anyway, those are our top three suspects. I mean, there are probably lots of others, and we'll keep adding to the list as we go, but I think we should start by talking to these three."

He nodded. "Let's talk with Professor Dupree first."

"Why her first?" Dawn asked.

Bryan shrugged, but he averted his eyes as he did so.

"It's because she's the safest, right? You don't want me around when you get to the others."

"She's not the safest if she turns out to be the killer. And frankly, I don't want you around any of them, Dawn." He sighed and began gathering up the papers. "First thing tomorrow, we'll head to the university and see if we can get a few minutes with her between classes."

"Aside from the risk we'll be taking of being seen, it's July, Bryan," Dawn reminded him. "Classes aren't in session—unless she teaches summer session, which I doubt."

"Yeah, well, summer session draws quite a few students, and she teaches straight through it."

"You know her?" Dawn asked.

"Know *of* her. I went to VSU, remember? It's where I met Nick. I never took a class with her, so I don't think she'd remember me. Of course, if she reads the papers, she'll know who I am, and you're right. It'll probably scare the hell out of her. She'll probably scream for campus security."

Dawn was picking up papers, organizing them, returning them to various file folders. "There's a home address for her right here. Nick was thorough when he checked her out the first time around."

"That address is sixteen years old," Bryan said. "We'll be better off starting at the university. She'll feel safer there, anyway. Can you imagine how you'd feel if a suspected serial killer showed up at *your* front door?"

"Good point," she said.

"Besides, I know my way around campus, so we can avoid being seen by too many people. If she's not there, we can probably at least get a phone number from the main office and call her, so she's not freaked out by us just showing up."

"If she's innocent."

"Right," Bryan agreed.

Dawn shrugged. "All right. But besides seeing her, what's the plan? Are we just going to come right out and ask her where she was on the nights of the last two murders?"

"We'll figure it out in the morning," Bryan said. "I'm beat."

"Okay." She fell silent as they finished picking up the mess, then looked at her suitcase, slung on the floor in the corner. The room had two beds. There was nothing, she told herself, to be nervous about. He hadn't made a move or a suggestive comment all day.

She'd been afraid he would, just like she'd been afraid of the ghosts she'd expected to show up the minute she set foot in this state. Neither fear had panned out.

Both those things had surprised her. And both left her feeling oddly disappointed. Funny, to miss something you thought you no longer wanted.

"You want the first shower?" he asked.

"Sure." She grabbed her suitcase and headed into the

bathroom, eager to give herself some space to think. To plan. What was she going to say if Bryan came on to her tonight? What was she going to do?

They had barely discussed their breakup. They hadn't talked about what had been between them, much less what still might or might not be. She didn't know if she wanted to stay here, even though the ghosts were no longer a problem, because she knew too well that they could reappear at any time, and she was still on the fence as to whether she wanted them to or not. She didn't know if she wanted to return to her old life and see what the future held in store there. She didn't know what the hell she wanted.

How could she give him an answer, if he demanded one? How could she know what to do if he put his arms around her? If he kissed her slowly, tentatively, awaiting her response to tell him whether or not to keep on going? How was she going to react?

She showered, and as she did, a dozen scenarios played through her mind. She imagined herself exiting the bathroom dressed in the T-shirt she used for a nightgown, her hair long and wet and hanging over her shoulders. Or maybe she should dry it first. Either way, he would stare at her, his eyes heating, sliding slowly down her body, lingering on her breasts beneath the fabric, noticing the obvious lack of any bra, then moving lower, as he wondered whether she was wearing panties.

She would stop there, halfway to the bed, frozen by his steady, intense gaze, and then he would get off the bed and come to her, and he'd say something about how good she looked, and how much he wanted her. How he'd been holding it in all day but just couldn't fake it any longer, much less deny himself the bliss of tasting just one more kiss from her. He would tell her that he had been dreaming of that for the past five years. And that it had never been the same with anyone else.

And then he would cross the room and pull her against him, and kiss her hard and deep, like at the end of a great romantic movie. He would kiss her, and she would probably be all stiff at first, wondering if this was the right thing to do, and then she would be so swept away by passion that she would surrender, melting in his arms and kissing him back.

They would end up in one of those beds, and they would make wild love for two solid hours before they stopped, exhausted, and, their sweaty bodies twined together, fell into a contented, sated, blissful sleep.

Yeah. Okay. That was the way she imagined it, and given the way she felt just thinking about it, she knew she wouldn't say no. She wouldn't make any promises or offer any explanations. But she damn well wasn't going to say no. She needed him.

She toweled off and wondered if there was even any point in putting on the T-shirt. Why pretend she didn't know what was going to happen between them? Why play games? Why not just walk out there in the towel and let it drop to the floor as he stared at her? Why even bother with the towel?

She closed her eyes and pulled on the T-shirt,

wishing she were bolder. She rubbed her hair partially dry, combed it out, brushed her teeth to be sure her breath would be infinitely kissable and straightened up the mess she'd made in the bathroom. And then, finally, she faced the door, drew a deep breath and told herself this had been a long time coming and that it was going to be good. Not a mistake. Not for the two of them. No matter how things ended up, this was not going to be a mistake. How could it be?

She lifted her chin, opened the door and stepped out of the bathroom, pausing in the doorway to set her bag down, deliberately not looking at him just yet. She would wait until he spoke and pretend to be surprised. She moved to her bed, certain his eyes were watching her every move, the heat in them building with every second. She sat on the edge of the mattress and then wondered why he still hadn't said anything.

Curious, and too eager to wait any longer, she lifted her head and turned slightly to look at him.

He was lying on top of his covers, sound asleep, his mouth slightly open, his eyes closed. And as she sat there, staring, burning with disappointment, he began to snore.

She bit her lip until it hurt. Between him and the damned ghosts, she was beginning to feel utterly unwanted.

"Keep your head down," she said for the tenth time.

Bryan wore a baseball cap and sunglasses, and

seemed to think that was enough to entirely change his appearance. It wasn't.

"You should have worn the hoodie," she added.

"And then I'd look just like the Unabomber. Besides, it's summer."

You wouldn't have known it to look around campus, though, Dawn thought. Summer session was in full swing. Students moved in groups of three or four, and in swarms of many more. The dorms were vacant, but workers in overalls buzzed in and out of them, getting them all spruced up for the fall semester.

"I thought there would be fewer people," she muttered, patting her hair lightly. She'd bundled her long locks up in a tight bun, then wrapped her head in a pretty silk scarf, knotted at one side, the end trailing down. She wore big sunglasses, like Bryan, and still she felt as if everyone they passed was looking at them, recognizing them and moving only just out of sight before pulling out their cell phones and dialing 9-1-1.

"Don't be nervous, Dawn. You look right at home on a college campus."

"Bull. I'm older than every student here. And I know I look it. The past five years haven't been good to me."

"Haven't they?" He shrugged. "I don't know. House near the beach, great-paying job, a boss that trusts you enough to do what yours just did for us? Sounds to me like the past five years have been just fine."

She shot him a quick look from behind her glasses. But of course she couldn't see his eyes through his.

"The job's great. So is the house. But I haven't been out there living the life of a surfer girl and rubbing elbows with the rich and famous. I've been in hiding, Bryan. I've been living in a constant state of…fear. And it shows on my face."

"You're a little touchy this morning. What's up?"

He'd paused just outside the double glass doors that read Miller-Freidman Building, English Department. "For what's it's worth, I think maybe it's those pills you've been taking that showed on your face. And maybe the stress and the worry. Being too far from your family for too long probably fits in there somewhere, too."

"Was that a lecture?"

"I was gonna point out that you look loads better just in the few days since you arrived. It's doing you good to be home, Dawn."

It was driving her crazy, being home, but she wasn't going to tell *him* that.

He shrugged, taking her arm and guiding her through the doors. "I just think you need to take better care of yourself."

"I thought that's what I *was* doing."

"You are, since you've been home. But what if the ghosts come back? What are you going to do then?"

She frowned up at him, knowing in that instant that there was more to the question than what was on the surface. She met his eyes, unable to reply. She didn't know what she would do if the ghosts came back—all of them, not just Bettina.

But he held her gaze, silently demanding an answer. And so she averted her eyes and said, "First thing I'll do if they come back is ask your girlfriend who killed her."

"She wasn't my girlfriend."

"I don't care what *you* call it—I guarantee you, *she* thought of herself as your girlfriend."

"Nice change of subject," Bryan said, and then he walked away from her, right up to the directory that was mounted on the wall across from the entry doors, in between two elevators. He ran his finger along the first row, stopping at the name, reading aloud. "'Professor Olivia Dupree—Room 317.'"

"I wasn't changing the subject."

"Did you think I was going to be a monk while you were on the other side of the country? Did you think I'd just put life on hold and wait to see if you ever came back?"

"Of course not." But she had done just that. And she was only now beginning to realize why. She'd been saving herself—for him. He was the only man she had ever wanted. And maybe she'd been punishing herself a little, too, for hurting him the way she had. And all the while, he'd been having sex with women he didn't even care for all that much.

She pressed the button on one of the elevators.

"Every time you mention Bette, you sound...pissed about it," Bryan said softly.

The elevator doors slid open. "Maybe I am, a little."

She stepped inside, turned and waited for him to join her.

He stared at her until the doors started to close, then stopped them with a foot and joined her. She hit the button, and they rode up to the third floor. "So *why* are you pissed?" he asked.

"I don't know."

"Are you jealous?"

"Maybe."

"Maybe that's why she won't talk to you, Dawn. You ever think of that?"

She gazed up into his eyes, mulling that over as the elevator stopped and the doors trundled open. "No, it can't be that. It's not just her, it's all of them. I haven't seen a ghost since I've been back."

A throat cleared, and they both turned, stunned. A woman stood just outside the elevator doors, apparently waiting for them to exit so she could board.

"Oh! Sorry." Dawn grabbed Bryan's arm and hurried out of the elevator.

"No problem."

The woman started to board, even as Dawn nodded toward the door on the opposite side of the hall. "Looks like she's not here." The door bore the gold digits 317, and underneath them, a name plaque. But the door was closed and the glass pane dark.

"That's because she's there," Bryan said, nodding toward the elevator.

The woman in the elevator stuck out a hand, holding the doors open. "You're looking for me?" she asked.

Dawn looked at her. "If you're Professor Dupree."

"I am." Sighing and glancing at her watch, she stepped out of the elevator, joining them in the hallway again. "I can give you ten minutes, assuming I can even help you at all. What's this about?"

"Bettina Wright," Bryan said.

The woman's face went slack. It bore no expression, just stillness. As if she were a photograph. She was a brown-eyed brunette, her hair in a tight bun, with a hint of Latina in her blood, Dawn thought. She didn't look her age, not if she'd been a grad student sixteen years ago, when the original murders had taken place. She didn't look a day over thirty.

She seemed to reboot herself then, giving a jerky nod and moving to her office door, fumbling with her keys and finally opening it. She flicked on the lights and motioned them inside.

It was an office, but it smelled like a classroom. Ink and paper and chalk dust. There were faint traces of coffee scenting the air, as well. She moved behind her giant desk, pulled out the worn leather chair and sat down. Dawn thought that was a little formal. She would have just sat on the edge. They were only talking ten minutes, after all.

Bryan and Dawn sat in the comfy chairs that faced the desk. Bookshelves lined the office, all of them filled. Dawn scanned them, seeing several volumes in a row by the same author, a famous recluse named Aaron Westhaven. She'd heard of him but had never read him herself. She continued scanning, her eyes stopping on a familiar title. Nick's book. Olivia had bought it in hardcover.

"So you're with the police?" the professor asked.

"He is. I'm just helping out."

Professor Dupree met Dawn's eyes. "I heard they'd brought in a psychic. Didn't believe it until now."

Dawn blinked. "I'm not a—"

"You read the article in the *Burlington Gazette?*" Bryan asked.

"I get my news from my iPhone. No time to read papers. No, this was just campus gossip. And then I overheard what you said about not seeing any ghosts." She shrugged. "So are you two supposed to be under-cover or what? Because really, those are terrible disguises."

"We just need to ask you a few questions, and it won't take long," Bryan said. "Did you know Bettina Wright?"

Sighing, she leaned back in her seat. "Of course I did. She was a student of mine." She licked her lips. "Look, I've discussed this at length with Nick Di Marco. You *do* know who he is, right?"

"Of course we do," Bryan said. "And I was aware he'd questioned you extensively about the original string of murders, but these new ones—"

"These?" She rose from her desk chair, moving as if it wasn't entirely her own idea. "You mean there's more than just Bette?"

Bryan and Dawn exchanged a quick glance. "I'm

sorry. There was another, night before last. Nadine Burmeister."

The professor lifted her hands to cover her mouth, almost as if an unwanted sound would have escaped if she hadn't. Dawn got up and went around the desk to put a hand on her shoulder. "I'm so sorry. We wouldn't have come if we knew you hadn't heard."

"I took a sick day yesterday, and I only came in today to collect a few papers. I haven't paid any attention to the news. I just—I can't believe this is happening again."

"So did you know Nadine, too?" Dawn asked.

Professor Dupree nodded hard. There were real tears brimming in her eyes. One even spilled over, and she dabbed it away. "She took one of my classes last semester. God, why didn't Nick tell me about this?"

From his chair, Bryan said, "You and Nick are… close?"

"Not like that." She licked her lips, opened a desk drawer and pulled out a whiskey bottle. Without explanation or apology, she poured some into a tiny shot glass, then picked it up and downed it as Dawn and Bryan gaped.

"I teach psychology as well as English. He teaches criminology and criminal profiling," Olivia Dupree said. "There's a lot of overlap. Especially in his class on serial killers, which is hugely popular here. We do a lot of lectures and workshops together. It's nothing more than that, but he would know I'd want to hear about this. He knew her, too."

She blinked and looked at them. They were both still staring at the now-empty shot glass in her hand. "What?" she asked.

"Where did you get that shot glass?" Bryan asked. Dawn could hear the change in his voice.

"I don't know. I've had it for years. Honestly, I don't remember—why are you so…?" She looked at the glass, and her eyes widened as she saw the scythe and the bleeding rose that were painted on its side. Her hand went lax, and the glass fell. "No, no, no, this isn't mine," she said, even as the glass hit the floor. It didn't break, just thudded on the carpet. The professor backed up a step, staring at it. "Mine's got a cactus and a roadrunner on it." She stared at the glass, her eyes seeming haunted. "He's been here. He's been in my office, hasn't he?"

Bryan got to his feet, grabbed a pencil from a cup on her desk, then crouched down and used the pencil to pick up the shot glass. "Have you got a Baggie or—"

"Yes, yes." She yanked open one drawer after another, finally locating a large envelope and holding it open for him. He dropped the shot glass inside. "What does this mean?"

"I don't know," Bryan said.

"Do you think I'm in danger? Do you think I could be next on this maniac's list? Do you—"

"I don't know," Bryan said again. "But I'm curious to know how you knew about Nightcap leaving glasses like that behind as a calling card. The book intentionally kept that quiet."

She met his eyes, her own stony. Then they shifted to something behind them.

All three of them snapped their heads toward the door, where Nick Di Marco had entered quietly and now stood there shaking his head. "Bryan, Dawn, good to see you again."

Dawn was so tense she thought her jaw might snap. "Nick. What are you doing here?"

"Came to tell Olivia about Nadine." He held out a hand. "Mind if I take that?"

The professor came around the desk, wobbly in her pumps, and handed him the envelope with the shot glass inside. "Nick, I swear to God, I never saw that before. The last time I used my shot glass, it *was* my shot glass. I don't know how that got into my desk."

Nick nodded as if he'd never once suspected otherwise. "When *was* the last time you used your shot glass, Olivia?" he asked.

"The day I found out Bette had been killed—and that it looked like Nightcap, even though he's dead. He *is* dead, isn't he, Nick?"

"Yeah. This is probably a copycat."

"Is he targeting me?"

"No, he's targeting her," he said with a nod toward Dawn. "And trying to frame him," he added, with an identical nod toward Bryan. "Which is why these two are wearing those lame-ass getups. You, Olivia, are not in any danger."

"How can you be sure?"

"You don't have the look. You used to, when your

hair was lighter, the first time around, but you've let your hair go back to its natural color now. None of the victims have been olive-skinned, not even a little. And they've all been in their early to mid-twenties. Frankly, you're too old, Liv."

"Never thought I'd be glad to hear a man tell me that," she said softly. "But the girls had both taken one of my classes. Nick, this killer is targeting girls I know."

"Girls *I* know," Nick said. "You just happen to know them, too."

"I knew them all the first time, too, though," she said. "You didn't even work here then. You didn't teach here then. Nick, why is he going after girls I know?"

"The first time he went after students here. You were a student here."

"I know."

"The first victim was—"

"I *know*." She held up a hand to make him stop talking. "Please."

"Look, Liv, if it's a new guy, a copycat, he'll stick to the M.O. of the original Nightcap Strangler, so you're safe. And if it's the same guy—"

"Or the same guy's ghost," she whispered with an odd look at Dawn.

Nick made a "that's ridiculous" face and went on. "If it's the same guy—which I don't see how it can be—he would've killed you a long time ago if he'd wanted to. He didn't. So again, you're safe."

"Then why did he leave the shot glass?"

"I don't know. I'll turn it in, we'll see if there are prints or anything and I'll let you know if—"

He was interrupted by a tap on the open office door. "Olivia, I—oh, sorry. Didn't mean to interrupt," said the short, round man with the bald head and wire-rimmed bifocals. "Hello, Nick."

"Hey, Jim." Nick glanced at Bryan and Dawn but apparently decided to skip the introductions. "Olivia needs a ride home," he said to the newcomer. "Why don't you take her in that monstrosity you call an SUV? Liv, I'm gonna send an officer over to check on you tonight, okay? I'll have them keep an eye on your place, and on you, until this animal is off the streets. But in the meantime, I need your office key, and, uh, you probably won't be able to use it for a few days. We'll need to get a team in here, go over things. You know the drill."

She nodded. "Thanks, Nick. Just let me gather up a few things." She took a canvas bag from the coat-rack just inside her office door and gathered up folders, books, papers. She vanished into a room off to one side that might have been a closet or storage area, and finally returned, apparently ready to go. She stretched out a hand to shake Dawn's. "I'm sorry I couldn't be more help."

Dawn took her hand to shake it and felt the little scrap of paper in Olivia's palm. She slid her palm over the other woman's, taking it and closing her fist around it so no one else would see. "I'm sorry we brought you such bad news."

"Be safe," Olivia said, and then she took her briefcase and left the office with Jim.

Nick waited until Olivia and Jim were on the elevator, then faced the two fugitives. "I knew you'd show up here to question Liv."

"How?" Bryan asked.

Nick tipped his head to one side. "It's what I would've done. You're a good cop. You're looking to solve this thing. You found a common denominator—Olivia. And so you came to talk to her."

"So why didn't the rest of the department figure that out?" Bryan asked.

Nick lowered his eyes. "The rest of the department are operating under the assumption that you're a suspect evading arrest. To me, you're a cop trying to solve a case. Big difference."

"Nick, we can't go back," Dawn said. "They'll arrest Bryan."

"Even more so now."

"What do you mean?" she asked.

Nick shrugged. "Bryan's here and the killer's calling card shows up at the same time. It doesn't look good."

"Do you have to tell them that?"

Nick grimaced, looked away, then faced them again. "*She's* gonna tell 'em. And if they ask her, she'll ID you, Bryan." He slanted a look at Dawn. "And *you*. Why don't you just paint a big bull's-eye on your forehead?"

She lowered her head, feeling guilty as hell.

Bryan wasn't so easily distracted. "Nick, how sure are you about this Olivia Dupree?"

"Sure."

"But she's known *all* of them."

"Some better than others. First one was her roommate."

That drew Dawn's attention away from her impending doom. She lifted her head and sucked in a breath. They hadn't gone back far enough in the case files yet to find that little detail.

"They were grad students, and they'd just moved into an apartment together off campus. Olivia came home to find her new roomie, Sara Quinlan, dead in her bed. Shot glass on the nightstand." He looked at the envelope in his hand, the one that held an identical shot glass. "This must have brought that all back with a vengeance, I'll tell you that much. Poor woman."

"But what if she did it?" Bryan asked. "What if she killed her roommate and has been killing ever since?"

"Not *ever* since," Dawn said. "She took a sixteen-year break."

Nick shook his head. "Her alibi for that night checked out. And besides, I saw her—I was the first cop on the scene back then. She was devastated. There's no faking that kind of shock." He shrugged. "Recheck everything if you want to, Kendall. You have my blessings. But you're wasting your time."

"Really? You don't mind?"

"Does it matter? You'll do it, anyway."

"If I'm not sitting in jail, I will."

"Well, you *will* be sitting in jail if you don't get the hell outta here, pal. 'Cause I've gotta call this in. I'm gonna say you took off on me. So take off. But on one condition."

"What is it?" Bryan asked.

"Call me." Nick dipped into his pocket, pulled out a cell phone, tossed it to Bryan. "It's clean, prepaid, untraceable. I've got one just like it in my pocket, and the number's already programmed into yours. So call me. I want to know where you're staying, what you're doing. And if I tell you it's time to come in, you come in. No questions asked. I'll work with you, Bryan, but only on those terms. I'm putting my ass on the line for you here. You'll do this for me?"

"Yeah. Thanks, Nick."

"Get outta here. And keep that girl of yours safe, you hear me?"

Bryan nodded. Dawn felt his arm come around her shoulders as he propelled her toward the door, but she pulled free and went around behind the professor's desk.

"What are you doing, Dawnie?" Nick asked. "Don't touch—"

Pulling her sleeve over her hand, she opened the drawer, reached in and pulled out the whiskey bottle. And then she held it up. "I think you're writing her off as a suspect *way* too easily," she said.

The label on the bottle was Glasgow Gold.

"You better bag this, too, Nick." She set the bottle on the desk, then joined Bryan and headed out the door.

9

Bryan didn't say a word all the way back to the car.

"Are you okay?" Dawn finally asked, as he maneuvered the vehicle onto the twisting campus roads and found his way to the main street beyond. "Bry?"

"Yeah. He just—sometimes he makes me feel like a rank amateur. So do you, for that matter. I didn't even notice the label."

"You were looking elsewhere, and she was turned at an odd angle. I'm not sure you could've seen it. And Nick has been a cop a lot longer than you have." She patted his hand on the steering wheel. "Besides, I'm not convinced he's right. Maybe if we dig into Olivia Dupree's background a bit, we'll find something he missed."

"Waste of time. If Nick didn't find it, there's nothing to be found."

"Yeah? Well, he didn't find *this*." She reached into her pocket, then opened her hand.

Frowning, Bryan glanced down to the tiny folded paper in her hand. "What's that?"

"Don't know yet. Olivia slipped it to me when she shook my hand."

Dawn unfolded the scrap, and unfolded it and unfolded it, until she finally saw what the professor had scribbled there.

"'Please call me. Tell no one. It's important. Olivia,'" she read aloud.

"Is that all?"

"No, there's a phone number. And *that's* all."

Bryan pulled the cell phone Nick had given him from his pocket and handed it to her.

"Let's give her time to get home first, okay?" Dawn suggested

"All right. We'll call her as soon as we get settled into the next motel."

Two hours later Dawn wadded up a pile of fast-food wrappers and stuffed them into an undersize wastebasket in a new motel room that wasn't much different from the last one. She wondered how long they would be forced to stay on the road.

Without her asking for it, Bryan handed her the cell phone Nick had given him. "Go ahead. Call her. See what this is about."

She nodded and took the phone from him, then quickly unfolded the scrap of paper she'd tucked back into her pocket and punched in the number.

Olivia Dupree answered on the second ring.

"I got your note," Dawn said.

"Good. I, um, I need to talk to you. Face-to-face, if that's possible."

Dawn met Bryan's curious gaze, but only nodded. "Sure it is. Can I ask what this is about?"

Olivia was quiet for a long moment. "Look, he's targeting you—according to Nick, anyway. Was he right about that?"

"I...wish I could say no, but I think he was."

"I'm sorry. Believe me when I tell you I know how terrifying that is. Because despite Nick's assurances, I think he might be targeting me, too. Why else leave that glass in my desk?"

Or my locket with the latest victim, Dawn thought.

"At the very least, he's tormenting me."

"At the very least, same here," Dawn said.

"Maybe we can help each other. I...I really want to meet with you. Privately. Please, please, say you'll see me."

Dawn licked her lips. For all she knew, this woman might *be* the Nightcap Strangler. And yet, even though she'd pressed Nick to pursue the possibility, she doubted it on a gut level. "It'll have to be somewhere fairly public. So we're both safe."

"I'm as afraid of you as you are of me," Olivia said. "Yes, somewhere public. But not too public. There's a park about five miles south of the university on Beckham Boulevard."

Dawn nodded. They'd driven past it on the way here. "The one with the swan pond and the little bridge?"

"Yeah. It's never deserted, but it's not crowded, either. Meet me there. One of the benches near the pond."

"When?" Dawn asked, glancing at the digital clock on the motel-issue nightstand. It was 3:27 p.m. They'd intended to question at least one more suspect this afternoon. "I can be there by nine."

"All right. I'll see you then. But come alone, or it's off."

"I will." Dawn cut off the call and handed the phone to Bryan.

"You can be where by nine?" Bryan asked, pocketing the cell phone.

"That park we passed, just south of the university. She wants me to meet her there—alone. I think I should go."

"I think you're out of your mind." He came out of the chair where he'd been sitting. "How do you know she's not the killer, or maybe the killer's girlfriend, or even, despite what Nick said, his next victim? You could get caught in the crossfire. You could be walking into a big trap, Dawn. And at *night…!*"

She licked her dry lips, loving that he was worried about her. That had to mean something, right?

"Bry, if Nightcap wants me—"

"Don't even say it." He held up a hand. "I don't like this. If I could go with you, yeah, but—"

"She won't talk to me if you come with me. Look, we wanted to question another suspect today. Why don't you drop me off at the park, and then go do that? I can tell Olivia to come meet me now, and you can go talk to Stokes's brother. Or Bette's Neanderthal ex, Jaycam."

"Out of the question."

"Bry, if she can help us clear your name, don't sabotage yourself trying to protect me."

He held her gaze, then lowered his.

"What are you going to do when this is over, Dawn?"

She blinked, stunned by the question, because it was so off topic. "I…I don't know."

He nodded. "Give it some thought, would you?"

"Sure." She tipped her head to one side, wondering if he might be asking for the reasons she hoped to God he was. "Why?"

He pursed his lips, his eyes roaming her face before looking away again. "We'll spend the afternoon here, out of sight, and then I'll drop you at the park and find a spot where I can keep my eyes on you, in case you need help."

"If she sees you…"

"I'm a cop. She's not gonna see me." He waited for her answer; then, when she didn't give one, he shrugged. "It's my best offer, Dawn. Take it or leave it."

Finally she nodded. "I guess I'll take it, then."

"Good." Then he looked down at himself and shrugged. "We should change. Just look slightly different than we did at the university today."

"I agree. But aside from the discount drugstore we passed on the way here, I don't know where we're going to shop for disguises."

"We'll make do."

* * *

Dawn waited on the park bench, tossing bread crumbs to the swans, and feeling ridiculous with her burgundy-red hair and black plastic-framed eyeglasses. Thank goodness the shampoo-in hair color was labeled temporary and would wash right out, according to the instructions. She barely resembled herself, and she did not like the new look.

Bryan was in the distance, sitting on a rock, apparently absorbed in a paperback. He'd tied a red bandanna around his head to hide his hair completely, and donned a pair of sporty sunglasses, even though it was dark outside. With his tank top and shorts, he looked as if he was taking a break from a daily run. Not watching for a serial killer to spring out at his onetime girlfriend.

Onetime.

Dawn felt a spike in her heart as she thought about what she'd thrown away, and why. And how maybe it had all been for nothing.

Damn, she'd missed Bryan more than she had ever allowed herself to admit—or *feel*.

Now, though—God, now she was swimming in regret. And he wanted her to say something. She knew it. He wanted her to tell him for sure whether she was staying or going when this was over, and she didn't think that was a fair question. How could she decide, when she didn't even know if he *wanted* her to stay? Or wanted her, period? Or if he would end up in prison? Or if the ghosts would come back or stay gone forever?

The evening breeze picked up, whispering through

the nearby trees and rippling the formerly glasslike water.

She needed to know those things she hadn't yet figured out—she needed to know *all* those things—before she could possibly decide if she were staying or going. Because all those things would impact her decision.

It wasn't fair of him to ask her to decide now, with so many pieces of the puzzle still missing.

Shoes tapping concrete drew her attention, and Dawn lifted her head to see Olivia Dupree walking toward her along the sidewalk that encircled the swan pond. She glanced up at Dawn on the bench, then quickly lowered her head and quickened her pace.

"It's me," Dawn said, realizing her disguise had thrown the other woman.

Olivia's head came up, and she frowned, then the frown eased. "God, I wouldn't have recognized you."

Dawn rose, saying, "I'm sorry about the disguise, I just—"

"You just figure if Nightcap can't recognize you, you might be safer. Believe me, the thought has crossed my mind, too." The other woman came closer and sank down onto the bench. "Do you think they arrested the wrong man? How horrible is that to think about? What if they killed an innocent man? I mean, that's what they did, really. He died in prison."

"He was no innocent man, Olivia. According to his record, he was a wife beater. Had six arrests for domestic violence before she finally left him. My personal opinion, the world is a better place without him in it, whether he was a serial killer or not. No harm, no foul."

Olivia blinked. "I know some law professors who would disagree with you on that." She paused, shaking her head slowly. "Do you think this could really be a copycat?"

"I don't know," Dawn said. "I wish I did."

"Part of me wonders if it might be—well, I guess it won't sound as stupid to you as it would to some. Part of me wonders if it could be a ghost. The ghost of Nightcap, returning to continue his work. Is that ridiculous?"

"I've thought the same thing," Dawn admitted. "With the timing—the murders starting up again just a month after his death. It *is* creepy, if nothing else."

Olivia nodded. "So, um, you're really psychic?"

Dawn lifted her head and met the woman's brown eyes. "I think medium is the technical term. I...I see dead people. Or I used to."

"Used to?"

"Yeah. I ran away from Vermont, and from my... gift, thinking I could hide from it. I've been on a tranquilizer, even done a little drinking when that wasn't enough, just to keep the ghosts away from me. But now that I'm back, now that I have a reason to want to talk to them, they're gone."

Olivia stared at her, searching her face. "Then... then you haven't been able to talk to any of the...the victims?"

"No. And I've tried, believe me. But no, it's like the ability just…evaporated."

Shaking her head, Olivia said, "No, it hasn't. It's like any muscle—you stop using it, it gets weak. But you start working out a little, and it can come back again." Then her eyes widened. "Though I don't recommend it. You ran away from this thing, and now it's gone. You've got your life back. Just let it be, so you can keep it that way."

She sounded almost as if she wanted to take back her earlier words.

"How do you know about this stuff?" Dawn asked.

"I teach psychology. Things like psychism and mediumship and the sixth sense have fascinated me from day one. I kind of minored in those areas. You know, trying to find ways to make sense of both ends of the psychological spectrum. The normal and the so-called paranormal."

"So-called?"

She nodded. "If it exists, it's normal. Natural."

"And you believe it exists?"

"Absolutely. That's why I wanted to talk to you. To see if any of the victims had…told you anything."

Dawn thinned her lips, wondering if she were imagining things, or if Olivia really was afraid of what one of the victims might have told her. It certainly seemed that way. The woman was fishing hard.

"Not a word," she said. "I wish they would."

Olivia nodded. "Then I guess this meeting was a waste of time." She started to get up.

"No, wait. I came here, I answered your questions. The least you can do is answer mine."

"All right." Olivia sat down again. "What do you want to know?"

"Tell me about Sara Quinlan. She was your roommate, right?"

"Why do you want to know?"

It was an odd question. Dawn frowned, and wondered why that would be Olivia's first response. "She was the first victim," she said, watching Olivia's face closely, because something was not right about her reaction. Her body language. She'd gone suddenly stiff and still, seemed guarded somehow. "I can't help but think the key to all of this is in her murder. So how well did you know her?"

"I didn't know her. Not at all."

"But she was your roommate—"

"We'd barely met. I'd only moved in a few weeks before—"

"A few weeks living with someone? Come on, Olivia, you must have known something about her. Anything. Where she was from, who her family were, anything at all?"

Olivia got to her feet. "Sara had the right look—the same look as all the other victims. And that's all. There was no more to it than that. And I can't talk about her." She hiked her bag higher on her shoulder. "I have to go." And she started walking away.

"You're running away from this conversation," Dawn said. "Why? Are you hiding something, Olivia?"

Olivia went still, her back to Dawn. "I don't want to talk about the woman I found dead in my home sixteen years ago, and you think I've got something to hide? It would be more suspicious, Dawn, if I *did* want to talk about her." She glanced back over her shoulder then. "I hope you stay safe."

"I hope you do, too," Dawn said.

And this time, when Olivia started walking, she didn't stop. Dawn waited where she was until Olivia was out of sight, then looked around to be sure no one else seemed to be watching. Finally she rose from the bench and headed for the street where they'd left the borrowed car.

She opened the passenger door and got in, then waited.

Five minutes later, Bryan slid behind the wheel and started the engine. He glanced at her, his gaze curious. "Well? What did she want?"

Dawn mulled the question for a moment. "I think she wanted to know if I'd talked to her dead roommate. I think she wanted to find out what I knew about Sara Quinlan."

He lifted his brows. "Really?"

"Yeah, and when I told her I hadn't, and that I didn't know anything, then asked her for information about Sara, she got all defensive, refused to give me anything and abruptly ended the conversation."

Bryan blinked as he processed that. "That's odd."

"She was hiding something, Bryan. Something to do with Sara Quinlan. I know it. I think that's where we have to focus our digging. On the first victim, on Sara."

He nodded slowly. "Okay."

She sighed. "She did say one useful thing, though. And then tried to take it back, so I think it slipped out unintended."

"Yeah? What was that?"

"She said that my gift is like a muscle. That when you don't use it, it gets weak. But if you just start flexing it again, it'll regrow, get strong and be as good as ever."

He stared at her for a long moment then finally spoke. "You're going to keep trying, then? To get the ghosts to come back to you?"

"I don't think I have a choice, Bry."

"Yeah, you do."

She sucked in a breath, then blew it out again and changed the subject.

"Let's get back to the room, really dig into the Sara Quinlan info in the files. I think her autopsy report was in there, wasn't it?"

"All of them were," he said. "But I don't know what that'll tell us. They all died the same way, strangulation and a lungful of Glasgow Gold."

"Still, we need to go over hers with a fine-tooth comb. Everything in her file. She was the first. She's our Ground Zero."

Sighing, he nodded. "Okay."

"So is it a plan, then?" she asked. "We research the hell out of victim number one tonight, and anything we can get on Olivia, as well? And we do it over something to eat?"

"All right, it's a plan," Bryan agreed. "But I don't want pizza or fast food for dinner again. My belly's asking for something legitimate for a change."

She looked at him. "You know, that sounds damn good to me."

"Does it?"

"Shit, yeah. Two stops and we've got it made. That drugstore we hit earlier—it had an electric two-burner cooking thingic."

"Yes, it did. What are you thinking?"

"I'm thinking with that, the motel room's microwave, a frying pan and ten minutes at a grocery store, we could have steaks and baked potatoes with sour cream for dinner."

"Are you trying to seduce me?" he asked with a broad grin.

She met his eyes and fell silent. Part of her wanted to look away, but some devil inside made her hold his gaze captive and say, "What if I was?"

Bryan's smile faded to black. He averted his eyes. "I, um, I don't think that would be...the best idea, Dawn."

"Oh." The hurt came through in that single syllable, she knew it did, but she couldn't help it. It was painful to think he didn't want her anymore.

"It's not what you think," he told her.

"It's okay. It doesn't matter."

"Dawn, I—"

"Don't." She held up a hand. "Just...don't. Look, there's a grocery store up ahead. Let's stop, okay?"

Bryan filled the cart. He picked out two giant-size Idaho russets, the two biggest T-bones in the case and a pint of sour cream. Then he added some extras. A pair of ready-made chef's salads from the deli, a box of Freihofer's chocolate-chip cookies, which he claimed were the best prebaked cookies on the planet, and a twelve-pack of Old Milwaukee.

Dawn was tossing stuff into the cart, too, but he paid very little attention to what. He was trying to pay very little attention to her altogether, but it was just about impossible. He knew he had hurt her by rejecting what had amounted to an offer of sex. But dammit, he had no choice. She'd stopped him from explaining that it wasn't that he didn't want her—because he did—but that it was a matter of self-preservation. And now that some time had passed, he thought that might be a good thing. Because if she knew how very much he'd wanted to say yes and to hell with the consequences, she wouldn't let up on him until he did just that.

And he couldn't.

He still felt too much for her. Way too much. More than before, even. Yeah, they'd been nuts about each other when they'd been teenagers. Thought they were in love, of course. But this...this was different. This was bigger and deeper and just...more. It was as if that old feeling had been Mossburg Creek, the tiny writhing strand that wound through Blackberry. And this new one was the Colorado River.

Or maybe the difference was just time. And how water cuts more deeply over the course of a few centuries.

All he knew was that no matter what she said, Dawn was going to bolt straight back to the West Coast if she saw another ghost. And he couldn't be sure that wouldn't happen. In fact, he was fairly certain it *would* happen. There was a look in her eyes, a new sort of determination, that told him she was going to keep trying until it did. And he'd never known Dawn to fail at anything she'd been determined to do.

I needed to take another victim.

I'd found her only twelve hours earlier, and I knew she would be next. She'd been walking along the sidewalk down Main Street, having just left the independently owned coffee shop on the corner. It wasn't a Starbucks or a Dunkin' Donuts or a Tim Hortons. It wasn't a chain. It was what they call a mom-and-pop business, even though its owners were a pair of female lovers who'd made enough money in Manhattan to escape it.

I love Vermont. I love Shadow Falls. There isn't a franchise in the town, not from one end to the other. Everything is independently owned. Everyone is unique, not following society's notion of how to live. It's the most idyllic place in the world. I *love* it here.

Her name was Sally. She was taller than Dawn Jones, and a little thinner. Definitely more sophisticated. Her shoes, sunglasses and handbag were matched, black with the same silver metallic trim—not too much, just enough—and bearing a designer's initials artfully entwined in strategic spots. Her hair had that ironed-straight look that didn't come naturally to anyone not of Asian descent. Her skin tone was so even that I knew she wore a lot of makeup, but because I couldn't see the makeup, I also knew it was expensive. I suspected she was a fairly recent transplant from a big city. New York or Chicago or L.A. Probably L.A. Her light brown hair had blond streaks, and her arms and legs were deeply tanned.

I was probably doing her a favor. A sun worshipper like her would look like a well-worn baseball mitt in a few years, anyway.

She's not what you want, and you know it. There's not enough fight in her, not enough life in her to even make it worth snuffing out. Look at her. She's tired. She's complacent. Content. Bored. She's going through life on autopilot.

I frowned at the voice in my mind. "Look, it doesn't matter what I want. I'm not doing this for gratification this time."

Bull-fucking-shit.

"I'm doing this because it has to be done. And as long as the rookie's on the loose, the crimes need to keep happening. It's the only way to make sure this goes down the way it ought to. It's the only way."

She's got no connection to the university. It breaks the pattern. The rules.

"It'll throw them a curveball, keep them guessing."

You'll get to Dawn Jones before this is over. You know you will.

"I won't. I don't want to kill her."

You want to kill her more than I do. It's keeping you awake nights, you want it so bad.

"You're the one who wants that. And you're the one keeping me awake nights. The one trying to turn this into something it's not. But I'm telling you, I don't *have* to kill. Not anymore. I'm over that. You don't control me the way you used to."

Right. You're killing again. At a rate you never came near before. Three in one week? Hell, man. You're relishing every freaking one like a blow job. But you're cured. Right.

"I'm not going to kill Dawn Jones."

You're going to kill her last of all. You're just building up to it, thrilling to it in your mind with every one of these substitutes you kill in her place. You're saving her for last, because you know she's going to be the best of all of them. The best you've ever had. You're going to kill her slowly, maybe revive her and kill her again, and again, until there's no bringing her back. That's how good she'll be. And that's why you're waiting. She's going to be the culmination of your career, my friend.

"No way. You're wrong."

We both know better. But let's get on with this. Your

*mark's going to get nervous if she discovers you follow-
ing her and arguing with yourself under your breath,
you know. Besides, she's getting too far ahead. We need
to know where she lives, so we can go visit her tonight.
Damn, I'm aroused just thinking about it. I love you,
you know. You give me so much freaking pleasure. I
love you.*

"And I hate you," I whispered, but I picked up the
pace all the same.

"Delicious," Bryan said as he picked up the paper
plates and carried them to the wastebasket.

"Yeah, it was good." But he'd only said it to soothe
her a little, Dawn knew that. The steaks had been tough
and the sour cream a tad too sour. Baked potatoes from
the microwave just didn't come close to the real thing.
No crispy skins or roasted flavor. The best part of the
meal had been the beer he'd tossed into their shopping
cart. She was on her third.

She was angry with herself for feeling petulant and
bitchy. If he didn't want her, he didn't want her, and
you couldn't get mad at someone for not wanting you.
It wasn't as if he had a choice. He felt what he felt.
More pertinently, he didn't feel what he didn't feel. The
thing was, why the hell had he been pestering her about
whether or not she was staying, if he was no longer interested? Why even ask?

Maybe he'd only been curious or asking as a friend—
a part of her family, really. Maybe she'd just read too

much into it. The look in his eyes. The way it felt when he touched her. Maybe he didn't feel any of that.

She was even angrier with herself for letting the way she was feeling on the inside bleed through to the outside, where he could see it and know. She was trying to fake it but failing pretty dismally. Hiding her feelings had never been one of her strengths.

She let him clean up, knowing it was his idea of a peace offering, and tried to focus on the autopsy report. There were lots of photos. It made her queasy, looking at photographs of the dead girl. It made her think about someone looking at photos of *her* dead body, if this murderous bastard ever caught up with her.

Right at that moment, a cold chill shot up her spine, the kind you feel when you suddenly realize that someone is standing close behind you. It hit so vividly that she gaped and swung her head around, expecting to see someone there.

No, not someone. *Him*. The Nightcap Strangler.

"Dawn? You okay?"

She pressed a hand to her heart, felt it racing. "He's going to come after me, Bryan. I feel it. He's going to come after me."

Bryan crossed the room and touched her shoulder. "That's why we're here. So he can't find you."

She nodded, closed her eyes and took a deep, slow breath. "I know."

"So is anything jumping out at you? From the autopsy report, I mean."

"No, nothing so far." She turned a little, enough

to make his hand fall from her shoulder, because she wanted a lot more from him than that. She tried to focus on the photos, the lists, everything in the report. "God, they've got everything here from the contents of her purse to what she was wearing. A New York Giants jersey. Wait a minute. *Wait a minute.*"

"What?" Bryan leaned over her, his warm breath on her neck too much.

She brushed a hand over her skin where his breath had touched her and flipped through the photos, setting aside the autopsy shots in favor of the ones of the crime scene. "There's New York stuff here, too. A Yankees cap on the bedpost. And look at the pennant above the bed where her body was found. Syracuse Orangemen."

"So?"

"So according to the police report, Sara Quinlan was from Chicago."

He looked, nodded and repeated, "So?"

"What do you mean, so? Why isn't there anything about the Bears or the Bulls or the White Sox?"

He shrugged. "Maybe she attended Syracuse University. She was a grad student, right?" Leaning over and reaching past her, a move that made his shoulder brush against hers, he fanned out papers until he found the background check that had been done on the victim. "Illinois State. Huh."

"There's no connection to Syracuse anywhere in here, Bryan."

"That's a little odd, but—"

"Who identified the body?"

Bryan grabbed a stack of papers and scooted around on the bed, so he was leaning back against the headboard with his legs stretched out in front of him and the pages on his lap. Dawn followed suit, grabbing a stack of what remained, taking up the same position beside him before thinking better of it, and started skimming.

"The 9-1-1 call was made by her roommate," she said, when she found the information she sought. "Olivia Dupree."

"The body was claimed by a cousin from out of state," Bryan said. "A Natalie Quinlan, as soon as it was cleared for release after autopsy. It was cremated." He lifted his head, met her eyes. "What are you thinking?"

"I don't know. I…I don't know. But this is odd enough to dig into a little more, don't you think?"

"It's probably nothing," he said.

"Then we'll find out it's nothing and move on. But we need to dig."

"Into what?"

He clearly thought she was off base, and she resented it. "Look, I have a feeling about this, okay? There's something not right about this body. Let's find someone who was there, strike up a conversation, see if anything seems…off."

"Find someone who was *where*, Dawnie?"

"The morgue. During the autopsy. When the body

was brought in, when it was released, anything. Bryan, this is important. I'm telling you, I *feel* it."

"Okay, okay, calm down. Let me make a call." He leaned over her, reached past her to snag the cell phone off the nightstand and flipped it open.

She covered his hand with hers. "Who can you call? They'll be monitoring Beth and Josh's incoming calls by now. And anyone who hears from you is going to report it, Bryan, not give us any answers."

"Not Nick."

She closed her eyes and sighed. "No, not Nick." Then she nodded. "Okay, go ahead."

She sat there, waiting while Bryan simultaneously placed calls and tapped keys on her computer, but she couldn't shake the feeling that there was a shadow hovering over her. Or that it was getting closer. She started putting the files back together, stacking them in the picnic cooler that had become their filing cabinet.

Within a couple of minutes Bryan was finished with his phone calls. He came back to the bed where she sat, pawed through the contents of an old evidence box and sat down beside her.

"Mission accomplished?" she asked.

"I got hold of Sara Quinlan's alma maters. Everything's automated these days, so I looked for back copies of various yearbooks from both. That's what took so long on the phone. I had to do a search to see which volumes she was in. And we're in luck. One has to be shipped, so I didn't order it. But the other, the one from Illinois State, can be downloaded directly from the Net. We'll get an e-mail with a password as soon as the credit card clears."

"You used a credit card?"

"Don't worry. It's Dad's card. He let me use it so much before I landed my job on the Shadow Falls P.D. that I know the numbers by heart."

"And what about the computer, Bryan?" she asked. "I mean, what if the cops figure out that you placed the charge? Won't they be able to track us if you get online?"

"What's it going to tell them? Not where we are, because we won't be here anymore. All they'll know is that your computer downloaded an old college yearbook. How is that going to hurt us?"

She nodded slowly, but her throat was dry. All of this was so damn scary. "And what about Nick?" she asked. "What did he have to say?"

"Nick's setting us up to meet the M.E. who was in charge back then. Didn't tell her who we are, of course. She'll probably figure it out when we get there, but…"

"When?" she asked. She'd absently picked up a piece of chrome, shaped like the letter *T,* that she'd found with the evidence, turning it this way and that, and watching the light glint off it.

"Tomorrow morning, if he can talk her into it. Probably at the county morgue."

"That's risky," she said. "Cops coming and going all the time…"

"Yeah, but Nick will help us." He nodded. "What've you got there?"

"Piece of trim off a Thunderbird. Sixty-something—'65, '66."

He blinked at her, then nodded and smiled. "According to the notes, which I've all but memorized, it took the department three weeks and five car experts to figure that out."

That made her laugh, though only a little bit. "So?"

"It was found on the road near one of the crime scenes. They don't know if it's related or not. Could have been there for days, for all we know."

"What made them collect it at all?" she asked.

"They collected everything—even cigarette butts and bottle caps off the ground near the crime scenes. Anything that looked fairly recent."

"Anyone report seeing a '65 T-Bird near any of the scenes around the time of the crimes?"

He nodded. "One neighbor reported seeing a— lemme see if I can remember the quote—an 'old car, like something you'd see at a car show,' near the home of victim number five, I think. Said it was red." He shook his head. "Aside from that statement and this one piece of chrome, there's no classic-car connection."

"Too bad," she said. "That's my area of expertise. I might have been more help there than I've been with everything else."

"You've been a ton of help."

She took a breath, let it out. "I'm tired."

"It's late," he said. "Let's get some rest."

She nodded and put the cover on the evidence box, then set it on top of the stack inside the cooler and closed the lid. And she didn't look at him, because it was starting to hurt every time she did.

At first she'd thought, deep down and even in spite of herself, that it was inevitable they would eventually be together again. They would work through all the garbage and end up writhing in each other's arms. She'd waited five long years for that, after all.

Now, though, looking at him brought a heavy sadness to her chest. She no longer believed it was inevitable that they would end up in each other's arms. More and more it seemed impossible instead. And her delusions of the night before were nowhere in sight this evening.

She left the cooler where it was and went into the small bathroom, washed up, brushed her teeth, put on her nightshirt and went back into the other room to crawl into bed.

"That was fast," he said when she settled onto her side with the blankets pulled up over her shoulder.

"Yeah. Night, Bry." She reached out and snapped off the lamp. There was still another one on, but it was on his side of the room. She ignored it, closed her eyes, covered her head and told herself she was tired enough to fall right to sleep.

It was a lie, but she told it to herself all the same.

10

Ten o'clock in the morning, and Bryan was sitting in a room in the county morgue, behind a glass door with wire mesh between the panes. He was thinking that mesh wasn't nearly enough between himself and the occasional police uniform moving through the hallway beyond.

Dawn sat across from him, her eyes wide, their movements jerky, as she took in the room. She hadn't slept well last night. Hell, he hadn't, either. All he'd wanted was to crawl into bed with her, pull her into his arms and kiss her the way he'd been dying to kiss her ever since she'd come home.

But he hadn't. Because he didn't think he could touch her and not fall head over heels in love again. And because he wasn't going to let that happen until and unless he knew for sure that she would stay. And because right now, he couldn't even promise her that *he* would stay, and it would be just as cruel if she fell hard for him and then he wound up serving life in prison.

So there was no choice but to keep things between them cool. No sex. No kissing. No passion and no love.

Although, most of the time, there was a tiny voice somewhere deep inside his brain, laughing at him for thinking he had any say in the matter. Those things were already happening in his imagination. In hers, too, he would bet.

He didn't like seeing her uncomfortable and it was clear this place made her antsy. There were six refrigerated "drawers" along one wall, situated in two rows of three. No way to tell if they were occupied, but at least there were no bodies lying around the room. No sheet-draped tables. Only bare, shiny ones. And equipment and cabinets and lights and tools.

Dawn was scared, though. Bryan knew her well enough to know that. There had to be a lot of ghosts in a place like this, and maybe they were finally communicating with her again. She looked about ready to jump off her stool and make a run for the door.

"You okay?" he asked softly. She met his eyes, nodded once.

Nick stood just inside the doorway, leaning back against it as if he would keep anyone from coming in. He'd hustled them in through a rear door, then led them down a single flight of stairs, through a dim hall and straight into this room after meeting them in a pay-parking lot a block away. It had taken him only five minutes to set this up and call Bryan back with the details.

The guy had clout.

Dr. Rita Westcott eyed Nick as if he were Bobby De Niro stepped right off the silver screen just to see her before returning her attention to the computer. "I'm taking a risk, giving you this information."

"Who, me?" Nick asked in apparent shock. "What risk? Haven't you heard? They reinstated me, Rita, just for this case. You can't get into any trouble for talking to a bona fide cop."

"And what about a bona fide suspect?" she asked, slanting a much less adoring look at Bryan, one that confirmed his theory that she would recognize him at first glance.

"Person of interest," Bryan corrected. "We don't say 'suspect' anymore, Doc."

The doctor remained stone-faced, then slowly smiled at him, and it even reached her brown eyes, crinkling the lines at their corners even deeper than they already were. "It's a good thing I've always liked you, Kendall."

It was mutual, but Bryan didn't say so. The woman was old enough to be his grandmother and had the brains of Albert Einstein to the tenth power. She was smart, sharp, serious, irreverent and funny. She ran the M.E.'s offices in several Vermont counties, pretty much only pretending to follow the rules handed down from on high. Which was why Nick had been sure she would help them out.

He hadn't been wrong.

"I pulled up my notes on victim one right after you

called," she said, hitting a button and calling up a file on the flat-screen monitor. "Just so we're clear, though, I did not perform the autopsy. That was the local coroner, a Shadow Falls doctor by the name of Carrie Overton. She was newly employed at S.F. General, and I believe that was her first job after med school, so I watched over things pretty closely."

"Understood. And I was there, remember?" Nick said.

She rolled her eyes at him, then returned her attention to the screen. "Sara Quinlan. Twenty-two. Grad student from Chicago. No living relatives—"

"I thought her body was identified by a cousin," Bryan injected.

Westcott nodded. "Yeah, I was getting to that. Stop interrupting." She refocused on the screen. "No living relatives we could find any mention of until the cousin came in to claim the body."

Dawn was still sitting on a tall stool, one leg crossed over the other. Her nervousness faded, Bryan thought, as she began to get drawn into the investigation. She loved solving crimes so much he wondered why he was the one wearing a uniform. Or at least who used to be the one wearing a uniform.

"Notes are fine, Dr. Westcott," Dawn said. "But personal recollection is so much more interesting. Do you remember her at all?"

"The victim?" Westcott asked.

"No, the cousin."

Westcott frowned. A door slammed from somewhere

down the hall, and Dawn jumped off the stool and onto her feet with a gasp.

Tipping her head to one side, Westcott said, "Being around the dead makes you nervous." It wasn't a question.

"Hell, no. I love corpses and morgues. They're my hobby."

Nick straightened away from the door and reached behind him to close the Venetian blind. "She's got reason to be skittish, Rita. It's not you." He shot Dawn a look that didn't need words.

"He's right," she said. "I'm sorry. I didn't mean to snap at you. The truth is, yeah, the dead and I don't…get along all that well. And just now I thought one of them was about to spring out of one of those drawers at me." She shook her head and managed a self-deprecating smile. "I know how ridiculous that sounds, believe me. I'll be all right."

She sat back down, recrossing her legs and breathing deeply, but Bryan could tell she was still on edge.

The doctor nodded. Bryan stayed where he was, saying nothing, just listening. "The body was brought here after being autopsied by Dr. Overton at Shadow Falls General. The cousin who showed up claimed it from me, and as I recall, there was nothing unusual about her. Slender build, average height, long dark hair. She looked as if she had a little Mediterranean in her blood. Greek, maybe. Or Italian."

"Would there have been any footage of her?" Bryan asked. "Security camera, anything like that?"

"We checked all that right after she claimed the body," the M.E. said. "But she kept her face averted from the security cameras. Did a good enough job at it that we thought it might have been deliberate. She had ID, but we didn't verify it or anything. It would have been easy enough to fake. We were a little lax back then."

Bryan tipped his head to one side. "Why were you even checking the footage, then? Did you have some reason to believe she wasn't who she said she was?"

Dr. Westcott sighed, nodded, took off her nearly square bifocals and massaged the bridge of her up-turned elfin nose. When she lifted her head again, she glanced at Nick.

He gave a nearly imperceptible nod.

Sighing, Westcott said, "We tried to locate the cousin again after the body had been released to her. As I was closing out the case, doing one last look at the autopsy report, as I always do, I found something I'd missed, buried near the end. I felt the cousin should know."

She looked up as the sounds of traffic passing in the hallway outside increased. Her voice much lower, she said, "The dead girl had given birth four to six weeks prior to her death."

Bryan snapped his eyes to Dawn's, and he saw her reaction. She blinked in shock, staring right back at him, then looked at Rita Westcott once more and said, "Sara Quinlan had a baby when she was killed?"

"She had given birth before she was killed. Those are the facts," Westcott said. "We wanted to find her cousin, her only living relative, and let her know there was a chance there was a living child out there somewhere, but we couldn't find her. And in fact, we became convinced in short order that there was no such person in existence."

"Holy shit." Bryan looked behind him at Nick, only just realizing he'd heard no sounds of surprise from his friend. He studied Nick's face for only a second or two, then said, "You knew about this."

"Of course I knew. It was my case, and since she was the first victim, I didn't know there would be more. I had to consider that the baby might have been a motive. But it was a dead end. No records of Sara at any hospital, no abandoned babies, no bodies, no clues. A little more digging, and it looked like the chick who claimed the body wasn't who she'd pretended to be. The phone numbers and addresses she gave us were bogus." He shrugged, shook his head. "At first I thought it had to tie in to the crime. But then more girls died, and we had a serial killer to contend with. The other women didn't have babies or imaginary cousins showing up to claim their remains. Clearly it was unrelated. So we let it go."

"You let a missing newborn baby go?" Dawn asked, rising slowly from the stool. "How could you do that?"

"We had no proof there had been a *live* birth," Nick said. "I tried to find out, get some information on the baby, believe me, but it was a dead end. Making it public would have done nothing for the kid. The press would have gone nuts over the whole thing."

"So you just let the baby go?"

Nick looked at Bryan as if seeking support, then he looked back at Dawn, and lifted his hands. "I know it seems like something, guys, but believe me, it's not. I've turned this over six ways to Sunday and never found a clue. She didn't want her kid found. Maybe it was still-born and she buried it somewhere. If that's the case, though, I think we'd have found the body by now—or we never will. I like to think she gave it to someone else to raise."

"Without a paper trail?" Bryan asked.

He shrugged. "I didn't say I thought she did it legally or even wisely. Just that it's possible. And hell, a high-end attorney can arrange a legal adoption and make it so private no one ever figures it out. Like I said, I never found any suggestion that the baby had anything to do with the killings. I doubt our Strangler even knew she'd had a kid. Or cared."

"Nick's right," Dr. Westcott said. "Chances are, she gave the baby away, maybe through private adoption or maybe something far less legal. Either way, I have to agree that it seems unrelated to the murder."

"Her roommate would have known if she'd had the baby with her," Dawn said. "How long did Professor Dupree say she'd been living with Sara?"

"A few weeks," Bryan said.

"So if she'd gotten rid of the baby, then she must have gotten rid of it at least three weeks before her murder.

You said she'd given birth four to six weeks prior. So that gives us a one- to three-week window."

Bryan nodded. "If we could backtrack, look into who she'd seen, where she'd been, in the time between having the baby and getting a roommate, maybe we could find something."

Nick rolled his eyes. "It's compelling, I know, but it's a waste of time. It's unrelated to the murders."

"I know you believe that," Bryan said, "and I know you're probably right. Hell, it's not that I doubt you, I just—"

Dawn interrupted. "I just don't know how anyone can be one hundred percent sure of that, Nick. Not without more information."

"Well, you've got nothing better to do. Unless you've stumbled onto a clue I don't know about?" Nick looked from Dawn to Bryan with his brows raised. They shook their heads in unison. "Fine. Then dig into this baby thing a little bit, if it'll ease your minds. But I'm telling you, you're wasting your time. I spent weeks trying to make it part of the case. It wasn't then, and it isn't now. But maybe while you're digging you'll stir up something else that *is* related."

Rita looked up toward the door as the noise in the hallway suddenly cranked up to a new level. Nick, who stood closest to the door, whirled to peer between the slats of the blind.

"Incoming," he said. "Get outta sight. *Pronto.*"

Bryan gripped Dawn's hand and pulled her across the room, looking for cover. Thinking fast, he pulled her up against the wall and yanked a gurney in front of them. "Crouch down."

She did, and Bryan quickly unfolded the sheet lying on the gurney, draped it over the table so it was hanging to the floor in front, then crouched down beside her.

Rita Westcott hovered, making adjustments to the sheet, even as the door burst open, and several people came flying in, pushing another gurney. Dawn's hand closed around Bryan's. He glanced at her, tried to nod reassuringly and then realized he could see through the white sheet well enough to know when the attendants hefted a body bag off the gurney and dropped it onto an autopsy table. He knew Dawn could see what they were doing, too, because he felt her cringe in reaction.

He squeezed her hand, ran his thumb over the back of it.

"What have we got?" Dr. Westcott asked. "Why didn't you take it to General, or even call it in? I wasn't expecting—"

"Chief ordered radio silence, said to bring her here," an attendant said.

"But why—"

"Ask him."

The attendant towed his now-empty gurney out the door and down the hall, following his coworkers, but before the door swung closed behind him, Chief MacNamara strode inside, spotted Nick and said, "Where the *hell* have you been, Di Marco? I've been paging you all morning."

Nick yanked his cell phone off his belt clip and

looked at it, feigning surprise that it was turned off, though Bryan suspected he'd done it on purpose, not wanting anyone to track him to Bryan.

Shaking his head, Nick said, "Damn thing shuts down when the battery gets low. Hell, I've gotta replace this relic. What'd I miss?"

"Not much. Just another one, that's all."

"Another one?" Nick looked sharply at the body bag on the table. "And you moved the body before I got the chance to—"

"You want in on things, keep your damned phone turned on. She was found at 6:00 a.m. when her housekeeper showed up. The crime scene was photographed, the evidence gathered. You're not the only one who knows what he's doing, Di Marco."

Dr. Westcott unzipped the body bag. "Let's get her out of here," she said. "Give me a hand." Nick and the chief got up closer, and the three of them lifted the body just enough to peel the bag out from underneath, then lowered it onto the stainless-steel table again.

Dawn turned her face into Bryan's shoulder. He closed his arms around her, moving carefully, slowly, so as not to jostle the gurney that hid them or move the sheet draped over it. Leaning closer to her, he whispered, "Are you seeing any...you know, dead people?"

She shook her head. "Just the one on the table. But *look* at her, Bry."

"I am." And he was. From this distance, with the thin sheet as a veil, he could have been looking at Dawn's lifeless body on that table. The lean length of her, the long, straight hair, the delicate facial features. At least there were no colors—all they could see was her silhouette, due to the sheet.

"She was found in her bed?" Nick asked.

"Yeah, just like all the others," MacNamara told him. "Shot glass beside her, whiskey in her mouth. Ligature marks suggesting strangulation."

Westcott was already flipping on the light above the table, leaning over the dead woman, getting far closer than Bryan ever would have wanted to. He needed to get Dawn the hell out of here. This wasn't anything she had to see. But they were trapped where they were, and she was starting to shake. He held her a little tighter and wished with everything in him that he could make this go away. He hated seeing her suffer this way. "Hold on," he whispered directly into her ear. "It won't be much longer."

She nodded and lifted her head, turning slightly and staring at the table through the sheet. Seeming to gird herself, she stiffened her spine; he felt it, and he saw her eyes narrow as she focused on the body.

He knew what she was doing then. She was trying to talk to the dead girl. And Bryan didn't know whether to hope she would succeed or pray she would fail. If she could get an answer, he might get his life back. But if she saw the dead again, she was probably going to run away when this was over. All the way back to the West Coast.

It was a no-win proposition for him either way.

Dr. Westcott was moving her gloved hands over the

corpse now, feeling the neck, the shoulders, the slender, still arms, all the way down to the dead woman's bagged hands. As she lifted one arm, even through the sheet Bryan saw the darker-colored bruising—or at least it looked like bruising—on the underside of it.

He knew Dawn saw it, too, when she tensed.

"He beat her," she whispered, lips moving near his ear, barely any breath emerging, barely any sound.

"No, Dawn. It's normal. Just the blood pooling at the lowest points. Gravity does that. He didn't do it."

"Why's she wearing a watch?" Dr. Westcott asked, interrupting their nearly silent conversation.

The chief shrugged. "It's what she had on when we found her."

"Who the hell wears a watch to bed?" Westcott asked. The flaring of her temper made both Nick and the chief look at her in surprise. She bit her lip, nodded firmly. "Sorry. I'm getting tired of cutting up gorgeous young women in their prime because of this jackass, whoever he is. Get him, will you?"

"You know we will," Nick promised, and he moved closer. "So, little lady, why were you wearing your watch to bed? Hmm?" He bent and stared at it, and then he straightened and shook his head. "She wasn't."

The other two both looked at him, and he nodded at the dead woman's wrist. "It's on upside down. She wouldn't have been able to read it. Someone else put this watch on her. Ten to one it was Nightcap. Gimme a bag, Rita."

Dr. Westcott was already striding away from the

table, and in an instant she handed Nick a pair of cutting pliers, then held the plastic bag for him. "Here, snip the band. Less chance of disturbing trace evidence that way."

He nodded, slid the shears underneath the watchband, snipped, then clamped the end of the pliers onto the cut band and held the watch up. Turning it slowly, he studied it. From his hiding place, Bryan did, too.

Dawn lifted her head from his shoulder to take a look for herself, and she kept on looking, even moving the sheet slightly so she could peer around it.

Nick dropped the watch into the waiting evidence bag and let the pliers clatter onto an otherwise empty instrument tray. "Take that back with you, would you, Chief?" he asked, handing the bag over and taking two steps toward the door, almost as if his motion would pull the chief along in his wake. "I want to hang out here a bit longer."

"Don't be long. I want you out at the crime scene ASAP." Yanking a pad from his pocket, he scribbled on it, tore off the top sheet and thrust it at Nick. "Here's the address. Be there within an hour."

"Sure."

The chief went out the door. Nick stood there, watching for a moment, then he turned and gave a nod. Bryan pushed the gurney away from them and stood, then helped Dawn get to her feet.

She was pale, and he thought he saw beads of sweat on her forehead.

"I know," he told her. "That was way too close."

"Yes, it was," she said. "But that's not what has me shaking like a leaf right now, Bryan." He frowned, tilting his head and scanning her face. Was it the dead? he wondered. Had the dead woman's ghost risen up and spoken to her? God, he couldn't imagine how frightening it must be to live with something like that.

Rita Westcott and Nick were staring at her just as intently, so he couldn't come out and ask. She pressed her lips together, swallowed, then spoke again. "It's not what you're thinking, either, Bryan. It was…it was my watch. That dead girl was wearing my watch."

Bryan drove, because Dawn was still shaking. She sat there, head back, eyes closed, telling herself it was stupid to be scared.

"What do you think about Nick's offer?" Bryan asked.

She felt her brows pull into a frown. "It's not my call, Bryan. I mean, you know him better than I do, and you're the one who's going to end up in jail if they find us."

"And you're the one who's going to end up—" He cut himself off, but she knew the next word, the one he hadn't spoken. *Dead.*

"Do you really think we can trust him not to rat you out if we stay in his cabin like he wants us to?" she asked. She didn't open her eyes, just waited.

"I trust him," Bryan said. "Nick Di Marco doesn't say anything he doesn't mean. If he says he'll keep it to himself, he will."

She nodded, mulling over their options. "Have you seen it? This cabin of his?"

"Yeah."

"So what's it like?"

He shrugged. "Isolated. It's out near the falls, a good distance from just about everything else."

"So it's either very safe or very dangerous."

"If no one knows we're there, we can lean toward 'very safe,'" Bryan said. "It's small, but nice. Got a fireplace, full kitchen, big front porch, bigger back one."

She opened her eyes. "Phone, Internet, indoor plumbing?"

"Satellite dish on the roof," he said. "That takes care of the TV and the Internet. No cell reception that far out of town, but there is a landline. And yes, it has fully functional indoor plumbing."

She sighed. "I *am* getting sick of takeout, and those microwaved baked potatoes were just sad. A real kitchen would be nice."

"So?"

She shrugged. "So I'll mull it over while we go talk to Olivia Dupree again."

"Good enough." He looked at her, then went quiet again.

She swallowed and nodded. "Yes, the watch was in my purse."

"But you went through the purse after the locket showed up on the last body. You didn't notice anything else missing," he said.

"I don't keep an itemized list of the contents of my

handbag, Bryan. So shoot me. I didn't notice anything else missing, but now I'm telling you that watch was in there. It needs a new battery, so I grabbed my spare and threw that one in, and then just forgot about it, with everything going on. There could be other things missing that I just didn't notice. A handbag is just a catchall to me, you know that."

"Okay, so it was in your bag, and there might be other things missing that we aren't yet aware of. Got it."

"That makes me doubly suspicious of Jaycam," Dawn said slowly. "He was there that day I left the car unlocked and came back to find my bag dumped all over the place."

Bryan sighed. "It doesn't make any sense, though. He doesn't even know you. Why would he want to torture you like this?"

"I don't know."

"It just feels…personal, you know? Maybe…maybe we should be looking at *your* enemies, Dawn. Maybe this whole thing is directed at you. Setting me up, knowing it would bring you back here, could have been the first step."

She frowned, as a dark fear settled even more deeply into her mind. "But who would want to do that to me?"

"Think about it. Do you have any unpleasant history with anyone?"

"You mean, besides you?" She said it as a joke, a lame attempt to lighten the mood, but his quick look told her it had missed the mark. "No, Bry, that's not what I meant. You know I don't believe you could have done any of this."

He nodded, but she could tell the barb still stung, even though she hadn't meant it that way.

"I haven't been as cruel to anyone as I was to you," she said quickly. "I hope I never will be."

He glanced at her again. "Is that an apology?"

"No. This is. I'm sorry, Bryan. I'm so sorry my cowardice hurt you the way it did."

"You're no coward, Dawn. That much I know."

"I ran away. I was too afraid to face who and what I was."

He shrugged. "It drove your father mad. Turned him into a killer."

She nodded and fell silent. But then she blinked and looked at him again. "Do you think there's any way he could have something to do with all of this?"

"Who? Mordecai?"

The sound of his name made her want to look around fast, to be sure it hadn't somehow summoned him. But there was no sign of her long-dead father. No sign of any ghosts.

"Dawn, he's dead," Bryan said softly. "He can't get to you anymore."

"He could before I left. What's changed so much?"

"I don't know. But I think if he could still get to you, he would. Don't you?"

She frowned, then nodded. "Maybe he's finally—I don't know—at peace or something."

"Or burning in hell." He bit his lip. "Shit, I'm sorry. I shouldn't have said that."

She shrugged. "I was thinking it, too. But…"

"But?"

She drew a breath. "It's like I'm afraid to say it. Afraid it will make it true. That's stupid, isn't it?"

"You're a lot of things, Dawn, but stupid isn't one of them. Tell me, what are you thinking?"

"Maybe…maybe he *can* still get to me. Maybe…this is how. Maybe it's the only way he still can."

"Dawn…"

"I think he…he wants me with him, Bryan. I think he's come back for me, and he's going to keep on killing innocent women until he gets the one he's come for. Until he—" She choked on the sob that blocked the rest of her words, then suddenly just burst into tears and covered her face with her hands.

"Oh, hell." Bryan slowed the car to a stop on the shoulder of the road, then turned and pulled her into his arms. "Come on, Dawn. Come on, baby, it's not that. You know it's not that."

"How?" she muttered, her words muffled by his shoulder. "How can I know?"

He ran a hand through her hair to push it out of her eyes and stared down into them. She blinked at him through her tears.

"I won't let him get to you. I won't let *anyone* hurt you, Dawn—living or dead. I promise."

"If it *is* him—"

"It's not."

"But if it is," she pressed, "then we can't beat him. You know that, Bryan. You knew him."

"Yeah. I knew him. But don't forget, Dawn, we beat him once already."

She blinked, oddly reassured by that simple reminder. "We did, didn't we?"

"And we can do it again. And I'll tell you something else, too. If we can take on your father and win, then there's no one else who stands a chance against us. Including the mortal human murderer who's behind all this."

She sighed, the tension leaving her all at once. "Thank you, Bryan. I don't deserve you."

"No. You deserve someone a whole lot better."

She lifted her eyes to his. "There isn't anyone better."

He smiled just slightly, and then his gaze locked on her lips. She closed her eyes, waiting for the kiss she knew was going to come.

But instead she felt his arms fall away as he put the car into gear again and started driving.

She'd lost him. She'd forgotten that for one precious moment. And she had no one to blame but herself. She'd walked away from the best man she would ever find. She never should have left him.

And she knew, right then, that she wouldn't make the same choice again. Not knowing what she knew now. She would face all the ghosts there were—she would face down Mordecai Young himself—if it meant keeping Bryan's love for her alive.

But she couldn't do it all over again. It was done. His love for her was dead; she'd killed it. And not even its ghost was going to come back to her now.

11

Professor Olivia Dupree did not look glad to see them, Bryan noted. Usually, when someone was unhappy to see the police, that meant they had reason to be. He, however, wasn't there in uniform. He was a murder suspect—person of interest, he corrected himself—so her grim expression at the sight of him was nothing to find suspicious.

Still, he'd thought she would be a little bit more receptive toward Dawn, since she'd been the one to initiate additional contact. And talk about being receptive to Dawn…

He'd almost kissed her back there in the car. He'd almost kissed her. And damn, if he had to spend much more time with her…

Hell.

It was no longer just that he knew damn well she would turn tail and run at the first sign of a ghost. And there would be more ghosts for her, he felt that right to his toes. There was also the possibility he might end up going to prison for life. Or he might get off on a technicality so shady that it ruined his career for good. He might even have to go on the run to avoid prison. He didn't have any business starting anything up with her, or any woman—not that there could be any other woman for him—with everything still unsettled.

Besides, the best thing he could do for Dawn right now would be to get her to leave here. To go back to the West Coast, to run as far from him as she could possibly go. She was putting her life in danger by being here with him. *He* was putting her life in danger.

One kiss, and he knew she would be even more unwilling to leave him than she already was.

Until the ghosts came back, anyway.

Professor Dupree opened the door of her neat white Cape Cod and then went as still as deepwater. No expression crossed her face. She just stood there, looking from one of them to the other, and then she said, "How do you know where I live?"

"Phone book," Dawn said, taking the lead when Bryan didn't. "Look, Professor Dupree—Olivia—we just have a couple more questions, and then, I promise, we'll leave you alone."

Olivia didn't open the door wider or say "Sure, come on in." She remained still, and then she shook her head. "I don't think I should talk to you," she said, and she started to back up, started to close the door.

"Please, Professor," Bryan said. "My life is on the line. Five minutes, I promise. And you don't even need to let us in. We can do this standing on the front step if you want."

She blinked at him and maybe saw some of the strain in his eyes. She'd probably questioned Nick about him. He knew she liked and respected Nick, so his reassurances probably went a long way with her. She would be scared if she thought there was any chance in hell he was a serial killer. She would be stupid to let him in if she thought that.

She wasn't stupid. And yet, she seemed to soften toward him, and he felt relieved.

She said, "Backyard. There are a table and chairs out there, on the deck. I'll be right out." Then she backed in and closed the door before either of them could reply.

Sighing, Bryan looked at Dawn.

She gave him a reassuring smile and gripped his upper arm, tugging him with her off the steps, down the walk and over the perfectly manicured emerald lawn to the back of the house.

They had to open a tall chain-link gate to enter the fenced-in backyard. There was a semicircular redwood deck off the back of the house, French doors going inside and a glass-topped, umbrella-shaded table off to one side. Bryan took it all in and nodded. "Nice," he said.

"It is," Dawn agreed as they traipsed over more grass toward the steps. "But watch where you walk."

He frowned, not clear what she meant, but then she nodded at the doggy door just to the left of the French doors, and he understood. The backyard was fenced in for a reason.

And just then those French doors shuddered, and he went stone still, because there was a small brindle-patterned pony on the other side of them, looking out at them.

No, not a pony. That thing was, apparently, supposed to be a dog.

Steam came from its nostrils, misting the glass, and then it bounded to the side and came lunging through its dog door too fast to allow either him or Dawn a chance to escape.

Bryan pushed her behind him and started backing up at a brisk pace. "Easy, boy. Easy. Easy now."

But the beast kept coming, bounding toward him, jowls flapping, reaching him in two leaps and then turning to one side just before crashing bodily into him. The dog pressed his side against Bryan, leaning into him with his full body weight—which was two hundred pounds if it was an ounce—wiggling and wagging, and panting a happy pant.

Bryan had to brace his legs hard to keep from being knocked over onto his backside, but even with that, his breath rushed out of him and he closed his eyes. "Okay, I guess he's not going to eat us."

"No," Dawn said. "Doesn't look that way." She reached out a hand to let him sniff. He licked it instead, and she laughed. "My God, what a dog. He's got a head the size of a bear's!"

"English mastiff. Biggest breed in the world."

They both looked up to see Olivia Dupree standing on the deck, carrying a tray that held three glasses full of dark liquid and clinking ice cubes.

She set the tray on the table. "As the lion is to the cat, the mastiff is to the dog. Or so someone is quoted as saying. Come here, Freddy."

The humongous beast bounded toward her, and she hugged his neck, without having to bend over very far to do so. Then she pulled out a chair and sat down.

Dawn and Bryan walked up the three steps onto the deck and joined her at the table, and the dog proceeded to move from one to the next in search of affection. Olivia set a glass in front of each of them. "Rum and Coke," she said. "I could use one."

"I know it isn't pleasant to keep dredging this up," Dawn said. "We really will try to be brief."

"All right." Olivia had, Bryan noted, a cell phone clipped to her pocket that hadn't been there before. She was taking precautions, just in case he *was* a killer. Though he thought the dog would have been plenty of protection even if he had been.

"Olivia, how well did you know your roommate, Sara Quinlan?"

She looked at her glass, not at Dawn. "I told you. Not well at all. I'd only moved in a few weeks before her death."

"Did you know she'd been pregnant?"

Olivia's head came up fast, and her brown eyes widened. It was a real reaction, too knee-jerk to be fake, Bryan thought.

"The autopsy report says she probably gave birth four to six weeks before she was killed. She never mentioned it to you?" Dawn went on.

"No. My God. And there was no baby. There was no baby stuff. No clue." She frowned and looked at Dawn. "What happened to the child? Was it stillborn?"

"Nobody knows," Dawn said.

"Someone knows," Bryan cut in.

"After Sara's body was claimed by a woman who said she was her cousin, the police tried to contact her, to tell her there might be a child somewhere. But they couldn't find any woman by the name she'd used."

Now Olivia turned to her dog, and she kissed his nose and stroked his head. "That's the oddest thing. Who would want to claim a body badly enough to lie about it?"

"That's what we'd like to know. Did you ever hear of a cousin?"

"No."

"Is there anything you can tell us about her, Olivia? Anything at all?"

She finally met Dawn's eyes again, then shook her head. "I can tell you that I knew nothing about any baby. I swear I didn't." Then she shifted her eyes to Bryan. "What's going to happen? I mean, now that the police know about this?"

"They've known all along," Bryan said. "They just didn't have any leads, didn't have anyone to contact, and let it drop."

"But there's a missing child out there somewhere."

"Missing sixteen-year-old now," Bryan said. "Unless it was stillborn and she just buried it or something."

"Why would she do that?"

He shrugged. "It happens."

She downed the rest of her drink. Then she took a breath and sighed. "So why are you asking me about it now?"

"Because I just found out myself. Nick never asked you?"

"No."

"I wonder why not."

"I don't know. Ask him. I certainly plan to." She looked at the sky. "It's going to be dark soon."

Dawn nodded and started to get to her feet.

"Wait," Olivia said. "Do you…do you want to stay and have something to eat?"

Dawn looked at her curiously.

"I've got some chicken soaking in barbecue sauce, and a salad. And a lot of questions, to tell you the truth. Why don't you stay?"

Bryan glanced at Dawn and knew they were both thinking the same thing. By staying they might glean some tidbit that Olivia hadn't told them already. By staying, they might find something out.

He had the feeling, though, that Olivia was asking them for the very same reasons they were saying yes. She was fishing, too. For what? he wondered.

"Okay. We'll stay."

It was surreal, Dawn thought. They were grilling chicken on a gas grill, and sipping rum and Coke under the stars. Crickets chirped and lightning bugs glittered, and the giant dog lay on the deck, snoring like a chainsaw.

It was an ordinary idyllic evening. And yet Bryan was being hunted by the police and Dawn by a crazed killer.

Surreal.

"I can't believe the police never told me. About… the baby, I mean." Olivia set a platter of chicken on the glass-topped table, beside the foil-wrapped baked potatoes and giant Pyrex salad bowl. "Help yourself."

Bryan stabbed a chicken leg before Dawn could even pick up her fork, and she managed to suppress a smile. His appetite almost never failed him, no matter how dire the circumstances.

He snagged a potato, too, then spent time carefully splitting it, so the steam wafted in his face while he dolloped a heaping spoonful of sour cream into the crevasse, before he returned to their earlier discussion. "Well, you weren't a relative," he said. "They wouldn't automatically inform you of stuff. They tried to find the child. Nothing but dead ends. What were they supposed to do?"

Olivia shrugged. "I don't know. Send someone back to where Sara came from—Chicago, right?"

"So we were told," Dawn said softly.

Olivia shot her a look. "So did they do that? Send someone to Chicago to ask around about her?"

"Nick says they did—discreetly," Bryan said. "That it was a dead end."

Olivia sighed and ate a piece of chicken.

"You had connections to Chicago, too, didn't you, Olivia?" Dawn asked.

Olivia choked. Her eyes widened and flooded with water, and she slammed her palm against her own chest repeatedly.

Bryan was up and moving behind her, no doubt about to deliver the Heimlich, when she held up her free hand, and waved him off. Blinking, she dabbed her mouth with a napkin, and took a drink of her rum and Coke.

"Damn," she muttered.

"You all right?" Bryan asked.

Olivia nodded. "Yeah, fine. It went down wrong."

"It wasn't something I said?" Dawn asked, her eyes watchful, because she knew damn well Olivia was hiding something. She just wasn't sure what.

"Of course not. As to your question, I've never even been to Chicago."

Dawn nodded. "Oh. I thought—well, I was noticing in the crime-scene photos that the bed where Sara was found had a lot of New York team paraphernalia, even some Syracuse University stuff, hanging near it. But no Chicago stuff. That was all on your side of the room."

Olivia narrowed her eyes and licked her lips. "You're very good at this, Dawn. None of the police ever picked up on that before. Not even enough to ask me about it."

"Oh?"

Olivia nodded. "The truth is, Sara was in my bed that night. I was staying over with friends, and when

I came home in the morning, that's where I found her. In my bed, dead."

"Why do you think she would have crashed in your bed, Olivia?"

Olivia shrugged. "She'd been complaining about her mattress, saying it needed to be replaced. Mine was brand-new. Maybe she just wanted one comfortable night."

"She didn't ask you first?"

"She knew I wouldn't mind."

"But you'd only been rooming together a few weeks. How could she know you that well so soon?"

Olivia sighed. "All right, look, I don't like to talk about this. It's a painful part of a painful childhood. But the truth is, I had met Sara once before. We…we shared the same foster home for a few weeks, years ago."

Bryan and Dawn exchanged a quick surprised look. "In Chicago?" Dawn asked.

Olivia shook her head hard. "In New York. We were both in our teens. It was only a few weeks, like I said. I have no idea how she wound up in Chicago. But when I came to Shadow Falls I saw her ad for a roommate, recognized her name and the rest…" She shrugged. "The rest is as I've told you. But she would have known I wouldn't care about her using my bed. We shared a bed in that foster home."

Dawn frowned. "Where were you the night she died, Olivia?"

Olivia sent her a sharp look. "I told you. I was with

friends. And before that I was at the park, near the pond, reading the latest Aaron Westhaven novel."

"That's pretty specific."

"His novels are important to me," Olivia said. "Getting a new one is an occasion. I wanted privacy and silence to read it straight through in a single sitting. And all of that should be in Nick's report, anyway."

"It was," Bryan said. "Almost word for word. And those friends you were with verified your story."

"What happened to Sara's stuff, Olivia?" Dawn asked then. "I mean, you know, her clothes, her photos, everything she had in the apartment?"

Olivia sighed. "I waited six months, then finally boxed it all up and took it to the Salvation Army drop box. I didn't know what else to do."

"You didn't save any of it? Not one single thing?"

She shrugged. "There may have been a handful of things I didn't pack up, but if there were, I left them behind when I moved out of the apartment six months later." She shifted her eyes to Bryan. "I just couldn't stay there."

"I understand," Bryan said.

Dawn turned her focus to the food. "The meal is delicious," she said.

"Thanks. Dawn, are the police going to start digging into Sara's past all over again now?"

Dawn watched her face, not answering. Bryan, though, did. "I don't think so. Nick pretty much told me it was a waste of time. I just had to know a little bit more before I could let it go."

"And now?" she asked. "Do you know enough now to let it go, Bryan?"

He held her gaze for a long moment, took a drink and set the glass down. "I don't know any more than I did before, so I guess not."

"Bryan," Dawn said, sliding a hand over his on the table. "Let's drop this topic, okay? It can't be a pleasant subject for Olivia, and I know I'd relish a break from it for a while."

He nodded. "For what it's worth, Olivia, I don't think he's going to come after you. And if he did…" He glanced down at the dog. "Well, if he did, I have a feeling you'd be all right."

"Freddy seems docile and friendly," she said with a nod. "But if anyone were trying to hurt me, he'd tear them limb from limb."

"Good."

"Does he have a brother?" Dawn asked.

They shared an uncomfortable laugh, and Dawn got to her feet. "Olivia, I need to use your bathroom, if it's okay."

"Straight in through the kitchen, down the hallway, second door on the right."

"Thanks." She got up and headed in through the French doors, sending a meaningful look at Bryan that she hoped to God he would get.

Just before the doors closed behind her, she heard Bryan say, "Does he know any tricks?"

Good, Bry. Keep her distracted.

Dawn didn't go to the bathroom. She walked fast,

opening doors, entering Olivia's bedroom. She hurried, knowing there wouldn't be much time, racing to the bed, dropping to her knees and looking underneath. Nothing there. The closet next. She opened the large sliding mirrored doors and scanned the racks, then yanked a chair from the vanity and stood on it to examine the topmost shelf.

If Olivia had keepsakes she didn't want anyone to see, the bedroom closet, top shelf, was where they would be, Dawn thought. In a box, probably pushed to the back.

She found a shoebox back there and felt sure it was what she wanted. Almost as if she *knew*. Just the same way she knew she was about out of time. Yanking it down, she didn't take time to go through it. Instead, she tucked it under her arm, then quickly closed the closet, replaced the chair and left the room looking exactly the way she'd found it. Then she dashed back through the house, pausing at the kitchen, to look to the left, toward the French doors and the deck beyond them.

Bryan and Olivia were not at the table. Which meant they wouldn't see her slip through the kitchen, but also meant she didn't know where the hell they were.

No time for cowardice. She ducked through the kitchen and found her way to the front door. She opened it, looking both ways and seeing no one, before dashing to the car. Quick as she could, she opened the passenger door and crammed the shoebox onto the floor, shoving car rubbish on top to conceal it. She closed the car door gently and ran back to the house, in through the front door, through the living room and into the kitchen.

Again she glanced toward the French doors. This time she could see Bryan and Olivia walking toward the deck across the grassy lawn, the dog lumbering close behind them with a Frisbee in his mouth.

She quickened her pace to cross the kitchen and quickly emerged onto the deck, trying to look entirely innocent.

"You oughtta see this guy at work!" Bryan exclaimed as he sank into his chair. "He didn't miss the Frisbee once! He can jump higher than my head for it."

Olivia was smiling, rubbing her dog's giant head as she reclaimed her own seat, and then looking up at Dawn as if she had forgotten her presence. "Oh, did you find your way all right?"

"Yeah, thanks." She sat down, avoiding Bryan's eyes. If she looked at him she would give herself away, and Olivia might see. The woman already looked nervous, glancing quickly toward the doors and back again.

"The meal was great, Olivia. Thank you," Bryan said. "And I'm glad I got to meet your, uh, dog."

Olivia's nervous expression eased. Like any red-blooded woman would, she was falling for Bryan. At least, falling under his spell. It wasn't his fault, Dawn reasoned. He didn't know he was doing it. But all his hometown, good-guy charm had been supercharged by this new wrongly accused hero ingredient. He was a whole different dish now, and a hard one to resist.

Olivia was a woman. Sixteen years older, maybe?

Sure, but still a knockout. Dawn felt a little twist of jealousy and tried to contain it. She didn't have any right to feel that way over Bryan. He's wasn't hers anymore.

"Thanks for the company," Olivia said. "I have to admit, I'm…I'm scared. I know, everyone keeps reassuring me that this guy isn't after me, but how can I be sure? How can anyone predict what a man capable of all this might do?"

"I thought Nick was going to send an officer by," Bryan asked. "In fact, I was surprised not to see one here when we arrived."

"Surprised and relieved, I'll bet," Olivia said. "Nick sent someone, but just to check in. They'll be back later on." She looked at her watch. "Pretty soon, as a matter of fact. You should probably go."

Frowning, Bryan looked around the table, snatched up a napkin, then turned to Dawn. "Got a pen?"

"Uh, yeah, in my bag." She scooped her purse up from where she'd hung it on the back of her chair, dug around and pulled out a pen.

"Thanks," Bryan said, taking it and bending to scribble on the napkin. "Olivia, I don't blame you for being afraid, and I agree there's no way to be sure he won't try for you. Just because he didn't before, that won't mean much if this isn't even the same guy."

"You're not exactly reassuring me here," she said with a weak smile.

"I want you to call this guy. His name is Rico, he was my partner on the force—will be again, I hope. He's beyond reproach. You tell him I said to call him.

He works days, same as you, so he can come around at night and keep an extra eye on you until this is over."

"You really think that's necessary?"

"I think it's better to be safe than sorry."

She nodded, taking the napkin, tucking it into a pocket. "Thanks. I wish I could have been more help to you."

"You might still be. Something could come to you later on."

"How will I let you know if it does?" she asked.

Dawn tipped her head to one side, thinking this professor was as clever as her title would suggest. "We'll call you in a day or two, just to check in."

Olivia nodded. "And to let me know if you've learned anything else…about Sara? Or…her baby?" she asked.

"Of course."

"Bye, Olivia." Bryan extended a hand, and she clasped it. "Thanks again," he said.

"You're welcome."

He smiled and then started around the house, even as Olivia sank back into her chair and reached for her glass.

"Flirt much?" Dawn asked, as they rounded the house and approached the car.

"Flirt? I wasn't—"

"You had her eating out of your hand. God, I thought you were going to propose there, once or twice."

"Oh, come on!"

She yanked open the car door and slid in, keeping

her feet off the box on the floor. Bryan got behind the wheel and started the engine. As he backed the car out onto the road, he said, "You don't really think I was flirting, do you?"

"I most certainly do."

"Well, I wasn't."

"You think she's hot?"

"Yes, I do. But I wasn't flirting. I was trying to be friendly and make sure she knew I wasn't the bad guy."

"You were flirting."

She bent and picked up the box now that they were a couple of blocks away. "Fortunately, *I* was working."

"What did you do, Dawnie?"

"I looked in the two places I would put something that I wanted to hide but didn't expect anyone to come looking for. Casual hiding places. Under the bed, and on the closet shelf, in the back. And I found this shoebox."

"What do you think it is?"

"I'm about to find out." She started digging.

12

Bryan kept his attention divided between driving the car back to their motel and watching Dawn dig through Olivia Dupree's shoebox. He wasn't expecting much. And he wasn't surprised.

"It's just keepsakes," she said. "Ticket stubs. A couple of group photos." She flipped over a snapshot of several young people. "No names or dates on them anywhere. They must be old friends."

"How old?"

"High school, maybe? Could be college age. Might even be former students."

"Former students who are dead, or former students who are alive?"

She looked up fast. "I hadn't thought of that. Don't we have a…a contact sheet somewhere with photos of all the original victims?"

"All we know about, yeah. It's in the file back at the motel."

"Okay, so we'll set the photos aside and move on."

She pulled out a dried rosebud, brown at the edges, its leaves ready to crumble to dust, and laid it on the seat beside her with care. She thinned her lips. "I feel bad about taking this stuff. I hope we can get it back to her before she knows it's gone."

"If we find something that can help solve this thing, or find Sara's missing baby—or both—then hurting Olivia's feelings is a small price to pay."

She nodded in agreement. "We've got to stop thinking of it as Sara's *baby,* though. The kid would be sixteen by now."

"I know." He glanced her way. "So what else is in there?"

She shrugged. "Some cards—tiny ones, like the ones you get with flowers." She frowned. "Wait a minute. Wait just a minute."

"What?" Bryan looked at her as she frowned down at the tiny card in her hand. "What is it, Dawn?"

"'To Sara—Congrats, Shelly.'"

"Sara?"

"Yeah. Why would Olivia have Sara's keepsakes?"

He shrugged. "Maybe she just didn't know what to do with them after she died. Maybe she wanted to keep something to remember her by."

"But then why lie about it?" She put the card back into the box and picked up one of the ticket stubs again. "This is from Wrigley Field. That's in Chicago, where Sara's from." Then she dropped the stub and grabbed the photo again. "And one of the kids in this shot is wearing an Illinois State sweatshirt. Bryan, I think this whole box belonged to Sara. These are Sara's keepsakes, not Olivia's."

He nodded slowly.

"Why would she keep this stuff? And then lie to us and say she hadn't? I don't get it."

"I don't know if we need to get it," Bryan said. "We might never know why, unless she decides to tell us. I'm not sure it matters."

"It means something. It has to."

He shrugged. "I'm not going to question your instincts, that's for sure." He looked at her, shook his head.

"What?"

"Well, you knew right where to find that box."

"I told you, I just looked in the most likely places."

"I think it might be a little more than that. You've done that a few times since you've been back. It's almost like you're…a little more tuned in than I am. Than… most people are."

She frowned at him, gave her head a quick shake and looked down at the box in her lap again.

"I'm serious, Dawn. Maybe your…gift…hasn't vanished. Maybe it's just changed a little."

"You think the dead are still talking to me, just very softly?" She rolled her eyes at the notion. "Or do you think I'm just coming down with a bad case of ESP?"

He shrugged. "Is it really so far-fetched? You've had far more unusual experiences in the past."

"Key phrase, there, Bry. 'In the past.' That's where it's staying. I promise you, I'd know if my hunches were coming from anywhere besides my own head. And they're not."

"Okay."

She looked at him. "They're *not,* Bryan."

"I said okay."

She nodded. "So what's the plan for the night, then?"

"I was thinking, head back to the motel, gather up our stuff and head over to Nick's cabin, start settling in."

"Let's not get too comfortable, though. We won't be there long."

"You're right. I sure don't want to risk Nick being brought up on accessory charges." He nodded in resolution. "So we give it a week. No more. After that, I'll just have to decide whether to turn myself in or head for points south."

"Points south?"

"Brazil. Argentina. Whoever has the toughest extradition restrictions. I'll get myself a fake ID and passport and— Hell, those things will take some time. Maybe I should start on that now, while—"

"Jeez, Bryan. Could you *be* any more negative?"

He shot her a quick look, surprised by her outburst.

"I meant," she went on, "that we won't be there long because we'll find what we need to nail this guy and clear your name, and we can go back to our everyday lives. God, try to have a little hope, would you?"

He smiled just slightly. "Sorry. You're right, I'll try."

"You do that." She put the rosebud back inside the shoebox, then put the lid on. "Do we tell Nick about this?"

He glanced at the box, shook his head. "Not yet. He and Olivia are friends. I don't want to go revealing that we snooped around her place, took things without permission, much less a warrant or even much of a reason. He'd be pissed."

"But if we find anything—"

"If it's pertinent, of course we'll tell him. While being careful not to screw up a friendship." He sighed. "I always wondered if the two of them would ever hook up."

She waggled her eyebrows. "Maybe they already have, even though she says not. She's gorgeous. And he's no slouch, except for that belly he's got going on."

"He'd tell you he's earned that belly."

She laughed a little. "I guess he has at that. Here's the motel."

Bryan nodded and pulled into the parking lot. Dawn opened the box one more time, retrieved the photos and took them with her into the room, going straight to the closet where they'd tucked the cooler with the file folders out of sight. He glanced at the unmade bed, the towels slung over the shower rod beyond the open bathroom door.

"Guess the maid honored our 'do not disturb' request," he said, dropping the little doorknob hanger onto the inside of the doorknob.

"Looks like." But she was only half listening. He could tell. She'd pulled out the contact sheet and was scanning the faces in the photographs for comparison. Then, shaking her head, she said, "No victims in this shot. Including Sara. But look, Bryan. Now that I have decent light, I can see there was something written on the back. It's so old it's faded."

"Lemme see that." He crossed the room and took the photo from her, holding it under the nearest lamp. "I don't think it's faded. It looks like it's been erased. Rubbed out. See those marks?"

She leaned in closer. "Yeah, like scuff marks. And only where there were words, nowhere else, so it's not normal wear."

"Got a pencil?" he asked.

She went to the bedside stand, rummaged around for a pencil, found one and handed it to him.

Bryan laid the photo on the nightstand, sat on the edge of the bed and, holding the pencil so its tip was nearly sideways, began rubbing it over the back of the photo. He took his time about it.

"Now she's sure to know we took this stuff," Dawn said.

He glanced up at her. "You kind of like Olivia, don't you?"

"Yeah. Yeah, I guess I do." Then she shrugged. "You almost have to like anyone with a dog like Freddy, right?"

He shrugged and went back to rubbing. "Okay, here we go. As good as new."

"What's it say?"

She sat beside him on the bed and leaned over him to see. Her side pressed against his, and her scent wrapped around his brain and squeezed. Damn, it was hard being this close to her and not—

"'Joey, Laura, Becky, Sara, Glenn.' There's a date, too. Seventeen years ago."

Their eyes met. "Then she *is* in this shot," Dawn said, even as Bryan was flipping it back over. He put his finger on the male face on the left, then touched each face, naming them as he went. "Joey, Laura, Becky... Sara?"

"Holy hell, Bryan. That's not Sara. That's...I think that's Olivia!"

"It's probably just a different Sara."

"Uh-uh. Look at her, Bryan."

Bryan did, pulling the photo closer, narrowing his eyes, recalling Olivia Dupree's face to mind. Her dark hair. Her brown eyes. The tiny mole on her cheekbone, the type glamour queens used to draw on with makeup and refer to as a beauty mark.

"What the hell?"

"Okay, okay, let's just take a step back. What does this mean?" Dawn asked. "At it's most basic, without speculation, what does this tell us?"

"That seventeen years ago, Olivia Dupree was calling herself Sara," Bryan said.

"Then why on earth is she calling herself Olivia now? Bryan, you don't think—"

"Boot up that laptop. We need to find a photo of Sara Quinlan taken sixteen years ago, or more, to be sure about this. Let's see if we can download that yearbook I ordered yet."

Nodding hard, Dawn returned to the closet, pulled down the notebook computer and waited for it to find the motel's wireless connection. "Okay, I'm on. Where'd you have the e-mail sent?"

He rattled off the info on the temporary account he'd set up, and she typed as quickly as he spoke.

"Yes, we got the e-mail with the password." She copied the nonsensical alpha-numeric code, returned to the University of Illinois Web site, found the pertinent page and pasted it in. Then she waited while the document downloaded.

"It's a PDF," she said at length.

While the machine worked, she drummed her fingers on the machine. Finally the pages finished loading, and she typed rapidly. "I'll just do a search under her name and…hello."

"What?"

She clicked on the thumbnail that had come up, a portrait taken at graduation. It enlarged to fill the screen. It was clearly the face of a much younger Olivia Dupree. But the name underneath it was Sara Quinlan.

Bryan looked up from the screen, his eyes locking with Dawn's. "Olivia Dupree is really Sara Quinlan."

"So then who did Nightcap murder sixteen years ago?" Dawn whispered.

"She was in Olivia's bed, with Olivia's memorabilia on her wall. It had to be the real Olivia Dupree."

"You think...Olivia—I mean, Sara—just switched identities with her?"

"It would have been hard," Bryan said, rising and pacing the room as he processed his thoughts out loud. "But not impossible. She was the roommate. How easy would it have been to identify the body as her own?"

"But someone would have known. Family or—"

"Olivia said she knew Sara when they shared a foster home. Maybe there wasn't any family to notice on either side," Bryan said. "And maybe the professor knew that. So she must have been the one who claimed the body, claiming to be a cousin. She had it cremated to end any chance of further investigation."

"Wouldn't there be records?" Dawn asked. "A driver's license, student ID?"

"No driver's license was ever issued for Sara Quinlan," Bryan said. "There should have been a student ID, though."

"Those have a photo on them. Wouldn't someone have asked for that?"

He nodded, thinking. "The murder was in July. Classes didn't start up until August. Maybe she didn't have it yet. Or maybe she did and the real Sara hid it, then said it was lost and got another one, with a new picture."

"Still, the police could have gotten a copy of the old

one from the school before she had a chance. It would have been on the computer."

"Yeah, but there was no need. Two people identified her, even if they were both one and the same. No reason to check. And you can bet if there ever was a copy of that ID on the college computers, the professor has found a way to delete it by now." Bryan shook his head. "Even then, I'm not sure she could have pulled it off alone. If she managed this, she almost had to have help. Powerful help, I think."

"What are you thinking?" Dawn asked softly.

He shrugged. "Nothing...nothing."

"What in the name of God could she have to hide, Bryan? Do you think—" She sucked in a breath and widened her eyes. "My God, do you think she really is the killer, after all? Do you think she's Nightcap?"

"So...she killed her roommate first, took her identity and then proceeded to keep on killing. Seventeen girls in a row. Then she just stopped for sixteen years before suddenly starting up again?"

Dawn looked up at him, and her stomach clenched. "We need to call the forensics team—well, have Nick do it. Have them review the trace evidence gathered from the most recent crime scenes. See if there were any dog hairs found at any of them."

"I just don't know what good it would do her to change her name. If she were wanted for anything, it would have come up. They searched far and wide for relatives, for history, for anyone with a motive to kill her—because no one knew it was a serial case at that point." He shook his head. "They found next to nothing. A small-time dope-dealer ex-boyfriend. But he was doing time—perfect alibi. I just don't get it."

"I don't either. Unless—"

"What?" Bryan asked. Dawn bit her lip, and he pressed her. "Come on, hon, you haven't been wrong so far. What?"

"Well, what if Sara Quinlan wasn't her real name, either? What if she killed the real Sara and took her name, just like she did with the real Olivia?"

"So maybe Sara—I mean, Olivia—*wasn't* the first victim?" Bryan thought on that. "Okay, okay, we can follow this string a little. So why kill all the others, since they were all local and she couldn't take their names without being caught?"

"Maybe she just developed a taste for it. Maybe she couldn't stop. And maybe, once Johnny Lee Jackson was convicted of her crimes, she didn't see any reason to change her name and run away. Maybe she'd built a good life here and wanted to keep it. And maybe she thought she'd finally beaten this thing. That she could stop killing."

"But then something set her off," Bryan said, picking up the thread. "And she started all over again." He lowered his head. "And what you just said might very well apply to Nightcap no matter who it is, if Johnny Lee really wasn't the guy."

Dawn closed her eyes for a moment. "What do we do now, Bryan?"

He sighed, knowing how much she would hate what

he was about to say. "We have to take this to Nick. We have to, Dawn."

"Couldn't we just talk to her first? Ask her why she's been lying all these years, see if she has some kind of reasonable explanation for it all?"

"We're going to go to a possible serial killer, tell her we know who she is and wait for her to come up with a logical explanation?" he asked. "And she will, she sure as hell will. She'll spin some fairy tale to buy a little time, and then kill us in our sleep before we have time to verify it. Or take off and start a fresh killing spree somewhere new. We can't risk that."

"I just can't believe Olivia would kill anyone."

"Sara. Her name is Sara. And killers don't always look like big bad boogeymen, Dawn."

"Hell, I know that. Look at my father. He was charming, charismatic—even handsome, according to some. But…but Olivia—Sara—she doesn't *feel* like a murderer to me." Then her head came up. "What about the baby? This means Olivia Dupree is the woman who gave birth before her murder. *Not* Sara Quinlan. The police were searching for the wrong set of relatives. Olivia might have piles of them who would want to know about the existence of this child. Aunts, cousins, grandparents. Not to mention that there must be a father somewhere."

He nodded. "That would explain why the professor was so upset by the news. She must be thinking the same things. That there's a child out there somewhere without a family, at least partly because of her lie."

"We have to go talk to her again, Bryan."

"No. We have to take this to Nick."

"No. Not before we talk to her."

"Dawn, if it's her, she wants you next. Don't you get that? She's been leaving items belonging to you with the bodies. She's warning you, toying with you like a cat with a mouse. I'm not willing to let you get within a hundred miles of this woman again. No. We take this to Nick."

She put her hands on her hips and glared at him. "How did she get the things from my purse? We didn't even meet her until after that started."

"Maybe she was there and you just didn't see her. Everette Stokes wasn't there, and he's still a suspect, too. It doesn't matter."

"Let's talk to her. What if all of this was—I don't know—an effort to get away from something? From some*one?* What if it has nothing to do with the Nightcap killings? What if—"

"What if she kills you? What if I lose you because you're here trying to help me? How am I supposed to live with that, Dawn? How?"

She blinked, lowered her head and tried to quell the rush of raw feeling that rose up in her chest at those words and, even more, at the emotion with which they'd been delivered. "I didn't think…about that."

"And how about what happens to me in all this? What if we tip her off just enough to let her get rid of all the evidence and leave me holding the bag for her crimes?"

"I'm sorry. You're right. I just didn't think—"

"About me. You didn't think about me, how it would impact me. Just like you didn't think about how it would impact me when you left without a word, or refused to see me or talk to me for the past five years. Just like you didn't think about asking me to help you through it, or even asking me to go with you. You just didn't think about me, Dawn. You never do."

He threw the photo onto the bed. It landed far too lightly to be satisfying. Then he returned to his former task of gathering up their things. "We're going to the cabin. And I'm calling Nick to have him meet us there."

She moved up behind him, slid a hand over his back, up to his shoulder, and let it settle there as he went still.

"I've been incredibly, unforgivably selfish. And shortsighted. And careless with your feelings, Bryan. I'm sorry. I'm really sorry. And I guess now I understand why you don't…feel the same way about me anymore. God, who would?"

He opened his mouth, but words failed him. He couldn't think of a damn thing to say and was, frankly, embarrassed by his emotional outburst.

"At least I get it now. I really am sorry, Bryan. Please believe that."

He sighed. "I didn't mean to lose my temper. I'm stressed out, that's all."

"It needed to be said. I deserved it and then some. But I promise, as badly as I treated you back then, that's not what I'm doing now. I want to help you, Bryan. I *am* thinking of you now. I'm not thinking of anything *but* you."

He turned then, searched her face. "And you're risking your life by being here, trying to help me. I know that. I'm sorry I lost it."

"It's been in there festering for five years. You had to lance the wound, I guess. Let the poison out. Maybe now it can…start to heal."

"Maybe."

"Go ahead. Call Nick."

He nodded, reached for the cell phone Nick had given him and prayed he was doing the right thing.

They drove up a meandering dirt road so deserted Dawn couldn't believe it led to *anywhere,* much less to anywhere she might want to be. She never would have followed through on this plan if Bryan hadn't been with her. Then again, she wouldn't have needed to, would she?

But he *was* with her. And that made it okay, somehow.

Maybe she'd better not explore that particular line of thinking to its conclusion just now. Better to focus on the matters at hand. They needed to solve the murders. They needed to keep Bryan out of police custody until they did. And they needed to be someplace where neither the cops nor the Nightcap Strangler could find them.

Whatever lay at the end of this twisting, tree-

smothered cow path would fulfill all those require-
ments. Even if she was beginning to expect a shack,
or maybe a lean-to, rather than the comfortable cabin
Bryan had described.

It was dark, and the going was slow. A Ford Taurus
was not built for off-roading, and that was what this
journey seemed like to her. They should have borrowed
a tank or a pair of ATVs or something.

They hit yet another hole in the road, and it jarred
her to her bones, even though the car was only moving
at sixteen miles per hour.

"How much farther?" she asked, and immediately
realized she sounded like an impatient child on her way
to Disney World. Might as well have asked, "Are we
there, yet?"

Bryan glanced her way and offered a strained smile.
"Not much," he said.

"That's good, because if this goes on much longer,
I think we'll be leaving car parts on the road behind
us."

His smile broadened. "You think this is bad, you
should see it in early spring."

"It's *worse?*" she asked incredulously.

"It alternates between mud pits deep enough to
swallow the tires, and humps that scrape along the
undercarriage and eat mufflers. It's way smoother in
the summer."

"What about winter?"

"They put up a sign at both ends—Road Closed. No
Maintenance. Seasonal Use Only."

She nodded. "Proceed At Your Own Risk. I'd Turn Back, If I Were You."

"Yep." Then he pointed. "Just around that next bend, and—oh, there you go. Look."

She looked, expecting to see the alleged *cabin,* but instead she saw three deer picking their way across the dirt track. A big fat doe and two smaller versions. No spots, but they had to be her offspring. And immediately a warm rush of familiarity rinsed through her, making her smile and feel like mush inside. "Been a long time since I've seen deer."

"I'll bet," he said. "I don't think city life agrees with you, Dawn."

"No?" She wanted to scowl at him but couldn't take her eyes off the deer. The mother had spotted the car now, and she froze, staring unblinkingly at their headlights. Then her tail flipped straight up, a white flag that got her offsprings' attention. They looked at her expectantly in the instant before she bounded away. One graceful leap and she vanished into the woods on the other side of the road, with her two fawns racing eagerly after her.

When they were gone, Dawn finally turned to look at him. "Why do you say city life doesn't agree with me?"

He shrugged. "You look way better now than you did when you first arrived."

"Is that an insult about how I looked then, or a compliment about how I look now?"

"Both?" he suggested, then made a face, as if

expecting her to punch him for the comment. When she didn't, he relaxed. "Your skin has more color. The dark circles are gone from underneath your eyes. Your hair's even shinier."

"I see. And your explanation for that?"

"I think you've been eating better. And I think those pills you were taking to fend off your...visions...were no good for you."

She nodded thoughtfully. "Anything else?"

"You belong here. In Vermont. In the mountains. In the fresh air. In the country. With family. It's all good."

"Right, except that there's a crazed killer after me."

"Right, except for that." He said it with a grin, but then his expression turned serious. "But I think it says a lot that you're healthier and better, even with a killer after you and on the run from the law, than you were just living an ordinary life in California. Don't you?"

She frowned as she mulled that one over, knowing deep down that he was right. But before she could construct a suitable reply, he was nodding toward the windshield. "There it is. Looks like Nick's already here."

She peered ahead and saw lights in the distance, the gleaming gold rectangles of several big windows. And then, as they drew nearer, she leaned forward, trying to get a better look at the place through the darkness.

There was a large gate in front, standing open, and a curved driveway that led to a log cabin that was far from the shack she had been expecting. Nick's car was parked in front of a wide front porch, two antique rocking chairs its only inhabitants. The cabin was a simple two-story square, with a peaked roof and large windows up and down. It looked cozy and even welcoming, and she breathed a sigh of relief as Bryan pulled the car up behind Nick's and shut off the headlights.

"This is really...nice."

"You sound surprised," Bryan said. "I told you it was nice."

"I was beginning to doubt you. Sorry about that."

He shrugged. "I'll get over it." He got out of the car, taking the keys with him, and Dawn followed, suddenly eager to see the inside. Bryan met her in front of the car and took her hand as they walked up the three broad steps to the porch, then to the door beyond, which was already swinging open.

Nick greeted them with a smile. "I was just starting to get worried about you two. Any problems?"

"Just trying to be gentle with the car," Bryan said. "It's not made for back roads."

Dawn was too busy looking around to make any snide comments about the so-called road. The huge fieldstone fireplace was aglow, even though it was a warm night, and the furnishings were rustic and male. Browns and greens. Typical guy stuff. The second floor was only a loft, with each stair made of a halved log, rounded on the bottom and flat on the top, and gleaming with layers of shellac. The main room had a cathedral ceiling, with a chandelier made of deer antlers as its focal point.

She grimaced a little at the antlers.

"They're fake, hon," Nick said with a deep chuckle.

She looked over at him quickly.

"And I took down the deer and moose and bear heads I had mounted around the place, in your honor."

Dawn smiled at him. "That was very thoughtful of you. Thanks. I wouldn't have been able to sleep with those marble eyes staring at me."

He laughed. "I picked up a few groceries, brought in some firewood. I know it's summer, but it gets chilly at night, and the fireplace is the only heat I've got here."

"It'll be plenty," she said. "Really, Nick, this is incredibly nice of you. I know you're risking a lot by helping us like this."

"What? My career as a cop? I'm retired, remember?"

Bryan shook his head. "She's right. You could go to jail."

"I don't even know you're here. I haven't been up here since spring turkey season. Never thought to check it out. Totally forgot you had a key." Then he dipped into his pocket and pulled out a key, handing it to Bryan. "Who's gonna say otherwise?"

"I'll never be able to repay you for this," Bryan said.

"Oh, you damn well *will,* Kendall. Trust me, I'll think of something." Nick slapped Bryan on the shoulder. "Come on, sit down by the fire."

It was only then that Dawn noticed the slice of a giant tree that served as a coffee table. There was a pot of coffee on it, along with three mugs and three small plates, each one bearing a heavy load of what looked like apple pie.

"You baked?" Dawn asked. "You *cook?*"

"Not unless forced. It's from the bakery in town. Fresh, though." Nick sat in an oversize chair, and picked up a plate and fork. Smiling, Dawn followed suit, taking a spot on the matching love seat. She sampled the pie and closed her eyes in ecstasy. "Mmmm."

"So what is it, Bryan?" Nick asked. "You said you'd learned something on the case. You have a lead?"

Bryan finally sank onto the love seat beside Dawn, but he didn't touch the pie. He leaned forward, elbows on his knees. "How well do you know Olivia Dupree?"

"I met her for the first time when I started investigating her roommate's murder. Didn't really see much of her after that, until I retired five years ago and took the job teaching at the university. We've become friends. I like to think I know her pretty well." He devoured another huge bite of pie, then set the plate down, pausing to chew. Finally he said, "Why?"

Bryan looked at Dawn. She gave him a nod to go on. "She's not who she says she is, Nick."

Nick's eyebrows went up, but he said nothing.

"We're pretty sure her name isn't Olivia Dupree. It's Sara Quinlan. The real Olivia was the one who was murdered back then. For some reason Sara took her identity. She might even have been the one who claimed the body. She might even—"

Nick held up a hand. "Stop right there."

"Look, I know you're friends with her. Maybe more than friends, but I have a photo that proves—"

"I'm not telling you to stop because we're friends—and yes, you're right, I'd have liked us to have been more than friends. It never happened, but that's kind of irrelevant here. I'm telling you to stop because you're on the wrong track here. Olivia—Sara—didn't change her identity to cover up a string of murders. She changed it 'cause she had to...to save her own life."

Bryan blinked, clearly shocked. Dawn set her pie plate down, and the fork clattered off the side and onto the table, smearing it with crumbs and apple goo. She stared at Nick, stunned, as she realized what she was seeing on his face—or, more accurately, what she *wasn't* seeing. Surprise.

She frowned at him. "You already knew," she said softly. "My God, Nick, you already knew."

Nick licked his lips and nodded. "I already knew. Finish your pie."

13

"What the hell do you mean, you already knew?"

Bryan shot off the love seat as if he'd been fired out of a cannon, completely blown away, Dawn thought, by his mentor's revelation. "You were a cop, for God's sake! If you knew, you'd have had to say so."

"Come on," Nick said with a grimace. *"Had to?"* He shook his head. "Come on, Kendall."

"Nick…"

Dawn got up and put a hand on Bryan's shoulder. He was clearly upset and, she could tell, about to get very angry. She didn't want to see that. He loved Nick—God, the man was like a second father to him.

Bryan snapped his head her way, but his face softened as soon as his eyes met hers.

She held on to that gaze and spoke slowly. "Maybe it would be better to get furious *after* we hear what Nick has to say about this?"

"There's nothing he *can* say."

"Hey, if you don't want to know—" Nick got to

his feet, as well, lifted both hands in surrender and shrugged. "I'm outta here."

"Nick, wait." Dawn let go of Bryan and rushed to Nick, clamping her hands on his shoulders. "Don't go. *I* want to hear what you have to say. I can't even imagine what Olivia—Sara—"

"Call her Olivia. It's important."

Dawn frowned. "Can you tell us why?"

He looked toward Bryan, who was still standing, his eyes seeming to be involved in some sort of inner search for understanding. Nick rolled his eyes, shaking his head, and focused on Dawn. "For you, hon, I'll stick around and give you the scoop. Just so no one mistakes me, though, I'm not explaining myself or defending my actions. I did what I had to do. Olivia would be dead by now if I hadn't."

"Olivia *is* dead." Bryan bit the words out.

Nick turned slowly, his face turning darker. "You want to stop acting like a ten-year-old, Kendall, and sit your ass down and listen? Or should I just cuff you and take you in, wash my hands of this whole damn thing?"

"That's what you want to do, be my guest," Bryan said, turning his back to Nick, his hands behind him, wrist against wrist.

"Oh, jeez, Bryan, would you knock it off?" Dawn pleaded.

"Fuck this." Nick stormed for the door. He got to it, yanked it open. "You know, kid, I never once doubted your word when you told me that you didn't kill Bettina

Wright. I never once, even for a minute, considered suspecting you. Calling you a liar. Questioning your decency. Never once. It'd be nice to have that favor returned."

"You broke the law," Bryan said. "You're a cop, and you broke the law, Nick."

"Like you're doing right now, you mean? Or like you were when you took all those files on the Nightcap case without telling anyone?"

"You know about that?" Bryan whispered, stunned.

"Of course I know about that. It was my case. And didn't you think they'd be looking for those files, once all this broke?"

"Do they know I have them?" Bryan asked.

"No. I've got them thinking the whole file was misplaced and digging through the archives looking for it. I was hoping I could get them back for you before they caught on, because they've been gone since before that first killing, and if they find out you took them, that makes you look even more guilty. To everyone but me. I figured you had a damn good reason. I figured you'd tell me when you were ready. I gave you the benefit of the doubt, Kendall. Because I trust you."

And then Nick turned, strode out of the cabin and slammed the door.

Dawn watched him go, then turned to stare at Bryan. "What the hell is the matter with you? Are you an *idiot?* He's one of the only people on this planet on your side.

Or he was. To tell you the truth, I'm starting to waver myself."

He sighed, tipped his head ceilingward. "He's not the man I thought he was."

"Yeah, because you made him into a hero. Some kind of flawless supercop. Now you find out he's a human being just like the rest of us, and you turn on him for that?"

He spun around to face her, blinking and looking as if he felt betrayed. "Whose side are you on?"

"Yours, Bryan. Always yours. The things is, so is Nick. You can't afford to turn on your friends right now. You don't have any to spare."

He shook his head slowly, then went to the door. "I'm going for a walk."

She didn't say anything, just crossed her arms over her chest and watched him go. But she resented it. She really resented him leaving her there alone, just because he was having a temper tantrum.

Ignoring the little voice that reminded her Bryan was wanted for a string of murders he hadn't committed, and that he had plenty of good reasons to be stressed out, she stomped deeper into the cabin for a look around. She found that the back half, the part under the loft, was a wide-open kitchen/dining area. Double glass doors at the back led onto a deck twice the size of the front porch, with lawn furniture and a gas grill. And beyond it, a breathtaking view, even in the gathering darkness, of Shadow Falls, ominous and eerie, cascading down from a high cliff and splashing furiously into the giant lake that lay at its feet.

"What it really needs is a hot tub," a voice said from behind her.

She damn near jumped out of her skin, even though it was Nick's voice and she recognized it immediately. She turned, smiling at her own nerves. "God, you scared the hell out of me."

"Sorry. I shouldn't have left like that. Where is he?"

"Went to walk off his temper."

"He left you alone?"

"Guess he thinks I'm safe here."

Nick held her gaze steadily, and she wondered what he was thinking. Was he thinking that Bryan didn't care much about her, if he would leave her unprotected like this? Or was that just her?

The screen door creaked. Odd that she hadn't heard it when Nick had come in, but she'd been deep in thought. "There he is," she said.

Nick lifted his brows and put a hand on the gun that was holstered under his left arm as he turned.

Dawn tensed behind him. Nick looked back at her. She was rubbing her arms and trying to suppress tears.

"Aw, come here, kid." Nick took a single step closer and wrapped his big arms around her, hugged her to his chest. She knew he was trying to comfort her, but she didn't feel at ease in his arms. Nerves, she decided. She was tense as a bowstring.

"Please, go see who it is. I'm feeling…odd."

"Sure, hon. Sure. You're shaking, though."

"I'll be all right."

"He likes that, you know. That fear his victims feel when they realize what he's going to do to them. It's what feeds him, like a drug he's addicted to."

"You should know," she said, and she pulled a little harder to free herself.

Nick drew back and looked at her with a frown.

"You wrote the book on the guy," she said. "At least, we think he was the guy."

"Yeah, even I'm starting to wonder at this point." He shook his head, but let his arms fall to his sides and turned toward the living room. "We're back here, Kendall."

She rolled her eyes. "You knew it was him the whole time?" she asked Nick.

"I'm only guessing. Bryan, stop scaring the hell out of your woman and answer me."

Footsteps came closer. "It's me, Dawn." And then Bryan stepped into view, and she met his eyes and let him see the fear and moisture in her own.

"I shouldn't have left you alone."

"Damn right you shouldn't," Nick said. "It could've been him who walked in on her just now instead of me. What the hell's wrong with you, Kendall?"

"Right now, Nick? You are." Bryan crossed the room, ran a hand over Dawn's face and said, "I'm sorry. Are you okay?"

She nodded. "I will be, if you two will just sit down

and talk." She hugged him, but only so she could get close enough to whisper, "He's more upset by this than you realize, Bry. He's sweating bullets. He really cares what you think of him."

Bryan nodded, one hand cupping her head as he did, so it seemed almost intimate. "I'm sorry I left you. I'm sorry—"

"*Listen* to him, Bryan."

Again he nodded, and she pulled away and decided to push them along. "What do you guys say we start this whole conversation over, okay? Tempers are raw, nerves are shot. You two know you love each other."

Nick rolled his eyes. "Women. It's always *love* with them."

Bryan slid an arm around Dawn's waist, which surprised her, and he turned her and walked back to the love seat, where they sat down.

Nick didn't. He paced, clearly still stirred up by what had happened. "Sara Quinlan was mixed up with a small-time dealer who was also a big-time asshole."

"What kind of dealer?" Bryan asked.

"Weed."

Bryan blinked—already, Dawn thought, doubting the story. Man, one slip and he was ready to doubt everything his former hero said? She guessed it was no wonder he still hadn't forgiven her for falling off her own pedestal.

But Nick was going on, and her attention was caught.

"She lived with the guy, and he beat the hell out of

her on a regular basis. Twice she tried to leave, twice he tracked her down and told her he'd kill her unless she came back. So she did. She was young. Scared. Believed him. I think she was probably right on that score."

Bryan shrugged. "She go to the cops?"

"He *was* a cop."

Now, finally, Dawn saw Bryan's eyes spark with interest. He looked Nick in the eye for the first time and paid close attention.

"They didn't take her complaints seriously. He always covered. Never left obvious marks, had a whole story going on, making her out to be mentally unstable, and set it up so early and so well that by the time Sara started filing complaints, everyone at the department already assumed she was nuts. But she knew she had to get out of there, and get out fast. So she started collecting information on his side business. Getting names, dates, listening to phone calls. When she put enough together, she sent it all to the DEA. And because he was a cop, they moved, and they moved *fast*. Once he was safely behind bars, she packed up her shit, emptied the bank accounts and skipped the state, coming here, far enough away from Chicago that she hoped he wouldn't find her for a while. When she got here, she found a girl she'd shared a foster home with. A girl with no family, just like her, and they hooked up again."

Nick paced to the fireplace, put a hand on the mantel. "When I arrived at the apartment, she was in a state of sheer terror. She was sure her ex had sent someone to murder her, and that they'd taken out the roommate in her place, by mistake. So she switched identities, told us the dead woman was Sara, claimed that she was Olivia, switched out their IDs and started using her roommate's driver's license and social security number. They didn't look alike, but she lightened her hair for the first few years, then let it go back when the license expired and a new photo had to be taken. And the change was complete."

"And when did you find out about it?"

Nick drew a deep, nasal breath and lifted his head. "Come on. You don't think she managed all that on her own, do you?"

"You helped her pull it off," Bryan muttered. "Dammit, Nick!"

"I checked out her story," Nick said quickly. "The guy was one badass, and he was out for blood, Kendall. Her blood. What would you have done if it were Dawnie, here, in that situation? I helped her. I had to. The asshole thinks she's dead. And no one got hurt by any of it."

"Except for the real Olivia's baby."

"The real Olivia had her baby before any of it happened. She put that kid where she wanted it to be."

"The kid must have a father, though," Dawn said. "Doesn't he have a right to know?"

"If I'd known about the baby, I would have handled things differently," Nick said. "But I didn't know. By the time I found out, I'd already dug myself in too deep to get out of it without destroying my career and putting that woman's life in danger. I knew she'd feel as badly about it as I did, so I never told her." He turned, spearing Bryan with his eyes. "But I swear to God, Bryan, I *did* try to find that kid. And to figure out who its father could have been, but I hit dead end after dead end. Decided maybe it wasn't meant to be known."

Bryan lowered his head.

"Just think about if it was Dawnie. What would you do to protect her?"

"It's different," Bryan said. "You didn't even know Sara. Dawn and I—" He shot her a quick look. "It's different."

"Not so different." Nick shrugged. "So that's the deal. That's the truth. You can share it with the world and maybe get a nice woman—an innocent woman—killed, not to mention destroy my career. Or you can keep it to yourself. Your call. Just know it's got nothing to do with the murders. And I felt like a real rookie when I found out it wasn't her ex who was behind her roommate's killing at all. Still, word of her murder made its way to him, just like we intended it to, so he's left her alone and will continue to do so, unless you expose her now."

He sat there, staring from one of them to the other. Bryan was silent and Dawn was tense, wondering what he would say. And when he didn't say anything at all as the seconds ticked past, she was too uncomfortable with the silence to let it draw out further.

"Maybe you should give us some time to process all this, Nick. It's a lot to—"

"It's not a lot. It's simple. You blow her cover, she

ends up dead. And it won't take long. Her ex isn't in prison anymore. He's a free man—and he's moved up in the criminal world, too."

Dawn frowned, her attention riveted. "You've kept track of him?"

"You're damn right I have. He even sniffs in this direction, I'll know about it. Olivia trusts me to keep her safe."

She nodded and studied his face, wondering if he realized that he was in love with the professor. Probably not. Men were notoriously dense about such things, weren't they? Hell, she should talk. She'd single-handedly ruined the best relationship she was probably ever going to have.

"You said he'd moved up in the criminal world," she asked. "How so?"

Nick's attention was on Bryan, but Bryan wasn't looking back at him. Sighing, Nick focused on her again. "Tommy Skinner's not a cop anymore. Doesn't have to maintain a phony facade. Even though he did time, he didn't rat out any of his contacts, and that gave him street cred with the bosses, so they brought him back in. He's pulling in the big bucks now, and he's got a lot of power, not to mention friends with even more."

"You're talking about organized crime," Dawn said.

Nick nodded.

"But how do you know he's still interested in her? Hasn't he got bigger things going on by now?" she asked.

"'Cause I know. I keep track. He's influential in Chicago. Anyone goes sniffing around asking questions about Sara Quinlan, he's going to know about it almost instantly."

"Shit," Bryan said softly. "Shit, shit, shit."

"What?"

He lifted his head, met Nick's eyes. "You'd better get someone out there to keep an eye on her place. Rico might already be there. I gave her his number. But if he's not, get him there."

"Why?" Nick asked, and the timbre of his voice seemed to hold a warning.

He sighed. "I ordered one of her old yearbooks."

"You mentioned Sara by name?"

Bryan nodded. "So I could find out the right year. I didn't know I'd be putting her in danger."

"You should have asked!"

"You should have told me! You knew I was digging into this! And don't get all self-righteous, Nick, when you're the one who's been breaking the law for the past sixteen years, maybe to the point where it's cost some father his own son, for crying out loud!"

"You—" Nick thrust a finger at Bryan as he spoke the single word, but it seemed the rest just deserted him. He closed his mouth, shook his head. "You're right. I should have told you."

"You're sure she had nothing to do with the murders?"

"I guarantee it. I checked that angle completely, believe me. She couldn't kill a flea, that one."

Bryan nodded. "Okay. Okay, I'll keep this to myself. But I still think you'd better—"

"Yeah, I'll get Rico on it, if he's not already there. I'll tell the chief I suspect Nightcap might go after her." Nick looked at him. "You really going to keep this to yourself, Bryan?"

Bryan nodded. "For now, at least."

Nick rolled his eyes, threw up his hands.

"What if he promises to talk to you first, Nick?" Dawn didn't think the two men were communicating on the same wavelength just now. "Bryan, you can promise that much, can't you? That you won't tell anyone else until you've given Nick fair warning?"

He nodded slowly. "Sure. Sure I can."

"That doesn't mean he's definitely going to blow it, Nick," Dawn added quickly. "Just give him some time to work through this in his mind."

"Yeah. Time. And a safe haven, and my help and un-wavering support. Just like always. Right, Kendall?"

Bryan looked at him, then dropped his gaze.

"Have a good night, you two." Nick turned and left them. He didn't slam the door. He didn't gun his engine or spin his tires. His anger was quiet, contained and somehow more potent in its silence.

Dawn sat on the sofa beside Bryan. She studied his face and she knew it was not the time to talk to him. He needed to mull this over on his own. He needed to figure it out for himself. He did not need her to say the words that were dancing on her tongue and knocking on her teeth to get out.

But she was going to say them if she didn't distract herself, and fast, so she patted his shoulder, just to let him know she was there if he needed her and not angry with him like Nick was.

Without lifting his head, he said, "What should I do?"

Dawn was stunned. "Bry, I can't tell you what to do. This is your deal, it's not—"

"Okay, suppose I do nothing? What are *you* going to do?" He lifted his head now, staring up at her.

"What do you mean?"

"I mean, it's all up to you, because I've thrown up my hands. So what do you do? Do you call the chief and tell him what you know about Olivia Dupree? Do you keep her secret and trust that she's really a good person? Do you go and talk to her again, and then decide? What?"

She shook her head rapidly. "Bryan, don't put this on me. I can't be the one to—"

"Please, Dawn, I'm begging here."

She met his eyes, saw the need in them and dissolved like sugar in boiling water. Sinking deeper into the sofa beside him, she nodded slowly, her mind working overtime. "All right. I guess, if it were me calling the shots—and it's not, but if it were—I guess I'd do some more investigating. If I could rule her out as the killer and verify what Nick told us about her ex-boyfriend, then I suppose I'd agree to keep the secret."

He nodded. "And if you couldn't rule her out as the Strangler?"

"Then I'd turn her ass in and make her my number-one suspect."

He listened, taking it in. Then he said, "What does your gut tell you about her, Dawn?"

"I think she's innocent," she said, without a hint of hesitation. "But that doesn't mean a damn thing. There's some kind of genetic, gender-based instinct inside me that wants to believe no woman could be capable of this. Of murdering other women so brutally."

"But you think she's innocent?"

It was as if he hadn't even heard the rest of her words after those. "Maybe I just hope she is."

He sighed deeply. "I think it's more than that. I know you don't think so, Dawn, but I do. I think you still have some kind of…connection."

"I don't. I don't have anything like that."

"We'll see."

She shrugged. "You're not going to be able to sleep yet. We should find something around here to do, take your mind off all this for a while."

He studied her face. "I'm so busy feeling my own turmoil, I'm ignoring yours."

"I don't have any turmoil."

"No? You've got a killer after you. And no turmoil?"

She shrugged. "I feel safe tonight."

"I'm glad you feel safe here."

"It's not the place, Bryan. It's the company."

His eyes darkened a little as they locked with hers, and she felt a familiar shiver up her spine. She wanted him. She felt the awareness of it like a rush of heated floodwaters. She wanted him so much. And she knew he still didn't trust her enough to try again.

She wondered if they could have sex without starting things up again—without reigniting the feelings they'd once had for each other. She doubted it. There was just too much history between them. Sex between them now would be like touching a match to dry tinder, and that could start a forest fire that would destroy them both.

"Why don't we walk down to that lake out back?" she suggested.

"It's a reservoir."

She looked toward the doors that led onto the deck, and through them to the glimmering water beyond. "It's the *size* of a lake. And the falls are spectacular."

He held her gaze for a moment longer, then broke eye contact, surging to his feet and nodding hard. "Good idea. In fact, I'll do you one better." As he spoke, he crossed the room, flung open a large closet door and rattled around inside it for a moment. Then he called, "Just one question. Do you want to do it on the dock or in the rowboat?"

Dawn's jaw dropped. She stammered for an answer. "I…don't… What… There's a rowboat?" It wasn't an answer, but it was the only thing she could think of to say.

"Yup." He emerged again, holding a tackle box in one hand and a pair of fishing poles in the other. "So, dock or boat?"

She shook her head and smiled. And then she

laughed. He was so good at that. At breaking her tension. At making her laugh. At helping her relax.

Always had been.

"Boat," she said. "If it's reservoir-worthy."

"It was the last time I was here." He nodded at the closet. "Grab a couple of hoodies. Gets chilly on the water at night."

She did, and then followed him through the kitchen and out the back door.

The air smelled like pine, and moonlight made it light enough to walk without flashlights. They crossed the broad redwood deck, then went down the steps at the far end to the ground. From there, a meandering but well-worn path wriggled down a slight incline to the shore. The reservoir had to be sixteen acres' worth of water, dark in the moonlight, glittering on the surface, frothy and foamy where the falls splashed down. A narrow wood dock jutted from the shore into the water, extending out about sixteen feet, its far end supported by floating barrels, so that it bobbed and dipped as they walked over it. Halfway along, a rowboat was tied to a post.

Bryan set the gear in the boat, then climbed in. He reached a hand up to her, and she took it. So strong, his hand. So big compared to her own. He helped her as she stepped off the wobbly deck and into the wobbly boat. She sat down on one of the seats, but he didn't let go of her hand as he sat opposite her, looked at her steadily.

"I don't know how I would have gotten through this if you hadn't come back, Dawn."

She gave him a half smile. "You haven't gotten through it yet, Bry. Maybe you'd better hold off on the gratitude until I've actually done something to help."

"You're helping. Believe me."

She shrugged. "You would do the same for me."

"Up to a week ago, I doubt it."

"You were still that angry?"

He nodded.

"And now?"

"You've made up for it—ten times over."

She frowned, tipped her head to one side. "Then you...you forgive me?" She turned her hand in his, laced their fingers and squeezed.

"I forgive you."

Her eyes fell closed, tears managing to slip between her lashes all the same. "God, I needed to hear that."

He ran a hand over her hair. "Maybe you can forgive yourself now, huh?"

"Maybe." But she didn't think so. As Bryan released her hand and rose to quickly untie the rope that held the little rowboat to the dock, she thought she would never be able to forgive herself. She'd lost his love. She'd ruined her chances with the only man she wanted a chance with. And she didn't think she would ever forgive herself for letting him go.

14

Bryan rowed the boat—rowed it hard, for a while—because once he got started, he realized the exertion was relieving his tension, at least a little, so he put way more effort into it than he really needed to.

Of course, sleeping with Dawn tonight would have relieved his tension, too—in spades—but he didn't want to do that. It would be self-destructive to the nth degree. He would end up falling as hard as he had before, and he knew too well what lay at the bottom of that fall. A bed of nails that would skewer him when she walked away again.

Maybe she wouldn't this time.

And how the hell could he be sure of that?

Maybe he should just ask her.

Right. Like he would get an honest answer. She was worried about him, had rushed to his side to help—out of guilt. And, okay, maybe a little bit out of caring. They had been special to each other, after all. They'd lost their virginity to each other. That had to mean something. They'd been friends. They were still friends.

And if he asked her to stay, she might not be able to say no to him, at least not today. But only out of guilt. Out of pity. Or based on the knowledge that he might soon end up in prison doing a term of twenty-five to life, so it might be his only chance at feeling alive until he came up for parole.

And she might be right.

"I think we're out far enough," Dawn said softly.

Bryan stopped rowing, glanced up to see how far they'd come, then turned and checked behind him. They were well beyond the middle of the lake and heading for the opposite side, where the water flowed out of the lake, between man-made concrete dams and into several swift-running streams, then on downhill. He nodded, pulled in the oars, dropped the tiny anchor to keep them from drifting with the current and reached for the tackle box. "No live bait," he said. "Nick has some rubber worms that are nearly as good, though."

"Hey, I'd far rather handle the rubber kind."

He smiled but didn't meet her eyes, not wanting her to see what he'd been thinking just a few moments ago. For the next several minutes he busied himself attaching the realistic rubbery worms, and half-red, half-white bobbers and tiny lead sinkers to their lines. Her pole ready, he handed it to her, then picked up his own.

"I haven't done this in…years. Not since I left, now that I think about it," she said. Then she drew the pole back and swung it forward, sidearming it rather than arcing it overhead. The line whirred through the air in a beautiful arch, then dropped into the water with a clean *plip*.

He watched, then nodded at her. "Nice."

"I guess you never forget some things."

She met his eyes, and his got stuck there. "I guess you never do."

He wasn't talking about how to cast a fishing pole. And he knew she knew it. He expected her to lower her eyes, look away, change the subject.

Instead, she said, "I never forgot *us*. That time, in the woods…"

He should have known she wouldn't back away from this conversation. He'd been avoiding it since she'd come home, but they both knew their time to talk things through might be rapidly approaching an end. He still wanted to avoid it. And yet, he didn't.

"Me, neither," he said, and then he cast his line in the opposite direction from hers.

"We didn't have a clue what we were doing. And yet…it was amazing."

He nodded, saying nothing.

"You've been with…a lot of women since I left."

He glanced at her. "I wouldn't say a *lot*. But yeah, there have been some." He met her eyes, then quickly lowered his. "Does that bother you?"

"If it did, I'd have no one to blame but myself, would I?"

He couldn't argue with that. Forcing an invisible

blockage from his throat, he said, "I imagine you've been with...other people, too."

"No."

He looked up sharply. "Come on, Dawn, you don't have to say that. I'm a grown-up."

She tipped her head slightly to one side, so that her hair slid lower on her shoulder. "I run, I work, I keep busy, and I...take care of any urges without need of a partner."

"But *why?*"

She shrugged. "It wouldn't be fair to have a relationship with a man when I knew I wouldn't stay with him. And I couldn't seem to embrace the idea of one-night stands. I don't know. For me, at least, sex is more about emotional connection than physical release."

"But..." He was thoroughly confused. "How did you know you wouldn't want to stay?"

"Because, to be honest, I've been homesick. I've missed the family. I've missed you." She shrugged. "I guess the truth of it is, I've never wanted anyone else."

There were tears in her voice, but they didn't show on her face. And in his mind, he was pleading with her, *Please, for the love of God, just tell me you won't leave again. That's all it'll take. Just say it. Say it. Say "I'll never run away from you again, Bryan."*

But she didn't say it. And just then the pole in her hands jerked, and she swung her head to the side. He followed her gaze in time to see her bobber vanishing beneath the waves. An instant later it reappeared.

"Whoa, that's a bite!" She waited, watching, and the minute the bobber vanished again, she gave the pole a quick jerk, then waited again, feeling. The end of the rod bowed, so she began reeling in the line as fast as she could.

Bryan knelt in the boat, snatching up a net, watching over the side for the catch to appear. It did, a big, black bullhead, and he quickly scooped it into the net and pulled it aboard.

"Beautiful fish," he said. "Damn, that's gonna taste good. I haven't had a bullhead all year." As he carefully gripped the fish underneath its spiked whiskers to keep himself from being jabbed, he fished a pair of needle-nose pliers from the tackle box, then easily removed the hook, rubber worm still intact.

She smiled. "This is fun. I'd almost forgotten how much fun we have together."

"Me, too." He put the fish onto a stringer and lowered it over the side. "I haven't been fishing with a girl since you left." Then he smiled a little sheepishly. "I guess that's not at good as not having sex with one, but…"

She shook her head. "I didn't expect you to join a monastery."

"On the upside, I'm probably better at it now than I was my first time out."

She went utterly silent, and he looked at her. Then, keeping her eyes glued to his, she said, "I still want you, Bryan. Just in case you didn't know that."

He nodded. "It's not that I don't…it's just that…"

"You said you'd forgiven me."

He nodded. "I have."

"Then why—"

The sound of a cell phone brought them up short. Bryan had totally forgotten that he'd brought it along. He pulled it out, saw "Private Caller" on the screen and frowned.

"Figures," Dawn said. "The middle of the lake is the one place up here with a signal."

Reluctantly, he flipped the phone open and brought it to his ear. A woman's voice came from the other end. "You've ruined my life, do you realize that?"

He licked his lips, met Dawn's eyes. "Olivia?"

"How could you do this to me?" Her voice was broken; she was obviously crying.

Bryan closed his eyes briefly. "Nick told you that I know who you are."

"And that you've been calling around, asking about me. Calling Chicago."

"To be fair, I didn't know it was you I was asking about. I thought it was a dead woman."

"Thanks to you, I probably will be!"

"Olivia, take it easy, will you? Look, I'm trying to find a killer before I get convicted of his crimes. My life is on the line here. And I had no way of knowing that yours was, too. I'm sorry."

"Sorry? I'm going to be dead by this time tomorrow—and you're *sorry?*"

"What do you mean? How do you—"

"He knows. He's found me. He just called."

"Who?"

"Tommy!" She gulped in a few breaths before she could speak again. Then she cleared her throat. "Thomas Skinner. My onetime beau and would-be... executioner. Who else? He managed to get my phone number—and probably my address, too."

"I only phoned your schools, and I used the automated system," Bryan said. "How could he—"

"That's how powerful he is now. That's the sort of connections he has."

Bryan met Dawn's eyes and could tell she was getting most of the conversation. She looked scared.

"Who called her?" she whispered. "Nightcap?"

He shook his head. "The ex."

"Oh, God."

"What did he say to you when he called, Olivia?"

"Nothing. He hung up when I answered. Probably just wanted to hear my voice—to verify it was really me. He's coming for me. I know he is."

"All right, all right, hang on. How do you know it wasn't just a wrong number? Or some kids playing a prank or—"

"Are you fucking kidding me?" Her voice rose, and he held the phone away from his ear as she raged, then brought it back.

"Is Nick there?"

"No." She sniffled loudly. "Officer Chavez is, though."

"Put him on the phone."

"Yes. But first—look, I didn't kill anyone, Bryan. I swear to you, I would never hurt anyone. If I were capable of that, Tommy Skinner would be long dead and I wouldn't be in this situation. Believe me. And I didn't know about the baby. I didn't know. It's haunting me now that I do, wondering if my actions cost a child its family. But I didn't know. I'm not a bad person."

"I hear you. I do. Just—please, put Rico on the phone, will you?"

He waited, and a moment later his partner's voice came on the line. "Hello?"

"Hey, Rico."

"Bryan? Holy shit, bud, do you have any idea how deep a hole you've dug for yourself? Everyone's looking for you."

"Yeah, and I'm putting your career at risk by talking to you. And I'm going to put it at more risk in a minute. But I don't want that woman getting killed because of me."

"Yeah, that I don't get," Rico said. "Nick says she's on the Strangler's hit list, but how could he know that? She's years older than he likes his victims. And she doesn't look like any of them, either. Besides, if he didn't kill her the first time around, why now?"

"It's a long story. But the short version is that you need to get her out of there. She needs to be someplace safe."

"So do you, bud. Are you?"

"Yeah."

"Then why don't I bring her there?"

Bryan was silent for a moment. He pulled the phone

away from his ear and hit the speaker button. "You want to bring her here?"

"If it's safe for you, it'll be safe for her, right?"

"I'm a fugitive, Rico. If I tell you where I am, you're going to have to turn me in."

"I won't do that."

"You could lose your job. Hell, they could charge you with—"

"Look, we're gonna to catch the real guy, bud. No one's gonna make too much of a stink about how we did it once it's done. Even if they do find out."

"I can't live with letting you risk so much, pal."

"Yeah? Can you live with another woman dying, when you could have saved her?"

Bryan blinked. He looked at Dawn.

She nodded, leaned closer to the phone. "Tell Nick to bring her to us," she said. "That way you're not involved."

"But Nick is?" Rico asked.

"She didn't say that," Bryan said quickly. "But we could tell him where we are, and then—"

"Bullshit. And thanks, partner. I just figured out where you are. We'll be there in an hour."

"Don't be followed, Rico," Bryan said. "Be safe."

"Understood." The connection was broken, and Bryan looked at Dawn.

"Are you sure you trust Olivia?" he asked her. "Enough to be out here in the middle of nowhere with you?"

"No. But it'll be a great way to find out. Just watch my back, and if she tries something—we'll know."

"Oh, *that's* a brilliant plan."

"I have another one," Dawn said.

"Yeah, what is it?"

She nodded at the oars. "Let that poor fish go and row us back to shore."

He sighed, but he complied.

Rico arrived with Olivia Dupree an hour later, as predicted. By then Dawn had made friends with the cabin's spotless kitchen. She'd figured out the coffeemaker and checked out the food Nick had stocked for them. So by the time she heard the knock at the cabin's door, the place was filled with the aromas of hot-from-the-oven cinnamon buns—the kind that came in the pop-open canister—and freshly brewed coffee.

"Kiss up, much?" Bryan asked when she dashed into the living room and caught up with him on his way to the front door.

"We put her life in danger. I hardly think snacks are enough to make up for that."

"If she's as innocent as she's claiming to be, that is," he said. He'd been busy bringing in more firewood from the pile outside and moving the car around to the back, where it wouldn't be easily seen from the road. Not that there would be any traffic to see it. But that was all the more reason. Anyone who *did* come driving up there might very well be there in search of them.

He reached for the doorknob, then turned to Dawn.

"Stay near me at all times, just in case you're wrong about her. Okay?"

Warmth flooded outward from the center of her chest. "Okay. But just so you know, I'd probably stay near you at all times anyway."

He smiled at that, and there was a moment when it felt…all right between them. Just a moment.

And then that moment was broken as he opened the door. Olivia stood on the other side. Her hand flashed out with the speed of a cobra and caught him across the face. Rico, just behind her, dropped the duffels he was carrying, gripped her shoulders and swore. But Bryan didn't react. Didn't pull back or slam the door or even shout at her. He just stood there, gave a slow nod as his cheek grew a red handprint, and drew a deep, slow breath probably meant to bank his temper.

When he exhaled again, he stood aside to let her in. It was Dawn who stepped directly into her path and stood nose to nose with her. "If that happens again, you're out of here and on your own. Killer ex or no."

"There would be no killer ex if not for the two of you!"

"There would be no killer ex if not for *you,* you mean. You're the one who hooked up with that lowlife to begin with. You're the one who stayed when you knew better. You're the one who didn't go buy a damn handgun and take care of your problem yourself. And you're the one who chose to live a blatant lie, not to mention let a good cop risk his career for you, by not facing up to the trouble you created. You, Sara. Not us."

Olivia/Sara didn't answer that. She dropped her gaze, and then her head followed. "You're right." She lifted her head again and turned to look at Bryan, but he was busy staring at Dawn in what looked like surprise.

"I'm sorry for hitting you," Olivia said, drawing Bryan's gaze back to her.

He nodded. "I'm sorry for blowing your cover." Then he glanced at Rico. "Since you're not peppering me with questions, I assume she filled you in on the way out here?"

"Yeah. I'm up to speed," Rico said.

"Well, you're here. Might as well come in." Dawn moved aside then, and the professor came in. Rico picked up the bags and followed, closing the door behind them.

The other woman looked at Dawn again. "I prefer to be called Olivia, not Sara."

"But that's not who you are."

"It's who I've been for the past sixteen years. It's who I intend to keep on being."

"Even once the threat is removed?" Dawn asked, searching the woman's face.

"Sara Quinlan died a long time ago. I remade myself when I took Olivia's identity. I'm different now. I'll never go back to what I was before."

It was absolutely true; Dawn sensed it. And it made her understand the other woman's violent reaction. She wasn't afraid of dying. She was afraid of losing the new life she'd created, of being forced to become Sara again.

And yet, no matter what her reasons, if she raised her hand to Bryan again, she was going find herself on the receiving end of a kick in the teeth.

"Something in here smells great," Rico said. It was a weak effort at breaking the tension in the room, but since they all wanted that, they let it work.

"Olivia fed us the last time we saw her. I figured reciprocation was in order," Dawn said. "I'll get it."

Bryan met her eyes, gave her an encouraging smile, then said, "Rico, why don't you pull your car around to the back, out of sight? That's where ours is. And, uh, Olivia, you can take your bag upstairs."

She looked surprised, and even Dawn sent him a frown before she realized why he hadn't offered to carry the bag himself. And it seemed Olivia understood, as well.

"You don't want me left alone with Dawn," she said softly. "You still don't believe I'm not the Nightcap Strangler."

"I don't believe you *are,* either," he returned, without missing a beat. "Until I'm sure one way or the other, I'm not taking any chances."

She nodded. "And yet you agreed to let me come here."

"Well, the possibility of you getting killed because of something I did isn't one I like much, either." He nodded at the staircase. "Top of the stairs, then to the left."

She picked up her bags and went up the stairs. Dawn

stood with her back toward the kitchen, arms folded. "That's the room I was going to use," she said.

"Well, there are only two bedrooms. You can't share with her, because she might kill you in your sleep, so it's me or Rico. I figured you'd prefer me. And if you tell me I'm wrong, my feelings are going to be hurt irreparably."

She shrugged as if she didn't much care either way and headed into the kitchen, where she started taking cups from the cupboard, lining them up on the counter, filling them with coffee. "So you expect her and Rico to share?"

"Either that or he can take the sofa."

"What if they share and you take the sofa?" she asked, teasing, not at all serious.

"You promised to stay close to me while they're here, remember?"

"I remember. And it's a promise I intend to keep." She turned, two filled mugs in hand, and saw the look on his face. He almost looked nervous.

She decided to give him a reason to be. After taking the mugs to the table, she went back for the other two, while Bryan followed with the tray of still-warm buns.

"To tell you the truth, Bryan, the idea of sleeping in your arms is pretty appealing right now." He opened his mouth, but she moved quickly closer and pressed a finger to his lips. "Even if that's all we do."

He met her eyes, and she lowered her finger. "It has to be," he said.

She shrugged and said nothing. But inside her mind, she heard a longing voice whispering, *God, I hope not.*

Olivia came back downstairs and joined them in the kitchen. She was quiet, but not in a despondent way. She seemed more watchful. Wary. Her wide eyes moved constantly, like those of a gazelle grazing a savanna full of sleeping lions. If she could have perked her ears, she would have, Dawn thought, suddenly reminded of Freddy.

The other woman sat at the table, sipped a cup of coffee, even tried a few bites of a cinnamon bun, but she was so stiff that Dawn thought she would break if she made a sudden move.

In an attempt to fill the silence, Dawn asked after the large mastiff. "Where's Freddy?"

"With a colleague," came the quiet reply. "I should have just brought him along. I hardly know what to do without him."

The sound of a car door closing out back preceded the thudding of Rico's footsteps on the deck.

Bryan flipped on the outside light, unlocked the patio doors and sent him a wave, but Dawn noticed that only from the corner of her eyes. She was too busy watching Olivia to fully look Rico's way. The other woman's tense expression tightened even more until the outdoor light revealed that it definitely was Rico approaching, and then it eased noticeably. She finally relaxed slightly in her chair and exhaled deeply.

Rico came in, tossed the keys on the counter, set down the heavy-looking duffel he was carrying and headed for the table as Bryan flipped off the outside light and locked the door.

"We have to go right back out there, pal," Rico said.

Bryan lifted his brows. "Why's that?"

"I brought a small arsenal." Rico shrugged. "Just in case."

"You signed them out? Rico, someone's gonna wonder what the hell you're up to if you—"

"Relax, Bry. It's my personal collection."

Bryan cocked an eyebrow at him. "I didn't know you had a collection."

"Neither did I," Olivia said softly.

"Why would you, Professor? We barely know each other."

"I'd have thought you might consider informing someone if you intended to drive them around in a four-wheeled weapon of mass destruction, Officer Chavez." Her tone might have been teasing—or not.

Rico grinned at her. "Don't worry, it's not a WMD. There wasn't a bullet in a chamber. All the ammo is in that duffel—" he nodded toward the bag he'd just brought in "—which was lying on the backseat. Guns are in the trunk."

"So what have you got?" Bryan asked.

"A 10, 12 and a 20 gauge, a .30-06, two .38s and a .44 Mag, plus my police-issue 9 mm."

Rico took a big bite of his cinnamon bun, closed his

eyes in pleasure, then washed it down with a swig of coffee. "Damn, that's good. You make that, Dawn?"

"The Doughboy did most of it," she said, but she couldn't help but feel a hint of pleasure at the praise, even though she was still shivering over the gun collection.

"So many guns," Olivia said with a visible shiver. "God, I hate guns. They're so dangerous."

"People are dangerous," Rico said. "Guns are tools."

"Weapons."

"Anything can be a weapon. A hammer can be a weapon."

"Yes, it can," the professor replied reasonably. "But that's not what it's made for. You can't pound a nail with a Glock. And…having all these guns around makes me a little…uncomfortable."

"Well, you might change your mind on that if your gangster boyfriend shows up to kill you," Rico pointed out.

She blinked across the table at him, then lowered her head a little. "I imagine you're right. I didn't mean to…judge. Actually, it's probably just that they remind me of…my old life. The one I left behind."

Rico's expression softened instantly. "I get that. I totally get that."

Bryan finished his bun, went to the door. "C'mon, *Suave,* let's get the guns inside in case we need 'em."

Rico shoved the remainder of the pastry into his

mouth, nearly more than it could hold, and surged to the door.

Bryan got as far as the door and then hesitated, turning back to Dawn.

She frowned and waved a hand at him. "It's sixteen feet away, for crying out loud. She couldn't strangle me that fast if I sat here and let her. Could you, Olivia?"

Olivia shot her a shocked look, and then she came very close to smiling. "I don't know. I never timed it."

Every eye swung toward her. Bryan and Rico looked dead serious. Only Dawn got the joke. She rolled her eyes as Olivia shook her head slowly. "I was kidding," she said.

"Go get the damn guns, guys," Dawn muttered.

Olivia nodded in agreement, and the two men went outside. Then Dawn got up and went to refill her coffee cup.

"You won't be able to sleep," Olivia said.

"That's kind of the plan." She turned, leaning her back on the counter and taking a sip. She saw Olivia's eyes dart toward the back door, then back to her, before her eyebrows went up and her lips pulled into a small smile.

"I really am sorry, Olivia," Dawn said softly. "I hope when all this is over, we can...put it behind us."

"If we both survive it," she said.

"You sound like you doubt that."

Olivia's face turned as expressionless as that of a figure in a wax museum. "If you knew Tommy, you'd doubt it, too."

"You're more afraid of him than you are of Nightcap, aren't you?"

The other woman nodded. "*Way* more afraid."

Dawn tipped her head to one side, studying the woman. Her hair pulled up, neat as a pin, her clothes conservative and no-nonsense.

"It's hard for me to imagine you being with someone like that," she said softly.

"Me, too," Olivia admitted. "It's like it all happened to a different person." She rose from the table, picking up her mug and carrying it with her as she moved closer to the door, and looked out at the starry night and the dark water beyond. The dull roar of the falls was barely audible, but it was still there, even with the doors closed. "I was young. Stupid. No self-esteem, no sense of…well, when I try to preach it to my students, I call it female empowerment."

"Girl power." Dawn raised a fist, feeling a deep connection with this woman, and growing more and more certain with every moment she spent with her that she was no killer. No threat.

The door swung open, and Bryan walked in with a long hard-shell plastic gun case in each hand. He set them down and glanced from one of the women to the other.

Dawn gave him a nod, and he turned and went back out.

She stayed where she was. "You must have found some kind of courage, though, turning him in the way you did."

"He'd have killed me if I hadn't."

"Because you wanted to leave him?"

Olivia met Dawn's eyes, shook her head. "Or because I stayed. Or because it rained outside. Or because he had a bad day. Tommy didn't need much of a reason."

Dawn had never knowingly met a woman who'd been a victim of domestic violence before. It was strangely compelling, and also tragic.

"I was down to a handful of options," Olivia said. "If I stayed, he'd have killed me sooner or later. If I tried to leave, he'd have killed me on the spot. All that remained was for me to kill him or turn him in. And frankly, I wish I'd had the strength to turn the tables on him, use…violence against him. But I didn't have it in me." She turned her eyes to the guns, still in their cases, leaning against the wall. "I don't know if that's still the case."

Dawn was stunned. But she didn't doubt it. The trembling in Olivia's voice told her the woman meant every word.

Rico came in then, carrying two more big gun cases. Bryan was right behind him, with a black suitcase.

He set the case on the table and then flipped it open.

Four handguns nestled in precisely shaped cutouts in a deep foam pad. He nodded. "Nice." Then he brought over the duffel bag Rico had carried in earlier, and removed several full clips and several boxes of ammo, lining them up on the table beside the suitcase.

Rico said, "Thanks. I think we should each keep a handgun on us at all times, just as a precaution."

Bryan nodded, glanced at Dawn. She nodded, too, and then Olivia reached out, and picked up the Glock 9 mm. She took a full clip, snapped it into the handle and worked the action, all in the space of a couple of seconds. Turning, she pointed the gun toward the patio door, her grip professional, her stance perfect. Then, nodding, she expelled the clip, ejected the chambered bullet and tucked the gun into her jeans. When she looked up to see everyone staring at her in stunned surprise, she said, "What? I said I didn't like them, not that I didn't know how to use them. I'll take this one, if you don't mind." She turned around and started to leave the room, but stopped short when Bryan walked right up behind her and pulled the gun out of her waistband.

"I do mind, actually."

She turned around slowly and met his eyes head-on, and her expression was stony. "That's right. *You* still think I might be a serial killer."

He flinched but stood his ground. "The more time I spend with you, the less likely that seems, Olivia, but I'm not taking any chances here."

"I get that. However, let's not forget that you're the number-one suspect. I'm not sure how comfortable I am with *you* being armed, either."

Dawn went up to him. "Olivia, I don't think you're a killer, either. But I know for sure Bryan isn't. We invited you here to keep you safe from Thomas Skinner, and you're going to have to play by our rules while you're here. Okay?"

Olivia met her eyes, nodded slowly. "Okay. Fine."

Dawn smiled to ease the worry from Olivia's face, and then she took the gun from Bryan's hand. "I'll keep this one. And Rico and Bryan will both be armed, and that'll have to be enough." Then she turned and handed the gun to Rico. "Actually, I think I'd prefer a shotgun. It's the only kind I've ever fired."

"I should put the extra weapons back in the car, then?" Rico asked.

Bryan nodded. "Seems like the best plan to me. Put 'em in the trunk and lock it up. And keep track of your key, okay?"

"Yes, Rico, you'd better make sure I don't pick your pocket when you're not looking. You wouldn't want me to go on a killing spree," Olivia said, and Dawn thought there was a hint of hurt in her voice. "I think I'm ready to turn in." She glanced at Rico. "You can share the room if you're not afraid of being murdered in your sleep. There are two beds." And then she walked out of the kitchen, through the living room and up the stairs.

15

Dawn hit the shower, then dug through her duffel bag in search of something even mildly sexy to wear to bed. Of course, she found nothing. She hadn't brought anything because she didn't *own* anything. Then again, she thought, she probably wouldn't have brought anything even if she had the entire Victoria's Secret collection in her closet. Seducing Bryan had been the furthest thing from her mind when she'd gotten on that plane. The possibility of being seduced *by* him might have fluttered through once or twice, but its wings had been weighted by doubt. No, not doubt. Certainty. Certainty that such a thing would never happen. Wasn't possible.

She hadn't been wrong. He was still telling her why they couldn't and why they shouldn't, but she was done listening. She had her own arguments to make tonight, and they were convincing ones.

Though they would be a lot more convincing in a sexy black negligee and a pair of thigh-highs to match.

The best she could do was a white tank-style under-shirt and a pair of red panties.

She stared at her reflection in the mirror as she brushed her still-wet hair. Reluctantly, and maybe partly because she was too nervous to face him just yet, she decided to blow it out, and took the hair dryer and round brush from her bag. As she worked, twisting the brush expertly through her hair, drying one section at a time to make it smooth and straight and sexy, she tried out her arguments on her reflection.

"'It's only sex,'" she whispered. "'It doesn't have to mean anything.'" She pursed her lips. "That sounds cold and kind of slutty. Besides, I know damn well it'll mean something to me. And I *want* it to mean something to him, too. Okay, ditch that one. How about, 'If you end up behind bars, we may never have another chance'?" She didn't really believe that one, either, though. She didn't believe for one minute that Bryan would go to prison. He was too good a person, and an innocent man to boot. She couldn't imagine this mess ending that way.

"Maybe I should try, 'If the killer catches up to us, I could end up dead. And I don't want to die without being with you again.'" She blinked and nodded, because that one tugged at her heart in a way that told her she wasn't making it up. She meant it. And she thought he would know that when he heard her say it. "Just one more time, Bryan," she whispered, staring at the bath-room door in the mirror now, speaking from her heart directly to him.

Nodding firmly, she finished drying her hair lock by lock, until finally there was no more dampness left. She'd already brushed her teeth. Already smoothed moisturizer into her face and shaved her legs. She'd done everything she could think of to do.

And yet she wasn't ready. Her rehearsed lines were already fading from her mind, and all she could think about was the feeling of his mouth on hers, the sensation of skin against skin. The way it was going to be when his arms finally closed around her body and pulled her close.

The knock on the bathroom door made her jump nearly out of her skin. She swung her head toward the door fast and barked, *"What?"* before she could stop herself.

"Uh, sorry, Dawn. I just…no hurry. Take your time. Save me some hot water, okay?"

She blinked. Great, she'd just bitten off the head of the man she intended to sweet-talk into her arms tonight. "I'm sorry, Bry. You startled me. I'll be right out."

She looked in the mirror, smoothed her hair, nodded firmly and, turning, yanked the door open.

Bryan was standing there, waiting. And he couldn't hide his reaction. Not even if he tried, and he did try, she thought, after that first surprised moment when his eyes went wide, and he sucked in a breath and took an actual step backward. Almost at the same instant, his gaze slid lower, tracing her body all the way to her toes and slowly back up again, before lingering on her face, her lips, meeting her eyes.

She couldn't keep her lips from curving into a tremulous smile. "It's all yours," she said.

He heard the double entendre but pretended not to. "Thanks."

He choked out the single word, and she was beyond gratified. He wanted her. He liked what he saw. And she thought maybe the tank was getting as good a reaction as any little black nightie ever could.

She made herself move, finally, tugging her feet from where they'd practically grown rooted to the floor and walking to the bed.

He turned, following every step until she sat down on the edge of the mattress, facing him again. "I'll be waiting," she said.

His look of pure appreciation changed then. It became one of pure fear. He turned away fast and darted into the bathroom as if someone were chasing him. The door banged closed.

Dawn lowered her head and blew every bit of air out of her lungs. He wasn't going to give it up easily, she thought.

Then she brought her head up fast as the door opened again. He looked out at her. She met his eyes, and if her own were expectant, she couldn't help it. He was going to say she looked great or something equally sweet.

He met her eyes. "I, um, I need to leave the door open while I clean up. Given that we don't know for sure if we're sharing space with a killer or not, I need to be able to hear you if you need me."

She sighed deeply, not trying to hide her disappointment, though she didn't expect him to understand its cause. "Or I could just lock the bedroom door," she suggested.

"Do that, too."

Still disappointed, she nodded.

"Don't tell me that little demonstration with the Glock didn't give you reason to rethink your assumptions about Olivia," he said.

She lifted her head. "Actually, Olivia was the last thing on my mind, Bry."

"Well, she shouldn't be."

She rolled her eyes, then turned her back on him to jerk down the covers of the only bed as if she were angry at them. "I wish whoever it was would just make a try for me already. I'm sick of this."

"I know. Hang in there, Dawn. It'll be okay."

"How? How's it going to be okay?"

He frowned at her, and she knew he thought she was behaving oddly. She was tense and nervous and almost weepy—probably because of the likelihood he would shoot her down tonight. She couldn't expect him to understand any of it. "Go take your damn shower. I'm locking the door." She crossed the room, turned the lock. "See?"

He nodded and backed into the bathroom, then pushed the door closed partway, just enough so he could stand on the other side of it, out of sight. She sighed and tromped back to the bed. Hurled her body onto it, punched the pillow into submission and then rolled onto her back and pulled the covers over her.

From that position she could see the mirror over the bathroom sink, and Bryan reflected in it. He'd turned on the shower and stripped off his shirt, and now he was just standing there behind the door, where he thought he was invisible. His bare chest was more magnificent than she could have imagined it. So defined and firm and broad. And then he undid his jeans and slid them down, and she saw boxer briefs covering up his small, hard tush and muscled hairy thighs.

He'd changed.

God, how he'd changed.

He'd been little more than a boy when the two of them had made love—that one and only time. He was a man now. He was *all* man now.

She rolled onto her side, propped her head on her hand and watched as he pushed the briefs down, catching only a flash of toned hip before he vanished behind the shower curtain.

But in her mind's eye, she was back there. All the way back there in time.

The Blackberry Inn had a grove out back, not quite part of the gargantuan state forest, but attached to it. Farther up the steep mountainsides, there were hardwoods surrounding clearings where the big stags held court. They especially liked the oak trees. But here, that sprawling forest was all conifers, towering pines and various types of spruce.

But not the little grove. It was all manmade. There were fruit trees—peach, apple, cherry—along with several varieties of flowering trees and a pair of weeping willows. In the center, a tiny pond lay dotted with lily pads and bright pink lotus blossoms. The willows dipped their fronds into the water, as if testing its temperature with their fingertips. So graceful.

Bryan and Dawn used to sneak out there in the dead of night, wrap up in each other's arms and kiss until they were both on fire. And that was all they did. Until that one night, when things went further.

That night their passionate makeout session had taken them to a place neither of them had been before. She smiled as she remembered how awkward it had been. How hesitantly he'd touched her breasts for the first time, after staring at them with such wonder and reverence in his eyes that she'd felt like the Mona Lisa. Touching, so careful, so fleeting. Kissing them, then. She'd been so incredibly shy of his lips on her until she felt them, and then tiny explosions just ripped through her body. From then on she was far too busy feeling to be shy anymore.

The clothes had come off slowly, while they kissed without pause and she realized how good this was going to be. It was only seconds later that, still kissing, he settled his body over hers, nudging his way inside her, a little bit, then waiting, then a little bit more, and then waiting, and then…

And then, when she started to squirm for something more and moved against him, encouraging him to do the same, he did. He thrust into her five or six times before he withdrew again, shuddering on top of her as hot semen shot onto her thighs in several bursts.

She remembered feeling…so turned on. So aroused. And so frustrated.

She thought he'd felt…wonderful, drained and happy. Though maybe he'd been worried, too, because he kept asking her if she was okay, if she'd enjoyed it, if he'd hurt her, and a dozen other things, until she'd cupped his head, and drawn his mouth to hers once more.

And whispered the words that came so easily to a teenage girl.

"I love you. I love you, Bryan Kendall. And I'll never, ever love anyone else. Not ever."

His smile had been quick and beautiful. "I love you, too."

The shower stopped running, and Dawn's awareness jolted from the past to the present in the space of a heartbeat. He was finished with his shower. He would be walking out of that bathroom any second now.

She bent one knee, letting it protrude from beneath the blankets, and tugged her hair so it hung over one shoulder.

Then she moved the blanket a little higher, baring her leg all the way to the thigh, wondering if the pose looked as sexy as she thought it did.

God, no, it was way too obvious!

She rolled onto her back instead, arms at her sides. But that made her look like a corpse waiting to be autopsied. So she rolled onto her other side and wondered if her butt looked huge from that angle.

Quickly she sat up, frustrated and wondering why a girl never had a porn director around when she needed one.

"You all right?"

She jerked her head up, and there was Bryan. She'd totally missed her cue. He was wearing clean boxer briefs and a T-shirt. A T-shirt, dammit. She really didn't want him in a T-shirt.

She sat up and braced her palms on the bed behind her, then tipped her head back a little. She bent her knee up and the covers slid off it, baring her thigh, and she imagined she looked just like the sexy female silhouette that adorned air fresheners in men's pickup trucks nationwide.

"Fine," she said. "Why do you ask?" And why, she wondered, do I suddenly feel just as awkward as I did five years ago?

"You were…tossing and turning…or something."

"Couldn't get comfy." He was trying too hard not to look at her, she thought. All right, enough with the porno pose. She gave up and fell back onto her pillows, then jerked the covers back up and patted the spot beside her.

He looked at the mattress as if it were a river hiding a killer croc just beneath the surface.

"Dawn, you know we talked ab—"

"I totally know what we talked about." She frowned at him. "What, don't you trust me? You think I'm going to—I don't know—force myself on you or something?"

He stood there, just looking at her for a long moment, and then he smiled and shook his head. "You couldn't if you wanted to."

And what the *hell* was *that* supposed to mean?

"Get in, then."

He got in. He lay on his back, head on the pillow, hands folded in an area roughly over his groin, almost as if they were protecting it.

She was insulted and almost told him so. Instead, she rolled over onto her other side, putting her back to him, and she *smoldered*.

Did he really think he was *all that?* That he had to sleep with his dick covered up to protect it from her inevitable attack?

Well, he'd better just damn well think again.

Jerk!

Hours later, she realized that in spite of her anger and frustration, she had managed to fall asleep. She opened her eyes to find her head resting on Bryan's chest and his arms wrapped around her. Without moving, she squinted at the glowing red numbers on the bedside clock—2:20 a.m.

He was sound asleep, no doubt. She felt his chest rising and falling, his heart thumping steadily beneath her head. And as miserable as she was, she lay there and let her body melt into him. Her top leg was bent, resting over his no-longer-protected groin. And she sighed in spite of herself as her leg moved higher, then lower again, all without her permission, rubbing over him.

And then she blinked, because he was hard beneath her thigh.

Maybe he wasn't asleep, after all.

Oh, hell, what should she do?

She lay still, holding her breath, wondering if she should pretend to be asleep or...

His hand moved, the one near the back of her head, his fingers threading very lightly into her hair.

Yup, he was awake.

It was too much. She lifted her head, turning her face to his, about to ask him if he were trying to kill her or just drive her mad.

But as soon as she turned, he lifted his head just enough to touch her lips with his. His hand in her hair tightened, pulling her closer, and she moaned as her lips parted and the kiss ignited everything in her. Their tongues met, and her hips arched instinctively against his hard thigh. She gripped the edges of his T-shirt almost angrily, tugging it up to bare his chest, and then she ran her hands over his skin, hungry for the feel of him. It was even better than she could have imagined.

She followed with her lips, kissing his chest, his nipples, his abs. Oh, they were incredible abs. She kept kissing as he rose up just enough to peel his shirt over his head, and then he tugged hers off the same way. Urgently. He gripped her waist and pulled her higher in the bed, stretching up to capture a breast in his mouth. She braced her hands on his shoulders and tipped her head back, her mouth opening as she sucked in breath after breath, the sensations too good to bear.

He arched up, and she realized she was straddling him now, feeling that hardness pressing up into her. Reaching down, she shoved his shorts lower, as low as she could reach, and he bent one leg and then the other to kick free of them. He was still focused on her breasts, licking at her, biting just a little, tugging. Every touch of teeth and tongue sent shock waves of pleasure radiating outward through her body. Holding his head where it was with one hand, she lifted her lower body and awkwardly struggled free of her panties.

If he stopped now she would kill him. As fast as she could, she lowered herself to him again, his cock, naked and hard, rubbing against her. Soft sounds of pleasure whispered from her lips, no words—just sounds that said more than any words could have. She parted her legs, rising up just a little, then lowering herself again, over him this time, taking him inside her, bit by bit. Slowly, experimentally, she took him deeper, and then deeper still, and she felt her body stretching to accept all of him.

It was good. It was so, *so* good.

His hands closed on her buttocks as she lifted and lowered her body slowly, gently, at first, but then with her pace growing faster and more urgent with every thrust. He arched to meet her, to drive himself into her, every time, and pulled her head down to his, taking her mouth with an urgency she'd never felt in him. He kissed her as if he would devour her whole, and she kissed him back with the same feverish need, as his body stroked the flames in her higher and higher.

And he seemed to know. He seemed to know as he clasped her more tightly, held her more firmly, thrust himself up into her more powerfully. In moments the climax broke inside her, and he swallowed her cries of pleasure and kept right on moving.

Then his movements slowed, his kisses gentled, his hands stroked slow, tender paths up and down her back, over her shoulders, her hips. Wrapping her more tightly in his arms, he rolled her over onto her back, body to body, flesh to flesh, never breaking that full-length contact. And then he was on top of her and she was parting her legs for him. Even as the shock waves of her orgasm began to fade, he resumed the frantic pace, pounding into her, holding her hips to make her take every thrust fully. She wouldn't have thought she was ready. And yet she was. Her body responded, and the fires raged all over again as he pushed her toward another orgasm. Again and again he drove into her, until she was crying out again, climaxing again, her entire body shivering and shuddering with the force of it.

As it rocked through her, every nerve ending seemed sensitized to the point that she couldn't possibly stand anymore.

And yet he gave her more. He wrapped his arms around her waist, anchoring her to him as he sat up, pulling her with him until her legs were wrapped around him and they sat face-to-face. He nuzzled and nibbled at her breasts, and she pulled back, because the sensations were too much.

His hands flatted to the small of her back and tugged her to him again, and this time his mouth was merciless as he pinched her throbbing nibbles between his teeth. She clasped handfuls of his hair and tried not to scream in exquisite pleasure.

Slowly this time, he led her back up toward ecstasy, his mouth relentless, tormenting, as he nibbled, then released, then licked at her nipples over and over again.

His erection, still rock solid and huge, moved in and out of her, but slower this time. She clung to him, desperate, drowning in sensation, her body clenching around him. She couldn't possibly come again, she thought. And then she whispered it. "I can't…I can't…"

"I think you can." He lifted her bodily off him, withdrawing completely as she whimpered in protest, and then he slid farther down in the bed, his mouth trailing kisses over her belly before he moved lower. Her thighs tried to close, because she was sure she couldn't take any more. But his hands pressed them wide, insistently, forcefully, and he bowed between her legs and worshipped her there with his mouth, with his tongue. He sucked at her, even bit her lightly, and she pulled a handful of blankets to her mouth to muffle her cries. Her pleas.

He laughed, then used his hands to spread her labia and captured her clitoris, sucking and nipping and tugging at it just as he had her breasts. There was nothing remaining of thought or sense or logic in her. She was nothing but pure sensation, sensation that exploded and screamed through her.

And then he was sliding up her once again, driving into her now-quivering and almost-too-wet body. His hands slid down her thighs, then lifted them until her legs were anchored over his shoulders, and he drove and drove until finally his entire body tensed and held, and she felt him throbbing into her.

He moaned deep in his chest and collapsed on top of her, wrapping her up tight and rolling onto his side, holding her tenderly.

Panting, their bodies damp with sweat, they lay there, clinging to each other as if…as if…

"Damn, I didn't want that to happen," he whispered.

"I could tell, the way you were covering yourself with your hands last night. I was pretty insulted, you know."

"Uh, that was to hide my…reaction to seeing you in nothing but a tank top and panties."

She giggled and nuzzled his chest. "Are you sorry?"

"Not yet."

She lifted her head, frowning at him. "What's that supposed to mean?"

He stared into her eyes, his own probing, searching, but she didn't know what for. "Nothing," he said at length. "I don't regret it. I'll remember it forever—no matter what happens."

She let her smile return, and, sighing, she dropped

her head to his chest again and closed her eyes. "So will I," she promised.

And she meant it.

But what she didn't say, what was clamoring to get out and only barely being restrained, was that she loved him.

It had been true when she'd said it so long ago. Truer than she had even known. She had never stopped loving him, not in five long years. She probably never would.

God, if only he could feel that way about her again. But no, not now. This was not the time to dump something that big and heavy on his powerful shoulders. He had more than too much to worry about already.

But *she* would worry about it. She would worry about it until she knew whether there was any chance for them at all, and what the future held.

If they even had a future by the time the Nightcap Strangler finished with them.

She fell asleep in his arms, and it felt so good that she didn't think it mattered if she never woke again. But then she was sinking deeper into the black velvet blanket of slumber and emerging on the other side.

She was still lying in a bed, but alone this time. She opened her eyes and realized she wasn't in the cabin. It was dark, this bed was smaller and the room around her was completely different. She smelled stale alcohol, which made her wrinkle her nose, and then she realized that she tasted it, too. Her mouth was dry, her stomach writhing, and her head, when she tried to move it to take in the room, pounded so hard she had to press her hands to it and close her eyes.

Where was Bryan?

Opening her eyes again, slowly, she noticed the room a bit more clearly as the mists cleared from her vision.

Wait a minute. This was Bryan's bedroom, in his little cracker-box house. What the hell?

Dawn moved her arm very slightly, lifting her hand and turning it. *Not my hand,* her mind whispered. And then she touched her own hair, patting it and feeling thick waves. Pulling a lock forward, she examined it.

Not my hair.

What is this?

She sat up slowly in the bed, and saw her own reflection in the mirror on the opposite side of the bedroom.

But it wasn't her reflection. It was Bettina Wright's face staring back at her; she'd seen her photo in the newspapers. And even as that realization made a home in her heart, she saw the dark form standing beside the bed, so close to the headboard that he was behind her. Mask, gloves, all dressed in black. He was a solid man with a bit of a paunch, and his eyes were glued to hers in that mirror. She opened her mouth to scream.

And then he moved, cutting off the sound before it was more than a breath. He twisted the black silk stocking around her neck and jerked it tight, cutting off her air. It hurt, and her head pounded with pressure. She clawed at the stocking but only managed to scratch her own flesh. Gaping, she tried to breathe and felt her tongue swelling in her mouth. Dizziness washed through her, and her wild kicking became, instead, a series of twitches and trembles.

The pressure eased. Widemouthed, she sucked in a breath. It hurt, and she knew her larynx was bruised, maybe crushed. But before she could draw a second breath, something cold touched her lips.

A glass. A tiny one. And as it tipped higher, the liquid it held poured into her mouth, choking her, burning. She tried to swallow, and it hurt more than anything had ever hurt in her life. Like swallowing broken glass. The whiskey bubbled in her throat as she gurgled and choked.

And then the stocking went tight again.

Oh, God, this was brutal.

Something hit her leg as her hands clasped uselessly at his gloved ones. Her eyes were watering so badly, bulging now, that she couldn't see. She wished she could just die and end this suffering. Her body twisted. But in the vague hope of finding a weapon she lowered one hand to her side, where something had landed on her, and closed her fist around something small and hard. Metal.

He pushed her down, bending over her, squeezing her life away. She saw tears in his eyes, those tiny black stones that showed in the holes of the ski mask. Flashes of multicolored light exploded behind her own eyes.

She was dying.

Bryan was a cop, she thought, and this guy had dropped a clue. Bryan would get him. He would get him—and she would help.

Desperately, she used the last bit of her strength to cram the tiny metal thing underneath the mattress. Then she let it go and withdrew her hand, and lifted her head for one last glimpse in the mirror, but there was only blackness before her eyes.

And, she realized, there was no more pain. No more struggling to breathe. No more pressure. The blackness cleared, and she looked down and saw her own body lying there, staring blankly. Lifeless.

I'm dead, she thought. She turned, sensing something behind her, and saw a nearly blinding light that grew larger. Compelled to go to it, she started to release the desire that held her there in the room, and immediately the light began to draw her closer with a force something like gravity.

And yet, just before she reached it, women appeared, lots of them, all young and beautiful, with soulful eyes full of pain. *Not yet,* they told her without moving their lips. *Not until he pays for what he did to us.*

He killed you, too? Unspoken, the question emerged all the same.

Yes, and he'll kill others. Stop him.

Stop him.

Dawn felt as if she were a spectator now, separating from the ride she'd been taking inside Bette's body. Standing apart from them all. Bette joined the others, turning to face her, and together they all repeated their plea, again and again.

Stop him. Stop him. *Stop him!*

16

She slept in his arms.

Bryan wished she hadn't. But by the time they had finally been too exhausted to move anymore, they'd also been too exhausted to stay awake. Much less to have a long and serious talk.

And he wasn't sure what the hell he would have said, anyway, or what he was going to say in a little while, when she rolled over and opened those eyes of hers and shot him straight in the heart. What was he going to say to her then?

Maybe he could slip away before that happened. Yeah, he knew it was a shitty thing to do, but he needed time to think. To figure out just what it was she was expecting him to say—no, what she *wanted* him to say. Or didn't want him to.

And maybe he ought to be more interested in hearing what she had to say on the subject, but hell, it didn't matter. It couldn't be—this thing between them just couldn't be. He couldn't let himself fall in love with her. Not again. Or maybe for the first time, because, really, could you fall in love at nineteen?

If you could, he had. God, she'd been everything to him then.

And she had known that. And still she had walked—no, run. She had run from him, from them, from the tender, innocent, wonderful thing they had. She hadn't even given it a chance.

He slid slowly out of her embrace and rolled onto one side, inching toward the edge of the bed, casting his eyes around the room to find something to put on. Anything. There. His jeans lay on the floor only a couple of feet from the bed. He stretched out an arm, grabbed them and started pulling them closer. He was too vulnerable to her naked. All she had to do was touch him and he would be a goner. After last night...

Suddenly Dawn sat up straight. Her eyes were wide-open but seemed unseeing, and she said, very clearly, "Stop him."

Bryan dropped the jeans in surprise. "What?" As he turned to face her more fully, he realized she was still asleep. And then she looked right at him, and he went ice cold. There was something *not Dawn* in those eyes.

"You have to stop him."

He frowned at her, lifted a hand to touch her cheek. "Are you okay?"

She blinked rapidly then, and when she looked at him again, he knew she was awake and aware. She held his eyes, and her brows drew together, and then she burst into tears, her hands covering her face, her head falling forward. Her shoulders shook as she sobbed and muttered "Oh, God, oh, God, *oh, God.*"

"Hey..."

She flung herself against him, and he had to wrap his arms around her, because what the hell else was he going to do? She was a mess. "Okay, baby, okay. I've got you. It's all right."

"Oh, God, Bry, I had the most awful dream!"

He came very near to sighing in relief. Very near. Because at first he'd thought all this emotion was her response to what had happened between them last night. And while he'd been dreading whatever her response would be, he hadn't expected anything quite *this* dramatic.

"But it was just a dream." He ran his hands up and down her unclothed back and, in spite of himself, let his head lean down on hers. "And it's no wonder you're having nightmares. With everything going on, all this stress and—"

"It was about Bette."

His hands stopped moving across her skin. "You dreamed about Bette?"

She nodded against his chest, then sniffled. "I dreamed about her murder. The whole thing. It was like I was right there."

Clasping her shoulders, Bryan moved her slightly away from him so he could look her in the eyes. "Are you sure it was a dream? I mean, are you sure it wasn't Bette? You know, talking to you?"

She sniffled again, and her nose twisted a little bit to one side. It made him want to smile and kiss the tip of it. But the pain in her eyes chased that impulse away.

"No. It wasn't like that. I wasn't seeing her. Or talking to her. It was like…it like I *was* her. I woke up in your bed, and I was in her body. I even saw her reflection in your mirror when I looked up. And then he was there, strangling me." As she spoke, her hands went to her neck, touching gingerly, and she flinched, as if it really did hurt. "It was so terrifying. And it hurt. It was brutal. He was cruel, Bryan. He was so cruel."

He nodded and pulled her close again. "It never happened that way before? When they used to talk to you?"

She shook her head. "No, it was always just like talking to a person, only less substantial. Like I had to listen with all my senses, not just my ears. And see them with my entire being, instead of just with my eyes. And even then, they would speak in whispers and be as delicate as mist." She took a breath. "But this was totally different."

"Still…"

"It was just a dream, Bryan."

"Okay. Okay." She sniffled again, and he held her tighter. "You're shaking like a leaf."

"It was horrible. He choked me—with a silk stocking. A black one. He choked me until I started to black out—and then he let up. Just when there was that tiny glimmer of relief from passing out and escaping the pain, he let up and poured that liquor down me. It *hurt!*

I couldn't swallow. I think I was drowning in it, and then he tightened that damned stocking again and—"

"Hey, take it easy." He frowned, genuinely startled by the way her voice had thickened, and become gruff and coarse, as if she had really lived that nightmare. As if she actually had been strangled and was feeling the physical repercussions.

And then it hit him how accurate her story was. It was precisely the way Nick had surmised the murders went down—the partial strangulation, then the nightcap, then the strangulation again.

"Dawn, do you remember what Bette was wearing?"

"Of course I do. She was naked." She scowled up at him. "But it was just a dream, Bryan."

"Are you sure?"

"Believe me, I know the difference."

"Okay."

"I wish it *had* been real. God, I wish it had."

"Why's that?"

She thinned her lips. "He dropped something—it fell, maybe from a pocket or something. Onto the bed. And she managed to shove it under the mattress before she died." She lifted her head.

He met her eyes. "And you're sure it was just a dream?"

It took her two heartbeats to respond. "Yes." And then, "Pretty sure."

"Then why is your throat sore?"

She swallowed hard and then pressed her fingertips

gently to her throat. "It *is* sore. But…it was a vivid dream. It's probably…just me believing it a little too much." She blinked, frowned, cleared her throat. "Still, maybe we ought to go back there. I think we have to go back and check underneath the mattress."

"I think *I* have to go back and check underneath the mattress," he said. "And I'm going to go right now, while it's still dark enough to provide some cover. You're going stay right here, where you're safe. I'll wake Rico before I go. He'll make sure you're protected. Okay?"

"But who's gonna keep *you* safe?" she asked.

He smiled gently at her. "I'm pretty good at that. I'll take a gun, okay? Will that make you feel better?"

"Not as much as if you'd let me go with you. Why won't you, Bryan?"

He kissed the top of her head, then reached down for the jeans and started pulling them on. "Because I don't want to risk your life by dragging you back out into the open."

"But you don't know I'm safe here."

"Yeah, I do."

She frowned as he zipped the jeans. "How? What if it's Olivia?"

"It's not."

"How do you know?"

"Because in the dream, it was a man."

She shook her head. "He wore a ski mask. I couldn't see—"

"You saw enough. You kept saying 'he.'"

She shook her head. "Bryan, I told you, it was just a dream."

"I don't think so."

"And you think you'd know better than I would? *I'm* the one who used to be able to see them. And this wasn't that."

"Then maybe it was something else. Maybe Bette— I don't know—sent you the dream. Or maybe it was just some kind of intuition. But it wasn't *just* a dream, Dawn."

"How do you know that?"

He crossed the room, found his shirt, put it on. "Have you read Nick's book yet?"

"No, not yet."

"Tell you what, you start reading it while I'm gone. It's amazing how closely his recreation of the old crimes, based on the evidence, matches the way it played out in your dream. It's eerie, Dawn. It had to be more than just a dream."

"Bryan, I really want to go with you."

"I know you do. I know. But…" He sighed, moved back to the bed and, reaching down, cupped the back of her head, pulling her close as he leaned down to kiss her hard on the mouth. "I need a little time. Can you… can you just give me a little time?"

Her face changed. She seemed to understand that they weren't talking about her dream anymore. Staring at him, a hundred questions swimming in her eyes, she nodded slowly.

"Yeah. I can give you a little time. Just…just be

careful, Bry. And if you get in trouble, call, okay? Just call, even if you only let it ring and hang up. Just let me know you need me, and I swear I'll get there." She lowered her eyes. "I'm not going to let you down again."

He glanced back at her and saw the sincerity in her eyes. "I'm not going to get into trouble. But yeah, if I do, I promise I'll call."

She surged out of the bed, as naked as the earth in earliest springtime, ran to him and hugged him hard around the waist. "Please be careful."

"I will. Be safe while I'm gone. I'll be back just as soon as I can."

"How long should I wait?"

If he didn't pry her off him before long, he was going to end up back in bed with her. "Before what?"

"Before I do…whatever I have to do to find you. If something goes wrong—and you can't get back and you can't let me know—how long should I wait?"

"If I'm not back by noon—"

"It's 4:00 a.m. That's eight hours!" She released him and took a step back, which left him standing there with a full view of her gorgeous body. "That's too long. I'll wait till 8:00 a.m. If you're not back by then, then we're coming to find you."

He nodded. "I'll be back by eight." He dropped his gaze, then lifted it and shook his head. "Sooner, if can manage it. Hell, I'll probably break the land speed record getting back to you."

The worry fled her face as a smile appeared like a sudden beam of light. "That was really sweet."

"I don't think 'sweet' is the word I'd use." He pulled her to him again and kissed her, slow and deep this time. And he thought about how screwed he was, because he couldn't keep himself from falling in love with her again—if he'd ever stopped at all. And he thought about how now he was the one ready to have that long talk. Because when she said she would never let him down, he thought she was trying to say more, maybe trying to tell him what he'd been so desperately needing to hear from her.

But now was not the time. So he lifted his head, taking his hungry lips from hers, forcing his arms to let her go and, turning, left the room.

"So what kind of a wild-goose chase is he on this time?" Rico asked.

The three of them were sitting on the deck at the rear of the cabin, sipping coffee, watching the mists rise off the lake and admiring the powerful, shadowy waterfall in the distance. The cabin sat so close to the lake that you could listen to the thunder of the falls anytime you were outside, and most of the time when you were inside, too. You could look out at the falls, which in turn looked down on the town that was their namesake.

"He didn't tell you?" Dawn asked.

"No. He only said not to let you two out of my sight, and that he'd be back as soon as he could, and that if you got antsy around eight, I ought to make you give him an extra hour before you sent out the National Guard." Rico smiled his most charming smile, and it seemed almost too white in the tanned skin of his face. He beamed it at Olivia more than at her, and Dawn was fine with that.

"So?" Olivia asked. "Where did he go?"

Dawn licked her lips, nodded firmly. "I had a dream. I saw the murder of Bettina Wright, and in the dream the killer dropped something in the bedroom before he left."

Rico frowned, glanced sideways at Olivia. She met his eyes, and then they both looked at Dawn. "So he's out chasing up a clue that you *dreamed?*" Rico asked.

"I know it sounds ridiculous. And I know it was just a dream, but he thought maybe…" She let her voice trail off and shrugged.

"He's more desperate than I thought," Rico muttered, shaking his head and looking at the floor. "Maybe it's all this stress."

"Or maybe he has good reason to think Dawn's dream might be more than just a dream." Olivia held her with a steady gaze. "Isn't that right, Dawn?"

Dawn closed her eyes. "How much of my story do you know?"

"I checked up on you after we first met," Olivia said. "And learned who your father was."

"Oh, that," Rico said, waving a hand dismissively. "Just 'cause her father was a self-proclaimed psychic, or whatever, that doesn't mean she is."

Olivia sent him a look meant to convey irritation with his interruption, then went on. "When your

father was killed in Blackberry, five years ago, it was
the biggest thing to hit Vermont since—well, since
the Nightcap murders. Everyone was talking about it.
Mordecai Young, charismatic cult leader turned self-
help author. Some said he was insane. Others said he
had an honest-to-God sixth sense, a connection that
couldn't be explained."

Dawn nodded slowly. "I think both were true. I think
he really did have some kind of extra…something. I also
think he was clinically insane, and those two things
were too twisted up to tell apart. The voices that told
him how to help people seemed to be coming from the
same place as the ones that told him which people to
kill. He obeyed them all, without question. Believed
them all to be one voice. The voice of God."

Olivia nodded. "A person could almost feel sorry for
him."

Dawn nodded, because she *did* feel sorry for her
father. And yet she also feared him. Still feared him,
even though he was dead. She was terrified he would
come to her again.

"And then after he died," Olivia said, "it was you
who helped solve another murder, clearing the man
who'd been wrongly accused and sent to waste away
in a mental ward. And some said you were only able to
do that because you had a direct line to the victim."

Rico swore under his breath. "What case—wait, are
you talking about River Corbett, the guy who was in the
loony bin for burning his house down with his pregnant
wife inside?"

Olivia nodded slowly.

Dawn drew a breath. "It's true. I used to be able to... pick up on things other people wouldn't be able to. And maybe I did inherit that from my father, which is why it terrified me so much that I ran away from it. But it faded, maybe from lack of use. I've been trying to get the dead girls to tell me who killed them ever since I got back here. And nothing. Not a word. The gift, or curse, or whatever you want to call it, is gone. It hasn't come back. This...this was just a dream."

"You're terrified that it wasn't, though, aren't you?"

Dawn looked up at Olivia and realized she was right.

"You know, your fear of this...gift... It could be the very thing that's keeping it from returning to you now when you need it most."

"You think?"

"Yes, I do. So maybe it's manifesting in other ways— because your mind is just too afraid to let it operate the way it did before."

Dawn looked thoughtful for a long moment. "It's possible, I guess. But I don't think so."

"But Bryan doesn't agree with you, does he?" Olivia asked.

Dawn shook her head. "No. And since the killer was clearly male in my dream, he no longer believes it was you, Olivia. Not that he ever *really* believed that, anyway. Neither of us did."

"That's a relief," Olivia said softly.

"And that's also why he's gone back to his place, to look under the mattress for whatever the killer dropped."

"You didn't see what it was…in the dream, I mean?" Rico asked.

"No."

"But you saw the killer?" he went on.

"No. He wore a ski mask, and he was dressed all in black, head to toe."

"But you saw the murder," Olivia whispered, and she probed Dawn's eyes, sympathy in her own. "I'm so sorry. That had to be…just awful."

"It was."

Olivia reached across the table, clasped Dawn's hand in her own, and Dawn knew in that moment that she had nothing to fear from this woman. That she was, in fact, going to become very close to her in time.

It was tough being back home, Bryan thought, as he ducked under the crime-scene tape and walked in through his own front door. It was tougher than he'd thought it would be. Because even though he and Bette hadn't been in love, they had been friends. Good friends. Intimate friends. They'd shared sex when they both needed release. They'd offered comfort to each other about the lovers they'd left behind—the ones they thought they would never get over. They'd shared a lot of laughs, a lot of good times. And he'd cared about her in a very real way.

Walking back into his home now brought back, all

too clearly, the memory of finding her there in his bed. A lifeless shell with sightless eyes and nothing of the warmth of who she really was left in her. Like a slab of meat, with a face and hair attached. There'd been nothing left of her.

Someone had taken it all away. They'd had no right to do that to her. To anyone. Dammit!

He'd been careful not to tear any of the crime-scene tape. The house was smudged with fingerprint dust. Empty spaces attested to items that had been taken as evidence. His computer. Every blanket and pillow in the place. A lot of the glasses and cigarette butts and ashtrays were missing. They'd left the dip to go sour, the chips to go stale.

His photo, the one of him and Dawn, was right where he'd left it, and a big pool of warmth bubbled up inside him as he caught sight of it. But that pool had fear-fish swimming restlessly in its depths. Back and forth, and jumping every now and then to send ripples through the water, keeping it from being as clear and calm as it should have been.

He moved down the hallway and into the bedroom. The bed had been stripped, but the mattress remained. Every item from the nightstands was missing. A big hunk had been cut from his carpet right where he supposed they estimated the killer had been standing while he strangled Bette to death.

Bryan stood beside the bed and turned his head to look into the mirror across the room. If only there were some way to see what that mirror had seen, some way to access the reflections from the mirror's recent memory, the way you could click through the memory of a computer for sites visited in the past.

The way you could sometimes still see the shape of the most recent scene after turning the television set off. The way it lingered, like an aura, fading slowly. Why couldn't mirrors work that way?

He imagined Bette seeing her own murder reflected in that mirror, probably through a veil of tears, a haze of panic. And her killer had been reflected there, too. Nightcap or his spawn. The bastard who'd taken her and turned his life upside down.

"You son of a bitch. I swear I'm going to make you pay for this."

He heard something—some*one?*—from just outside, jerking him to attention. Apparently he had even less time than he'd thought in which to do what he'd come here to do.

He checked under the mattress. Nothing. He moved quickly but silently to the other side of the bed, then thrust a hand beneath the mattress again, feeling around. When he felt nothing, disappointment rinsed through him. He was feeling an urgency to leave. To just slip into the bathroom, out the window and be gone before whoever was outside made their way in.

But dammit, he couldn't give up. Dawn's dream had to be more than just a coincidence. It *had* to be. Because if it wasn't, then he had nothing. No hope.

He picked up the mattress and leaned it against the headboard. Tugging his penlight from a back pocket, he flicked it on and aimed it at the area underneath. It was a platform bed, with a heavy sheet of plywood laid to support the mattress.

He frowned, leaning closer as his light reflected off something caught between the edge of the frame and the plywood. Something shiny.

He pried at it with a fingertip and slid it slowly upward. Finally it was free, and he let it fall into his palm. Straightening, eager, he opened his hand to stare down at his prize.

It was a small metal charm, the kind you found hanging from a key chain, but in this case the chain was missing. All that was left was…a tiny version of an old classic car.

He tensed as something knocked at the back door of his brain. And then he realized he was no longer alone in the room, and a surge of panic raced up his spine.

He jerked his head around, then sighed in automatic relief as he spotted Nick standing there.

"Jeez, you scared the hell out of me," he muttered.

"Did I? Sorry about that." Nick lifted his chin, eyes on Bryan's hand. "What you got there?"

"Damnedest thing," Bryan said. "Dawn had a dream—she saw the killer drop something, saw Bette shove it under the mattress. I just couldn't let it go without checking."

"Because she used to be psychic. And apparently still is." Nick smiled and shook his head. "Who'd have figured? You found something?"

"Yeah." Bryan was still holding the little car balanced

on his open palm. "Hey, can you get me a bag or something? We don't want to smudge any prints. There should be one in the kitchen—the drawer to the left of the sink."

"Sure, sure. But wait, I think I've got something right here." Nick fished around in a pocket, came out with a paper envelope and said, "This'll do for now." He squeezed it so that it opened, and Bryan dropped the car inside.

"What is it, anyway?" Bryan asked.

"What, you don't recognize it?" Nick grinned that grin that was so typically his own, the one that crinkled his entire face, and said, "I'll bet your girlfriend would. It's a '65 T-Bird, pal. I used to have one just like it."

Something in Bryan went ice cold. He lifted his head, looked his mentor, his hero, right in the eyes, and saw something cold there. Something he had never seen before. His mind was shuffling through hundreds of tidbits—the neighbor who'd seen an old red-and-white car at one crime scene. The metal *T* that had been found at one of the other crime scenes. The one that came from a 1965 Ford Thunderbird. And now this piece of a key chain. And Nick saying he used to have a car just like it.

"You…you did?" It was the only thing he could think of to say.

And even as Bryan frowned, trying to make sense of the impossible notion his brain was screaming at him, Nick's other hand came around in a powerful, sudden, gun-wielding arc.

"Still do," Nick added, just before the blow fell.

Bryan felt the explosion of the impact, and then he dropped to his knees and began to topple sideways. He never felt himself hit the floor.

17

"He should have been back by now."

Dawn scanned the living room, as restless as the storm now raging outside. Thunder pounded the skies with an unending fury. Every flash of lightning, every howl of the wind and every single crack of a falling tree limb seemed like an omen of doom.

Rico had finished checking the area and was now in the kitchen, cooking something that smelled great and included bacon, while Olivia was upstairs having a shower. Dawn had decided to pass the time by reading, so she'd been sitting by the fire with Nick's book, devouring it and trying not to look up at the clock every time she turned a page. It shouldn't have been as hard as it was to stay focused. The book was a page turner. But despite that, it was tough to focus on anything other than the fact that the man she loved was out there, somewhere, looking for evidence against a crazed killer, while the entire Shadow Falls Police Department was trying to hunt him down and put him behind bars.

Time and pages passed. The accounts of the murders gave her chills, and after experiencing one so personally—even if it had been just a dream—she finally couldn't handle reading any longer. She tucked the jacket flap between the pages to hold her place, but before she closed the book she noticed the author photo on the jacket and smiled slightly.

Nick, sixteen years younger, had been a real hottie. No beer belly back then. Dark hair, piercing eyes and a sensual, full mouth. He knew it, too. He was one hundred percent the cocky, full-of-himself supercop, leaning on the front fender of a car. He looked as if he belonged in a cop show on TV. She frowned at the car, which caught her interest, as cars usually did. It was clearly a classic—a Ford, she thought—but it was tough to tell more with just that tiny bit of fender and part of one headlight visible.

Sighing, she closed the book and then looked up at the sound of footsteps on the stairs. Olivia, back in her nightgown and a fluffy robe, padding down to join her. "He's not back yet?"

"No. And it's getting close to nine." Dawn glanced at the clock on the wall.

"It's eight-twenty," Olivia said. "Give him until nine, hon. You said you would."

"I said I'd give him until eight," Dawn corrected her. "He added that extra hour."

"Still…"

"I think I should at least call him."

"What if he's trying to keep from being discovered at

the crime scene, or is creeping around watching someone suspicious? You want to give him away by ringing
his phone?"

"If he's creeping or watching, he should know enough
to put the damn phone on vibrate." Dawn rolled her eyes
and resumed pacing. "He *does* know enough. He's a
cop." Setting the book on the coffee table, next to a
boxful of evidence and a huge stack of files from the
original series of murders, she sat down on the sofa and
reached for a telephone that looked as if it was left over
from the fifties. She picked up the heavy handset and
poked a finger into the dial, then went still. "Shit."

"What's wrong?"

"No dial tone." She set the handset down, and looked
at the tall windows and the rain that pelted them from
the gloom beyond. "Must be the storm."

"I'll get my cell phone."

"No, there's no point. No signal out here. The only
place we've had service so far is in a rowboat out in the
middle of the lake."

"Well, we're sure not going out on the lake in *this,*"
Olivia said. And then she smiled. "Is that where you
were when I called you?"

"Yeah. Fishing." A warmth flooded Dawn's belly,
and she went soft inside. "It was nice."

"You two…you have a history, I guess."

Dawn nodded. "I walked out on him. Ran out,
really."

"Why?"

Lowering her head, Dawn said, "To get away from

the 'gift' my father passed on to me—the ghosts who were constantly trying to talk to me—and the memory of my father, all of it. And it worked. I got rid of them. But in the process, I lost the best thing I'll ever have. And I still don't know if I can ever get it back again."

Olivia lifted her brows. "Well, from the sounds coming from that bedroom last night, I think you already have."

Dawn pressed her hands to her cheeks. "Oh, God, you heard us?"

"Don't be embarrassed. I think it's fantastic. You two are good together."

"But we're *not* together."

"No?"

Dawn shook her head sadly. "He still wants me. Physically. But sex isn't love. He loved me once, though."

Olivia tipped her head to one side. "But you don't believe he still does?"

"No."

"Well, don't be so sure. He's made himself a fugitive—and somehow I just don't think he's the type to run from justice, innocent or not. He's a cop, and by all accounts, he loves being a cop. Seems to me he'd be more apt to stick it out, do the whole thing by the book and face the consequences. I think he took off to protect you. Not himself."

Dawn looked at her. "I think so, too. But that doesn't mean he loves me."

"If it doesn't, then I really don't know what does." Olivia sighed and nodded. "Besides, I see the way he looks at you. Trust me on this, you two are going to be fine."

"I hope you're right, and if we both get through this in one piece, maybe we'll still have a shot. God, what am I going to do until nine?"

"I suggest we just make some hot cocoa and keep each other company until he gets back," Olivia said almost cheerfully. "And he will. He'll be back any minute now."

Again Dawn looked at the clock. "If he's not back soon, I'm going out looking for him."

"Okay, okay, and if you do, my intrepid bodyguard and his arsenal and I will go with you."

Dawn smiled. "I'm really sorry we caused trouble for you, Olivia. I really am."

Olivia just nodded and pulled her robe more tightly around her as she headed to the kitchen to make the promised cocoa.

Bryan's first sensation was of pain in his head, and then, gradually, his awareness spread out from there. His head was leaning over to one side, resting on something hard. He was sitting upright, his legs out in front of him, his backside on a hard floor, and his hands...

His hands were cuffed behind his back.

He lifted his head slowly, blinked his eyes open, tugged at his wrists to confirm what he already knew. And then his vision came slowly into focus on the gleaming machine only a few feet away from him. He was in a garage with an immaculate 1965 Ford Thunderbird. It was red and white, its chrome and shiny paint bearing not so much as a speck of dust or a smudge of dirt.

He could hear a storm raging outside but couldn't see any flashes of lightning. And as he looked around, he saw that the windows were shuttered, the garage locked up tight. And it wasn't the garage at Nick's house. Bryan had been inside his garage many times. They'd shared beers, worked on cars together. Nick definitely had a garage, but this wasn't it.

Damn, how could Nick do this?

"Hey, you're awake. Good. I wanted tell you how sorry I am about all of this before—well, you know."

He turned slightly in the direction of Nick's voice.

"You?" Bryan whispered. "No...God, Nick. *You're* the Nightcap Strangler?"

Nick came closer, across the concrete floor, and hunkered down in front of him. Nick Di Marco. God, he was the one. He was the Strangler. How could it be? Bryan just couldn't believe it.

"Not me, really. It's him. Nightcap. He's..." Nick gestured toward his forehead. "He's in here, but he's not me. You know?"

"No," Bryan said. "I don't have a fuckin' clue, Nick. Or are you setting yourself up for an insanity defense?"

"I won't need to." Nick sighed. "It's hard to explain. But still, he says we don't have any choice here, and even though I've tried and tried, I just can't see any other option."

"Any other option besides what?" Bryan asked.

"You going to kill me, Nick? You're gonna *kill* me?
Me, Nick?"

The older man nodded. "It's not like I'm happy about
it. But I have to. You're my protégé. You were familiar
with every aspect of the case, even stuff only I knew.
That's what I'll tell them, anyway. You're the only one
who could have pulled off a string of copycat crimes
this convincing."

"So you're going to frame me and *then* kill me?"

Nick nodded again. "Yeah. I got a fresh one just
down the block. Took her last night. I'll position your
body there, say I caught you in the act, had no choice
but to fire my weapon. The press will find it ironic. My
own protégé, my own biggest case, and I end up being
the one to take you down. Hell, I bet I'll get another
book out of this one. Maybe they'll make a sequel to
the movie. Maybe get De Niro again, huh?"

"What time did you kill her?"

"Doesn't matter. Doesn't matter at all, Kendall."

"Sure it does. Dawn knows what time I left. She'll
alibi me and shoot your story all to hell."

He shrugged. "Yeah, but she's in love with you. And
she's got no credibility, anyway. She's been helping you
run from the police, hiding you, aiding and abetting and
all that." He shook his head. "There'll be enough evidence at the scene to make it clear she's lying to protect
you."

"Yeah? Too bad we had company stay over with
us at the cabin last night, pal." Bryan met Nick's eyes
and smiled. "The chief might not believe Dawn all by

herself, but he's damn well gonna believe Rico and Olivia. I even woke Rico before I left. We checked the time together, so they'd know how long to wait before getting worried. Before sending help. They know when I left, Nick. So if you killed another woman last night, I'm solidly covered. In fact, this murder will be the one that clears me of all of them. You stupid son of a bitch, you've fucked yourself."

Nick closed his eyes. It seemed as if he was experiencing some kind of pain—or ecstasy. Bryan couldn't tell which.

"You might as well just let me go, Nick. It's over. You put in all this work setting me up, and then you made one huge mistake and undid it all. It's over. You can see that, can't you?"

Nick stood still, eyes closed, head tipped back. A small smile began to appear on his lips.

"Look, Nick, just get out of town. Get out of the country. I'll play dumb until you've had enough time to get clear, okay? Isn't that the best way to handle this? Isn't that the easiest way? You don't have to kill me. You don't have to hurt anyone ever again."

"I do, though. I do." It was a whisper.

"No, man. You don't. You controlled it for sixteen years. You said it in the book, and you were right and everyone else was wrong. You were *right,* man. You proved it—a serial killer *can* stop killing. He can control it. You stopped. You held it in check."

"I did. But then…it came back." His smile grew into a replica of his usual, but there was something way off about his eyes. "I told you," he said, but the voice was off, too. Not quite Nick's. "I told you we'd have to kill her. Last of all, best of all, that's what I said. And you kept arguing with me. You kept saying you weren't going to do that, that you liked Dawn." He tipped his head back and laughed and laughed and laughed, and in between the gusts of laughter, he coughed out more words. "And now...now...we have—*ah-ha-ha*—no choice."

"Shit, Nick, stop it. You're freaking me out, okay?"

Nick kept on laughing, a staccato percussion from deep in his chest, utterly devoid of joy. "You *should* be freaking out." He shook his head, then suddenly bent down, gripped Bryan by the front of his shirt and pulled him to his feet. Then he opened the car door and shoved him in, so that Bryan fell across the backseat, unable to catch himself. Nick shoved Bryan's feet inside, and Bryan could feel the man he'd thought of as a friend tying his ankles together before he let go and slammed the door. Then he got behind the wheel and started the engine. It didn't purr, it growled, deep and powerful and somehow very dark.

Bryan struggled into an upright position, turning as best he could to look out the rear windshield, and saw the garage door rising behind them, revealing the pouring rain beyond. Then Nick hit the headlights, and Bryan swung his head to the front again, still trying to get a handle on where the hell they were so he could lead the police back here later—on the off chance he survived.

His gaze fell onto the rear wall of the garage, which was completely covered in photographs. They looked as if they'd been decoupaged onto the wall with some sort of polyurethane. Rows and rows of photographs, all of young women. Young, beautiful women. Some matched the photos of Nightcap's victims, but there were others, too. There were women he'd never seen before.

God, how many? Bryan tried to count as the car began backing up. He only got to thirty before he couldn't see anymore, because his gaze was stuck on one.

The photo drew his eyes, gleaming more than all the others, because the coating was shinier—still wet, Bryan thought. And then he felt the life sucked out of him as if by an oversize vacuum.

That photo was of Dawn.

Nick put the car in Reverse and backed it out of the garage into the rain, then hit a button, and the door began closing again. As they backed onto the road, then started moving forward, the wipers beating at high speed, Bryan looked at the building. A storage unit in the middle of hundreds just like it. And as they drove he saw a sign. EZ RENT Storage Units: 555-9EZ-RENT.

They were sipping cocoa. Olivia was searching through the contents of the evidence box, fingering one item after another, while Dawn pored over the evidence list and police reports yet again. Five minutes to nine. Five more minutes, and then they could go after Bryan. God, why wasn't he walking in that door? She tried to tell herself that he might have found a clue that led him to another and maybe another, and that he would have phoned if the phone weren't out. But she wasn't buying it. Something was wrong.

"What's this from?" Olivia asked. She was holding up a piece of silver metal shaped like a *T,* and her intent, Dawn knew, was to distract her from worrying.

Dawn smiled. "If I'd been here, I could have told them what it was immediately. I wasn't, though. Took the cops three days and five classic-car experts—or maybe it was five days and three experts—to get a positive ID on that little thing. It's from a '65 Thunderbird. They found it on the road in front of one of the original crime scenes sixteen years ago."

"You would have known it on sight?"

"I've always been a car buff, and I've spent the past five years restoring old classics for a living."

"I didn't know that." Olivia smiled, setting the piece on the coffee table. "Didn't turn out to be much of a clue, though, did it?"

"They don't even know if it's a clue at all. Just because a T-Bird drove past the victim's house and lost a piece of trim, that doesn't mean the killer was driving it. They couldn't even be sure it wasn't dropped there days before the murder."

Olivia nodded. "I'm surprised the department let you

guys have all this stuff—I mean, being that Bryan's a suspect."

"He wasn't a suspect when he got all this out of storage."

"He wasn't?"

"No. He was actually doing some research on the case and trying to keep it very hush-hush." She leaned closer. "It doesn't seem to matter much now, but Nick's getting the Vermont Law Enforcement Lifetime Achievement Award next month. The committee asked Bryan to present it."

"And Nick doesn't know?"

"Nope. It's always a secret. Bry's supposed to give a big speech, and he figured he'd pepper it with highlights from Nick's career, particularly stuff having to do with his most famous case." She lowered her eyes then. "Guess that's all out the window now, though. Unless we can clear Bryan's name and find the real killer by then."

Olivia tipped her head to one side. "It's a real coincidence, isn't it? The timing of all this?"

"How so?" Dawn asked.

"Well, just that right at the time Bryan started digging out the old case files on the murders, the murders started up again." She shook her head. "And that the first victim was his friend, killed in his house. And that he's the only real suspect, at least as far as the cops are concerned." She lifted her gaze slowly and met Dawn's eyes. "Dawn, don't you think that's way too much to be coincidental?"

Dawn averted her eyes. "It's either coincidental or he's guilty. And I *know* he's not guilty, so don't even—"

"I don't think he's guilty."

"He's not." Rico's voice came from the kitchen, where he had apparently just finished cooking. He was coming toward them, plates holding steaming omelets in his hands. "Breakfast is served, but I'm not doing cleanup," he said. "Bryan's not back yet?"

Dawn quickly said, "Not yet. We were just talking about—"

"Yeah, I heard you. It's either coincidence or he's guilty, you said. And we know he's not guilty." Rico set their plates on the coffee table and went back for his own. When he returned, Olivia was digging in. But Dawn's stomach was tied in so many knots with worry that she didn't think she could eat a bite, though it looked and smelled delicious.

"You're right, Dawn," Rico went on. "It's way too much to be coincidental. So that means there has to be a third option. A cause-and-effect thing going on. So what happened first?"

"First...Johnny Lee Jackson died in prison," Dawn said.

"And then Bryan found out he was going to have to present the Lifetime Achievement Award to Nick and he had to keep it secret," Olivia said.

"And then Bryan took the files and evidence from the Nightcap Strangler case," Rico said. "Without permission or even signing them out properly. Which makes it look really suspicious." He took a big bite of his omelet, chewed and swallowed. "And then his girlfriend was murdered in his bed."

"She wasn't his girlfriend," Dawn said, the words popping out before she could even try to bite them back. She cleared her throat. "None of this makes any sense. Why would any of it cause someone to start recreating Nightcap's crimes?"

"It wouldn't," Rico said with a sigh.

Shrugging, Olivia got to her feet and turned toward Rico. "Cocoa?"

"Sure."

She went to get it, and Rico raised his voice so she would be able to hear. "What if it's not a copycat?" Rico said.

Dawn swung her head toward him as if he were insane. Olivia stepped back through the doorway, brows raised.

"Just say, what if? What if Johnny Lee Jackson wasn't the real killer? What if the real killer set him up, way back when, and then, for whatever reason, he just stopped killing?"

"I didn't think serial killers *could* stop," Dawn said.

Rico shook his head. "Nick thinks they can. He mentions it in the book—he says anyone can have a bad impulse, but the strong can control them, the weak can't, and that's what separates good people from bad ones. He didn't want anyone feeling sorry for Johnny Lee Jackson for being overruled by his impulses. He

believes a man always has the final say in what he
chooses to do and not to do. He said a man of character
can overcome anything. So that begs the question, what
if he was right about that? Or at least partially right.
What if Nightcap did manage to control his impulse to
kill—for sixteen years?"

Dawn nodded. "Okay, so if Johnny Lee Jackson was
innocent, then Nightcap was on the loose but no longer
killing."

"And thinking he was completely in the clear. And
then, all of a sudden, here's a rookie cop, taking out all
the old files. Going through all the old evidence. Apparently being kind of shady about it, too."

Olivia and Dawn both gasped aloud as they finally
understood what Rico was getting at. Dawn shook her
head. "But no one knew Bryan had taken out those
files."

"What if someone did?" Rico took the cocoa from
Olivia as she reentered the living room, then started to
pace. "What if Nightcap knew, and what if he thought
Bryan was on to him? How would he deal with that?
He's been in the clear for sixteen years. He's got a lot
to lose. So what would he do?"

"Kill Bryan and make it look like an accident?"

"Yeah. Or give in to the urge he's been suppressing
all these years, now that he has the perfect excuse. Kill
again, frame Bryan, let him take the fall and once again
be in the clear."

"But who?" Olivia asked softly.

"Someone would have to know he took those files,

and they'd also have to know the case inside and out."
Rico frowned as he spoke, and Dawn could tell he didn't
like what he was thinking. He didn't have to say it. This
had to have been an inside job. Someone either in the
department or with intimate knowledge of both it and
the old case.

"I don't know who it is, Rico." Dawn set her cup
down firmly on the coffee table. "But I'm done waiting.
Bryan's not here, and I'm worried about him. I have to
go find him. And I'm going to have to take your car,
because he has ours."

"We'll go with you," Olivia said. "Just give me two
minutes to get dressed."

Headlights cut through the murky morning, and
Dawn felt every muscle in her body go as soft as heated
candle wax. "Oh, thank God," she said, the words rushing out of her on a relieved sigh. "He's back."

She closed her eyes momentarily in relief. "I wonder
if he found anything." Then, bending, she picked up
her fork and took a big bite of the luscious omelet, no
longer too nervous to eat. As she relished it, she grabbed
the tiny metal *T* and reached across the coffee table to
drop it into the evidence box. And then she froze, her
muscles going taut and cold again.

"Oh, my God."

"What?" Olivia rushed closer.

Dawn dropped the *T* and grabbed Nick's book, flipping it open and staring at the photo on the jacket. Her
eyes narrow, she ran her forefinger over the tiny bit of

fender she could see, the shape of the headlight, the chrome around the edge.

"It's a Thunderbird."

"What is?" Olivia leaned over her, and Rico rushed closer.

Dawn pressed her forefinger to the car in the photo. "It's a Thunderbird," she said. "And I'm pretty sure it's a '65."

Olivia's soft gasp was interrupted by Rico saying, "Be cool. Be cool everyone. Just be cool."

Dawn frowned up at him, then followed his gaze to the front door, which was even then swinging open to admit a gust of rain-soaked wind and Nick Di Marco, a small black case tucked under his left arm. He met their eyes, his hair wet, his big smile dying slowly. "Why does everyone look so worried? Huh? Aren't you glad to see me?"

He pulled a gun from behind his back and, without so much as a single word of warning, leveled it and fired.

Rico never even had a chance to react. His head snapped with the impact, a spray of blood and bone exploding from the back of his skull as the bullet exited. Dawn and Olivia screamed, jumping back, Dawn falling over the arm of the sofa and landing on the floor on the other side.

Gasping for a breath that didn't seem willing to come, Dawn stared in wide-eyed horror at Rico, who'd fallen almost straight down, legs buckling, body following, like a skyscraper brought down by expertly placed charges. Now he lay there on the floor, a pool of blood spreading beneath his head.

Dawn's heart was pounding so hard she thought it would burst, but she managed to tear her gaze from poor Rico and look beyond him to Olivia. She was pressed back against the wall, one hand on her face, one on her stomach, and her gaze met Dawn's. And then, slowly, they both looked toward Nick again.

He waved the gun at them. "Let's go, ladies. Upstairs. Shame about Chavez. Unavoidable, though."

Dawn shook her head. "Nick? God, Nick, it *can't* be you. It *can't* be."

"Been me the whole time, sweetie." He glanced at Olivia. "You don't fit the profile. You're gonna be a fly in the ointment, but I think my theory will be that he had to eliminate every witness. He probably came out here to kill her, not expecting to find you and Rico, as well. Last-minute decision. He was forced to break his pattern. To improvise."

"What the hell are you talking about?" Olivia shook her head. "You're talking about killing us? Killing *me,* Nick? As close as we've been to each other all these years?"

"Look, I helped you change your identity to elude your lunatic ex. You've been friendly to me out of gratitude. And that was that."

"I cared about you, Nick. I've...God, I've considered you one of my best friends. I *trusted* you."

"Whatever. Quit interrupting. I need to get this straight in my head. He shot Chavez, 'cause really, what else was he gonna do? And then he figured he was going to have to kill you, anyway, Olivia, so he might as well do it his way. Sure, you don't fit the profile, but he'll get his kicks on that score with Dawnie here." He smiled at Dawn. "You have to be last."

"Why's that, Nick?" She kept her voice as calm as she could manage, while her mind scrambled for a solution, a way out.

"You're the best, baby. You're the one we've been looking for all this time."

"We?" She didn't know what that meant, didn't even pretend to, and found herself looking beyond him, toward the darkness and pouring rain, beyond the still-gaping front door.

"Where's Bryan?" she asked, trying to sound calm, trying not to set him off. He was clearly insane, and she knew insanity. She knew it all too well. As she stood there facing Nick, she felt as if her father had found a way to return to her, after all. But she shook that notion away. This wasn't Mordecai. This was nothing to do with Mordecai.

Mordecai would never have hurt her. Not on purpose, anyway.

"I need to know if Bryan's alive, Nick. Will you do that for me, give me that one thing, before you go any further with this? Please?"

Nick stared at her, and his features seemed to soften just slightly. She thought he liked her. She could use that.

"I didn't kill him."

She nodded. "But…you will. Won't you, Nick?"

"I have to, Dawnie. I don't have a choice." He lowered his head, his guilt not allowing him to look her in the eye. Another weapon she could use, she thought. He actually felt remorse about what he was planning to do.

"I was on my way to his place—had some evidence to plant there from this latest one—and I saw him sneaking in. He found my key ring under the damn mattress." He met her eyes again, then shook his head. "You still have something, there, Dawnie-girl. It wasn't just a dream, after all."

"But…Bryan loves you, Nick. He'd never turn you in. You don't have to kill him."

"Yeah, I do. I have to pose him, set it up, make sure it's obvious he was the Strangler. Or a weak copy of the Strangler, anyway. I'll say I burst in here to save the day, after finally figuring out it was him. He'd already killed Rico and Olivia. I caught him in the act of strangling you, Dawn, and I had to shoot him to try to save you, but my valiant effort was just too damn late." He finally looked at her again when he'd finished.

"So where is he now?"

"What difference does it make?"

"You…brought him with you. You must have, if you intend to…to do what you just said."

He tilted his head to one side, studying her. "I forgot how smart you are. You're stalling. Buying time in hopes some kind of help will arrive. But it won't, Dawn. No one's going to attempt this road in this kind of weather.

This is over." He waved the gun at the stairway. "Go on now. Both of you. Upstairs. There's no point in making this harder than it has to be."

Swallowing hard, Dawn turned and started toward the stairway, but she froze in place when Olivia shouted, "No!"

"Olivia," Dawn pleaded, "just—"

"No!" the other woman cried again. "What's he going to do, shoot me where I stand? That would ruin his little plan! Wouldn't it, Nick? Your neatly staged little crime scene would be all messed up. Shooting me wouldn't fit into the story you're weaving. So what are you gonna do?"

He surged across the room at her, swinging the gun as he went. Dawn lunged to get between them, but she was too late. He brought his hand around and clocked Olivia with the pistol butt. She hit the floor hard, landing on her knees, one hand pressing to the side of her head, which was bleeding. She'd landed so close to Rico's body that her fingertips were almost touching his blood. She jerked backward when she saw that and raised her head slowly. "No man will ever hit me again and live to tell about it." She started to get up, and Dawn knew she was going to attack him.

He raised his hand again, and Dawn wedged herself between them, arms on his shoulders. "Don't! Just don't! She's going to cooperate, okay?"

"The hell I am!"

"The hell she is." He repeated it deadpan, then shrugged and pushed Dawn out of the way, then crammed the gun barrel into the back of Olivia's neck. And then he shoved the little black case he'd been carrying at Dawn. "Carry this up the stairs. You miss one step, I blow her head off. Got it?"

Dawn nodded, her motions jerky.

"Move."

She moved. Nick bent over Olivia, who tried to scramble backward, crablike, but she was up against the wall and there was nowhere to go. She sent Dawn a pleading look. *Help me.*

Dawn tried to send her a silent promise, then turned away and marched up the stairs, leaving Nick trying to get a solid grip on the twisting, writhing Olivia with one hand while holding his gun in the other.

Dawn reached the top of the stairs and turned toward her bedroom—where there was a shotgun in the closet.

"Hey!" Nick shouted. "Hey, where are you going so fast? You wait for me, Dawnie!"

She didn't turn to face him. There were only two more steps to the bedroom door. She lunged, turning them into one, and lurched into the bedroom, slamming the door behind her, throwing the lock. She hurled the little black vinyl case away from her as if it were contaminated and spun toward the closet, yanking it open and wrestling the shotgun into her arms. Bullets, bullets, bullets, where the hell were the— Top shelf!

Something slammed into the bedroom door. "Don't fuck with me, Dawnie Jones. Don't even try!" Nick bellowed, and then he hit the door again.

Dawn reached the box of slugs, ripped it open, spilled half of them, but managed to slide two into the pump-action shotgun.

He slammed into the door again. It would break with one more blow. There was no more time. She worked the pump action, pulled the gun up to her shoulder, leveled it at the door and waited for him to burst in, so she could blow him away.

But he didn't. Silence came from the other side. She was shaking so hard she could barely hold the gun in position. Where was he?

A car door slammed. Had someone else arrived? Was help here at last? She lowered the gun only slightly and ran to the window to look outside.

The Thunderbird sat there in the rain, red and white and dripping wet. Nick was leaning into the back and tugging something out. Feet. Legs. He held a rope that was tied around his captive's ankles and kept pulling.

The torso slid out of the car, then the shoulders, arms pinned behind the body. She stiffened, knowing it was Bryan even before his head dropped from the edge of the seat, hitting the side of the car and then the muddy driveway. He didn't fight; his eyes were closed as the rain beat down on him. Unconscious? God, she hoped he was only unconscious.

Nick stopped and looked up at her in the window. "You gonna keep fucking with me?" He screamed the question so loudly that she could hear him clearly over the storm and through the closed window. She lifted a trembling hand to her lips as he slammed Bryan's legs to the ground, stomped to the car and returned with a tire iron. "Are you?" he shouted, lifting the iron and bringing it down hard across Bryan's lower legs. "Are you?"

She lifted the gun to take aim, wondering even then if she would hit Bryan by mistake. But even as she did, Nick lifted his own gun and pointed it at Bryan's head.

"No!" She screamed the word, then leaned the gun on the wall and flung open the window. "No, Nick! Please don't hurt him!"

"He's gonna kill him, anyway," Olivia said. Her words were slurred. She'd apparently made her way up the stairs and spoke from the other side of the closed bedroom door. "We've got to get out of here."

Sniffling, Dawn went to the door and opened it. "I figure you've got about five minutes before he realizes you're gone," she said.

Olivia lifted her brows. "Gone where?"

"Back door, down to the dock, there's a rowboat. Take your phone. Go, try to get help. Row out to the middle and you can get a signal. I'll try to stall him long enough for you to get clear."

"I can't leave you!"

"He's gonna kill you first, remember? Besides, I'm not leaving Bryan. Get the hell out. You're our only hope, Olivia. Please!"

Nodding, Olivia turned and stumbled dizzily back down the stairs. Dawn turned toward the open window. "I don't know what you want me to do, Nick," she called, raising her voice so he could hear. But as she spoke, she picked up the shotgun and examined the bed where he would kill her, if he got that far. The bed where he would strangle her.

With the memory of Bette's death playing through her mind, she leaned the shotgun up against the headboard, on the opposite side from where he had stood to murder Bette, and then she adjusted her floor-length Blackberry Inn bathrobe over the bedpost to cover it. She reminded herself to stay near that side of the bed when he tried to do her in.

"What the hell do you want me to do?" she called, searching the room and spotting his stupid black case again. "I can't just let you kill me. I'm not a sheep, and I'm not a victim. I'll fight for my life, Nick. I don't think I could do otherwise, even if I tried."

He would choke her unconscious, she realized, as she moved to where she'd thrown the case, picked it up, opened it and saw the black silk stocking, the bottle of Glasgow Gold and the shot glass inside. And then he would wake her and pour that burning whiskey down her throat. And finally he would choke her again, so she drowned in the liquor.

"The hell you will," she whispered.

He didn't answer her, and she got worried. She took the shot glass and the whiskey bottle with her to the window, and glanced down even as she went to hurl the bottle out. And then she would flush that damned stocking down the toilet.

Bryan wasn't lying on the ground by the car anymore. Where was he? God, where was he?

She'd paused with her arm in midswing, and then a powerful wet hand snapped up from outside to clasp her wrist, and with a low growl Nick pulled himself, dripping, up over the windowsill and into the room with her.

"No! No, dammit, no!"

He backhanded her. "Don't even try to outsmart me in my own fucking house! We're *doing* this! We're doing it *now!* Where's that bitch Olivia? Where is she?"

He was still holding her wrist, pulling her arm above her head, but she was still clutching the bottle in her other hand. Furious, she brought it around hard and smashed it against his head. She watched it explode. The glass shattered, and the whiskey soaked his face and hair, and spilled onto the floor, forming an amber pool on the hardwood.

He swore a blue streak, but he didn't let her go.

"I asked you where Olivia is," he said, his tone dangerous and deep.

"She's right where you left her, you animal! She's dead. She was your friend, and she's dead! You killed her, just like you killed Rico, and just like you killed Bette and all the others. You're a murderer, Nick. You're a cold-blooded killer, and this stupid plan of yours isn't going to work. It'll never work, because you're wrong. Your whole theory is wrong. You can't stop. You can't control it. Not ever."

"I can stop. I stopped before."

She pulled and twisted, and he tried to hold her, but she managed to get her foot near enough to the shot glass to kick it against the wall, where it broke into several large chunks.

"You're ruining everything!" he shouted. "And you're wrong. I can stop whenever I want. I *did* stop."

"You *didn't* stop, Nick! You're still killing. How is that stopped?" She was shrieking at him, shouting more loudly than he had as she methodically tried to shake him from his cool, calculating state of disassociation. She knew that state, had seen it in her own father. You had to rattle them, get to them, make them feel something. That was when they were weakest.

"I stopped for sixteen years."

"You paused. You took a break. But you *never* stopped being a serial killer. A predator. An animal."

"Shut up! Shut the hell up!"

She'd found his weak spot. She knew it and pressed on. "You can't control it, Nick. *It* controls *you*. That beast inside you, *he's* the one in charge. You don't even have any say in the matter. You're too weak to have any say. You don't have enough man in you to beat it."

"You're wrong. I'm in charge."

"Are you? Then why the hell did you kill Bette? Why, Nick?"

He threw her backward on the bed. "I didn't have a choice!"

"Why? Because Bryan took out those files on the original case? Because you thought he was on to you?

Is that why? So you killed his girlfriend, Nick? How much sense does that make?"

"Shut up! Shut up!" He punched her in the face, and she wasn't expecting it. Her head snapped back, hit the headboard so hard it left her dizzy, weak, near the edge of consciousness.

Then he turned, scrambling for something on the floor.

Rolling onto her side, she reached up, toward the gun, but he was back before her fingers found it, shoving her down again.

"Wouldn't it have been easier just to kill Bryan? Maybe even make it look like an accident? Why start this whole Nightcap bullshit all over again? You couldn't have picked a more complicated way to cover your tracks, Nick, don't you realize that?"

He straddled her body and slid the black stocking around her neck, even as she gripped it with her hands, holding on for dear life. He pulled it tight, and she kept her fingers between it and her skin, fighting hard to loosen it, kicking her feet at him in a vain attempt to buck him off.

"And all the time you didn't even *need* to cover your tracks, because Bryan didn't suspect anything. He took those files to honor you, you asshole. Not to nail you."

He released the stocking, backhanded her across the face, then grabbed it again, jerking it tight and hard and so fast this time that it nearly broke her fingers. She felt her own knuckles sinking into her throat, into her windpipe, helping the silk to crush it. She couldn't breathe. She couldn't taunt him anymore. Her eyes watered, her heart pounded hard, but no matter how it tried, it couldn't get oxygen to her brain.

He pulled tighter. "Die, dammit!"

Bryan managed to get himself into a sitting position on the ground beside the house, where Nick had dumped him, his hands still cuffed behind him, legs tied together at the ankles, rain pouring down on his already-soaked body. He didn't know where the hell Nick had gone, but he knew the man's ultimate goal. He was going to kill Dawn—just the way he'd killed Bette. And Bryan would be damned if he would let that happen.

He'd heard a gunshot just after they'd arrived and Nick had gone inside. And up until just a moment ago, when he'd heard Dawn's voice taunting Nick from the bedroom window, he'd been unsure she was still alive.

Nick had done him a huge favor by dragging him out of the locked car. The bastard had given him a fighting chance. Now he lay on his side and curled up as tightly as he could, finally finding the knotted rope with his teeth. It was damn near backbreaking, but he worked it, tugging the knot, pulling it until his teeth seemed on the verge of coming loose, but finally it gave. He got the knot untied and his legs were free. Next he braced his back against the wall of the house and forced his cuffed hands downward, over his buttocks and under his thighs; then, twisting his knees to one side and bending almost double, he worked and worked, trying to get the cuffs past his feet, one at a time, so at least his hands would be in front of him rather than behind. He twisted and pulled until the metal cut into his wrists and his shoulders were straining against their sockets. Blood flowed, staining his shirtsleeves, and the muddy, wet ground made it hard to get any leverage. But still he pulled and contorted himself despite the pain.

Finally one foot snapped through. The second was easier, and then he was up on his feet, and running toward the car. He quickly opened the front door, then the glove compartment, where he found exactly what he'd known he would find. A .44 Magnum. Nick always carried a spare weapon in the glove compartment.

No handcuff key, though.

And no time.

He backed out of the car, leaving the door open, and ran toward the house. Up the steps to the front door. It was ajar, and he peered through, gun at the ready. When he didn't see anything, he pushed the door wider and stepped inside, and then he saw a nightmare.

Rico! Oh, hell, Rico. He barely restrained himself long enough to look left and right, then raced over to Rico, but he knew his friend was dead even before he knelt beside him. Goddammit. That bastard Nick had killed his best friend.

A thump from the bedroom, springs squeaking. Dawn!

He had to set the gun down long enough to dig into

Rico's pocket for his key ring. He knew his friend well. He found a generic handcuff key, along with Rico's car keys and a dozen others. No time to free himself, though. He pocketed the keys, then headed upstairs, trying to move as fast and keep as quiet as he could.

He reached the bedroom door, leveled the gun and sprang inside. Nick was on top of Dawn, choking her life away. Bryan leveled the gun. "Get off her! Get the fuck off her! *Now!*"

Nick turned, one hand snatching his own gun from where it lay on the nightstand, aiming it at Bryan. Bryan desperately wanted to fire, but he was afraid of hitting Dawn, and in that moment of hesitation, Nick got off the first shot.

Bryan ducked, then rose and aimed again, but Nick was already clambering out the window. Bryan got off one shot, not knowing if he hit the man or not, and then ran to Dawn, kneeling on the bed beside her. "Baby! Dawn, come on. Be okay. Be okay." He untwisted the stocking and pulled it away from her neck, wincing at the deep red mark it had already left there, and then he patted her cheek firmly and shook her. "Dawn, dammit, wake up. Talk to me. Show me you're alive, baby, come on."

She choked but didn't open her eyes.

Bryan let go of her, relief flooding him that she wasn't dead. Nick hadn't killed her. Thank God. *Thank God*.

But Nick was still out there, the bastard. And he was armed. And he had nothing to lose now.

Bryan rose from the bed and ran to the window, to look out and see where Nick had gone. But the man was nowhere in sight.

"Dammit!"

Rushing back to the bed, he shook her shoulders. "Dawn. Dawn, you gotta wake up. Come on. I need you."

She blinked, opened her eyes, focused on him. "You're alive…." Her voice was hoarse and choked, and it made him furious.

He helped her sit up, handed her the gun. "Watch my back while I get these cuffs off."

She nodded jerkily and sat up straighter, steadying the gun. He wrestled the keys from his pocket and tried to unlock himself, but then she took them from him. "You hold the gun. I'll unlock you."

In seconds the cuffs sprang free, and then she wrapped her arms around him and held on tight.

"Okay. Okay, baby, I know. I know." He hugged her back, keeping one eye on that window, then nervously glancing at the door. "But we have to get out of here."

"I know."

"Where's Olivia?"

"I told her to take the boat and go for help. She took her phone, but I don't know. In this weather, I just don't know. I hope she made it. Rico…oh, God, Rico…"

"I know. I know. I saw. Come on, we have to go, baby. We have to get out of here."

"But he's out there. He's still out there!"

"We have to go."

"No! No, we don't. We…we can lock ourselves in here. Just wait for him to try to come in and…and…and shoot him." She reached over to the bedpost and pulled a shotgun from beneath the bathrobe that hung there. "Just close the window and lock the door and—"

"And he'll wait us out. Or burn us out. We have to get out of here, baby. We have to."

"He tried to kill me."

"I know."

She pressed her hands to his cheeks. "I love you, Bryan. I love you, and I mean that, and I'll never, ever run away from you again. And I'm so sorry. I'm so sorry I hurt you. I swear, it'll never, never happen again. Please, believe that."

He nodded and felt a bigger flood of emotion than he could ever have imagined. So big he couldn't speak. So he held her a little tighter, kissed her gently, then pushed her away. "Come on. We have to get away."

"He'll be waiting."

He kept an arm around Dawn and moved to the window, glancing out. He didn't see Nick. Or his car.

"Did he leave? Did he…did he leave?"

"I don't know. Maybe." Bryan held her close to his side and turned toward the bedroom door. He peered out, reluctantly taking his arm from around her. Then he handed her the .44, and gently took the shotgun from her. "I've got Rico's keys in my pocket," he said. "We're gonna go out the back door, get in Rico's car and get the hell out of here. Okay?"

"Do you think Olivia—do you think she made it in this storm?"

"I think she's fine. Come on."

Arm in arm, they moved slowly into the hallway, eyes open and alert, listening for any sound, watching for any movement. Bryan could feel Dawn's entire body shaking, and her breaths weren't breaths at all but hic-cuplike sobs. She was on the edge of hysteria.

There was nothing in the hallway. No sound, no presence.

Step by step, they moved to the top of the stairs. He couldn't see any sign of Nick. God, please, let him have gone. Let him have gone. Let him have gone.

They began to walk downstairs. First one step, then the next. And then another. Still no sound, nothing but silence from below. And the smells—the gunpowder and fresh blood.

He did his best not to look at Rico, but when he glanced at Dawn, he found her gazed fixed on the dead man. "Don't look there, Dawn. Keep alert. Watch for Nick."

She nodded and tore her eyes from the body.

They moved through the living room. The front door still stood open. It was nerve-racking to go the other way, toward the back, through the open archway, into the kitchen area, half expecting to be jumped from behind with every step. But they weren't.

There was only the patter of the rain on the roof. The mournful whining of the wind through the pines. The falls' roar, almost lost behind noises of the storm.

They crossed the kitchen, and he scanned every inch of space. Nothing. No one.

And then they moved on to the French doors that led to the deck.

He hesitated there, looking out. He could see Rico's car, right where it was supposed to be. Across the deck, four steps down and a dash of maybe five yards to the vehicle.

It was murky and dismal outside, the sky obliterated by the storm clouds and visibility further diminished by the pouring rain. Even so, it wasn't quite the deluge it had been earlier.

Bryan wanted to flip on the outside light, to illuminate whatever might be out there. But if Nick hadn't really left, that would give away their position and their intent. It would allow Nick to get in between them and their only means of escape.

So the light was off-limits.

He opened the door and pulled Dawn with him as he stepped through it. She planted her feet, resisting.

"We just have to make it to the car. Just to the car, baby."

"No. No. Bry, no. I don't want—"

"I think he's gone. Come on, hon, it's only a few yards. Come on."

She was shaking even harder than before, and he didn't think she could hit the broad side of a barn with the handgun. So he picked up the pace as he pulled her along beside him across the deck. They made it to the steps and down to the grassy lawn. Bryan pointed the key ring and hit the button to unlock the car.

She burst into a run then. Racing across the grass to the car, jerking open the passenger door, Bryan no more than a step behind her.

And that was when Nick rose up from the other side of the car, leveling his gun at her.

"Not so fast, sweetie pie."

"Nooooooo!" Bryan lunged even as Nick pulled the trigger. He pushed Dawn to the ground, firing the shotgun as she went down and feeling the white-hot bullet rip into his chest.

"Bryan!" Dawn shrieked his name, crawling over the wet grass to him. He felt his blood pulsing, felt his life ebbing.

"Dawn—Nick. Careful." And then there was only darkness.

Bryan.

All she wanted was to stay by his side, but she knew what he'd been telling her, knew she had to creep around the car and see whether Bryan's frantic shotgun blast had hit its mark. Whether Nick was dead—or waiting to finish his gruesome task.

She let Bryan's head rest on the ground and then, cradling the .44, crept on her knees along the side of the car, shaking from head to toe. She reached the front and peeked quickly around. Then crept farther, inching along the grille, to the other side. And finally, shaking so hard she could barely believe she could still move, she darted forward, took a furtive peek, then jerked back again.

Nick was lying on his back on the ground.

Holding the gun, pointing it ahead of her, she leaned forward again. His arms were spread out on the grass above his head. His gun lay several feet away from them. There was a massive hole in his chest. She didn't think anyone could survive such a blast.

But she pointed the gun at his head, just in case, and without hesitation, she pulled the trigger.

Assured now that he was dead, she scrambled back to Bryan. But what she saw stopped her in her tracks.

Bryan was standing there, smiling, holding out his hands to her.

But his body was still on the ground.

"No…" The gun fell from her limp hands to the wet ground. "No, no, no. Bryan, don't be…"

A trembling hand flew to her lips as her gaze shifted from the Bryan lying on the ground to the Bryan standing before her, semitransparent and perfect in every way.

"No. Oh, no no no no."

"I love you, too," he said. The words echoed and whispered, as if they were part of the rain-soaked morning. "I never stopped. You need to know that. I need to tell you that."

"Bryan…you listen to me! You get back into your body *right now!* You aren't leaving me, do you hear? Come back. Bryan, please, please, come back to me!"

He looked down at his own body, then back at her,

shaking his head sadly. A bright light appeared just beyond him. Blindingly bright. She'd never seen anything so bright before, she thought. And she cried out, "No! No, you can't have him! No!"

And then she heard the chopper blades, and the light got closer and began sweeping the ground.

"Oh, God, it's a helicopter. It's a helicopter. Bryan, it's…"

But he was gone. His body still lay in the wet grass, but he no longer stood before her.

She fell on her knees beside him, sobbing, clinging. "Don't leave me. Please, don't leave me."

And then she felt something amazing. One of his hands rose, weakly, then landed in her hair. And that was all.

Epilogue

There were press everywhere as Dawn helped Bryan into the car outside the hospital. She supposed it was appropriate. The biggest case Vermont had ever seen had just been solved by a rookie cop. *Her* rookie cop. And everyone wanted to know what he was going to do now.

She was more curious than any of them.

Thank God Olivia had managed to make it far enough out on the lake to get a weak signal, even in the storm, and had called for help. When she'd told them an officer had been shot, all hell had broken loose.

And it was a good thing. Bryan wouldn't have survived his gunshot wound if he'd had to wait any longer for treatment.

As for Olivia, her secret remained just that. The only people who knew her true identity, besides the two of them, were dead. And they had vowed never to tell. There had been no more hang-up calls, and Olivia thought perhaps she was still safe in her false identity, after all.

Dawn helped Bryan out of his wheelchair, waved at the reporters and said a cheerful "No comment" as she reached past him to open the passenger door of his Mustang, which they'd finally reclaimed.

But Bryan didn't get in. He turned, one hand on the top of the car door, and held up the other hand. "I guess we can take one or two questions. Uh, you there, with the baseball hat."

The reporter in the hat met Bryan's eyes and winked; then, with a huge smile, he shifted his focus to Dawn. "Ms. Jones, my question is for you, actually."

"Hello, Mr. Brown. Good to see you again," she said.

"Good to see you alive," he replied. "So, do you plan on staying here in Vermont, now that all this is over?"

She smiled, but she was puzzled and couldn't hide it. "Oh, I'm staying. This is my home." And she meant it. She hadn't seen any more ghosts since seeing Bryan's. She didn't know if she ever would. Bryan thought her gift had transferred itself into a heightened sense about things, but she wasn't so sure. What she *was* sure of was that it didn't matter. She would never leave him again. No matter what she had to face in order to stay by his side.

"And a follow-up, if I may?" Mitch Brown went on.

"Of course."

The reporter grinned wider. "As long as you're hanging around, would you consider marrying this hero cop?"

She blinked in shock as the words processed through her brain, and then she frowned hard. "What?"

"He asked if you'd marry me." Bryan pulled a ring from his pocket and held it in front of her nose. "I told him to."

She melted right there in front of the car, so thoroughly that she was surprised not to find herself blinking up from a little puddle on the ground. Then she smiled, wrapped her arms around his neck and kissed him senseless, saying, "Yes!" repeatedly, in between kisses. And then she stopped kissing him long enough to hold up her left hand.

Bryan slid the ring onto it. She blinked through a rush of hot tears at the sparkling little stone. And then she flung her arms around his neck and kissed him some more.

"I think that's a yes, guys," the reporter shouted.

A great big cheer went up as Bryan deepened the kiss, bending her backward and holding her closer. She'd been given a second chance at life. They both had, thank God. And she wouldn't blow it. Not this time.

Not ever again.

* * * * *

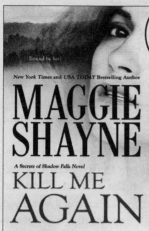

**Look for all 3 books in the brand-new trilogy
from *New York Times* and *USA TODAY*
bestselling author**

HEATHER GRAHAM

July

August

September

Available wherever books are sold!

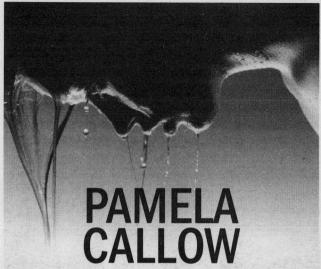

REQUEST YOUR
FREE BOOKS!

2 FREE NOVELS
FROM THE SUSPENSE COLLECTION
PLUS 2 FREE GIFTS!

YES! Please send me 2 FREE novels from the Suspense Collection and my 2 FREE gifts (gifts are worth about $10). After receiving them, if I don't wish to receive any more books, I can return the shipping statement marked "cancel." If I don't cancel, I will receive 3 brand-new novels every month and be billed just $5.74 per book in the U.S. or $6.24 per book in Canada. That's a saving of at least 28% off the cover price. It's quite a bargain! Shipping and handling is just 50¢ per book.* I understand that accepting the 2 free books and gifts places me under no obligation to buy anything. I can always return a shipment and cancel at any time. Even if I never buy another book, the two free books and gifts are mine to keep forever.

192/392 MDN E7PD

Name   (PLEASE PRINT)

Address   Apt. #

City   State/Prov.   Zip/Postal Code

Signature (if under 18, a parent or guardian must sign)

Mail to **The Reader Service:**
IN U.S.A.: P.O. Box 1867, Buffalo, NY 14240-1867
IN CANADA: P.O. Box 609, Fort Erie, Ontario L2A 5X3

Not valid for current subscribers to the Suspense Collection
or the Romance/Suspense Collection.

Want to try two free books from another line?
Call 1-800-873-8635 or visit www.morefreebooks.com.

* Terms and prices subject to change without notice. Prices do not include applicable taxes. N.Y. residents add applicable sales tax. Canadian residents will be charged applicable provincial taxes and GST. Offer not valid in Quebec. This offer is limited to one order per household. All orders subject to approval. Credit or debit balances in a customer's account(s) may be offset by any other outstanding balance owed by or to the customer. Please allow 4 to 6 weeks for delivery. Offer available while quantities last.

Your Privacy: Harlequin Books is committed to protecting your privacy. Our Privacy Policy is available online at www.eHarlequin.com or upon request from the Reader Service. From time to time we make our lists of customers available to reputable third parties who may have a product or service of interest to you. If you would prefer we not share your name and address, please check here. ☐

Help us get it right—We strive for accurate, respectful and relevant communications. To clarify or modify your communication preferences, visit us at www.ReaderService.com/consumerschoice.

MSUS10R

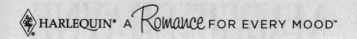

MAGGIE SHAYNE

32618	BLOODLINE	__	$7.99 U.S. __	$8.99 CAN.
32498	ANGEL'S PAIN	__	$7.99 U.S. __	$7.99 CAN.
32243	THICKER THAN WATER	__	$5.99 U.S. __	$6.99 CAN.
32266	TWO BY TWILIGHT	__	$5.99 U.S. __	$6.99 CAN.
32518	LOVER'S BITE	__	$7.99 U.S. __	$7.99 CAN.
32497	DEMON'S KISS	__	$7.99 U.S. __	$9.50 CAN.
32906	PRINCE OF TWILIGHT	__	$7.99 U.S. __	$9.99 CAN.
20944	COLDER THAN ICE	__	$6.99 U.S. __	$8.50 CAN.
32229	DARKER THAN MIDNIGHT	__	$6.99 U.S. __	$8.50 CAN.

(limited quantities available)

TOTAL AMOUNT	$ _____
POSTAGE & HANDLING	$ _____
($1.00 for 1 book, 50¢ for each additional)	
APPLICABLE TAXES*	$ _____
TOTAL PAYABLE	$ _____

(check or money order—please do not send cash)

To order, complete this form and send it, along with a check or money order for the total above, payable to MIRA Books, to: **In the U.S.:** 3010 Walden Avenue, P.O. Box 9077, Buffalo, NY 14269-9077; **In Canada:** P.O. Box 636, Fort Erie, Ontario, L2A 5X3.

Name: _____
Address: _____ City: _____
State/Prov.: _____ Zip/Postal Code: _____
Account Number (if applicable): _____

075 CSAS

*New York residents remit applicable sales taxes.
*Canadian residents remit applicable GST and provincial taxes.